The
Crucifix
Killer

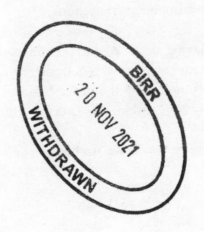

About the author

Born in Brazil of Italian origin, Chris Carter studied psychology and criminal behaviour at the University of Michigan. As a member of the Michigan State District Attorney's Criminal Psychology team, he interviewed and studied many criminals, including serial and multiple homicide offenders with life imprisonment convictions.

Having departed for Los Angeles in the early 1990s, Chris spent ten years as a guitarist for numerous Glam Rock bands before leaving the music business to write full-time. He now lives in London. *The Crucifix Killer* is his first novel.

Visit www.chriscarterbooks.com

The Crucifix Killer

Chris Carter

SIMON &
SCHUSTER

London · New York · Sydney · Toronto

A CBS COMPANY

First published in Great Britain by Simon & Schuster UK Ltd, 2009
A CBS COMPANY

Copyright © Chris Carter, 2009

1 3 5 7 9 10 8 6 4 2

Simon & Schuster UK Ltd
1st Floor
222 Gray's Inn Road
London WC1X 8HB

www.simonandschuster.co.uk

Simon & Schuster Australia
Sydney

A CIP catalogue record for this book
is available from the British Library

Trade Paperback ISBN 978-1-84737-538-4
Hardback ISBN 978-1-84737-622-0

Typeset by M Rules
Printed in the UK by CPI Mackays, Chatham ME5 8TD

To Samantha Johnson, for simply being everything.

Acknowledgements

Writing is always regarded as a solitary occupation, but I owe a great debt to several people who have generously given me their time and input, in so many areas.

My love and thanks to Samantha Johnson, the most giving and understanding person I know, and who tirelessly read and re-read the initial manuscript so many times, even I lost count.

Thank you also to Coral Chambers for the encouragement and for pointing me in the right direction and to Andrea McPhillips for the corrections and the chats.

My sincere thanks also goes to all the incredible people at Simon & Schuster UK who have done an outstanding job and to my phenomenal editors, Kate Lyall Grant in the UK and Pia Götz and Sybille Uplegger in Germany, whose great input and valuable suggestions made the story and the characters in this thriller come alive.

Words can't express how thankful I am to the most passionate, dedicated, thoughtful, determined and extraordinary agents any author could ever hope for – Darley Anderson and Camilla Bolton. I'm the lucky one.

To the fantastic team of extremely hard-working people at the Darley Anderson Literary Agency, my eternal gratitude.

One

'Hello . . . Detective Hunter speaking.'

'Hello, Robert, I have a surprise for you.'

Hunter froze, almost dropping his coffee cup. He knew that metallic voice very well. He knew when that voice called it meant only one thing – a new, mutilated dead body.

'Have you heard from your partner lately?'

Hunter's eyes quickly searched the room in vain for Carlos Garcia.

'Has anyone heard from Garcia this morning?' he shouted across the office after pressing the mute button on his cell phone.

The other detectives exchanged silent, puzzled looks and Hunter knew the answer even before it came.

'Not since yesterday,' Detective Maurice said shaking his head.

Hunter pressed the mute button once again.

'What have you done to him?'

'Do I have your attention now?'

'What have you done to him?' Hunter demanded in a firm voice.

'As I've said, it's a surprise, Robert,' the metallic voice said

laughing. '*But I'll give you another chance to make a difference. Maybe this time you'll put more effort into it. Be at the laundry room down in the basement of the old number 122 Pacific Alley in South Pasadena within the hour. If you bring back-up, he dies. If you don't make it within the hour, he dies. And trust me, Robert, it'll be a very slow and painful death.*' The line went dead.

Two

Hunter raced down the stairs of the old building in east LA in giant leaps. The deeper he went, the darker and hotter it got. His shirt was covered in sweat, his tight shoes crushing his feet.

'Where the hell is this laundry room?' he whispered as he reached the basement.

A glimmer of light was coming from underneath a closed door at the end of a dark corridor. He ran towards it calling his partner's name.

No answer.

Hunter pulled out his Wildey Survivor double-action pistol and positioned his back against the wall to the right of the door.

'Garcia . . .'

Silence.

'Rookie, are you in there?'

A muffled thud came from inside the room. Hunter cocked his gun and took a deep breath.

'Fuck it!'

With his back still against the outside wall, he pushed the door open with his right hand and in a well-rehearsed move rotated his body into the room, his gun searching for a target. An unbearable smell of urine and vomit forced him to take a step back coughing violently.

'Garcia . . .' he called again from the door.

Silence.

From outside Hunter couldn't see much. The light bulb that hung from the ceiling above a small wooden table in the center of the room was too weak to illuminate it properly. He drew another deep breath and took a step forward. What he saw made his stomach churn. Garcia had been nailed to a life-size cross inside a Perspex cage. The heavy bleeding from his wounds had created a pool of blood at the base of the cross. He was wearing nothing but his underwear and a barbed-wire crown around his head, the thick metal spikes clearly piercing his flesh. Blood streaking down his face. Garcia looked lifeless.

I'm too late, Hunter thought.

Approaching the cage he was surprised to see a heart monitor inside it. Its line peaking slightly and at steady intervals. Garcia was still alive – just.

'Carlos!'

No movement.

'Rookie!' he shouted.

With great effort Garcia managed to half open his eyes.

'Hang in there, buddy.'

Hunter surveyed the dimly lit room. It was large, fifty-five feet by forty-five he guessed. The floor was littered with dirty rags, used syringes, crack pipes and broken glass. In the corner, to the right of the entrance door he could see an old and rusty wheelchair. On the wooden table in the center of the room sat a small, portable cassette tape recorder and a single note that read *play me first* in large red letters. He pressed the play button and the now familiar metallic voice came blasting out of the tiny speaker.

'*Hello Robert, I guess you've made it in time.*' Pause.

'*You have no doubt realized that your friend needs your*

help, but for you to be able to help him you have to play by certain rules ... my rules. This is a simple game, Robert. Your friend is locked inside a bullet-proof cage, so shooting it won't help you. On its door you'll find four colored buttons. One of them opens the cage, the other three – don't. Your task is quite simple – pick a button. If you press the correct one the door will open, you'll be able to free your partner and walk out of the room.'

One chance in four to save Garcia – definitely not great odds, Hunter thought.

'Now here comes the fun part,' the tape recorder played on. *'If you press any of the other three buttons an uninterrupted high-voltage current will be sent directly to the wire crown on your friend's head. Have you ever seen what happens to a human being while he's being electrocuted?'* the voice said with a chilling laugh. *'His eyes burst, his skin crinkles like bacon, his tongue recoils into his mouth ready to choke him to death, his blood boils, bursting vessels and arteries open. It's quite an exquisite scene, Robert.'*

Garcia's heartbeat went into overdrive. Hunter could see the line on the heart monitor screen peaking faster.

'And now for the really fun part ...'

Somehow Hunter knew that the electric current trick wouldn't be the only twist in that room.

'Behind the cage I've placed enough explosives to obliterate the room you're in. The explosives are attached to the heart monitor and if it gets to read a flatline ...' a longer pause this time. Hunter knew what the metallic voice was about to say next.

'Boom ... the room blows. So you see Robert, if you press the wrong button, not only will you watch your friend die knowing that you've killed him, but you'll get to die soon after.'

Hunter's heart was now beating viciously against his chest, sweat dripping from his forehead and stinging his eyes, his hands shaky and clammy.

'But you have a choice Robert. You don't have to save your partner, you can just save yourself. Walk away now and leave him to die alone. No one will know except you. Can you live with that? Will you gamble your life for his? Pick a color, you've got sixty seconds.' A loud beep came from the tape recorder before it went silent.

Hunter saw a red digital display above Garcia's head light up 59, 58, 57 . . .

Three

Five weeks earlier.

Jenny rubbed her eyes as she got up from the busy table at the Vanguard Club in Hollywood, hoping she didn't look as tired as she felt.

'Where're you going?' D-King asked, sipping his champagne.

Bobby Preston was the best known dealer in northwest Los Angeles, but no one ever called him by his real name, everyone knew him as D-King. The 'D' stood for 'Dealer' as he would deal in just about anything: drugs, girls, cars, guns – for the right price he'd supply you with whatever you wanted.

Jenny was by far his most stunning girl. Her body was flawlessly toned and tanned and her perfect face and smile could charm any men on this earth, D-King was sure of it.

'I just need to retouch my make-up. I'll be right back babe.' She blew him a little kiss and left the exclusive VIP area still holding her champagne glass.

Jenny couldn't handle any more alcohol, not because she was feeling drunk, but because this was her fifth successive night out partying and she'd had enough. She didn't think her life would turn out this way. She never thought she'd become a hooker. D-King had always assured her that she wasn't a working girl. She was a high-class entertainer for gentlemen with extremely good taste and obviously a lot of money, but at the end of the day she was having sex for cash. To her that made her a hooker.

Most of Jenny's clients were perverted old millionaires looking for something they couldn't get at home. Sex was never your normal run-of-the-mill missionary position. They all wanted their money's worth. Bondage, BDSM, spanking, watersports, strap-on sex, it didn't matter. Whatever they were into, she had to provide, but tonight was no working night. She wasn't being paid by the hour. She wasn't out with one of her deadbeat clients. She was out with the boss and she had to party until he said it was over.

Jenny had been to the Vanguard Club plenty of times. It was one of D-King's favorite hangouts. There was no denying that the club was a magnificent luxurious extravaganza. From its enormous dance floor to its laser-light show and great stage. The Vanguard could hold up to two thousand people, and tonight the club was packed to capacity.

Jenny made her way towards the bar closest to the ladies' room where two barmen seemed rushed off their feet. The entire club was a tremendous buzz of beautiful people, the great majority of them in their twenties and early thirties. Jenny was oblivious to the pair of eyes that followed her from the VIP area to the bar. Eyes that had been on her all night. In fact, they'd been following her for the past four weeks, from nightclub to nightclub and hotel to hotel. Watching her as she pretended to have a good time, as she pleasured each and every one of her clients.

'Hi, Jen, are you OK? You look a bit tired,' Pietro, the long-haired barman, asked as Jenny approached the bar. He still spoke with a slight Spanish accent.

'I'm OK, hun, just too much partying I guess,' she said unenthusiastically after catching a glimpse of herself in one of the bar mirrors. Her hypnotic blue eyes seemed to have lost some of their sparkle tonight.

'No rest for the wicked, huh?' Pietro's comment came with a shy smile.

'Not tonight,' Jenny smiled back.

'Can I get you anything?'

'No, I'm OK. I'm still struggling with this one.' She raised her champagne glass giving him a sexy wink. 'I just needed to get away from the party for a little while.'

Pietro and Jenny had flirted a few times but he'd never made a move on her. He knew she belonged to D-King.

'Well, if you need anything just give me a shout.' Pietro went back to preparing cocktails and flipping bottles. A dark-haired woman who had been standing on the other side of the bar dying to get his attention gave Jenny an evil look that said 'Back off, bitch, I saw him first.'

Jenny swept a hand through her long, wheat-blond hair, placed her champagne glass on the bar counter and turned around to face the dance floor. She enjoyed the club's atmosphere. All those people having fun, dancing, drinking and finding love. OK, maybe not love, she thought, but at least they'd be having sex for pleasure, not money. She wanted to be just like them. This was definitely not the beautiful Hollywood life she'd dreamed of when she left Idaho six years ago.

Jenny Farnborough's fascination with Hollywood started at the age of twelve. The movie theater became her shelter from the never-ending rows between her submissive mother and her overly aggressive stepfather. Films became her escape route, the vehicle that could take her places she'd never been before and she wanted to be a part of it.

Jenny knew that the Hollywood dream was nothing more

than a fantasy. Something that existed only in clichéd romantic books and films, and she'd read and watched plenty of those. She had to admit she was a dreamer, but maybe that wasn't such a bad thing. Maybe she'd be the lucky one. She had nothing to lose.

At the age of fourteen she started her first job as a popcorn girl. Jenny saved every dime she earned and by her sixteenth birthday she had enough saved up to leave that godforsaken town behind. She swore she'd never go back to Idaho. Jenny never found out about her mother overdosing on sleeping pills only a week after she'd left.

Hollywood was everything she'd expected it to be. A magical place full of beautiful people, lights and fantasies, but the harsh reality of life in the City of Angels was a far cry from the illusion she'd created. Her savings didn't last long and with no professional training the rejections started piling up like dirty laundry. Her beautiful dream slowly began to turn into a nightmare.

Jenny was introduced to D-King by Wendy Loutrop, another struggling wannabe actress. At first she'd rejected every proposition he'd made her. She'd heard all the stories about beautiful women coming to Hollywood dreaming of becoming a star only to end up working the streets or for the porn-movie industry. Jenny was determined not to give in. She didn't want to become just another failure story, but her pride had to play second fiddle to her survival instinct, and after several months of phone calls and expensive gifts D-King had himself a new girl.

Jenny never noticed the hand pouring a colorless liquid into her champagne glass. Her eyes were still set on the dancing crowd.

'Hi there, babe, can I buy you a drink?' a tall, blond man standing to her right asked with a bright smile.

'I already have a drink, but thank you for the offer anyway,' she replied politely without locking eyes with the stranger.

'Are you sure? I can order us a bottle of Cristal. What do you say, babe?'

Jenny turned and faced the tall blond man. He was smartly dressed wearing a dark-grey Versace suit, a crisp white shirt with a stiff collar and a blue silk tie. His green eyes were his most striking feature. Jenny had to admit he was an attractive man.

'What's your name?' she said forcing a smile.

'I'm Carl and it's a pleasure to meet you,' he said offering his hand.

Instead of shaking it Jenny had a sip of her champagne. 'Look Carl, you're quite a handsome guy, I'll give you that' – her voice now taking a very sweet tone – 'but trying to pick up a girl by flashing your money around is not a great idea, especially in a place like this. It makes us feel cheap, unless you are looking for a bimbo – is that what you are looking for? A pro?'

'Oh . . . No!' Carl fumbled with his tie nervously. 'Sorry, that's not how I meant it, babe.'

'So you ain't looking for a party girl to show you a *really* good time?' she asked having another sip of her champagne, her eyes now fixed on his.

'No, of course not, hun. Just trying to have a friendly drink, and if there's any chemistry between us . . .' He left the sentence hanging in the air with a shrug of his shoulders.

Very gently, she ran her fingers down his tie before pulling him closer. 'It's a pity you're not looking for a party girl,' she whispered into his left ear.

Carl's smile evaporated into a confused look.

'I could've given you my pimp's number, he's right over there.' She pointed to the VIP area with a sarcastic smile on her lips.

Carl half opened his mouth as if about to say something but no words came out.

Jenny drank the rest of her champagne and gave him a sexy wink before moving away from the bar and into the ladies' room.

The eyes still followed her.

It won't be long now. The drug will soon show its effect.

Jenny was re-applying her lipstick when she started to feel faint. She knew something was wrong. All of a sudden she felt hot and feverish. The walls seemed to be closing in on her. She found it hard to breathe and moved towards the door as quickly as she could. She needed to get out of there.

As she stumbled out of the ladies' room the entire place spun around her. She wanted to go back to D-King's table but her legs weren't responding. Jenny was about to collapse on the floor when a pair of hands grabbed her.

'Are you OK, babe? You don't look so good.'

'I don't feel too well. I think I need . . .'

'You need some air. It's too stuffy in here. Come with me, I'll help you. Let's step outside for a while.'

'But I . . .' Jenny had started to slur her words. 'I need to tell D . . . I have to go back to . . .'

'Later, babe, now you just need to come with me.'

No one noticed Jenny and the stranger walking towards the club exit.

Four

'Yes, Detective Hunter speaking.' Hunter finally answered his cell phone after the sixth ring. His voice was deep and the words came out slowly, giving away how few hours sleep he'd had.

'Robert, where the hell have you been? The captain's been after you for two hours.'

'Rookie, is that you? What time is it?' Hunter's new side-kick, Carlos Garcia, had been assigned to him only a week ago after the death of his long-term partner.

'Three in the morning.'

'What day?'

'Shit man . . . Monday. Look, you'd better come and have a look at this, we've got a really screwed up homicide on our hands.'

'We're Homicide Special Section 1, Carlos. Screwed up homicides is all we do.'

'Well, this one's a real mess and you'd better get here quick. The captain wants us to run this show.'

'Uh-huh,' Hunter replied indifferently. 'Gimme the address?'

He put his cell phone down and looked around the small, dark, unfamiliar room. 'Where the hell am I?' he whispered.

The thumping headache and the terrible taste in his mouth reminded him of how much he'd had to drink the night before and he sunk his head deep into the pillow hoping that would soothe the pain. Suddenly there was movement next to him on the bed.

'Hi, does that phone call mean you have to go?' The woman's voice was soft and sexy with a hint of an Italian accent. Hunter's surprised eyes fell over the half-covered body lying next to him. Through the little light coming into the room from the lamp posts outside the window he could just about make out her outline. Quick memories of last night flashed through his mind. The bar, the drinks, the flirting, the cab ride to a stranger's apartment and the long dark-haired woman whose name he couldn't remember. This was the third woman he'd woken up next to in the past five weeks.

'Yeah, I do have to go. I'm sorry,' he sounded casual.

Hunter got up and started looking for his trousers; his headache was more prominent now. His eyes quickly got used to the dimly lit room allowing him to see the woman's face better. She looked to be thirty or thirty-one years old. Her silky, dark hair hung about four inches past her shoulders framing a heart-shaped face with delicate sculpted nose and lips. She was attractive, but not in a Hollywood-movie-star way. Her uneven fringe suited her perfectly and her dark-green eyes carried an unusual and captivating sparkle.

By the bedroom door Hunter found his trousers and under-wear – the pair with blue teddy-bear prints.

Too late to feel embarrassed now, he thought. 'Can I use your bathroom?' he asked zipping up his trousers.

'Sure, it's the first door on the right as you come out of the room,' she said sitting up and resting her back against the head-board.

Hunter entered the bathroom and closed the door behind him. After splashing a handful of cold water onto his face, he stared at his reflection in the mirror. His blue eyes looked bloodshot. His skin paler than normal. His face unshaven.

'That's great, Robert,' he said to himself, splashing some more water onto his tired-looking face. 'Another woman who you barely remember meeting, never mind coming back to her apartment. Casual sex is great. It's even better when you can recall having some. I have to cut down on this drinking business.'

After squirting a little toothpaste on his finger he tried to finger-brush his teeth. Suddenly, a new thought entered his mind. *What if she's a hooker? What if I owe her money for something I don't even remember doing?* He quickly checked his wallet. The little money he had was still there.

He hand-combed his short blond hair and returned to the bedroom where she was still sitting against the headboard.

'Were you talking to yourself in there?' she asked with a shy smile.

'What? Oh yeah, I do that sometimes, it keeps me sane. Look . . .' He finally managed to find his shirt on the floor next to the bed. 'Do I owe you any money?' he asked sounding breezy.

'What?' You think I'm a prostitute?' she replied clearly offended.

Oh shit! He knew he'd blown it. 'No, look . . . It's not like that, it's just . . . It's happened to me before. Sometimes I drink too much and . . . I didn't mean it as an offence.'

'Do I look like a hooker to you?' she asked in an annoyed voice.

'Definitely not,' he replied firmly. 'It was stupid of me thinking such a thing. I'm sorry. I'm probably still half drunk,' he back-paddled as fast as he could.

She regarded him for a moment. 'Look, I'm not the kind of

woman you clearly think I am. My job carries a lot of pressure and it's been tough the last few months. I just wanted to let out some steam and have a few drinks. We got talking. You were funny, nice, quite charming even. You could actually hold a decent conversation. Unlike most of the other jerks I meet when I go out. One drink led to another and we ended up in bed. Obviously a mistake on my part.'

'No . . . Look . . .' Hunter tried to find the right words, '. . . sometimes I say stuff without thinking. And the truth is . . . I don't remember much of last night. I'm really sorry. And I feel like an asshole now.'

'So you should.'

'Believe me, I do.'

Her eyes were fixed on Hunter. He sounded sincere.

'Anyway, if I were a hooker, judging by your underwear and clothes I don't think you'd be able to afford me.'

'Ooh. That was low punch. I was already embarrassed enough without you mentioning it.'

She smiled.

Hunter was glad his back-paddling had worked. 'Do you mind if I make myself a quick cup of coffee before I go?'

'I don't have any coffee, only tea, but you are more than welcome to it if you like. The kitchen is just down the hall.'

'Tea? I think I'll pass. I need something stronger to wake me up.' He finished buttoning up his shirt.

'You sure you can't stay?' She pulled the covers back revealing her naked form. Great curves, nicely formed breasts and there was no hair anywhere on her body. 'Maybe you could show me how really sorry you are for calling me a hooker.'

Hunter stood there for a moment as if debating what to do. He bit his bottom lip and shook the thought from his head. His headache reminded him not to do that again.

'I promise you, if I could stay, I would.' He was now fully dressed and ready to go.

'I understand. Was that your wife on the phone?'

'What? No, I'm not married. That was work, trust me.' The last thing Hunter wanted was for her to think he was a cheating husband.

'OK,' she said matter-of-factly.

Hunter's eyes ran the length of her body once again and he felt an exciting tingle. 'If you give me your number, maybe we could meet up again sometime.'

She studied him for a long moment.

'You're thinking I won't bother to call right?' Hunter said sensing her reluctance.

'Oh, you read minds as well? That's a neat party trick.'

'You should see what I can do with a deck of cards.'

They both smiled.

'Plus, there's nothing I like more than proving people wrong.'

She reached for the notepad on her bedside table with a smirk on her face.

Hunter took the piece of paper from her hand and kissed her right cheek. 'I gotta go.'

'That will be one thousand dollars, babe!' she said gently running her fingers over his lips.

'What?' he asked with a shocked look. 'But . . .'

She was already smiling back at him. 'Sorry. I couldn't resist after you called me a hooker.'

Outside her apartment Hunter unfolded the piece of paper in his hand. Isabella! Sexy name, he thought. He searched the street for his old Buick Lesabre. The car was nowhere to be seen.

'Shit! I was too drunk to drive,' he cursed himself before flagging down the first cab he saw.

*

The directions Garcia had given him took Hunter to the middle of nowhere. Little Tujunga Canyon Road, in Santa Clarita, is eighteen miles long running from Bear Divide to Foothill Boulevard in Lakeview Terrace. Almost all of it is within the Angeles National Forest. At times the woodland and mountain views are simply breathtaking. Garcia's directions were precise and soon the taxi was driving down a tiny, bumpy, dirt road surrounded by hills, bushes and rough terrain. The darkness and nothingness was overwhelming. Twenty minutes later they finally came to an uneven lane that led up to an old wooden house.

'I guess this is it,' Hunter said handing the driver all the money in his pocket.

The lane was long and narrow, just wide enough to fit a standard-size car. Surrounding it were dense, impassable shrubs. Police and official vehicles were crammed everywhere making it look like a traffic jam in a desert.

Garcia was standing in front of the wooden shack talking to an agent from the crime lab, both of them holding flashlights. Hunter had to negotiate his way through the carnival of cars before joining them.

'Jesus, talk about a place out of the way – any further and we'd be in Mexico . . . Hi there, Peter,' Hunter said, nodding at the crime lab agent.

'Rough night, Robert? You look just like I feel,' Peter said with a sarcastic smirk.

'Yeah, thanks, you look great too. When is the baby due?' Hunter asked tapping his hand over Peter's beer gut. 'So what have we got here?' He turned to face Garcia.

'I think you better see it for yourself. It's hard to describe what's in there. The captain's inside, he said he wanted to talk to you first before letting the boys tag and bag the place,' Garcia said looking unsettled.

'What the hell is the captain doing here? He never comes out to crime scenes. Does he know the victim?'

'I'm as much in the dark as you are, but I don't think so. She's not exactly recognizable.' Garcia's statement made Hunter's eyes squint with a new worry.

'So it's a female body?'

'Oh, she's female alright.'

'Are you OK, rookie? You look a little shook up.'

'I'm fine,' Garcia reassured him.

'He's been sick a couple of times,' Peter commented with a new sneer.

Hunter studied Garcia for a moment. He knew this wasn't his first murder scene. 'Who found the body? Who called it in?'

'Apparently it was an anonymous call to 911,' Garcia answered.

'Oh great, one of those.'

'Here, take this,' Garcia said handing Robert his flashlight.

'Would you like a barf bag as well?' Peter joked.

Hunter paid no attention to the comment and took a moment to study the house from the outside. There was no front door. Most of the wooden planks from the front wall were missing and grass had grown through the remaining floorboards, making the front room look like a private forest. He could tell the house had once been white from flecks of peeled paint on the remains of windowsills. It was obvious that no one had lived there for a long time and that bothered Hunter. First-time killers didn't go to the trouble of finding such a secluded place to commit murder.

Three police officers stood to the left of the house discussing last night's football game, all three holding steaming cups of coffee.

'Where can I get one of those?' Hunter asked pointing to the coffee cups.

'I'll get you one,' Garcia replied. 'The captain's in the last room on the left, through the corridor. I'll see you in there.'

'Working hard, guys?' Hunter shouted to the three officers who glanced at him indifferently before carrying on discussing the game.

Inside the house a peculiar smell hung in the air, a mix of rotten wood and raw sewage. There was nothing to see in the first room. Hunter turned on his flashlight and moved through the door at the far end into a long and narrow corridor that led to four other rooms, two on each side. A young police officer was standing outside the last door on the left. As Hunter made his way down the corridor, he quickly peeked inside each room he passed. Nothing except for spider webs and old debris. The creaking floorboards gave the house an even more sinister feel. As Hunter approached the last door and the officer standing guard he felt an uncomfortable chill. The chill that comes with every murder scene. The chill of death.

Hunter produced his badge and the officer stepped to one side.

'Go right ahead, detective!'

On a table just outside the door Hunter found the customary overalls together with blue plastic shoes and head covers. Next to them a box of latex gloves. Hunter got himself ready and opened the door to face his new nightmare.

The shocking image that met his eyes as he stepped into the room sucked all the air out of his lungs.

'Jesus Christ.' His voice was just a weak whisper.

Five

Hunter stood at the door of a large double room illuminated only by two moving flashlights – Captain Bolter and Doctor Winston. Surprisingly the room was in much better condition than the rest of the house. A giant pit welled in his stomach as he stared at the image before him.

Directly in front of the bedroom door and about three feet from the back wall, the naked body of a woman hung from two parallel wooden posts. Her arms spread as wide as they'd go, her knees bent as they touched the floor placing her in a kneeling Y position. The rope restraining her wrists against the top of the poles had cut deep into her flesh and dark lines of dried blood now decorated her thin arms. Hunter stared at the dead woman's face. His mind struggling to understand what his eyes were seeing.

'Sweet God in heaven!'

An incessant swarm of flies were swirling around her body creating a relentless buzzing sound, but they left her face alone. Her skinless face. A shapeless mass of muscle tissue.

'Hunter! You finally decided to show up.' Captain Bolter was standing across the room next to Doctor Winston, the Chief Medical Examiner.

Hunter stared at the woman for a few more seconds before diverting his attention to the captain. 'Somebody skinned her?' he questioned from the doorway, his voice carrying a tone of disbelief.

'Alive . . . someone skinned her alive,' Doctor Winston's calm voice corrected Hunter. 'She died hours after her skin had been ripped off her face.'

'You've gotta be kidding me!' Hunter studied the faceless woman. The absence of skin made her eyes puff out of their sockets and they seemed to be staring straight at him. Her mouth hung open. No teeth.

Hunter guessed her age to be no older than twenty-five. Her legs, stomach and arms had defined muscle tone and it was clear she'd taken pride in her appearance. Her hair was golden blond, long and smooth, falling halfway down her back. Hunter was sure she'd been a very attractive woman.

'There is more. Have a look behind the door,' Doctor Winston said.

Hunter stepped into the room, closed the door and stared at it confused for a couple of seconds.

'A full-length mirror?' he said quizzically staring at his reflection. Suddenly he stepped out of the way and the woman's body came in full view on the mirror.

'God! The killer made her watch.' Her body had been positioned directly in front of the door.

'That's what it looks like,' Doctor Winston agreed. 'She probably spent her last living hours staring at her disfigured reflection in the mirror – mental torture as well as physical.'

'This mirror doesn't belong on this door . . .' Hunter said looking around, '. . . or in this room. It looks brand new.'

'Exactly, the mirror and those wooden posts were placed in here for a reason – to increase her suffering,' Doctor Winston confirmed.

The bedroom door swung open in front of Hunter breaking

his stare from the mirror. Garcia walked in holding a cup of coffee. 'Here you go,' he said handing it to Hunter.

'I think I'll pass, rookie, my stomach has seen better days and I'm very much wide awake now,' Hunter replied with a dismissive gesture.

Captain Bolter and Doctor Winston both shook their heads indicating they didn't want any either. Garcia reopened the door.

'Here you go,' he said to the young officer standing outside. 'You look like you could use a drink.'

'Uh! Thank you sir.' The officer looked surprised.

'Don't mention it.' Garcia closed the door and approached the victim with Hunter. A pungent smell filled their nostrils forcing Hunter to place a hand over his nose. The woman had been kneeling in a pool of urine and faeces.

'She was kept tied to those posts for several hours, maybe even an entire day. That was her toilet,' Doctor Winston explained pointing to the floor.

Garcia grimaced in disgust.

'How long has she been dead for, doc?' Hunter questioned.

'It's hard to be precise at this moment. The human body drops approximately 1.5 degrees in temperature every hour after death. Her body has dropped around twelve degrees which could mean that she's been dead for eight hours, but that depends on the circumstances. The summer heat would've no doubt slowed the process down and during the day I'm sure this room feels like a sauna. I'll have a better idea of the time of death once I get her into my autopsy room.'

'There are no cuts, no bullet wounds, no strangulation marks. Did she die from her facial injuries?' Hunter asked, looking at the woman's torso and waving his hands to get rid of some of the flies.

'Again, without an autopsy I can't be certain, but my guess would be heart failure induced by pure pain and exhaustion. Whoever did this to her, kept her in this position inflicting more and more pain until she was gone. The killer wanted her to suffer as much as possible, and suffer she did.'

Hunter looked around the room as if searching for something. 'What's this other smell? I can smell something else, something like vinegar.'

'You've got a good nose, Hunter,' Doctor Winston said pointing to one of the corners of the room. 'That jar over there, it was full of vinegar. You can also smell it over her body, predominantly on the top half. It looks like the killer poured it over her skinless face at set time intervals.'

'Vinegar also works as a fly repellent,' Hunter said.

'That's correct,' Doctor Winston confirmed. 'Now just imagine the sort of pain she had to go through. All the nerves around her face were completely exposed. Even a small gust of wind would've caused unbearable pain. She probably passed out several times, or at least tried to. Remember, she had no eye lids – no way of keeping the light away, no way of resting her eyes. Every time she regained consciousness, the first image she'd see would be her disfigured naked body. I'm not even gonna go into what sort of pain the acidity of vinegar poured over open flesh causes.'

'Jesus!' Garcia said taking a few steps back. 'Poor woman!'

'Was she conscious when she was skinned?' Hunter asked.

'Not without being anesthetized, but I don't think she was. I'd say she was drugged, knocked unconscious for several hours while this psycho went to work on her face. After he was done, she was brought up to this house, tied to the posts and tortured some more until she died.'

'What? You don't think she was skinned in this house?' Garcia asked, looking confused.

'No,' Hunter replied before Doctor Winston had a chance to do so. 'Look around. Check any room you like. Not even a speck of blood anywhere except directly under her body. True, I'm sure the killer cleaned up after himself, but this isn't the place. Correct me if I'm wrong, doc, but skinning a human being is a complicated process.'

Doctor Winston nodded in silence.

'The killer would need surgical equipment, operating room lights, not to mention a lot of time and knowledge,' Hunter continued. 'We're talking about one highly skilled psychopath here. Somebody with a great knowledge of medical practices. She wasn't skinned in this house. She was tortured and killed here.'

'Maybe the killer is a hunter. You know, knowledge of skinning animals?' Garcia suggested.

'Could be, but that wouldn't have helped,' Hunter replied. 'Human skin doesn't respond the same way animal skin does. Different elasticity.'

'How do you know that? Do you hunt?' Garcia asked intrigued.

'No, but I read a lot,' Hunter replied casually.

'Plus animals are dead by the time they're skinned,' Doctor Winston carried on. 'You can simply rip the skin off with no concern for the animal's life. Our killer kept the victim alive and that is a very delicate procedure in itself. Whoever this person is, he knows medicine. In fact, he'd make a very good cosmetic surgeon, except for the job on her teeth. They were simply pulled out, no finesse, but maximum pain.'

'The killer didn't want us to identify her,' Garcia concluded.

'He left her fingers intact,' Hunter shot back after quickly checking her hands. 'Why take the teeth and leave the fingerprints?'

Garcia nodded in agreement.

Hunter walked around the two wooden poles to have a look at the woman's back. 'A performing stage,' he whispered. 'A place where the killer's evil could come alive. That's why she was brought here. Look at her, her position is ritualistic.' He turned to face Captain Bolter. 'This killer's done this before.'

Captain Bolter didn't look surprised.

'No one could've handled this sort of pain in silence,' Garcia commented. 'This is the perfect place, totally secluded, no neighbors, no one to walk in on the killer. She could've screamed her lungs out and no one would've come.'

'The victim, do we have anything on her? Do we know who she is?' Hunter asked, still examining the woman's back.

'Nothing so far, but we haven't run her prints through yet,' Garcia answered. 'Our first look through this house has given us zip, not even a piece of clothing. She obviously didn't live here and searching the house for any clues on her identity is probably a waste of time.'

'Do it anyway,' Hunter said firmly. 'How about missing persons?'

'I've fed her initial description into the Missing and Unidentified Persons Unit database,' Garcia replied. 'No matches yet, but without a face . . .' Garcia shook his head as he considered the impossible task.

Hunter took a few seconds to look around the room before his eyes rested on a window on the south wall. 'How about tire tracks on the outside? There looks to be no other way of getting to this place except for that narrow lane. The killer must've driven up here.'

Captain Bolter nodded slightly. 'You're right. That lane is the only access to this house and all the police and forensic units have driven up and down it. If we had anything, it's been covered up. And I'll be having some asses for this.'

'Great!'

The room fell silent. They'd all seen it before. A victim that had no chance against a deranged opponent – a blank canvas painted with the striking colors of death – but this seemed different, it felt different.

'I don't like this,' Hunter broke the silence. 'I don't like this at all. This isn't your regular spur of the moment homicide. This was planned and for a fucking long time too. Just imagine the kind of patience and determination it takes to pull something like this off.' Hunter rubbed at his nose. The stench of death now getting to him.

'A crime of passion perhaps? Maybe someone just wanted revenge over a broken affair,' Garcia offered a new opinion.

'This is no crime of passion,' Hunter said with a shake of the head. 'No one that'd been in love with her would be able to do something like this. No matter how hurt he was, unless she was dating Satan himself. Just look at her, this is simply grotesque and that worries me. This ain't going to end here.'

Hunter's words sent a new chill into the room. The last thing the city of Los Angeles needed was another psychopath killer on the loose, someone wanting to be the next Jack the Ripper.

'Hunter's right, this isn't a crime of passion. This killer has done this before,' Captain Bolter said finally, moving away from the window. His statement stopped everyone in their tracks.

'Do you know something we don't?' Garcia asked the question on everyone's lips.

'Not for long. There is one more thing I want you to see before I let the forensic boys in here.'

Hunter had been intrigued by that since his arrival. Usually the forensic team checks the scene before the detectives are allowed to walk all over the evidence, but today the captain wanted Hunter in there first. Captain Bolter rarely broke protocol.

'On the back of her neck, have a look,' he said tilting his head towards the body.

Hunter and Garcia exchanged a concerned look before approaching the dead woman once again.

'Give me something to lift her hair up with,' Hunter called to anyone in the room. Doctor Winston handed him a metal retractable pointer.

As his flashlight illuminated her now exposed neck Hunter's mind went into a whirlwind of confusion. He stared at it in disbelief – the color drained from his face.

Garcia didn't have a clear view from where he was standing, but what disturbed him was the look in Hunter's eyes. Whatever Hunter was staring at, it had scared him soundless.

Six

Despite being thirty-nine years old, Robert Hunter's youthful-looking face and impressive physique made him look like a man who'd just hit thirty. Always dressed in jeans, T-shirt and a beat-up leather jacket, Hunter was six foot with squared shoulders, high cheekbones and short blondish hair. He possessed a deliberate controlled strength that came across in every movement he made, but it was his eyes that were most striking. An intense pale blue that suggested intelligence and an unflinching resolve.

Hunter grew up as an only child to working-class parents in Compton, an underprivileged neighborhood of South Los Angeles. His mother lost her battle with cancer when he was only seven. His father never remarried and had to take on two jobs to cope with the demands of raising a child on his own.

From a very early age it was obvious to everyone that Hunter was different. He could figure things out faster than most. School bored and frustrated him. He'd finished all of his sixth-grade work in less than two months and just for something to do he'd sped through seventh-, eighth- and even ninth-grade books. Mr Fratelli, the school principal, was amazed by the child prodigy and arranged an appointment at the Mirman School for the Gifted in Mulholland Drive, North West Los Angeles. Doctor Tilby, Mirman's psychologist, ran him through a battery of tests and Hunter was pronounced 'off the scale.' A week later, he'd transferred to Mirman as an eighth-grader. He was only twelve.

By the age of fourteen he'd glided through Mirman's high-school English, History, Biology and Chemistry curriculum. Four years of high school were condensed into two and at fifteen he'd graduated with honors. With recommendations from all of his teachers, Hunter was accepted as a 'special circumstances' student at Stanford University. The top psychology university in America at the time.

In spite of Hunter's good looks, the combination of being too thin, too young and having a strange dress sense made him unpopular with girls and an easy target for bullies. He didn't have the body or the aptitude for sports and preferred to spend his free time in the library. He read – chewed up books with incredible speed. He became fascinated with the world of criminology and the thought process of individuals dubbed 'evil'. Maintaining a 4.0 Grade Point Average during his university years had been a walk in the park, but he soon grew tired of the bullying and of being called 'tooth-pick boy'. He decided to join a weights gym and started taking martial art classes. To his surprise, he enjoyed the physical pain of the workouts. He became obsessed with it and within a year the effects of such heavy training were clearly visible. His body had bulked up impressively. 'Tooth-pick boy' became 'fit boy' and it took him a little less than two years to receive his black belt in karate. The bullying stopped and all of a sudden girls couldn't get enough of him.

By the age of nineteen Hunter had already graduated in Psychology and at twenty-three he received his PhD in Criminal Behavior Analysis and Biopsychology. His thesis paper titled 'An Advanced Psychological Study in Criminal Conduct' had been made into a book and it was now mandatory reading at the FBI National Center for the Analysis of Violent Crime (NCAVC).

Life was good, but two weeks after receiving his PhD Hunter's world was turned upside down. For the past three and a half years his father had been working as a security guard for the Bank of America branch in Avalon Boulevard. A robbery gone wrong turned into a Wild West gun-fight and Hunter's father took a bullet to the chest. He fought for twelve weeks in a coma. Hunter never left his side.

Those twelve weeks sitting in silence, watching his father slip away little by little each day transformed Hunter. He could think of nothing else but revenge. That's when the insomnia started. When the police told him that they had no suspect, Hunter knew they'd never catch his father's killer. He felt utterly helpless and the feeling disgusted him. After the burial, he made a decision. He wouldn't only study the minds of criminals anymore. He'd go after them himself.

After joining the police force, he quickly made a name for himself and moved through the police ranks at lightning speed making detective for the LAPD at the early age of twenty-six. He was soon recruited by the Robbery-Homicide Division, being paired up with a more senior detective – Scott Wilson. They were part of the Homicide Special 1 Division, dealing with serial killers, high-profile and other homicide cases requiring extensive time.

Wilson was thirty-nine at the time. His six-foot-two build was complimented by three hundred pounds of muscle and fat. His most distinctive feature was a shining scar that graced the left side of his shaved head. His menacing look had always played in his favor. No one would mess with a detective that looked like a pissed-off Shrek.

Wilson had been in the force for eighteen years, the last nine of them as a detective for the RHD. At first he'd hated the idea of being paired up with a young and inexperienced detective, but Hunter was a fast learner and his powers of deduction and analysis were nothing short of astounding. With every case they solved Wilson's respect for Hunter grew. They became the best of friends, inseparable on and off the job.

Los Angeles had never lacked in gruesome and violent homicides, but it did lack in detective numbers. Wilson and Hunter frequently had to work on up to six different cases at once. The pressure never bothered them; on the contrary, they thrived on it. Then a Hollywood celebrity investigation almost cost them their badges and their friendship.

The case had involved Linda and John Spencer, a well-known record producer who'd made a fortune after producing three consecutive number one rock albums. John and Linda had met at an after-show party and it had been one of those flash romances, within three months they were married. John had bought a magnificent house in Beverly Hills and their marriage seemed to have come straight out of a fantasy book, everything looked and felt perfect. They loved entertaining, and at least twice a month they'd throw an extravagant party by their piano-shaped swimming pool. But the fantasy story didn't last long. By the end of their first year of marriage the parties had started to die down together with the romance. Public and domestic rows became a common thing as John's drug and alcohol addiction took over his life.

One August night, after another heated argument, Linda's body was found in their kitchen with a single .38 caliber revolver shot to the back of the head, execution style. There was no sign of a struggle or break in, no defense wounds or bruises on Linda's arms or hands. The evidence found in the crime scene together with the fact that he had disappeared after his argument with Linda made John Spencer the primary and only suspect. Hunter and Wilson were assigned to the case.

John was only picked up days later drunk and high on heroin. In his interrogation he didn't deny he'd had another row with his wife that night. He'd admitted their marriage had been going through a rough phase. He remembered the argument and leaving the house angry, agitated and drunk, but what he couldn't remember was what had happened to him for the past few days. He had no alibi. But he also sustained that he would never hurt Linda. He was still crazy in love with her.

Homicide investigations involving celebrities in Hollywood had always attracted a lot of attention and the media was quick to create their own circus – 'FAMOUS AND RICH PRODUCER MURDERS BEAUTIFUL WIFE IN JEALOUS RAGE.' Even the mayor was calling for a swift resolution to the case.

The prosecution showed that John did own a .38 caliber revolver, but it had never been found. They also had no problem getting witnesses to testify to all the public rows John and Linda used to have. In most cases, John did all the yelling while Linda just cried. Establishing that John Spencer had an aggressive temper had been child's play.

Wilson was convinced of John's guilt, but Hunter was sure they had the wrong man. To Hunter, John was just a scared kid who had got rich too fast, and with the money and fame came the drugs. John had no history of violence. In school he'd been just another regular geeky-looking kid – torn blue jeans, strange haircut, always listening to his heavy metal music.

Hunter tried reasoning with Wilson many times.

'OK, so he had rows with his wife, but you find me a marriage without them,' Hunter argued. 'In none of those rows had he ever hit or hurt Linda.'

'Ballistics proved that the bullet that killed her came from the same stash found in John Spencer's office desk drawer,' Wilson shouted.

'That doesn't prove he pulled the trigger.'

'All the fibers found on the victim came from the same clothes John was wearing the night we found him. Ask anyone who knew the couple. He had a foul temper on him, shouting at her all the time. You're a psychologist. You know how these things escalate.'

'Exactly, they escalate. Gradually. It doesn't usually just jump from heated arguments to shooting someone in the back of the head in one single step.'

'Look Robert, I've always respected your assessment of a suspect. It has guided us in the right direction many times, but I also like to follow my gut. And my gut tells me this time you're wrong.'

'The guy deserves a chance. We should carry on with the investigation. Maybe there's something we missed.'

'We can't carry on.' Wilson laughed. 'It ain't up to us to make that decision. You know better. We've done our part. We followed the evidence we had and we apprehended the suspect we were after. Let his attorneys deal with it now.'

Hunter knew what killers were made of and John Spencer simply didn't fit the bill, but his opinion alone meant nothing. Wilson was right. It was out of their hands now. They were already behind on five other cases and Captain Bolter threatened Hunter with suspension if he wasted any more time in a case that was officially closed.

The jury took less than three hours to reach the verdict of guilty as charged and John Spencer was sentenced to life imprisonment. And life's what he got. Twenty-eight days after his conviction John hung himself using his bed sheet. In his cell, next to his body a single note that read *Linda, I'll be with you soon. No more arguments, I promise.*

Twenty-two days after John Spencer's suicide, their pool cleaner was picked up in Utah. In his car they'd found John's .38 caliber revolver together with some jewelry and lingerie that had belonged to Linda Spencer. Subsequent forensic tests showed that the bullet that had killed her had come from that same revolver. The pool cleaner later confessed to shooting her.

Hunter and Wilson came under severe scrutiny by the media, the Chief of Police, the Police Commissioner and the Mayor. They'd been accused of negligence and failure to conduct a proper investigation. If Captain Bolter hadn't intervened in their favor and accepted half the blame they would've lost their detective badges. Hunter never stopped blaming himself for not having done more. His friendship with Wilson took a huge knock. That had been six years ago.

Seven

'What is it? What can you see?' Garcia asked moving towards his partner, who still hadn't said a word. Hunter stood motionless and wide-eyed, staring at something carved onto the woman's neck, something he'd never forget.

After tiptoeing to raise himself above Hunter's shoulder, Garcia got a better look at the dead woman's neck, but it still didn't settle his confusion. He'd never seen the carved symbol before.

'What does that mean?' he asked, hoping for an answer from someone.

Silence.

Garcia moved closer. The symbol looked like two crosses in one, one right side up and the other upside down ‡, but the crossbars seemed quite far from each other, almost at the extremities of its vertical beam. To him it meant absolutely nothing.

'Is this a sick joke, Captain?' Hunter finally snapped out of his trance.

'It's sick alright, but no joke,' the captain replied in a stern voice.

'Will somebody fucking talk to me?' Garcia's impatience was growing.

'Shit!' Hunter blurted, letting the woman's hair fall back onto her shoulders.

'Hello!' Garcia waved his hands in front of Hunter's eyes. 'I don't remember taking my invisible pills this morning, so will somebody let me know what the hell this is all about?' His irritation was barely disguised.

To Hunter the room had just gotten darker, the air heavier. His headache now hammering his brain made it hard for him to think. He rubbed his gritty eyes in a last hope that this had all been just a bad dream.

'You'd better fill your partner in, Hunter,' Captain Bolter said bringing Hunter's senses crashing back to the room.

'Thank you,' Garcia said, relieved to have found an ally.

Hunter still paid Garcia no attention. 'You know what this means, Captain?'

'I know what it looks like, yes.'

Hunter ran his fingers through his hair. 'The media will have a field day when they get hold of this,' he continued.

'For now the media won't get hold of anything, I will take care of that,' the captain reassured him, 'but you better find out if this is the real deal.'

'What real deal?' Garcia shouted.

Doctor Winston cut in. 'Well, whatever you have to do, could you do it outside. I need to get the boys in here so they can start processing this room. I don't really wanna lose any more time on this.'

'How long to process this place? How long until we know something?' Hunter asked.

'I'm not sure, but judging from the size of this house, most of the day, maybe even into the night.'

Hunter knew the procedure well, there was nothing he could do but wait.

'On your way out, tell the crime lab team to come in will you?' the doctor asked, walking towards the victim's body.

'Yeah, we'll do that,' Hunter said nodding at Garcia who was still looking like a lost kid.

'Nobody's told me shit yet,' he protested.

'C'mon, if you drop me by my car we can talk on the way there.'

Hunter had one more look at the mutilated body tied to the wooden posts. It was hard to imagine that only a few days ago that body had belonged to a woman full of life. Hunter opened the door and stepped out of the room, Garcia right on his heels.

Outside the house Hunter still looked unsettled as they approached Garcia's car. 'So where is your car?' Garcia said opening the door to his Honda Civic.

'What?' Hunter's thoughts seemed to be someplace else.

'Your car? Where is it?'

'Oh! In Santa Monica.'

'Santa Monica! Damn that's all the way across town.'

'Do you have anything else to do?'

'Not anymore,' Garcia replied with a foolish look. 'Where exactly did you leave it?'

'Do you know the Hideout bar?'

'Yeah, I know it. What the hell were you doing there?'

'I don't even remember,' Hunter replied with a slight shake of the head.

'It's gonna take us around two hours to make it to Santa Monica from here. At least we'll have plenty of time to talk.'

'Two hours?' Hunter sounded surprised. 'What do you have under that hood? A scooter engine?'

'Did you notice the bumpy roads all around this place? This is a new car. I ain't screwing my suspension up, so until we clear the lunar surface-like roads, we'll be going real slow.'

'Whatever.' Hunter got into the car and buckled up. He looked around at an obsessive compulsive cleaner's paradise. The car's interior was spotless. No potato chip bags on the floor, no coffee spills on the carpet or seats, no donut smudges, nothing.

'Damn rookie, do you clean this car every day?'

'I like my car clean, it's better than a pigsty of a car, don't you think?' Garcia sounded proud.

'And what the hell is this smell? It's like . . . tutti frutti.'

'It's called air freshener. You should try one inside that old beater of yours.'

'Hey, there's nothing wrong with my car. Old yes, but built like a fortress. Not like these cheap imports.'

'This car wasn't cheap.'

'Yeah right,' Hunter replied with a short laugh. 'Anyway, I'm impressed. Do you clean houses as well? There is a big market out there in Beverly Hills if you ever decide to pack up the detective's job.'

Garcia ignored Hunter's comment, started the engine and maneuvered through the few police units that were still parked in front of the old house. He tried his best to avoid brushing his car against the dense shrubs bordering the narrow path and cursed when he heard the sound of wood scraping against metal. Garcia drove slowly at first, trying to minimize the bumpy ride. They were both silent until they reached the main road.

Hunter had driven along Little Tujunga Canyon Road many times. If you are looking to unwind it's an astonishing drive with heart-warming views.

'OK, I'm all ears,' Garcia broke the silence. 'Enough with the bullshit. What the hell does that weird carving on the back of the victim's neck mean? You've obviously seen it before, judging by your reaction.'

Hunter searched for the correct words as old images came into his mind. He was about to bring Garcia into a nightmare – one he was trying to forget.

'Have you ever heard of the Crucifix Killer?'

Garcia cocked an eyebrow and looked inquisitively at Hunter. 'Are you joking?'

Hunter shook his head.

'Yeah, of course I have. Everyone in LA has heard of the Crucifix Killer. Damn, everyone in the entire USA has heard of the Crucifix Killer. I actually followed the case as closely as I could. Why?'

'What do you know about him? What do you know about the case?'

'Are you trying to brag now?' he asked with an uncomfortable smile as if waiting for the obvious answer – he got none. 'Are you serious? You want me to talk to you about the case?'

'Humor me.'

'OK,' Garcia replied with a *whatever* head movement. 'It was probably your biggest case. Seven horrific homicides over a two-year period. Some crazy, religious fanatic. You and your ex-partner caught the guy about a year and a half ago. He was picked up driving out of LA. If I'm not mistaken, he had a shitload of evidence inside the car with him, victim's belongings and stuff like that. Apparently even his interrogation didn't take that long; he confessed straight away, didn't he?'

'How do you know about his interrogation?'

'I'm still a cop remember? We get some good inside information. Anyway, he got the death penalty and the lethal shot about a year ago, one of the quickest executed sentences in history. Even the president got involved right? It was all over the news.'

Hunter studied his partner for a moment. Garcia knew the story as it'd been told by the press.

'Is that all you know? Do you know why the press called him the Crucifix Killer?'

It was now Garcia's turn to study his partner for a quick second. 'Have you been drinking?'

'Not for a few hours,' Hunter said instinctively checking his watch.

'Yes, everyone knows why. As I've said he was a religious fanatic. He thought he was ridding the world of sinners or some crap like that. You know – prostitutes, drug addicts – whoever the little voices in his sick mind told him to kill. Anyway, the reason he was called the Crucifix Killer was because he branded a crucifix on the back of every victim's left hand.'

Hunter sat in silence for a moment.

'Wait a second! Do you think this is a copycat case? I mean – carving that strange symbol on the back of that woman's neck. It did look like some sort of crucifix if you think about it,' Garcia said, picking up on Hunter's hint.

Hunter didn't answer back. Silence took over for another two or three minutes. They'd now reached Sand Canyon Road, an exclusive neighborhood in Santa Clarita and the view had changed to large houses with impeccably treated lawns. Hunter was glad to be back in civilization again. Traffic was getting a little busier as people made their way into work. Hunter could see businessmen and women stepping out of their front doors in their nice suits ready for another day at the office. The first rays of sunlight had just graced the sky in what was already promising to be another scorching hot day.

'Since we're talking about the Crucifix murders, can I ask you something?' Garcia ended the silence in the car.

'Yeah, shoot,' Hunter replied in a monotonous tone.

'There were rumors going around that either you or your partner never believed that the guy you caught was the killer – despite all the evidence found in his car and despite his confession – is that true?'

Old images of Hunter's only interrogation session with the so-called Crucifix Killer started playing in his mind.

Click . . .

'Wednesday 15th of February – 10:30 a.m. Detective Robert Hunter initiating the interrogation of Mike Farloe concerning case 017632. The interviewee has declined the right to counsel,' Hunter spoke into the old-fashioned tape recorder inside one of the eight interrogation rooms in the RHD building.

Opposite Hunter sat a thirty-four-year-old man with a strong jaw, protruding chin covered in three-day-old stubble and dark eyes as cold as black ice. His hairline was receding and the little black hair that remained was thin and combed back. His cuffed hands were placed over the broad metal table that sat between him and Hunter, palms down.

'Are you sure you don't want to have a lawyer present?'

'The lord is my shepherd.'

'OK then. Your name is Mike Farloe is that correct?'

The man lifted his stare from his cuffed hands and looked straight into Hunter's eyes. 'Yes.'

'And your present address is number 5 Sandoval Street in Santa Fe?'

Mike was strangely calm for someone who was facing a multiple homicide charge. 'That's where I used to live, yes.'

'Used to?'

'I'm gonna live in prison now, isn't that right detective? At least for a little while.' His voice was dull and steady.

'Do you wanna go to prison?'

Silence.

Hunter was the best interrogator at the RHD. His knowledge of psychology allowed him to extract extremely valuable information from suspects, sometimes even confessions. He could read a suspect's body language and tell-tales like a billboard. Captain Bolter wanted every little piece of information he could get from Mike Farloe – Robert Hunter was his secret weapon.

'Can you remember where you were on the night of 15th of December last year?' Hunter was now referring to the night before the last Crucifix Killer's victim was found.

Mike was still staring straight at him. 'Yes I can . . .'

Hunter waited a few seconds for the remainder of the answer. It never came.

'And where were you?'

'I was working.'

'And what is it that you do?'

'I clean the city.'

'You're a garbage collector?'

'Correct, but I also work for Our Lord Jesus Christ.'

'Doing what?'

'I clean the city,' he repeated calmly. 'I rid this city of filth – sinners.'

Hunter could feel Captain Bolter shifting in his chair inside the observation room on the other side of the two-way mirror mounted on the north wall.

Hunter massaged the back of his neck with his right hand. 'OK, how about the . . .' – he flipped through a few notes he had with him – '. . . 22nd of September, do you remember where you were on that night?'

Inside the small observation room Scott looked puzzled. '22nd of September? What the hell happened on that day? There was no victim found on that date, or even close to it. What the fuck is Hunter doing?'

The seven Crucifix Killer dates had been imprinted into Scott's brain, and he was sure Hunter knew them by heart, no need to check any notes.

'Let him do his job, he knows what he's doing.' The answer came from Doctor Martin, a police psychologist also observing the interrogation.

'The same. I was doing exactly the same thing,' Mike replied convincingly. His answer caught everyone in the observation room by surprise.

'What?' Scott mumbled. 'Is there a victim we don't know about?'

Captain Bolter's answer was a simple shrug.

Hunter had been observing Mike Farloe's reactions, trying to get an insight into his thoughts, trying to read his tell-tale signs. Text-book behavior psychology told Hunter to monitor Mike's eye movement – up and to the left meant he was accessing his visual constructive cortex, trying to create an image in his mind that didn't exist before, a clear indication of lying – up and to the right meant he was searching his memory for visually remembered images, therefore, probably telling the truth – there was no movement whatsoever, his eyes were as still as a dead man's.

'How about the items that were found in your car, can you tell me about them? How did you get them?' Hunter asked, referring to the passport, the driver's license and the social security card that had been found inside a paper bag hidden away in the spare tire compartment of Mike Farloe's 1992 rusty Oldsmobile Custom Cruiser. Each of the items belonging to a different victim. Inside his trunk the police had also found some bloody rags. The blood on them matching the DNA on three of the victims.

'I got them from the sinners.'

'The sinners?'

'Yes . . . don't play dumb, detective, you know what I mean.'

'Maybe I don't. Why don't you explain it to me?'

'You know the world wasn't meant to be this way.' The first hint of emotion from Mike finally coming through – anger. 'Every second of every day a new sin is committed. Every second of every day we disrespect and disregard the laws that were given to us by the highest power of all. The world can't go on like this, disrespecting Our Lord, disregarding his message. Someone has to punish them.'

'And that someone is you?'

Silence.

'To me all those victims were just normal people, not great sinners.'

'That's because your eyes have been glued the fuck shut, detective. You've been so blinded by the filth in this city that you can't see straight anymore. None of you can. A prostitute selling her body for cash, spreading disease throughout the city.' Hunter knew he was talking about the second victim. 'A lawyer whose sole purpose in life was to defend scumbag drug dealers just so he could pay for his playboy lifestyle. A person with no morals,' referring to the fifth victim. 'A high city roller who fucked her way to the top, any cock would do as long as it moved her up a step . . .' the sixth victim. 'They needed to pay. They needed to learn that you can't just walk away from the laws of God. They needed to be taught a lesson.'

'And that's what you were doing?'

'Yes . . . I was serving Our Lord.' The anger was gone. His voice as serene as a baby's laughter.

'PSYCHO.' The comment came from Scott inside the observation room.

Hunter poured himself a glass of cold water from the aluminum jug on the table.

'Would you like some water?'

'No thanks, detective.'

'Can I get you anything . . . coffee, a cigarette?'

His response was a simple shake of the head.

Hunter still couldn't read Mike Farloe. There were no variations in his tone of voice, no sudden movements, no change in facial expressions. His eyes remained deadly cold, devoid of any emotion. His hands remained still. There was no increase in perspiration on his forehead or hands. Hunter needed more time.

'Do you believe in God, detective?' Mike asked calmly. 'Do you pray to repent your sins?'

'I believe in God. What I don't believe in is murder,' Hunter replied evenly.

Mike Farloe's eyes were on Hunter as if the roles had reversed, as if he were the one trying to read Hunter's reactions. Hunter was about to pop another question when Farloe spoke first. 'Detective, why don't we cut the bullshit and go straight to the point? Ask me what you are here to ask me. Ask and you shall be answered.'

'And what is that? What is it that I'm here to ask you?'

'You wanna know if I committed those murders. You wanna know if I am who they call the Crucifix Killer.'

'And are you?'

Farloe shifted his stare from Hunter for the first time. His eyes now rested on the two-way mirror on the north wall. He knew what was happening on the other side. The anticipation inside the observation room now growing to eruption point. Captain Bolter could swear that Farloe was staring straight at him.

'I didn't choose that name for myself, the media did.' His eyes had returned to Hunter. 'But yes, I freed their souls from their life of sin.'

'I'll be damned . . . we've got a confession.' Captain Bolter could hardly hide his excitement.

'Hell yeah! And it only took Hunter about ten minutes to get it out of him. That's my boy,' Scott replied with a smile.

'If you are the Crucifix Killer, then you did choose your name,' Hunter continued. 'You branded the victims. You chose your mark.'

'They needed to repent. The symbol of our Lord freed their souls.'

'But you are no God. You don't have the power to free anyone. Thou shall not kill, isn't that one of the commandments? Doesn't killing these people make you a sinner?'

'No sin shall be when done in the name of the divine. I was doing God's work.'

'Why? Did God call in sick that day? Why would God ask you to kill in his name? Isn't God supposed to be a merciful being?'

Farloe let a smile grace his lips for the first time showing yellow cigarette-stained teeth. There was an evil air about him. Something different, something almost inhuman.

'This guy gives me the creeps. Shouldn't we just stop this interview, he's already confessed, he's done it, end of story,' Scott said clearly irritated.

'Not yet, give him a few more minutes,' Doctor Martin replied.

'Whatever . . . I'm out of here, I've heard enough.' Scott opened the door and stepped into the narrow corridor on the third floor of the RHD building.

Hunter grabbed a piece of paper, wrote something on it and slid it towards Farloe over the table. 'Do you know what this is?'

Farloe's eyes moved down to the paper. He stared at it for about five seconds. By the movement of his eyes and imperceptible frown Hunter knew Farloe didn't have a clue what the figure on the paper meant. Hunter got no answer.

'OK, so let me ask you this . . .'

'No, no more questions,' Farloe cut in. 'You know what I've done, detective. You've seen my work. You've heard what you wanted to hear. There's no more need for questions. I've said my piece.' Farloe closed his eyes, placed his hands together and began a whispered prayer.

'Yes it's true. I never believed he was our killer,' Hunter finally answered Garcia's question, snapping back from his memory flash.

Even though it was just past six in the morning the day was already warm. Hunter pressed the button on the passenger's door and his window rolled down smoothly. The scenery had changed from the luxurious houses of Santa Clarita into noisy traffic as they drove down San Diego Freeway.

'Do you want me to turn on the air con?' Garcia asked fiddling with his dashboard.

Hunter's car was an old Buick and it didn't have any of the luxury gadgets of modern cars. No air conditioning, no sunroof, no electric windows or mirrors, but it was a Buick, pure American muscle as Hunter liked to call it.

'No. I prefer it like this, natural polluted LA air – you just can't beat it.'

'So why did you think you had the wrong guy? You had all the evidence found in his car, plus the guy confessed. What else did you need?' Garcia asked bringing the subject back to the Crucifix Killer.

Hunter tilted his head towards the open window letting the air brush through his hair. 'Did you know we never found any evidence at any of the seven crime scenes?'

'Again, I've heard rumors, but I thought that was just you guys playing your cards close to your chest.'

'It's true, Scott and I fine-combed every inch of those crime scenes and so did the forensic team. We never found a thing – not a fingerprint, not a strand of hair, not a fiber . . . nothing. The crime scenes were like forensic vacuums.' Hunter paused, letting the wind hit his face once again. 'For two years the killer never made a mistake, never left anything behind, no slip-ups . . . the killer was like a ghost. We had nothing, no leads, no direction and no idea of who the killer could be. Then, all of a sudden he gets caught with all that shit in his car? It didn't add up. How the hell does anyone go from being probably the most thorough criminal in history to being the sloppiest one?'

'How did you catch him?'

'An anonymous phone call just a few weeks after the seventh victim was found. Someone had seen a suspect car with what seemed to be blood smudges on the outside of its trunk. The caller had managed to note down the license-plate number and the car was picked up on the outskirts of LA.'

'Mike Farloe's?'

'Exactly, and inside his trunk it was like Christmas time for our investigation.'

Garcia frowned. He was starting to follow Hunter's line of thought. 'Yeah, but several major criminals have been caught out just like that, out of a traffic violation or some minor contravention. Maybe he was thorough at the crime scene, but sloppy at home.'

'I don't buy that,' Hunter replied with a shake of the head. 'He also kept on calling me "detective" throughout the interrogation.'

'And what's the problem with that?'

'The Crucifix Killer used to call me on my cell phone and let me know about the location of a new victim, that's how we

found them. I was the only one who'd had any contact with
him.'

'Why you?'

'I never found out, but every time he called me he'd always
use my first name, he'd always call me "Robert", never "detective,"' Hunter paused. He was about to drop an atomic bomb
on Garcia's lap. 'But the turning point was when I asked him
about the crucifix mark branded on the victims' hands. In a
way he accepted it, he said that the symbol of our Lord could
free them or something like that.'

'Yes, so he was a religious psycho – what's your point?'

'I showed him a drawing of the symbol used by the Crucifix
Killer and I'm sure he didn't recognize it.'

'He didn't recognize a crucifix?' Garcia arched both eyebrows.

'The Crucifix Killer never branded a crucifix on the back of
the victim's left hand. That was just a story we fed the media to
avoid the copycats, the attention seekers.'

Garcia held his breath in anticipation and felt an uncomfortable shiver down his spine.

'What the Crucifix Killer did was carve a strange symbol,
something like a double-crucifix, one right side up and the
other upside down on the back of the victim's neck.' Hunter
pointed to the back of his own neck. 'That was his real mark.'

Hunter's words caught Garcia totally by surprise. His mind
flashed back to the scene in the old wooden house. The
woman's body. Her skinless face. The carving on the back of
her neck. The symbol of the Crucifix Killer. 'What? You've
gotta be kidding me.' Garcia took his eyes off the road for an
instant.

'Watch the road!' Hunter realized they were about to run a
red light. Garcia's attention switched back to the road once

again and he slammed down on the brakes throwing Hunter's body forward like a torpedo. Hunter was held by his seatbelt which brought him crashing back to his seat, his head jerking back violently and hitting the headrest.

'Damn! That brought my headache back, thanks,' Hunter said, rubbing his temples with both hands.

The last thing in Garcia's mind was his partner's headache. Hunter's words were still echoing in his ears. 'So what are you saying? That someone found out about the real Crucifix Killer's signature and is using it?'

'I doubt it. Only a handful of people knew about it. Just a few of us at the RHD and Doctor Winston. We kept all information about the killer sealed tight. The symbol we saw today, it's identical.'

'Fuck, are you trying to suggest that he's back from the dead or something?'

'What I'm trying to say is that Mike Farloe wasn't the Crucifix Killer as I'd always suspected. The killer's still out there.'

'But the guy confessed. Why the hell would he do that when he knew he would get the shot?' Garcia asked, almost shouting.

'Maybe he just wanted the notoriety, I'm not sure. Look, I have no doubt that Mike Farloe was mentally fucked up, he was a religious psycho, just not the one we were looking for.'

'But then, how the hell did all that evidence end up in his car?'

'I'm not sure, framed probably.'

'Framed? But the only one who could've framed him was the Crucifix Killer himself.'

'Exactly.'

'And why now? Why would he be back now?'

'I'm trying to figure that out myself,' Hunter replied.

Garcia sat immobile staring at Hunter. He needed time to take all that in. That would explain Hunter's reaction to the symbol carved on the woman's neck. Could it be true, the Crucifix Killer had never been caught? Was he still out there? Had the State sent an innocent man to his death? Since Mike Farloe's conviction the killings had stopped, which indicated that he was the Crucifix Killer. Even Hunter had started to believe it.

They sat in silence. Hunter could feel Garcia trying to process all the new information, trying to understand why someone would confess to a crime he didn't commit.

'If this is the real deal, I guess we will find out soon enough,' Hunter said.

'Really, how? How will we find out?'

'Well, for starters, if this is the same killer, the forensic team will come up with nothing, another clean-as-a-whistle crime scene . . . Green light.'

'What?'

'The traffic light, it's green.'

Garcia shifted his Honda Civic into gear and stepped on the gas. Neither said a word until they reached Santa Monica.

The Hideout bar is located right at the beach end of West Channel Road. Santa Monica beach itself is literally just across the road, making the Hideout bar one of the most popular nightspots in Westside Region. Garcia had only been once. Swaying curtains separated the nautically themed bar area from the main lounge, which was decorated with images of Santa Monica in the 1920s. The second floor was a loft that over-looked a low-back-chair-filled rear patio. It was a very popular place with the younger crowd and definitely not the type of bar Garcia would picture Robert Hunter hanging out.

Hunter's car was parked just a few yards from the bar's entrance. Garcia parked right behind it.

'I'd like to take another look in that house after the forensic team is done, what do you say?' Hunter asked, getting his car keys out of his pocket.

Garcia was unable to meet Hunter's gaze.

'Yo! Rookie, are you OK?'

'Yeah. I'm good,' Garcia finally replied. 'Yeah, that's a good idea.'

Hunter stepped out of the shiny Honda and opened the door to his old beat-up Buick. As he started his engine there was only one thought in his mind.

This shouldn't be his first case.

Eight

D-King didn't take too kindly to any of his girls doing a disappearing act on him. Jenny had walked out on his party at the Vanguard Club three nights ago and he hadn't heard from her since. D-King differed from other sex dealers in Los Angeles in that he wasn't violent with his girls. If any of them decided that they'd had enough and wanted out, he'd be fine with that, as long as they didn't go to work for another sex dealer or run away with his money.

Finding new girls was the easiest aspect of his business. Every day hundreds of beautiful girls arrive in Los Angeles looking for the Hollywood dream. Every day hundreds of dreams are shattered by the harsh reality of the City of Angels. It's just a matter of knowing which girls to approach. The desperate and totally broke – the ones that need to get a fix – the ones that craved the lifestyle D-King had to offer. If any of his girls wanted out, all they had to do was say it and a replacement would be just around the corner.

D-King sent his main bodyguard, Jerome, to find out what had happened to Jenny. Why hadn't she called back? Worst of all, why hadn't she turned up for her appointment with a client last night? D-King didn't tolerate letting a client down. It didn't reflect well on his business and even a crooked business depended on reliability. D-King suspected something wasn't right. Jenny was his most reliable girl and he was sure that if she had run into any trouble, she would've called.

The truth was he had a soft spot for Jenny. She was a very sweet girl, always with a smile and a fantastic sense of humor – qualities that went a long way in her line of work. When Jenny first started working for D-King she told him she'd only do this job until she had enough money to stand on her own two feet. He respected her determination, but for now she was one of his most profitable girls, a very popular choice among the rich and ugly scumbags that made up his client list.

On Jerome's return D-King was doing his morning exercise – twenty-five laps of his half-Olympic-size swimming pool.

'Boss, I am afraid I ain't got good news.' Jerome was a scary looking man. African American with cropped Afro hair and a crooked nose that had been broken so many times Jerome had lost count. He was six-foot-three and weighed three hundred and thirty pounds. He had a square jaw and cotton-white teeth. Jerome had been tipped to become the next heavyweight champion of the world, but a car accident had left him almost paralyzed from the waist down. It took him four years to be able to walk properly again. By that time, his shot at the title had come and gone. He ended up working as special security for a nightclub in Hollywood. D-King offered him a job and a substantial salary raise after he saw Jerome single-handedly take care of a group of seven football players who were looking for trouble one night.

D-King stepped out of the swimming pool, grabbed a clean white bathrobe with the word 'King' in big golden letters on the back and sat down at the table by the side of the pool, where breakfast was waiting for him.

'That ain't what I want to hear, Jerome. I don't wanna start my day with bad news.' He poured himself a glass of orange juice. 'Go on, nigga, spill it out.' His voice was as calm as it'd always been. D-King was not the type of person to lose his coolness easily.

'Well, you told me to go and check on Jenny, see why she'd disappeared for a few days.'

'Yeah?'

'OK, it looks like she didn't only disappear from the club, boss, she simply disappeared.'

'What the fuck is that supposed to mean?'

'It doesn't look like she's been home at all in the past few days. The building concierge hasn't seen her either.'

D-King put down his glass of orange juice and studied his bodyguard for a few seconds. 'How about her things? Were they still in the apartment?'

'Everything – dresses, shoes, handbags, even her make-up. Her suitcases were all stacked up in the wardrobe too. If she split, it was in a fucking hurry, boss.'

'She has nothing to be running away from,' D-King said as he poured himself a cup of coffee.

'Does she have a boyfriend?'

'Does she what?' he asked, making an 'I don't believe you' face. 'You know better than that, nigga. None of my girls have relationships, it's bad for business.'

'Maybe she met someone that night at the Vanguard.'

'And what?'

'I don't know. Maybe went back to his place.'

'Hell no, Jenny doesn't do freebies.'

'Maybe she liked the guy.'

'She's a hooker, Jerome. She'd just come out of a five-night working week. The last thing she would've wanted was to go to bed with someone else.'

'Private clients?'

'Say what? All my girls know what would happen if I found

out they were trying to run a little parallel business. Jenny ain't the type, she ain't stupid.'

'Maybe she's just staying with a friend,' Jerome offered one more option.

'Again, not like her. She's been one of my girls for what, almost three years? She's never given me any trouble. She's always on time for her appointments. No, Jerome, this is messed up, something's wrong.'

'Do you think she might be in trouble, financially I mean, gambling or something like that?'

'If she is she would've come to me, I know that. She would-n't just run away.'

'What do you want me to do, boss?'

D-King had a sip of his coffee, thinking about his options. 'First check the hospitals,' he finally said. 'We've gotta find out if something's happened to her.'

'Do you think someone might've hurt her?'

'If someone did . . . that motherfucker is dead.'

Jerome wondered who'd be stupid enough to hurt any of D-King's girls.

'If the hospitals come up blank we'll need to check with the police.'

'Shall I call Culhane?'

Detective Mark Culhane worked for the Narcotics division of the LAPD. He was also in D-King's dirty-cop pay list.

'He ain't the sharpest of minds, but I guess we'll have to. Warn him not to go snooping around like a lost dog though. I wanna keep this on the "low low" for now.'

'I've got you, boss.'

'Check the hospitals first, if you come up empty – call him.'

Jerome nodded, leaving his boss to finish his breakfast.

D-King had a bite of his egg-white omelet, but his appetite

had gone. After over ten years as a dealer he'd developed a nose for trouble and something didn't smell right. He wasn't only well known in Los Angeles, he was also well feared. Once someone had made the mistake of slapping one of his girls across the face. That someone was found three days later inside a suitcase – his body separated into six parts, head, torso, arms and legs.

Nine

Carlos Garcia was a young detective who'd worked his way up through the police ranks almost as quickly as Hunter. The son of a Brazilian federal agent and an American history teacher, he and his mother moved to Los Angeles when Garcia was only ten years old, after his parents' marriage collapsed. Even though he'd lived in America most of his life, Garcia could speak Portuguese like a true Brazilian. His father was a very attractive man with smooth dark hair, brown eyes and olive skin. His mother was a natural blond with light-blue eyes and European-looking fair skin. Garcia had inherited his father's olive-tone skin and darkish brown hair, which he let grow slightly longer than his mother would've liked it. His eyes weren't as light blue as his mother's, but they had definitely come from her side of the family. Despite being thirty-one years old, Garcia still had a boyish look. He had a slim frame, thanks to years of track and field, but his build was deceptive and he was stronger than anyone would've guessed.

Jennet Liams, Garcia's mother, did everything in her power to persuade him not to pursue a career as a police officer. Her marriage to a federal agent had taught her plenty. It's a dangerous life. Few human beings can endure the kind of mental pressure that comes with it. Her family and marriage suffered because of her husband's profession. She didn't what her son and his future family to have the same fate. But by the age of ten, Garcia had made up his mind. He wanted to be just like his hero – his father.

He'd dated the same girl since high school and marriage came almost immediately after their graduation. Anna was a sweet girl. One year younger than Garcia with magnificent dark hazel eyes and short black hair, her beauty was unconventional but mesmerizing nevertheless. They had no children, a decision they'd made together – at least for the time being.

Garcia spent two years as a LAPD detective in north Los Angeles before being given a choice: a position with the Narcotics department or one with the Homicide division. He decided to take the Homicide job.

On the morning of his first day with the RHD Garcia had woken up a lot earlier than usual. He'd tried to be as quiet as possible, but that didn't keep him from waking Anna. He needed to report to Captain Bolter's office at eight-thirty, but by six-thirty he was already dressed in his best suit and found himself killing time in their small apartment on the north side of LA.

'How do I look?' he asked after his second cup of coffee.

'It's the third time you've asked me the same question,' Anna laughed. 'You look fine, babe. They are lucky. They are getting the finest detective in LA,' she said as she softly kissed his lips. 'Are you nervous?'

Garcia nodded and bit his bottom lip. 'A little bit.'

'There's no need. You'll be great.'

Anna was an optimist; finding the positive side to just about anything. She was happy for Garcia; he was finally achieving what he'd always wanted, but deep inside she felt scared. Garcia had experienced some close encounters in the past. He'd spent a week in hospital after a .44 caliber bullet shattered his collar bone and she'd spent a week in tears. She knew the perils that came with his job and she knew he would never shy away from danger, and that petrified her.

At exactly eight-thirty Garcia was standing in front of Captain Bolter's office in the RHD building. He found it funny that the name on the door said 'KONG.' He knocked three times.

'Come in.'

Garcia opened the door and stepped inside.

Captain William Bolter was now in his mid-sixties but he looked at least ten years younger. Tall, strong as an ox and sporting a full head of silvery hair together with a thick mustache, the man was a menacing figure. If the stories were true, he'd taken over twelve bullets in his time, and he was still standing.

'Who the hell are you, Internal Affairs?' His voice was firm but not aggressive.

'No sir . . .' Garcia stepped closer, handing over his forms. 'Carlos Garcia, sir, I'm your new detective.'

Captain Bolter was sitting in his imposing high-backed swivel chair behind his rosewood desk. He flipped through the forms looking impressed at times before placing them on his desk. He didn't need any paperwork to tell him Garcia was a good detective. No one was assigned to the RHD if they hadn't shown a high level of competence and expertise, and according to Garcia's track record, he had plenty.

'Impressive . . . and you are exactly on time. Good start!' the captain said after swiftly consulting his watch.

'Thank you, sir.'

The captain walked up to the coffee machine in the far corner of his office and poured himself a cup, Garcia didn't get offered one. 'OK, first things first. You gotta lose that cheap suit. This is the Homicide division, not the fashion police. The guys out there are gonna crucify you.' He gestured towards the detectives' floor.

Garcia looked down at his suit. He liked that suit – it was his best suit – his only suit.

'How long have you been a detective now?'

'Two years, sir.'

'Well, that's remarkable. It usually takes a detective at least five to six years on the job before he's even considered for the RHD. You either kiss a lot of ass or you are the real thing.' With no reply from Garcia the captain continued. 'Well, you might've been a good detective out there working for the LAPD, but this is Homicide.' Sipping his coffee, he walked back to his desk. 'Holiday camp is over, sonny. This is harder and definitely more dangerous than anything you've done before.'

'I understand, Captain.'

'Do you?' He pinned Garcia with his intense gaze. His voice took a more ominous tone. 'This job will mess with your head, kid. You'll make more enemies than friends as a Homicide dick. Your old friends at the LAPD will probably hate you from now on. Are you sure this is what you want? Are you sure you are strong enough? And I'm not talking about physical strength here, sonny. Are you sure you're ready?'

Garcia had half expected the *dangerous job* speech; every captain has one. Without turning away from the captain's stare, he replied in a steady voice and with no vacillation. 'I'm ready, sir.'

The captain looked back at Garcia, searching for a hint of fear, self-doubt maybe, but years of experience in character judging told him this kid wasn't scared, at least not yet.

'OK then, we're done here. Let me introduce you to your new

partner,' he said, opening the door to his office. 'Hunter . . . get in here,' his loud voice resonating through the busy floor.

Hunter had just walked in. He was sitting at his desk stirring a cup of strong black coffee. His sleep-hangover made the captain's voice sound like a heavy metal band. He calmly had a sip of the bitter-tasting liquid and felt it burn his lips and tongue. In the past few months Hunter's insomnia had gotten worse, fueled by the constant nightmares. He'd sleep a couple of hours every night if he was lucky. His daily routine had become lethargic – bad headache, strong boiling-hot coffee, burnt mouth and onto the pile of second-rate cases on his desk.

Hunter didn't knock, he simply opened the door and stepped inside. Garcia was standing next to the rosewood desk.

'Yo! Captain, you've got the wrong man, I'm not in trouble with Internal Affairs,' Hunter said biting the loose skin on his burnt top lip.

Garcia looked down at his suit again.

'Sit down, Hunter, he isn't IA.' The captain paused, holding the suspense for a few seconds. 'Meet your new partner.'

At first those words didn't seem to register in Hunter's ears. Garcia took two steps in Hunter's direction and offered his hand. 'Carlos Garcia, it's a pleasure to meet you, Detective Hunter.'

Hunter left Garcia's hand hanging in the air; in fact he didn't move at all except for his eyes. Garcia could feel Hunter analyzing him, trying to size him up. It took Hunter twenty seconds to make his mind up about his new partner.

'No thanks, Captain, I'm doing quite well on my own.'

'The hell you are, Hunter!' the captain said calmly. 'Since Wilson's death what have you been doing, office work and helping the LAPD with shoplifting and petty theft cases? Gimme a goddamn break. Anyway, you knew this was coming. Who did you think you were, Dirty Harry? Look, Hunter, I'm not gonna give you the bullshit speech about how great a detective you are and how you're wasting your talent. You're the best detective I've had under my command. You can figure things out that no one else can. Sixth sense, detective's intuition, whatever you wanna call it; you've got it like no one else does. I need you back in Homicide and I need you sharp. You know I can't have a Homicide dick on the streets on his own, it's against regulations. You're no use to me the way you are.'

'And how's that, Captain?' Hunter shot back in a half-offended tone.

'Have a look in the mirror and you'll find out.'

'So you gonna pair me up with a rookie?' He turned to face Garcia. 'No offense.'

'None taken.'

'We were all rookies once, Hunter,' the captain said running his fingers over his Santa Claus mustache. 'You sound just like Scott did when I told him I was getting him a new partner. He hated your guts at first remember? You were young and inexperienced . . . and just look at how you turned out.'

Garcia bit his lip trying not to laugh.

Hunter regarded him once again. 'Oh, you think this is funny?'

Garcia tilted his head in a *maybe* gesture.

'Tell me, what sort of experience do you have?' Hunter asked.

'I've been a detective for the LAPD for two years,' Garcia replied cheekily.

'Oh, a local boy.'

Garcia nodded.

'Why are you so nervous?'

'Who said I'm nervous?' Garcia said defiantly.

Hunter gave Captain Bolter a confident smile. 'The knot on your tie is too tight, but instead of loosing it up you keep on faintly rotating your neck hoping no one will notice. When you tried to shake my hand earlier, I noticed how moist your palm was. This room ain't hot enough, so I'm guessing nervous perspiration. And since I walked into the office you keep on shifting your weight from one leg to the other. You either have a lower back problem or you're feeling a little uncomfortable. And since you wouldn't make detective with a back problem . . .'

Garcia frowned and shifted his stare to Captain Bolter who gave him a quirky smile.

'A word of advice,' Hunter continued. 'If you're feeling nervous it's better to sit down instead of standing up. It's a more comfortable position and it's easier for you to hide your tell-tale signs.'

'He's good, isn't he?' Captain Bolter asked with a chuckle. 'Anyway, Hunter, you know you don't have a say in this, I'm still king of this fucking jungle and in my jungle you'll take a partner or you'll walk.'

Garcia finally understood the nameplate on the door. He waited a few seconds before extending his hand again.

'As I've said, Carlos Garcia, it's a pleasure.'

'The pleasure is all yours nervous boy,' Hunter replied, leaving Garcia's hand hanging for a second time. 'You've gotta lose that cheap suit, rookie, who do you think we are, the fashion police?'

Ten

As night fell over LA, Hunter and Garcia went back to the old wooden house. The forensic team had already left and the place was deserted. The lack of sunlight and the impenetrable surrounding vegetation meant that exploring the outside at this time was impossible, but Hunter was sure the perimeter had already been meticulously searched by a team of specialized officers. Hunter and Garcia concentrated on the house, but after a couple of hours, both were ready to call it a night.

'There's nothing here. If there were, the forensic guys must've picked it up,' Garcia said, sounding hopeful.

Hunter could see fine, green fluorescent powder that had been applied to several surfaces around the house. The special green powder is always used in conjunction with lasers and low-powered ultraviolet lamps to allow the visualization of latent prints which would otherwise go undetected. Hunter had a feeling the forensic team hadn't found anything either. 'Let's hope Doctor Winston has some good news for us in the morning,' he said, grabbing Garcia's attention. 'There's nothing else we can do here tonight.'

It was past midnight when Hunter turned his old Buick into Saturn Avenue with Templeton Street in South Los Angeles. The entire street was in desperate need of refurbishment with its ageing buildings and neglected lawns. Hunter parked in front of his six-floor apartment block and stared at it for a moment. Its once striking yellow color had now faded to un-appealing pastel beige and he noticed that the light bulbs above the doorway had been broken again. Inside the small entrance hall the walls were dirty, the paint had peeled off and gang graffiti made up most of its decoration. Despite its terrible state, he felt comfortable in the building.

Hunter lived alone; no wife, no kids and no girlfriend. He'd had his share of steady relationships, but his job had a way of taking its toll on them. The dangerous RHD lifestyle wasn't easy to cope with and girlfriends always ended up asking for more than he was prepared to give. Hunter didn't mind so much being alone any more. It was his defense mechanism. *If you have no one, they can't be torn away from your life.*

Hunter's apartment was located on the third floor, number 313. The living room was oddly shaped and the furniture looked as if it had been donated by Goodwill. A couple of mis-matched chairs and a beaten-up black leatherette sofa were placed against the far wall. To its right, a small badly scratched wooden desk with a laptop computer, a three-in-one printer and a small table lamp. Across the room a stylish glass bar looked totally out of place. It was the only piece of furniture Hunter had purchased brand new and from a trendy shop. It held several bottles of Hunter's biggest passion – single malt Scotch whisky. The bottles were arranged in a peculiar way that only he understood.

He closed the living-room door behind him, turned on the lights and moved the dimmer switch to the 'low' setting. He needed a drink. After pouring himself a double dose from the twenty-year-old bottle of Talisker, he dropped a single cube of ice in the glass.

He couldn't shake the faceless woman's image from his

mind. Every time he closed his eyes he could still see the carving on the back of her neck; he could still smell the pungent odor from that room. *Could this be happening again? Could this be the same killer? And if yes, why has he started killing again?* The questions kept coming and Hunter knew the answers wouldn't follow at the same speed. He stirred the ice cube once around the glass with his index finger and brought it to his lips. The sour, peppery taste of the Talisker relaxed him.

Hunter was certain that this would be another sleepless night, but he needed to somehow rest. He turned on the lights in the bedroom and emptied his pockets onto the bedside table. Car keys, house keys, some pocket change and a small piece of paper that read *Call me – Isabella.* A smile played on his lips as he remembered the whole morning incident.

'*I can't believe I suggested she was a hooker to her face,*' he thought and the smile turned to laughter. He liked her sense of humor and her wit. She had thrown his sarcasm straight back at him. She was certainly different from most of the dull women he met in bars. He checked his watch. The time was coming up to one in the morning – too late. Perhaps he'd call her some other time.

He walked to the kitchen and pinned Isabella's note on a corkboard next to the fridge, before making his way back into the bedroom ready to fight insomnia.

From the parking lot, hiding in the shadows a dark figure avidly observed the flicker of lights coming from the third-floor apartment.

Eleven

Hunter managed to doze off a few times during the night, but that was the best he could do. By five-thirty in the morning he was up and feeling like he'd been hit by a truck. Gritty eyes, dry mouth and a nagging headache that would be with him throughout the rest of the day – all the signs of a sleep hang-over. He poured himself a strong cup of coffee and considered adding a quick shot of whisky to it, but that would probably make him feel worse. By six-thirty he was dressed and ready to leave when his cell phone rang.

'Detective Hunter speaking.'

'Robert, it's me, Carlos.'

'Rookie, you gotta stop calling me so early in the goddamn morning. Do you ever sleep?'

'Sometimes, but last night it was hard to.'

'You can say that again. So what's up?'

'I just talked to Doctor Winston.'

Hunter quickly glanced at his watch. 'This early? Did you wake him up as well?'

'No, he's been up most of the night. Anyway, he said his team of forensic examiners didn't come up with anything from the wooden house either.'

Hunter ran his hand over his chin. 'Yeah, I was half expect-ing that,' he said disappointedly.

'He also said that there's something he wants to show us, something important.'

'There always is. Is he in the Coroner's office now?'

'Yep.'

'OK, I'll meet you there . . . half an hour?'

'Yeah, that's enough time, see you there.'

The Los Angeles County Department of Coroner is located on Mission Road. As one of the busiest Coroners in the entire United States, it can receive anywhere up to one hundred bodies a day.

Hunter parked next to the main building and met Garcia by the entrance door. He'd seen his fair share of dead bodies after ten years as a detective, but Hunter still felt uneasy walking down the corridors in the Department of Coroner. The smell was like a hospital, but it had a different sting to it, something that burnt the inside of his nostrils and irritated the back of his throat.

Yesterday's victim's autopsy had been conducted in a small separate room in the basement of the building. Doctor Winston had been the medical examiner during the Crucifix Killer case; if anyone could identify the same modus operandi, he could.

'Why are we going downstairs – aren't all the autopsy rooms on the first floor?' Garcia asked intrigued, as they reached the bottom of the stairs that led to an empty and creepy basement corridor.

'This is the same autopsy room that was used during the Crucifix Killer's investigation. As the captain said, he wants this whole thing kept under wraps. Those goddamn reporters pay informers everywhere and this place is no different. Until we make sure the nightmare hasn't started again the captain has asked the good old doctor to use the same precautions as the original case – and that includes no access to the victim's body by anyone except the doctor himself and us.'

As they reached the room at the end of the narrow, well-lit corridor, Hunter pressed the intercom button on the wall and smiled a silly smile at the camera mounted just above the door. Seconds later Doctor Winston's voice cracked through the small wall speaker.

'Robert . . . let me buzz you in.'

A loud buzz echoed through the basement corridor followed by a clicking sound. Hunter pushed the heavy metal door open and stepped inside the room with Garcia.

A gleaming stainless-steel table with a sink at one of its ends was positioned close to the far wall. A large surgical light above the table illuminated the entire room. A tray which was used for placing organs as the examiner removed them from the victim's body sat close to the sink. The drainage tube from the organ tray was stained orange-brown. The stinging smell was stronger inside the room. Two large surgical saws and several blades of different shapes and sizes were neatly arranged over a small table up against the west wall. The faceless woman's body lay on the steel table.

'Come in,' Doctor Winston said, showing them into the room.

Garcia's gaze rested on the motionless corpse and the hairs on the back of his neck stood on end.

'So, what do you have for us?' Hunter asked quietly as if scared of waking her up.

'Unfortunately, not much,' Doctor Winston replied as he slipped on a brand-new pair of latex gloves. 'My team didn't manage to lift a single fingerprint from the house and given what we might be facing again, I'm not surprised.'

'Yes, Carlos told me,' Hunter said, letting out a disillusioned sigh. 'How about fibers or something that can give us some sort of start?'

'Sorry, Robert, the house has given us zilch.'

'How can that be?' Garcia asked. 'The killer has obviously spent hours torturing that woman in that house. How come he left nothing behind?'

'You said it before, rookie,' Hunter explained. 'A secluded location. The killer had all the time in the world to torture her uninterrupted. After she died the killer had all the time in the world to go over the entire house and make sure nothing was left behind. Time is on his side.'

Doctor Winston nodded.

'How about her?' Hunter asked tilting his head towards the body. 'What can you tell us about her, doc?'

'Twenty-three to twenty-five years of age, very healthy. She took very good care of herself. Her body fat was around 14.5 percent, which is athlete low. You don't need me to tell you about her muscle tone, which means she was probably a gym rat. No operations or implants either, she still had her tonsils and appendix and her breasts were her own. Her skin still feels very smooth even after rigor mortis and the lab analysis showed a high content of humectants, emollients and lubricants.'

'What?' Garcia asked frowning.

'Moisturizer,' Hunter replied, trying to end Garcia's confusion.

'So she moisturized, most women do.'

'Don't I know it?' Doctor Winston replied in a mocking voice. 'Trisha spends a fortune on creams that have absolutely no effect; it's all a big con if you ask me, but the thing about our victim is that the tests have shown a very high-quality grade of it, in other words, she used the very expensive stuff . . . just like Trisha. My confident guess is that she was well off.'

'Why? Because she used expensive moisturizers?' Garcia asked.

'Do you have any idea how much they cost?'

Garcia raised his eyebrows indicating he didn't.

'A hell of a lot I can tell you. Also have a look at her nails, both hands and toes.'

Hunter and Garcia checked her hands and feet. Her nails looked very nicely kept.

'I had to remove her nail varnish, standard procedure,' the doctor continued. 'Once again, the tests showed a very high-quality product. Her nails were professionally done, judging by the smoothness of the cut and cuticle. Now, manicure and pedicure isn't really an expensive treatment, but it highlights how much importance the victim paid to her appearance. The hair analysis showed another high-quality-grade product and judging by its condition she probably had a hairdresser's appointment at least once a month.'

'Is her hair dyed?' Garcia asked.

'No, she's a natural blond. Whatever she did for a living, I'd say her appearance played a major part in it.'

'Rich husband maybe?' Garcia suggested.

'No wedding band and no signs that she'd ever worn one either,' the doctor quickly dismissed the suggestion.

'So she made good money on her own?'

'It looks that way, yes.'

'Was she raped?' Hunter asked.

'No, no sexual intercourse for at least forty-eight hours – no lubricant in her vagina or anus, which rules out the possibility of sex with prophylactics – the killer wasn't after sexual pleasure.'

'Any identifying marks?'

'Nothing . . . she's got no tattoos, no birthmarks, no scars.'

'Fingerprints?'

'I faxed them to your captain last night so you'll have them when you get back to your precinct, but I can also access the Central Fingerprint Database from here – no match, she's not in the system and as you know we've got no chance of getting an ID from her dental records.' Doctor Winston walked over to his desk and quickly fumbled through a few loose pieces of paper. 'As I'd suspected, she'd been drugged. I found traces of gamma hydroxy butyrate in her stomach, better known in clubs as GHB.'

'I've heard of that,' Garcia said. 'The new date-rape drug right?'

'Well, it's not really a new drug. Kids use it in small doses to get high, but an overdose would produce an effect very similar to Rohypnol,' Hunter clarified.

'Which is like a blackout?'

'That's correct,' Doctor Winston said this time. 'Once the subject regains consciousness they can't remember anything that has happened to them while under the effect.'

'Can we trace it?' Garcia asked.

Hunter shook his head. 'I doubt it. GHB is basically degreasing solvent or floor stripper mixed with drain cleaner; anyone can make it at home, and you can get the correct mixing dosage over the internet.'

'Kids are mixing degreasing solvent with drain cleaner and taking it as a drug?' Garcia enquired in surprise.

'Youth has come a long way since we were kids, detective,' the doctor replied, patting Garcia on the back.

'How about the cause of death?' Hunter asked.

'Heart, liver and kidney failure. Her body just couldn't cope anymore. A combination of the tremendous pain she'd suffered together with dehydration and starvation. If she hadn't been in such good physical condition she would've probably lasted only a few hours.'

'How long did she last?'

'Anywhere between ten and sixteen hours. She died sometime between 8:00 p.m. on Sunday evening and 1:00 a.m. Monday morning.'

'She was tortured for almost sixteen hours? Jesus Christ!' Garcia commented.

The room went quiet for a moment. Doctor Winston was the first to speak again. 'We have also analyzed the rope that was used to tie her to the posts.'

'And?'

'Nothing special there either. Regular nylon rope; it could've been bought in any hardware store.'

'How about the mirror on the bedroom door, it looked new; did we get anything from it?'

'Not really. We found very old traces of chemicals consistent with mirror adhesives.'

'So what does that mean?' Garcia asked.

'That the killer didn't buy that mirror – he took it from another door somewhere. I don't think anyone would've reported a stolen door mirror, so tracking it down would be almost impossible,' Hunter said.

'And the vinegar in the jar?'

'Your most common type of vinegar, found in any supermarket.'

'In other words, we've got absolutely nothing,' Hunter concluded dryly.

'Oh we've got something alright, but you're not gonna like it . . . let me show you.' Doctor Winston walked over to the east end of the room where a few photographs were scattered over a small desk, Hunter and Garcia right behind him.

'This is the carving on our victim's neck.' The doctor pointed to the first picture on the left. 'All the other pictures you see here are from the Crucifix Killer's case. The carvings are consistent, I'd say with a fair degree of confidence that they were made by the same person, probably with the same sharp instrument.'

The small ounce of hope Hunter had of a copycat killer was crushed. The photographs brought back a hurricane of memories.

This was the first time Garcia had seen any of the forensic evidence of the original Crucifix Killer's case. He could easily see the similarities in all the photographs.

'Can you tell us anything about the skinning of her face?' Garcia asked.

'Yes, this is where the killer shows us how good he really is, it's surgically precise – the way the skin had been cut away, the way the lean tissue and ligaments had been left intact – fantastic work. He must've spent a fair amount of time operating on her face. I wouldn't be at all surprised if whoever did this was a surgeon or something along those lines. But then again, we knew that much about the Crucifix Killer.'

'What do you mean?' Garcia looked confused.

'The Crucifix Killer always removed a body part from his victims – an eye, a finger, an ear – human trophies in a way,' Hunter explained. 'It's one of his signatures, together with the carving on the back of the neck and the stripping of the victim. According to the doctor, the removal of the body parts was always surgically precise, and apparently they had always been done while the victims were still alive.'

'It seems the killer's got better at it,' Doctor Winston concluded.

'Why would the killer take a part of a victim's body?' Garcia asked.

'To remind him of the victim,' Hunter replied. 'It's quite common when it comes to serial killers. Their victims mean a lot to them. Most of the time the killer feels there's some sort of bond between him and the victim. Some killers prefer to take a piece of clothing, usually an intimate piece of clothing. Some go for a body part.'

Garcia studied the photographs. 'I'm assuming the original investigation checked for doctors as probable suspects.'

'And medical students, nurses, and so on and so forth. It didn't lead us to anyone,' Hunter answered.

Garcia moved back towards the body. 'You said there are no birthmarks, no tattoos. Is there anything that can help us identify the body?'

'We can try her face.'

Garcia stared at Doctor Winston sullenly. 'Are you kidding?'

'This is the twenty-first century, detective,' the doctor said, his mouth twisted in what might've been a trace of a smile. 'Computers can perform miracles nowadays. They've already been working on it upstairs for an hour and we shall have some sort of computer image ready any minute now. If we're lucky you can pick it up on your way out.'

'Judging by how much effort she put into her appearance I'd say she was either a model or an aspiring actress,' Hunter suggested.

'Or a high-class hooker, perhaps even a porn actress. They can make a lot of money you know,' Garcia complemented Hunter's suggestion.

'How do you know? Dated a porn star recently, have you?' Hunter smiled.

'Um . . . it's common knowledge.'

'Of course it is. So who's your favorite star?'

'I'm married.'

'Oh yeah. That makes a difference, I forgot. Married men don't watch porn. Let me guess. You probably like Briana Banks.'

'She *is* hot,' Garcia said and immediately froze.

'You walked straight into that one,' Doctor Winston said padding him on the back.

Both detectives regarded the body in front of them for a while. She looked different now. Her skin seemed rubbery and paler and her mutilated face looked like a mask – a well-made-up actress ready to shoot a horror scene in some Hollywood production – an image of almost pure evil.

'We'd better go check up on that computer image, doc, or is there anything else you'd like to show us?'

'No, Robert, I'm afraid there isn't much else I can tell you about her.'

'Are you keeping her in this room?'

'As requested by your captain . . . yes, we have our own cooling chamber in here. Let's just hope we don't have to fill it up with any more bodies.'

Hunter and Garcia buzzed themselves out of the autopsy room and walked up to the computer tech lab in silence.

'Can I ask you something?' Garcia asked.

'Shoot.'

'How come no one believed you when you told them that Mike Farloe wasn't the Crucifix Killer?'

'I never said that. In the end Captain Bolter and my ex-partner, Scott, saw my reasoning. But with all the evidence found in Farloe's car, coupled up with him confessing to the murders, there wasn't much we could do. It was in the DA's hands. And they didn't wanna hear any reasoning.' Hunter looked down debating if he should carry on. 'Maybe the truth is that we all wanted it to end,' he finally said. 'It had gone on for too long.

Deep inside I secretly wished Farloe was the real killer. And now the nightmare is back.'

For Garcia the nightmare was just starting. For Hunter this was the worst kind, a recurring one.

Twelve

Excluding children's and psychiatric, there were eight hospitals in total in the central Los Angeles area, but only four of them showed Jane Doe entries for the past few days. Posing as the boyfriend or as a work colleague, Jerome visited all four with no luck. If Jenny had been admitted into a hospital, it hadn't been one in downtown LA.

Jerome had thought about extending his search to places like Santa Monica, San Diego, Long Beach, Santa Ana, but that would've taken him an entire week and he didn't have that kind of time. He decided to get in contact with Detective Culhane.

Mark Culhane hated receiving payments from a criminal, a drug lord, but he couldn't deny the money came in handy; it was more than twice his Narcotics Division pay. In return, he was expected to look the other way during major drug deals, slightly mislead investigations and provide inside information every now and again. It's a corrupt world and it didn't take much effort from D-King to find Mark Culhane.

Jerome and Culhane met at the In-N-Out Burger restaurant in Gayley Avenue, one of Jerome's favorite burger joints. By the time Culhane arrived, Jerome had already devoured two Double-Double burgers.

Culhane was forty-nine years old, five foot six, with a receding hairline and a frightening beer belly. Jerome had always wondered what would happen if Culhane had to chase a suspect on foot.

'Culhane . . . sit down,' Jerome said, eating the last of his fries.

Culhane sat opposite Jerome in the small old-fashioned diner booth. He looked older than Jerome remembered. The bags under his eyes had gained some extra weight. Jerome had no time for pleasantries and he slid a brown-paper envelope towards the detective. Culhane grabbed it and brought it close to his chest, holding it like a hand of poker. He had a quick look at the photograph inside.

'She's missing,' Jerome carried on.

'So? Talk to missing persons, I'm Narcotics remember?' Culhane replied, clearly irritated.

'Was that attitude?' Jerome asked, having another swig of his giant-size root beer.

Culhane kept silent.

'Let's just say D-King considers her to be a special girl.' He slid another envelope towards the detective. 'This is extra.'

This time Culhane didn't have to open it to know what was inside it. He picked the envelope up and placed it in his pocket.

'What's her name?' he sked, his irritation dissipating.

'Jenny Farnborough.'

'Did she run out on him or you think it might be something else?'

'We're not sure, but we don't think she's a runaway. She's got nothing to run away from. On top of that all of her belongings are still in her apartment.'

'Is she hooked? Could she just be tripping out somewhere?'

'I don't think so. She does coke every now and then, you

know, to keep her going, but she is no junkie. She wouldn't work for the boss if she was.'

'Boyfriend? Family?'

'No boyfriend – her family lives in rednecksville somewhere in Idaho or Wyoming, but she doesn't get along with them anyway.'

'When was the last time you saw her?'

'Last Friday night. She was out partying with the boss and a few other girls; she went to the bathroom to retouch her make-up, and that was it.'

'She might've been arrested and she's just cooling off in a cell somewhere.'

'She would've called if that was the case and I don't know what she'd be arrested for, but I guess you better check that out too.'

'Can I get you anything?' The question came from a young brunette waitress who'd approached their table.

'No, I'm OK thanks,' Culhane said with a dismissive hand gesture and waited until the waitress was out of earshot. 'Is there anything else I need to know?' His attention was back on Jerome.

'Nope, I guess that's all.'

'Did she steal any money or something that would've given her a reason to disappear?'

'Not from us.'

'Gambling debts?'

'Not that we know of.'

'Was she involved with anyone else, maybe one of D-King's competitors?'

'Nah-ah,' the reply came with a shake of the head. 'She was a good girl, probably his best girl. She had no reason to run away.' He had another sip of his root beer.

'The good ones are usually the worst.' Culhane's comment failed to amuse Jerome. 'How long has she been with D-King?'

'Almost three years.'

'Maybe she'd had enough and she wanted out.'

'You know the boss doesn't mind if any of his girls want out. If she'd had enough all she had to do was say it. Plus as I've said, she didn't take any of her stuff with her.'

'OK, give me twenty-four hours and I'll see if I can come up with anything.' Culhane got up ready to leave.

'Culhane.'

'Yeah,' he said turning to face Jerome.

'D-King wants to keep this quiet, so don't go flashing her picture around like a pair of tits.'

Culhane nodded and made his way to the door while Jerome reopened the menu on the desserts page.

Sitting inside his car, Culhane had another look at the picture Jerome had given him. The girl was stunning, the sort of girl he'd have to pay a lot of money to sleep with. He tapped the other envelope inside his pocket. *Hello, new car,* he thought with a wide smile.

Culhane guessed the girl in the photograph was in trouble. D-King was good to his girls, the nice apartments, the expensive clothes, the free drugs, the superstar lifestyle. He'd never heard of any of them running away.

He could start with a hospital search, but that would take way too long. After thinking about it for a few seconds he reached for his cell phone and dialed Peter Talep, a good friend of his who worked for the missing person's department of the LAPD.

'Pete, it's Mark from Narcotics, how're you doing? I need a small favor . . .'

*

The LAPD Missing Persons Unit was established in 1972. The unit has citywide responsibility for the investigation of adult missing persons with over twenty-five investigative detectives. Peter Talep was one of them.

Peter met Culhane at the lobby of the South Bureau Police Department in 77th Street. Culhane needed a good story to get Peter to search the missing person's database without raising any eyebrows or putting in an official request. He claimed Jenny was one of his major narcotic informers and sometime in the past seventy-two hours she'd gone missing. Culhane wanted Peter to use his department's access to check the hospital files.

'So, do you have a picture of this girl we're looking for?' Peter asked.

'Unfortunately I don't, that's why I have to go through the records with you, keeping pictures of informers can lead to a lot of trouble,' Culhane lied. If D-King wanted to keep this quiet, handing Jenny's picture to Peter wasn't a great idea.

'OK, so what am I looking for?'

'Caucasian female, around twenty-three, twenty-four, blond hair, blue eyes, stunning looking, if you see her picture you'd probably know,' Culhane said with a malicious smile.

'When was the last time you had contact with her?'

'Last Friday.'

'Do you know if she has any family around, someone that might've reported her missing?'

'No, I don't think so, she lived alone. Family are from out of town.'

'Boyfriend, husband?'

'No.'

'So nobody would've reported her missing? You're the first one?'

'Yep,' Culhane agreed.

'So if she went missing on Friday, it'll be too soon,' Peter said, shaking his head.

'What do you mean? What'll be too soon?'

Peter rolled his chair away from his computer. 'All the records we have in our database are from missing persons that have been reported in by someone – family, boyfriend, whatever. People will usually bring in a picture and fill in a missing person's report, you know the protocol. Anyway, that record is then fed into the Missing and Unidentified Persons Unit database. If no one's reported her missing, there will be no record.'

'Yes, but how about hospital patients, you know, Jane Doe's?'

'Well, those are quite rare.'

'Yeah, but they do happen?'

'Yes, but she needs to be either unconscious or have lost her memory. If that's the case the hospital would usually wait anywhere between seven to fifteen days before considering the patient a proper Jane or John Doe and reporting them to us. We then compare the picture the hospital sends us with what we have in our database and check for a match. If there isn't one the patient is then inserted into the MUPU database as unidentified. If she went missing on Friday and no one has reported her missing, that's way too soon. If she is unconscious in a hospital somewhere or has lost her memory, you'll have to wait until she regains consciousness, check hospital by hospital for a Jane Doe or wait up to two weeks and check back here with me.'

'Shit!'

'Sorry, Mark, there isn't much I can do for you.'

'That's OK, thanks anyway.'

Outside the South Bureau Police Department, Culhane sat in his car pondering his options. He sure as hell wasn't about to go on a hospital tour of LA just to find some hooker for D-King. The past weekend arrests' report he'd requested had just been sent to his car fax machine. Six girls matched the description. Three had already made bail. He had a hunch none of the remaining girls would be the one he was looking for, but he had to check them.

It took around five minutes for the pictures to come through. As he'd suspected none of them was Jenny. There was one more thing left to do – check for a dead body.

He could try and ask for information from the Homicide Division, but there has always been animosity between Homicide and Narcotics detectives. More often than not one type of investigation would lead into the other. In LA, drugs and murder walked side by side.

Screw the Homicide division, Culhane thought. If Jenny was dead, there was only one place she'd be – the morgue.

Thirteen

The technicians at the County Department of Coroner had used a software program specially developed to reconstruct full images from partial ones. The program is similar to the ones used by film studios on the latest computer-animated motion pictures. The basics are simple – in the animation process, the designer first creates a wire frame of the character as a base and then covers it with a 'skin' layer. The process used by the Coroner's technicians followed the same steps, although no wire frame was needed. Their base was the victim's skinless face image.

This process is mostly used to re-create an image out of bone structure – a body that has been discovered in a very advanced or complete state of decomposition. In the case of last night's victim, the process was made easier because the muscle tissue around her face was almost intact. The computer didn't have to calculate the fullness of her cheeks or the shape of her chin and nose. It only needed to apply a skin layer over the already existing lean tissue, calculate skin age and pigmentation and Hunter and Garcia had a face.

Hunter was right, she'd been a beautiful-looking woman. Even though the computerized image made her look like a character out of the Final Fantasy video game series, Hunter could easily see the soft lines, the model-like features that made up her face.

From his car, on the way back from the Coroner's office Hunter called Captain Bolter.

'Hunter. Tell me something good.'

'Well, the computer guys at the Coroner's office managed to re-create the victim's face using some fancy computer program, that should help us identify her.'

'That's good news, what else?'

'That's about as far as the good news go,' he paused to take a deep breath. 'According to Doctor Winston, it's more than probable that we're dealing with the same killer as before.'

Silence followed. Captain Bolter had expected this since finding the double-crucifix on the back of the victim's neck.

'Captain?'

'Yeah, I'm here. This is like the fucking twilight zone.'

Hunter agreed but said nothing.

'I'm setting you and Garcia up in a separate office, away from the main floor. I don't even want the rest of the RHD detectives to get involved in this.'

'That's fine by me.'

'The last thing I need in my hands right now is widespread panic around this city because some shitty reporter got hold of this story.'

'Sooner or later some shitty reporter will get hold of this story, Captain.'

'So let's try and make it a lot later than sooner shall we?'

'You know we'll be doing our best, Captain.'

'I need more than your best this time, Hunter. I want this killer caught, and I mean the REAL one.' The anger in his voice was undeniable as he slammed the receiver down.

Fourteen

The office Captain Bolter supplied for Hunter and Garcia was located on the top floor of the RHD building. It was a medium-sized room, thirty-five feet wide by twenty-five with two desks facing each other in the center of it. A computer, a telephone and a fax machine had been set up on each desk. The room was well lit, courtesy of two windows on the east wall and several fifty-watt halogen dichroic light bulbs on the office ceiling. They were surprised to see that all the original files from the Crucifix Killer's case had already been gathered and placed over their desks making two enormous piles. A corkboard had been mounted onto the south wall. The photographs of all seven of the original Crucifix Killer's victims, together with the new faceless one, had been pinned onto it.

'What, no air con, Captain?'

Captain Bolter took no notice of Hunter's sarcasm. 'Have you been brought up to speed with the situation yet?' his question was directed at Garcia.

'Yes, Captain.'

'So you understand what we might be dealing with here?'

'Yes,' Garcia answered with a hint of trepidation in his voice.

'OK, over the desks you'll find everything we had on the old case,' the captain continued. 'Hunter, you should be familiar with those. The computers on your desks have a T1 internet connection and each of you have a separate telephone and fax line.' He walked towards the photographs on the corkboard. 'This case is to be discussed with no one inside or outside the RHD. We need to try and keep this as quiet as possible for as long as possible.' He paused and looked at both detectives with a hawk-sharp glare. 'When this case goes public I don't want anyone to know that we might be dealing with the same psychopath that did this,' he said pointing to the victims' photographs. 'So, I don't want anybody referring to this case as the Crucifix Killer. For all purposes, the Crucifix Killer is dead, executed about a year ago. This is a brand-new case, is that understood?'

Both detectives looked like school kids being reprimanded by their principal. They nodded and looked at the floor.

'You guys are exclusively on this, nothing else. You better live, breathe and shit this case. I wanna report of the previous day's events on my desk every day by 10:00 a.m. until this killer is caught, starting from tomorrow,' Captain Bolter said, walking towards the door. 'I wanna know everything that's going on in this case, good or bad. And do me a favor, keep this fucking door locked, I don't want any leaks.' He slammed the door behind him, the loud sound reverberating inside the room.

Garcia walked over to the photographs and stared at them in a macabre silence. This was the first time he'd been presented with the Crucifix Killer's police evidence. This was the first time he'd ever seen any of the killer's original evil. He studied them feeling faintly ill. His eyes taking everything in, his mind trying to reject it. How could anyone be capable of this?

One of the victims, male, twenty-five years old, had his eyes compressed into his skull until they'd burst from the pressure. Both of his hands had also been crushed to the point of pulverization of the bones. Another victim, this time female, forty years old, had her abdomen sliced open and disemboweled. A third victim, another male, African American, fifty-five years old, had a laceration that ran the length of his neck; his hands had been nailed together as in a prayer position. The other pictures were even more gruesome. All that pain had been inflicted on the victims while they were still alive.

Garcia remembered the first time he'd heard about the Crucifix killings. It had been over three years ago and he hadn't made detective. Research has shown that there are around five hundred serial killers active at any one time in the United States, claiming something in the region of five thousand lives every year. Only a very small number of them get media recognition, and the Crucifix Killer had gotten more than his share of it. At the time, Garcia had wondered what it would be like to be a detective in such a high-profile investigation. To follow the evidence, analyze the clues, interrogate the suspects and then put everything together to solve the case. If only it was that simple.

Garcia became a detective shortly after the first victim was found and he followed the case as closely as he could. When Mike Farloe was arrested and presented to the media as the Crucifix Killer, Garcia had wondered how could someone that didn't seem to be intelligent had managed to evade the law for such a long time. He remembered thinking that the detectives assigned to the case couldn't have been very good.

Looking at the pictures on the corkboard, Garcia's feelings were a mixture of excitement and fear. Not only was he now a lead detective in a serial-killer investigation, he was one of the lead detectives in the Crucifix Killer's case. Ironic he thought.

Hunter fired up his computer and watched the screen come alive. 'Are you gonna be OK with all this, rookie?' he asked, sensing Garcia's uneasiness at the pictures.

'What? Yeah, I'm good,' Garcia turned and faced Hunter. 'This is some different kind of evil.'

'Yes, I guess you can say that.'

'What would motivate a person to commit crimes like these?'

'Well, if you go by the textbook definition of why someone would commit murder, then we have: jealousy, revenge, to profit, hatred, fear, compassion, desperation, to conceal another crime, to avoid shame and disgrace or to obtain power . . .' Hunter paused. 'The basic motivators for serial crimes are manipulation, domination, control, sexual gratification, or plain simple homicidal-mania.'

'This killer seems to enjoy it.'

'I agree. Gratification, but not of the sexual kind. I'd say he loves watching people suffer.'

'He?' Garcia questioned.

'Judging by the nature of the crimes, the logical conclusion is that the killer is male.'

'How so?'

'To start with, the overwhelming majority of serial killers are male,' Hunter explained. 'Female serial killers have a tendency to kill for monetary profit. While that can also be true their male counterparts, it's very unlikely. Sexual reasons top the list for male serial killers. Case studies have also shown that female killers generally kill people close to them, such as husbands, family members, or people dependent on them. Males kill strangers more often. Female serial killers also tend to kill more quietly, with poison or other less violent methods, like suffocation. Male serial killers, on the other hand, show a greater tendency to include torture or mutilation as part of the process of killing. When women are implicated in sadistic homicides, they've usually acted in partnership with a man.'

'Our killer works alone,' Garcia concluded.

'Nothing indicates otherwise.'

Both detectives fell silent for a while. Garcia turned around and faced the photographs once again. 'So what do we have on all the old victims, what sort of connection?' he asked, eager to get started.

'None that we've found.'

'What? I don't believe that,' Garcia said, shaking his head. 'You're not trying to tell me that you guys spent two years investigating this case and you haven't come up with a connection between the victims?'

'Well, believe it.' Hunter got up and joined Garcia in front of the corkboard. 'Look at them and tell me this – what would you say the age bracket of the victims was?'

Garcia's eyes moved from picture to picture, pausing on each one for only a couple of seconds. 'I'm not sure, early twenties to mid-sixties I guess.'

'Kind of broad, don't you think?'

'Perhaps.'

'And what would you say is the main type of victim, old, young, male, female, black, white, blond, brunette or what?'

Garcia's eyes were still studying the pictures. 'All of those judging by these.'

'Again, kind of broad, isn't it?'

Garcia shrugged.

'Now, there's something else you can't get from these pictures, and that's their social class. These people came from all different walks of life – poor, rich, middle class, religious and non-religious, employed and unemployed . . .'

'Yes, what's your point, Robert?'

'My point is that the killer doesn't go for a specific type of victim. With every new victim, we spent days, weeks, months trying to establish some sort of link between any of them. Work place, social clubs, nightclubs, bars, universities, lower and high school, place of birth, acquaintances, hobbies, family trees, you name it, we've tried it and we came up with a big fat zero. We'd find something that would link two of the victims together but not the others, nothing would stick. If we managed to start a chain with two victims, the link would be broken on the third and fourth one sending us back to square one. From what we know these people could've been chosen completely at random. The killer might as well have flipped through a phone book. In fact, if the killer hadn't carved his symbol on the back of their necks these could've been seven different victims from seven different killers – eight with our new one. Nothing is the same, except the level of pain and torture he puts them through. This killer is a new breed of serial killer. He's unique.'

'What sort of links are you talking about when you say you managed to establish a link between two victims but not the rest?'

'Two of the victims lived in South Central LA just a few blocks from each other, but the others were scattered all over town. Two other victims, number four and number six,' Hunter pointed to the photographs on the board, 'went to the same high school, but not at the same time. The links seemed more coincidental than a breakthrough. Nothing concrete.'

'Did he follow a certain time interval between kills?'

'Random again,' Hunter said. 'They go from a few days between the third and fourth victims to months, and on this last case, over a year.'

'How about body locations?' Garcia asked.

'There's a map over there; I'll show you.' Hunter unfolded a large map of Los Angeles with seven red dots the size of a dime scattered around it, a number next to each one.

'These are the locations and sequence in which each body was found.'

Garcia took his time going over the marks. The first body had been found in Santa Clarita, the second one in downtown Los Angeles with the other five spread all over the map. Garcia admitted that at first glance they looked pretty random.

'Again, we've tried everything, different sequences and patterns. We even brought in a mathematician and a cartographer. The problem is that when you look at random points on a piece of paper for long enough, it's like looking at clouds in the sky, sooner or later you start seeing shapes and images, nothing real, nothing that could lead us anywhere, just your mind playing tricks on you. The only solid conclusion is that the bodies were found in and around Los Angeles. This is his burial ground.' Hunter sat behind his desk while Garcia continued studying the map.

'He's gotta have a pattern, they all do.'

Hunter leaned back on his chair. 'You're right, they usually do, but as I've said, this guy is different. He's never killed two victims in the same manner, he tries new things, different things – it's like he's experimenting.' Hunter paused for a few seconds to rub his eyes. 'Killing another human being isn't an easy task, no matter how experienced someone is, ninety-five percent of the time the killer is more nervous than the victim. Some killers like to stick with the same MO simply because it's worked before and they feel comfortable with it. Some move in a progression and the MO may change from crime to crime. Sometimes the offender may find that his particular course of action wasn't very effective, wasn't what he was looking for. Maybe too noisy, too messy, too hard to control or whatever. The killer then learns to adapt and tries new methods to see if they work better for him. Eventually he'll find an MO that he's comfortable with.'

'And he'll stick with it?' Garcia commented.

'Most of the time yes, but not necessarily,' Hunter said, shaking his head.

Garcia looked puzzled.

'Serial killers are usually after satisfaction . . . a sick kind of satisfaction, but satisfaction nonetheless. It could be sexual fulfillment, a sense of power, a God feeling, but that's only half of the satisfaction.'

'The kill itself?' Garcia's voice took on a grave tone.

'Correct. It's like taking drugs. When you first start, you only need a little hit to achieve the high you want, but soon, if you carry on, that little hit won't be enough and you'll go for more, you start chasing the high. In the case of a killer, the murders become more violent, the victims have to suffer more so the killer can get the satisfaction he needs, but again, just like drugs, there's usually a steady progression.'

Garcia shifted his stare back to the photographs. 'What's the progression here? They all look just as violent, just as monstrous.'

Hunter's agreement came with a nod.

'It's like he jumped straight into the deep end. Which leads us to believe that his progression of violence came earlier on in his life,' Garcia concluded.

'Correct again. You catch on quick, but you can read all that on the case files.' Hunter tilted his head towards the two large piles of paper on his desk.

'None of these were fast kills either.' Garcia's attention was back on the corkboard.

'That's right. This guy likes to take his time with his victims. He likes to watch them suffer, he wants to savor their pain. He's getting his satisfaction. This killer doesn't rush, he doesn't panic and that's his greatest advantage over us.'

'When people panic, they make mistakes, they leave things behind,' Garcia commented.

'Exactly.'

'But not our guy?'

'Not so far.'

'How about this symbol, what do we know about it?' Garcia asked pointing to a picture of the carving on the neck of one of the victims.

'Here comes confusion.' Hunter's lips tightened. 'We brought in a symbologist when the first victim was found.'

'And what did he have to say?'

'The symbol seemed to be a return to the original design of the double-crucifix, also known as the double-cross or the cross of Lorraine.'

'Original?' Garcia shook his head.

'The double-crucifix in its original version consisted of a vertical line crossed by two smaller horizontal bars evenly spaced and of the same length. The lower bar used to be as close to the bottom of the vertical line as the upper was to the top.'

'Why do you say used to?'

'Through the years, its design morphed. The lower bar became longer than the upper one, and both crossbars are now nearer the top of the vertical line.'

Garcia turned to analyze the photographs for a few seconds. 'So this is the old version?'

Hunter nodded. 'Its origin is thought to date back to pagan times. At least that's where history believes it was first used. Back then it was also known as the double-edged sword.'

'Yeah, history aside, what does it mean?' Garcia made a hand gesture urging Hunter to move on.

'Psychologically speaking, it's believed to represent someone with a double life. The double-edged sword cuts both ways, right? That's exactly it, duality, good and evil, white and black all in one. Someone who has two totally opposite sides.'

'You mean someone that could be a normal law-abiding citizen during the day and a psychotic killer at night?'

'Exactly. This person could be a community leader, a politician, even a priest doing good deeds today; tomorrow he could be slashing someone's throat.'

'But that's the textbook definition of schizophrenia.'

'No, it isn't,' Hunter corrected Garcia. 'That's a mistake most people make. Contrary to popular belief, people with schizophrenia do not have *split personalities*. Schizophrenics suffer from problems with their thought processes. These lead to hallucinations, delusions, disordered thinking, and unusual speech or behavior. They usually aren't dangerous people either. What you're thinking of is dissociative identity disorder, also known as DID. People with DID display multiple distinct identities or personalities.'

'Thank you, professor Hunter,' Garcia said, putting on a silly child's voice.

'But I don't believe our killer suffers from DID.'

'And why not?' Garcia asked intrigued.

'DID sufferers have no control of when one personality takes over the previous one. Our killer is fully aware of what he's doing. It pleases him. He ain't struggling with himself.'

That thought silenced Garcia for a few seconds. 'How about a religious meaning? It looks like a religious symbol to me.'

'Well, that's where it gets even more complicated,' Hunter replied massaging his closed eyes for an instant. 'There are two main theories according to scholars. One is that the double-crucifix was the first-ever symbol of the anti-Christ.'

'What? I thought that was supposed to be an inverted cross.'

'That's the symbol as we know it today. It's believed the double-crucifix was first used by some of the early prophets when they prophesied about the end of time, when an evil being would come to end the world.'

Garcia shot Hunter an incredulous look. 'Hold on, you ain't gonna start talking about someone with 666 marked on his head and little horns, are you?'

'It wouldn't surprise me,' Hunter said, shifting his eyes back to the photographs. 'Anyway,' he continued, 'when they prophesied about such an evil being, they said he would bring with him the symbol of pure evil. A symbol that would mean God in reverse.'

Garcia's eyes went back to the photographs before widening in surprise. 'I'll be damned. Two crosses touching each other,' he said finally understanding it. 'One right side up and the other upside down?'

'Bingo. The symbol of Jesus opposed by the same symbol of Jesus. The anti-Christ.'

'So we really could be dealing with a religious fanatic here?'

'An anti-religious fanatic,' Hunter corrected him.

A few silent seconds followed. 'And what's the second?' Garcia asked.

'Excuse me?'

'You said there were two theories concerning religious meanings; what's the second one?'

'Get ready for this. The killer could believe he's the Second Coming.'

'What? Are you joking?'

'I wish. Some scholars believe the early double-crucifix is not one cross right side up and another upside down, but one cross over another, meaning the second son of God. The Second Coming.'

'But these are two totally opposite theories. One says he's the anti-Christ and the other says he's the second Christ.'

'That's true, but remember these are only theories based on what the double-crucifix symbol could mean according to history and academics. It doesn't necessarily mean that they apply to our guy. For all we know, he could've just picked that symbol because he liked the look of it.'

'Is the double-crucifix used by any religious groups or cults?'

'The morphed design, with both crossbars closer to the top of the vertical line, has been used by several groups over the years, religious and not. It's even part of the American Lung Association's logo.'

'And the old design. The one our killer uses?'

'You'd have to go back over one hundred years to find anything. And nothing that could be relevant to the case.'

'What's your gut feeling on this?'

'Gut feelings don't matter in this case, as I've found out.'

'C'mon, humor me. From what I've heard, you have a kick ass intuition,' Garcia said.

'The truth is that I'm not sure. This killer's displayed some classic disturbed behavior like most serial killers. Some of the things he does are textbook perfect, too perfect, as if he wants us to believe he's a typical serial killer.' Hunter pinched the bridge of his nose and closed his eyes for a few seconds. 'Sometimes I think we are dealing with a religious freak, sometimes I think he's some sort of a crime genius fucking with us, pulling the right strings to send us in the wrong direction. Playing a game where only he knows the rules, and he can change them any time he feels like it.' Hunter took a deep breath and held it for a few seconds. 'Whoever he is, he's very intelligent, very clever, very methodical and as cold as ice. He never panics. But what we need to do now is concentrate on the new victim, maybe she'll be the one that'll lead us to him.'

Garcia nodded. 'First we need to fax her photograph to as many model and acting agencies as we can. Having the victim's identity would be a great start . . .'

'Sure, we'll do that, but there's something I'd like for us to check first.'

'And what's that?'

'Remember what Doctor Winston said about the victim?'

'Which part?'

'The *gym rat* part.'

Garcia raised his eyebrows. 'Good thinking.'

'The problem is, there're over a thousand gyms scattered around this city.'

'For real?' Garcia asked surprised.

'Yes, this is LA, the city where to get even a waiter's job you need to look your best. Fitness is big business here.'

'In a country where the obesity rate is off the charts?'

'As I've said, this is LA, the city of the fit and beautiful.' Hunter smiled as he flexed his bicep mockingly.

'Yeah, in your dreams.'

'We should check out some of the bigger, more famous gyms,' Hunter paused for a moment. 'The doctor said she liked to use expensive stuff right? So she obviously spent money on herself.'

'And I bet that with a body like that she liked to be noticed,' Garcia cut in.

'I agree.'

'So if you wanted to show off your body, which gym would you go to? Since you are the expert.'

'Well, Gold's Gym is our best bet, there are two branches in Hollywood where we'll find a lot of famous and "in" people, and then there's the Arnold Schwarzenegger famous Gold's Gym in Venice Beach.'

'I think we should check them out.'

'Grab that computer image, we're gonna go visit the big boys.'

As Hunter reached their office door his cell phone rang. 'Yes, Detective Hunter speaking.'

'*Hello, Robert, did you miss me?*' the robotic voice asked.

Fifteen

Garcia was still walking towards the stairs when he realized Hunter wasn't with him. He stopped and looked back. Hunter was standing in front of their new office holding his cell phone to his right ear. By the look on his face Garcia could tell something wasn't right.

'Robert, what's wrong?'

Hunter didn't reply. He instinctively shook his head – just a slight movement, but enough for Garcia to figure out what was happening.

'Damn!' Garcia said under his breath and quickly moved to Hunter's side tilting his head towards the phone trying to listen in.

'*I trust you have seen my latest work?*'

Hunter's mind went blank, his heart speeding like a racing bike.

'*Aren't you gonna answer me, Robert?*'

It had been almost two years since Hunter had heard that robotic voice. 'What was there to miss?' he replied with a calm voice.

Laughter – '*Well, maybe the thrill, the adventure. I give purpose to your job.*'

'To tell you the truth, I was hoping you were gone.'

Another laugh. '*Oh, c'mon Robert! I know you didn't really believe the guy you caught was me.*'

Hunter stepped back into his office, Garcia still with him. 'So he was just another one of your victims?'

'*I didn't kill him.*'

'You framed him, which is basically the same thing.'

'*In truth I did you a favor. He was just another dirty sack o' shit . . . a pedophile.*'

Despite his hatred, Hunter knew that the longer he kept the killer talking, the more chances he had of forcing a mistake, a slip of the tongue.

'So you decided to come out of retirement?'

The laughter was more enthusiastic this time. '*I guess you could say that.*'

'Why now?'

'*Patience. All will be revealed in good time, Robert. Anyway, I'd love to chat for longer, but you know I can't. I just wanted to make sure you knew the games have started again, but don't worry, I'll be calling you again soon enough.*'

Before Hunter had a chance to say anything else the line went dead. 'Shit!'

'What did he say?' Garcia asked before Hunter could return his phone to his pocket.

'Not much.'

'So there's no doubt anymore, it's him, it's the Crucifix Killer.'

With frustration in his eyes Hunter could only manage a slight nod.

'We'd better tell the captain.'

Hunter registered a certain excitement in Garcia's voice. 'I'll call him from the car; we need to go check those gyms – you drive.'

Hunter's conversation with Captain Bolter was quick. He told him about checking out a few gyms and about the killer's phone call. The captain had cogitated the idea of placing a listening device in Hunter's cell phone, but they'd tried it before with no luck. The caller had used a tracer scrambler device that bounced the call through twenty locations around the globe. For now, there was nothing anyone could do.

Their visit to the gyms in Hollywood came up empty. Neither the reception nor the fitness staff had seen a woman that resembled the computer-generated portrait. They'd need a warrant and a lot of man hours to go through all the member files in the gym's database, and that would still be a shot in the dark.

The Gold's Gym branch in Venice Beach is arguably the most famous gym in the world. It shot to fame with the release of the film *Pumping Iron*, starring Arnold Schwarzenegger in 1977. From professional bodybuilders to movie stars and celebrities, Gold's Gym in Venice Beach is the place to be if you want to show off your body, but their luck didn't change. No one recognized the woman in the picture there either.

'There's no way we're gonna go around LA checking all the gyms,' Garcia said as they reached his car.

'I know, this was a long shot anyway, but we had to try it,' Hunter said rubbing his tired eyes. The previous sleepless night was starting to show its signs.

'So what's next, model and acting agencies?'

'Not yet.' Hunter was deep in thought for a moment. 'Doctor Winston said he was confident our victim had money and she spent quite a lot of it on pampering herself remember?'

'Yeah, so?'

'If she was a struggling actress or model . . .'

'One thing she wouldn't have a lot of would be money,' Garcia picked up where Hunter left off.

'You're getting good at this – ever thought about becoming a detective?' Hunter said derisively.

Garcia lifted his right hand and showed Hunter his middle finger.

'There's someone else I'd like to visit.'

'Who?' Garcia asked intrigued.

'If she was a struggling actress or model she'd still be able to make quite a lot of money by doing something else. You mentioned it before.'

Garcia frowned. After a few seconds he snapped his fingers and pointed at Hunter. 'Hooker,' he said triumphantly.

Hunter gave him an approving smile. 'And I know just the guy we need to talk to.'

'Let's go then,' Garcia said sounding eager.

'Not now, he's only around at night – are you busy tonight?' Hunter said with a quick wink.

'Are you asking me out on a date?'

It was Hunter's turn to flip Garcia the middle finger.

Sixteen

George Slater left his office at the renowned Tale & Josh law firm at the usual time of six-thirty in the afternoon. His wife Catherine knew she wouldn't be having dinner with him as it was Tuesday night, 'poker night.'

George was an average-looking man. The kind that would never attract much attention in a crowd through looks alone, but no one could deny he was charming. Five foot nine with dark-brown eyes and hair to match, his impeccable dress sense had always managed to conceal his thin frame.

After leaving his office George sat listening to the radio news as he drove his luxurious M-Class off-roader Mercedes-Benz to a small rented apartment in Bell Gardens. He'd found the apartment over the internet and dealt directly with the owner avoiding the estate-agent middleman. In exchange for discretion, George had offered to pay the landlord cash – one whole year in advance.

Two copies of a hand-drafted agreement and a receipt for the amount paid were the only existing documentation of the transaction. No lengthy contracts, no traceable paperwork. Even the name on the contract was fictitious – Wayne Rogers. George took no chances. The property could not be traced back to him.

The apartment was located in a very quiet street just on the edge of Bell Gardens and that suited George just perfectly. It meant fewer people to witness him coming and going and the building's underground garage offered him even more shelter from prying eyes.

The single-bedroom apartment wasn't very spacious but it served its purpose. It certainly wasn't luxuriously decorated. The entrance door opened straight into a small living room painted white. A three-seat black-leather sofa had been placed a little off the center of the room facing an empty wall. There was no TV set, no paintings, no rugs or carpet. In fact, apart from the sofa, the only other piece of furniture in the living room was a magazine holder. The kitchen was small and very clean. The cooker had never been used. The contents of the fridge were restricted to twelve bottles of beer, some chocolate bars and a carton of orange juice. The apartment wasn't used for living in.

An en-suite double bedroom was located at the end of a small corridor. Inside it, an extravagant bed with a pompous iron-frame bedstead had been positioned against the wall directly opposite the door. To the left of the bed an all-mirrored-door wardrobe. The room had been fitted with a dimmer switch, or as George liked to call it – the mood switch. This was the most important room in the apartment.

George closed the door behind him, placed his briefcase on the floor next to the sofa and walked into the kitchen. After grabbing a beer from the fridge and twisting its top off he returned to the living room. The beer tasted ice-cold and it relaxed him on a desperately hot day. George drank half the bottle down before sinking himself into the sofa and grabbing his second cell phone from his briefcase. Very few people knew about his extra phone; his wife wasn't one of them. George had one more sip of his cold beer before rereading the latest text message.

I'll be with you around 9:15. Can't wait to see you.

The message wasn't signed, but there was no need. George, or Wayne as he was known, knew exactly who it was from – Rafael.

George had met the six-foot-one man of Puerto Rican descent through a male escort agency a year ago. At first their relationship was professional, but it soon developed into a forbidden affair. George knew Rafael had fallen in love with him and though his feelings for Rafael were very strong, he couldn't call it love – at least not yet.

George checked the time – ten past eight. He had an hour before his lover was due to arrive. He finished his beer and decided to go for a shower.

As the water massaged his tired body, George fought a guilty feeling. He loved Catherine, and he loved making love to her on the few occasions he was allowed to. Maybe if they'd stayed in Alabama things would've been different, but LA had offered him something new. In today's society being bisexual would be considered by some as quite normal, but certainly not by Catherine.

Catherine Slater was born Catherine Harris in Theodore, Alabama. Her upbringing by her excessively religious family had been very strict. She was an avid churchgoer, sometimes five to six times a week. Overbearing and opinionated, she firmly believed in no sex before marriage, and even then she believed sex shouldn't be used as an instrument of carnal pleasure.

Catherine and George met during their freshman year of law school at Alabama State University. Both straight 'A' students, it didn't take long for their classmate friendship to develop into an impossible, sexless romance. Blinded by his enormous desire to be with her, George asked for Catherine's hand in marriage one month after their graduation.

Soon after their wedding George was offered a position with a very well-known law firm in Los Angeles, Tale & Josh. Catherine's vision of Los Angeles was that of a degraded and violent city fueled by sex, drugs and greed, but after two months of discussions and promises she accepted that George's job opportunity was too good to pass.

Catherine wasn't bothered by the fact that her own professional future wasn't involved in the move to Los Angeles. She'd never expected to be a career woman. Her parents had brought her up to be a good wife, to take care of her home, her children and her husband, and that was exactly what she wanted to do. She also believed George wouldn't take to LA and after maybe a year or two he would grow tired of the 'big city, bright lights' lifestyle – she was wrong.

After winning his second case for his new law firm, George's client invited him to a private party to celebrate the victory. *Don't bring your wife with you. You'll have more fun on your own, if you know what I mean.*

George was intrigued by the mysterious invitation. He gave Catherine the typical 'working late' excuse and turned up at a luxurious mansion in Beverly Hills. What he saw changed his life forever.

George's only porn experience had been in high school. One of his friends had managed to get his hands on an old VHS movie and some adult magazines during a weekend when his parents were away. George had never forgotten it, but this was no movie, this was no acting. In one clean swoop George was introduced to BDSM, partner swapping, gloryholes, spanking, sex slavery, golden showers – things he'd never even dreamed of. He discovered a world he'd never thought existed outside adult books and sleazy films. Free sex, free drugs – a place where all his fantasies could come true, where his darkest sexual desires could be exposed with no guilt. It was there, inside the dungeon room of the luxurious mansion that George had had his first sexual experience with another man, and he'd loved it. After that, he couldn't get enough of his new-found underground life. He loved the parties, the people, and the secrecy of it all.

George dried himself slowly before wrapping the towel around his waist. The anticipation of seeing Rafael again turned him on. In the kitchen he grabbed another beer and checked the wall clock – 8:45, not long now. He toyed with the idea of getting dressed again, but he enjoyed the excitement of greeting his lover with nothing on but a towel.

One thing they both enjoyed doing was role-playing and George had a story all worked out for tonight. In the bedroom he slid open one of the mirrored wardrobe doors to reveal an amazing variety of BDSM props – whips, chains, ropes, gags, leather straps, handcuffs, anything his imagination could come up with.

He carefully chose the toys he needed for his scenario and placed them on the bed, his excitement starting to show through his bath towel, but was interrupted by a knock on the door. He checked his watch – 8:53. He is early, George thought, maybe he's as eager as I am.

George couldn't conceal the satisfied smile that came to his lips as he opened the door.

'Who're you?' His smile evaporated into a worried frown.

The answer came as a punch to the stomach, powerful and precise. George contorted in pain as the air drained from his lungs, his eyes wide open and terrified. Gasping for oxygen, he took one step back, but it wasn't enough to avoid the second blow. This time a kick straight between his legs. As the intruder's foot made contact with George's genitals, he fell backwards, his bath towel dropping to the floor. George wanted to speak, to fight back, but he had no strength left.

The intruder calmly closed the apartment's door and approached George's contorted body on the floor. George couldn't make any sense of what was happening. He gurgled, unable to breathe and his heart skipped a beat as he saw the syringe. With a quick arm movement the intruder plunged it into George's neck and all of a sudden there was no more pain, no more struggle. Only darkness.

Seventeen

Chris Melrose had been working for the County Department of Coroner for the last three years. From a very young age Chris had been fascinated with death, with everything morbid. His initial plan was to become a forensic scientist, but his poor school grades kept him from getting a place at university.

Chris's first job was as a jack-of-all-trades in a mortuary. His duties ranged from funeral arrangements to lining the inside of coffins and preparing bodies, but that just wasn't enough. Chris wanted the life he'd always dreamed of. He wanted the blood-stained rags, the stainless-steel tables, the stinging and intoxicating smell of death. He wanted to work with bodies in their raw state, before they were cleaned up and made ready for the funeral. After applying for almost every lower-level position with the County Department of Coroner he was finally offered a job as a lab porter. His new duties included cleaning autopsy rooms, moving bodies to and from the cooling chambers and making sure that all equipment was clean and ready to be used. The medical examiners in the Coroner's office had never seen anyone take so much pride in his work. Chris was in everyone's good books. What he loved doing more than anything else was sitting in on autopsies. None of the examiners minded.

Chris's night shift went from 7:30 p.m. to 7:30 a.m. He liked to take his first break just before midnight; it gave him a chance to light up a cigarette and have a quick banana, peanut-butter and honey sandwich.

Chris took a last drag of his cigarette and flicked the butt in the air and watched it produce a dim, yellow arc. He got up from the small bench he'd been sitting on, folded his empty plastic sandwich bag and started walking back towards the Coroner's building. A cold hand grabbed his left shoulder.

'Hi there, Chris!'

'Jesus Christ!' Chris jumped and turned to face the figure standing behind him, his heart halfway up his throat. 'Are you crazy? You scared the fuck out of me.'

Mark Culhane gave Chris a rehearsed yellow smile.

'If I had a gun, you could be dead right now. How do you get off on sneaking up on people like that?' Chris asked placing a hand over his chest, his heart pounding against it.

'I'm a detective, I love sneaking up on people,' Culhane said with a new smile. 'Besides, why the fuck would you carry a gun? Everyone you deal with is already dead.'

'Everybody packs these days, this is LA remember? Anyway, I haven't seen you for a while, what the hell do you want?'

Chris was in his early thirties, a few pounds overweight with straight dark-brown hair that he kept quite short. He had strange cat-like brown eyes, a reddish complexion and a prominent nose.

'Oh, Chris, that's no way to greet an old friend.'

Chris didn't answer back. He simply raised his eyebrows waiting for Culhane to state his business.

'I need to check whatever new entries you've had in the past few days,' Culhane finally said.

'By entries, you mean bodies?'

'What else would I mean, smart ass?'

'Why don't you just put in a request, you're a cop, aren't you?'

'This is a friend, not necessarily official business.'

'A friend?' Chris's voice took a dubious tone.

'Are you training to be a cop? What's with all the goddamn questions? Just show me the bodies, will you?'

'And if I told you I couldn't do that because it's against regulations?'

Culhane placed his right arm around Chris's neck and pulled him closer. 'Well, that would certainly piss me off, and I don't think you'd wanna do that, do you?'

Silence.

Culhane tightened his grip.

'OK . . . OK, I was going back in anyway,' Chris said, lifting both hands.

'Adda boy,' Culhane said, letting go of the headlock.

They both walked back to the Coroner's building in silence. One of the advantages of visiting Chris at this hour was that Culhane wouldn't have to go in through the front door; the building would be a lot quieter, no badges needed to be shown, no papers to sign – less suspicion.

They reached the staff entrance door on the south side of the building and Chris punched a six-digit code into the electronic keypad. The thick metal door buzzed open.

'Wait here, I'll be right back,' he said and quickly disappeared into the building leaving Culhane standing outside with a curious look on his face. Less than a minute later Chris re-emerged carrying a standard coroner's white overall. 'Put this on, it should fit. It's the largest one I could find.'

'Are you trying to be funny?'

The last thing Chris wanted was for anyone to find out he'd allowed a stranger into the building without signing in at the front desk, even if that stranger was a cop. He guided Culhane through the deserted lower-floor corridor, through a pair of heavy swing doors and up the staircase to the first floor. Culhane had walked these corridors more times than he cared to remember. It still made his stomach turn inside out. Culhane would never have admitted it, but he was glad he wasn't alone. They reached the last room at the end of the hall.

After every autopsy, the bodies were brought to the cold-storage room, or as everyone in the Coroner's office called it 'the big chill.' The room had enough freezer space on its west wall to store over fifty bodies. Culhane and the other detectives from the Narcotics division had their own name for that room – 'the honeycomb of death.'

Chris locked the door behind him so they wouldn't be interrupted and walked over to the computer desk at the far end of the room.

'OK, let's try an initial search . . . male or female?' he asked wasting no time. The faster he got rid of Culhane the better.

'Female.'

'Is she white, black . . .?'

'Caucasian, blond, blue eyes, slim and very attractive.'

Chris gave Culhane a coy smile. 'OK, from what date would you like me to search from?'

'Let's try from last Friday.'

Chris instinctively looked at his watch. 'That'd be . . . June 1st right?'

'Yeah, that's right.'

'OK.' Chris typed in the information and hit the enter key. It took less than five seconds for the computer to return an answer.

'Yep, we've got sixteen matches. Do you have a name?'

'Yes, Jenny Farnborough, but I'm sure she won't show up on your screen.'

Chris's eyes quickly searched the list. 'Nope, you're right, she's not on this list.'

'Any unidentified female bodies?'

Chris checked the list once again. 'Yep, we've got four.'

'Let's check them.'

After a few mouse clicks they had a printout. 'OK, let's go have a look,' Chris said, walking towards the freezers. They stopped in front of the door marked C11, the first one on his list. It took them a little more than five minutes to go through the four unidentified bodies. Jenny Farnborough's wasn't one of them.

'Are these all the bodies? I mean, is there another cold-storage room in the building?' Culhane asked.

'Yes, there's another one in the basement, but I have no access to it,' Chris replied.

'What do you mean, why not?'

'It's a sealed-off area.'

'Why is there a sealed-off area in a Coroner's?'

Chris was glad to offer an explanation to something an LA detective didn't know. 'Certain cases can still be too dangerous – radiation, poison victims, high risk of contamination – cases like that. In those circumstances, the autopsy is conducted in the sealed-off area by the chief medical examiner.'

'And do you know if there's a body down there at the moment?'

'Doctor Winston was working on an autopsy in there until really late last night. The body has never come up to this room, so I'm pretty sure it's still down there.'

'But the body has to come up to the honeycomb right?'

'Honeycomb?' Chris frowned.

'This room . . . the fridge.' There was a hint of irritation in Culhane's voice.

'No, that room has its own storage area. The body can stay down there indefinitely.' Chris's answer added to the detective's irritation.

'Are you sure you can't get me in that room?'

'No chance, only Doctor Winston has the key and he keeps it on him at all times.'

'Isn't there a way around it?'

'Not really. The door is alarmed and there is a camera on the wall. If you ain't invited, you ain't getting in.'

'How many bodies are down there?'

'Only one that I know of.'

'Have you got a picture of the body or any records on your computer?'

'No, Doctor Winston keeps everything related to the cases that go into the sealed-off area in there. They don't even get added to the main database until they're cleared by the doctor himself. Anyway, even if I had a picture of the body I don't think it would help you.'

'And why's that?'

'Well, rumor has it the body's unrecognizable, something to do with it having no face.'

'What? Really?'

'That's what I've heard.'

'Decapitated?'

'I'm not sure, I just heard the body had no face. It could've been blown off by a shotgun. It's not unheard of,' Chris said shaking his head.

Mark Culhane took a moment to think about the situation he'd been presented with. In his mind, the odds of the only body in the sealed-off area being of Jenny Farnborough were quite skinny. He saw no point in pursuing it.

'Thanks, Chris. Do me a favor will you? Keep an eye out for

any bodies matching the description I gave you, if anything comes in, give me a shout, it's important.' Culhane handed Chris one of his cards.

Chris regarded the card for a moment. 'Sure, anything for the LAPD.'

'I'd better get going. Do you mind if I get out through the same door we came in?'

'That's fine by me. I'll have to walk down with you, there's a code to the door.'

They left the cold-storage room and walked back in silence. As they reached the door, Culhane handed the overall back to Chris who punched the code into the metal keypad. Culhane was glad to see the outside world again.

Sitting inside his car, Culhane lit a cigarette. There were another two Coroner offices in Los Angeles, one in Santa Clarita and one in West Lancaster, but he wasn't sure if it was worth the trip. He finished his cigarette and decided he'd done all he could do to find this Jenny Farnborough girl; she was only another hooker anyway. In the morning he'd call Jerome and let him know. For now, he had more important things to do.

Eighteen

West Sunset Boulevard is one of the most famous streets in Los Angeles, but its best-known portion is the mile and a half stretch between Hollywood and Beverly Hills that has been dubbed 'The Sunset Strip.' The Strip embraces a premier collection of rock clubs, restaurants, boutiques, and Hollywood nightspots. It's been known as 'the place to be seen in LA' since the early seventies. Every evening, the Strip becomes a vibrant slash of gaudy neon, with traffic almost coming to a standstill as huge numbers of cars cruise down a people-packed boulevard. From celebrities to celebrity wannabes, from tourists and people-watchers to sleazy sex dealers, the Sunset Strip is definitely the place to be if you're looking for action in the City of Angels.

'Remind me again who're we here to see at this time?' Garcia asked as Hunter parked his car on Hilldale Avenue, just around the corner from the Strip.

'A scumbag called JJ,' Hunter replied getting out of the car and grabbing his jacket from the back seat.

Juan Jimenez, better known as JJ, was a low-life, small-time pimp who liked to conduct his business around Sunset Boulevard. He exploited his girls, all five of them. His trick was to keep them hooked on some sort of 'class A' drug. JJ was a violent man, and every now and then one of his girls would turn up in hospital with cuts and bruises, sometimes even broken bones. 'I tripped and fell' was always the lame explanation.

JJ had been arrested several times, but none of his girls had ever had the guts to press charges. His most powerful weapon – fear. 'Cross me and I'll cut you open.'

'And he can help us?' Garcia asked.

'He knows these streets and the girls that work them better than anyone. If our victim was a pro, he should be able to tell us. We might need to use a little "persuasion" though.'

They walked up Sunset Strip through the never-ending bustle of people trying to get into the already packed bars and clubs.

'So where're we going?' Garcia asked, looking around like a kid in a playground.

'There it is,' Hunter pointed to the colorful sign that hung above number 9015 West Sunset Boulevard.

The Rainbow Bar and Grill has been a hangout for rock musicians since the seventies and not much has changed. Gold records, guitars, photos and autographs from a variety of bands and solo artists adorned the walls. Rock music blasted through its speakers while a mixture of long-haired guys and peroxide blonds wearing next to nothing surrounded the bar and occupied the tables inside and outside.

'Is this JJ character into Rock?' Garcia asked.

'You better believe it.'

'I thought he was from Cuba or something like that.'

'Puerto Rico.'

'Aren't they all into salsa or meringue or something?'

'Not JJ.'

Garcia looked around the place and although they stood out from the crowd no one had taken any notice of them. 'Can you see him?'

Hunter quickly scanned the bar and tables. 'Not yet, but

this is his favorite hangout, he'll be here. Let's grab a drink and wait.' Hunter ordered an orange juice and Garcia a Diet Coke.

'They actually cook a great steak in here if you're ever hungry,' Hunter said, lifting his glass as if proposing a toast.

'Been here much?' Garcia asked with a contemptuous expression.

'A few times.'

'Wow, the Hideout Bar in Santa Monica, the Rainbow in Sunset Strip. You're a bit of a party animal, aren't you?'

Hunter didn't reply and concentrated his attention on the bar entrance. He hadn't seen JJ for the best part of five years, but the tall, very slim, dark-skinned Puerto Rican was an easily recognizable figure, with black pearl eyes, appallingly large ears and crooked teeth.

A tall, blond woman wearing overly tight leather trousers and a cropped top with the words 'Rock Bitch' across the front approached the bar and positioned herself to Hunter's right. She ordered a 'Slow Comfortable Screw up Against the Wall' and gave Hunter a sensual smile. Hunter smiled back and for a split second his eyes fell on her cleavage.

'Do you like them?' she asked with a sweet voice.

'Uh . . . like what?' Hunter tried to play dumb.

She looked down at her breasts which seemed about to explode out of her top. 'My tits silly . . . I saw you looking at them.'

'Busted,' Garcia said with an animated laugh.

No point being embarrassed now, Hunter thought. 'They look . . . very nice.'

'They're brand new,' she said proudly.

The barman came back with her cocktail and without breaking eye contact with Hunter she wrapped her red lips around the double straw and slowly sipped her drink.

'Is that nice?' Hunter asked.

'A slow screw is always nice,' she said having a second sip before moving closer. 'Maybe I could show you sometime,' she whispered into his ear while she ran her hand over his right bicep.

It all happened too fast. JJ had barely stepped into the Rainbow when his eyes met Hunter's and all of a sudden he was back outside; his legs moving like a quarterback's going for the touchdown that could win them the Super Bowl. Hunter sprung into action. He had no time to alert his partner whose undivided attention was on the tall blond's new pair of breasts. In a split second he was outside chasing JJ down Sunset Strip.

Hunter was fast despite his heavier, muscular frame, but JJ was skinnier, lighter and moved with the agility of a rat. Hunter decided to try the friendly approach first.

'JJ, I just wanna talk to you, slow down goddammit.'

JJ paid no attention to Hunter's call and in a semi-suicidal move crossed the Boulevard, disregarding traffic and heading towards Frankie and Johnnie's NY Pizza place.

Hunter followed him, but his run was slowed down by the street crowd and the constant people swerving. Twice he had to perform a quick and awkward left-right-left dance to avoid bumping into street punters.

Two blocks past the Rainbow and moving even faster, JJ swung left in front of the famous Whisky A Go Go bright-red building. Hunter was breathing down his neck, but again he had to zigzag around clubgoers and an uneven piece of side-walk caused him to take a false step. He felt his left foot twist at the ankle. A sharp pain shot from it quickly consuming his entire leg. His run faded into an awkward hop.

'Shit!' he yelled as he watched JJ disappear in the distance.

Suddenly, out of the corner of his eye, Hunter saw a figure

come past him with incredible speed. Garcia was moving like an Olympic champion. With just a few steps he had left Hunter behind and was fast gaining ground on JJ who had turned right into a small alleyway next to a large warehouse. Hunter limped his way after them.

Up ahead, it didn't take long for Garcia to be within an arm's length of the tall Puerto Rican. He reached out and grabbed him by his jacket's collar.

'OK, OK I give up,' JJ said slowing down and putting both of his hands up but it was all too late. Garcia spun him around and threw him against the wall, twisting his right arm behind his back. JJ screamed in pain.

'Running away from armed police officers, have you always been this stupid or is it a new affliction?' Garcia asked, catching his breath.

'Let me go ese, I haven't done nothing.'

It took Hunter thirty seconds to reach them.

'Are you OK?' Garcia asked still holding JJ's arm.

'I'm fine. Twisted my ankle back there.'

'Let go of my arm.'

'Shut the hell up.' Garcia slammed JJ's body against the wall once again.

Hunter turned to face JJ. 'What the hell were you doing? What's with all this running crap?'

'Force of habit, homie. What's this all about? Let me go man!' He twisted his body trying to escape Garcia's tight grip.

Hunter gave Garcia a nod who let go of JJ's arm.

'You can't do that man, I'm a legal citizen now,' JJ said, massaging his right wrist with his left hand and stepping away from the wall.

'Do we look like immigration to you? Damn, you're as dumb as you look,' Garcia snapped.

'Legal citizen? You're a pimp JJ, last time I checked prostitution was still illegal in the state of California, we can take your ass straight into prison right now,' Hunter said pushing JJ back to the wall.

'Enough with the wall slamming, homie,' he protested.

'If my ankle swells, so will your face,' Hunter threatened.

'Ain't my fault, homie.'

'Of course it's your fault HOMIE. If I didn't have to chase you like a fucking rabbit I wouldn't have twisted my foot.'

'Why you chasing me man? I didn't do nothing.'

'Exactly. We just wanna ask you a few questions.'

'Why didn't you say so in the first place?'

Hunter gave him an evil look before pulling the computer portrait out of his pocket. 'We need to find out who this woman is, if she is a pro or not.'

JJ stared at the picture for a few seconds.

'Yeah, I have her at home in a video game,' he said with a smirk.

The slap to the back of the head came from Garcia, throwing JJ's head forward with a loud thud. 'You wanna be a smart ass? I'm really starting to dislike you.'

'Hey, man, this is police brutality. I can press charges you know?'

This time the slap to the back of the head came from Hunter. 'Does this look like play time to you? Look at the picture – do you know who she is?' Hunter's voice was more menacing now.

JJ looked at the picture once again concentrating harder this time. 'Maybe . . . I can't be sure,' he said after a few seconds.

'Try.'

'Is she supposed to be a hooker?'

'That's a possibility, JJ. We wouldn't be asking you if she was a lawyer, would we?'

'Oh, you're funny.' JJ took the picture from Hunter's hands. 'She looks too pretty to be a street girl, not that my girls aren't beautiful.'

'Uh-huh,' Hunter tapped his index finger on the picture three times forcing JJ's attention back to it.

'If she's a pro, she plays for the big boys – first class.'

'And how can we find that out?' Garcia asked.

'A girl this pretty would only work for one guy around here – D-King.'

'Elvis came back from the dead to become a pimp?' Garcia asked narrowing his eyes.

'Not the King, D-King, homie.'

'D-King? What kinda name is that?' Garcia frowned.

'The kinda name you don't wanna fuck with.'

'Big-time pimp and drug dealer,' Hunter cut in. 'Rumor has it that he also deals in guns, but he runs a very tight operation. Everything very much underground. That's why you wouldn't have heard of him. He controls everything from afar, except his girls, where he prefers a hands-on approach.'

'And where can we find him?' Garcia asked.

'You won't find him on the streets, his business is high class.' JJ scratched the small scar over his left eye. 'What's in it for me?'

'You get to keep all your ugly teeth and not bleed all over your cheap suit. Sounds like a good deal to me,' Garcia said pushing JJ against the wall one more time.

'Who the hell's this guy?' JJ asked Hunter taking a step away from Garcia.

'I'm the guy *you* don't wanna fuck with,' Garcia said, stepping closer once again.

'He's my new partner JJ and I don't think he likes you very much. Last guy he took a dislike to still can't eat anything more solid than yogurt.'

'Can't you keep him on a leash?'

'Sure I can. The leash is in the car. I'll go get it. You guys will be OK by yourselves for ten minutes or so, right?'

'Wait, wait. OK, man. No need to leave me alone with monster-cop here. Friday and Saturday nights D-King likes to go to the Vanguard Club in Hollywood. You'll find him in the VIP area.'

'How about tonight, right now, where can we find him?'

'How the hell should I know, homie? I'm doing you a favor here, man, the Vanguard Club Friday and Saturday nights, that's all I know.'

'You better not be messing with us, JJ.' Garcia's tone was threatening.

'Why the fuck would I do that? If I never see you two again, that'd be too soon.'

Hunter placed his hand on JJ's left shoulder squeezing it. The pressure made JJ contort in pain once again. 'I really hope you're not sending us on a bogus chase, HOMIE.'

JJ tried in vain to escape Hunter's grip. 'I'm telling you the truth man. For real ese.'

Hunter let go of JJ who started dusting his jacket with both hands. 'Look at what you've done to my suit man, these things don't come cheap you know.'

Garcia checked his pocket change. 'Here.' He extended his hand towards JJ. 'A dollar ninety-five. Go buy another one.'

'He needs to see somebody, like an anger management person or something. Don't you guys have shrinks in the police?'

'No one good enough to cure him,' Hunter laughed.

JJ muttered something in Spanish as he walked away from both detectives. Garcia returned his change to his pocket and waited until JJ was far enough. 'What do you think?'

'I think you're pretty good in the bad, angry cop role. What a transformation! Even I believed it.'

'Last guy I disliked still can't eat anything more solid than yogurt?' Garcia asked, arching his eyebrows.

'Well, I wanted to make it convincing,' Hunter smiled.

'So what's next?'

'I guess we're going clubbing this Friday,' Hunter said reaching for his car keys.

Nineteen

Hunter pumped the gas pedal four times, placed his key in the ignition and turned it. The engine made a coughing noise followed by a rattling sound, the dashboard lights flickered but the car didn't start. Hunter returned the key to its original position, pumped the gas a couple more times and tried it again. This time he kept the key turned for about twelve seconds pressing the gas pedal gently. The engine coughed again and made the dreaded locomotive sound.

'You ain't serious,' Garcia said, staring at the dim flicker of the dashboard lights.

'Chill out, it's OK. This engine is just temperamental,' Hunter replied, avoiding Garcia's stare.

'By temperamental you mean old, right? Anyway, the problem isn't your engine. It sounds like a dead battery to me.'

'Trust me, I know this car, it'll be OK.' Hunter tried once again and this time the engine made no sound. The dashboard lights flickered only once and then . . .

'Umm! I guess you better call your road rescue service.'

'I don't have one.'

'What? Please tell me you're joking,' Garcia said, leaning against the passenger door.

'No I'm not.'

'Are you crazy? You have a car that's . . . How old is this car?'

Hunter screwed up his face trying to remember the exact year of fabrication. 'About fourteen years old.'

'You have a fourteen-year-old car and no road rescue plan? You're either very optimistic or a mechanic, and I don't see any grease on your hands.'

'I'm telling you, I know this car. We just gotta give it some time and it'll start, it always does. So coffee or beer?'

'Sorry?'

'Well, we've gotta kill some time . . . twenty or so minutes. We could just sit in here and shoot the breeze, but since we're on Sunset Strip, we might as well grab a drink while we wait, so do you prefer coffee or beer?'

Garcia looked at Hunter in disbelief. 'I don't see how waiting any amount of time will recharge your battery, but coffee will do for me.'

'Beer it is then,' Hunter said, opening his door and slipping out of the car.

'Shall we go back to the Rainbow? Maybe you can continue your very interesting conversation with the "Rock Bitch" blond babe,' Garcia taunted.

'It's OK, I got her phone number,' Hunter teased back.

They found a small, quiet bar on Hammond Street. It was just past one in the morning and most punters were getting ready to go home. Hunter ordered two beers and a bag with ice for his ankle before taking a table towards the rear of the bar.

'How's the foot?' Garcia asked as they sat down.

'Fine. It's just a simple twist,' he said after a quick examination. 'The ice will keep it from swelling up.' He placed the bag of ice over his foot and rested it on an empty chair to his left. 'I won't be able to run for a couple of days but that's all.'

Garcia nodded.

'I've never seen anybody run the way you did, were you in the Olympics or something?'

Garcia smiled, showing glistening white and perfectly aligned teeth. 'I used to be in my university's track and field team.'

'And you were very good at it by the looks of things.'

'I've won a few medals.' Garcia sounded more embarrassed than proud. 'How about you? If you hadn't twisted your foot you would've gotten to him easily. He was half your weight.'

'I'm not as fast as you, I can tell you that,' Hunter replied with a tilt of the head.

'Maybe one day we'll find out,' Garcia said with a challenging smile.

A loud crashing noise came from the bar catching their attention. Someone had slipped from his bar stool, smashing his beer bottle and plummeting to the floor.

'Time to go home, Joe,' a short brunette waitress said, helping the man back to his feet.

'There's something that bothers me about this case,' Garcia said following Joe out of the bar with his eyes.

'Everything bothers me about this case, but let's hear yours,' Hunter replied, having another sip of his beer.

'In this day and age, how can the killer not leave anything behind? I understand that the killer also has a lot of time to clean up the place before he leaves, but we've got lights and chemicals and different gadgets that can reveal a speck of dust on the floor. We've got DNA tests; we can convict someone by his saliva. Hell, if the killer had farted in that house the forensic team would probably have some gadget that could pick it up. How can the crime scenes be so clean?'

'Simple, the killer never works on a victim at the location where the victim is found.'

Garcia half nodded accepting Hunter's theory.

'Our victim for example. She wasn't skinned at that old wooden house. The killer surely has a very secure place, a killing place, a place where he feels safe, where he can take his time with the victims, where he knows no one would ever interrupt him. So all the messy stuff, the blood, the noise, the fibers are all left somewhere else. The killer then transports the victim to the place where he wants them to be found, usually a secluded place where the risk of being seen by a member of the public is very slim. All the killer has to do is wear some sort of overall that sheds no fibers.'

'Like a plastic suit?'

'Or a rubber suit, diving suit, something like that. Something the killer could've made himself at home, impossible to trace really.'

'How about transporting the victim?'

'Probably a van, something common, something that wouldn't raise any suspicions, but big enough to transport a body or two in the back.'

'And I bet the van's interior is completely covered in plastic sheets or something the killer can easily remove and burn, avoiding leaving any traces behind in case the van is ever found.'

Hunter nodded and had another sip of his drink. They both went silent and Hunter started playing with his car keys.

'Have you ever thought about getting a newer car?' Garcia asked cautiously.

'You know, you sound just like Scott. I like that car, it's a classic.'

'Classic piece of junk maybe.'

'That's a true old-fashioned, all-American car. None of this Japanese- or European-made flimsy stuff.'

'Japanese cars will run forever, they've got amazing engines.'

'Yeah, now you're really sounding like Scott, he used to drive a Toyota.'

'Intelligent man.'

Garcia pressed his upper teeth against his lower lip. He wasn't sure how Hunter would react to his next question, but he decided to go for it anyway. 'What happened to Scott? I was never told,' he tried to sound casual.

Hunter placed his beer back on the table and looked at his partner. He knew that sooner or later that question would come up. 'Do you want another beer?' he asked.

Garcia looked at his half-full bottle. It was obvious Hunter was trying to avoid the question. He decided not to push it. 'No, I'm not really a beer guy, I prefer whisky.'

Hunter lifted his eyebrows in surprise. 'Really?'

'Yeah, single malt is my weakness.'

'OK, now you're talking.' Hunter gave Garcia a quick nod. 'Do you think they have any decent single malt in this joint?'

Garcia realized Hunter was about to go back to the bar. 'Probably not, but hey, I don't wanna get started on whisky, not at this time,' he said quickly glancing at his watch. 'This beer will do. I wanted coffee remember.'

Hunter gave Garcia a quick smile and finished the rest of his beer in one go. 'Boat accident.'

'What?'

'Scott and his wife died in a boat accident, right after Mike Farloe was sentenced.' Hunter's statement caught Garcia by surprise. He wasn't sure if he should say something or not and took another swig of his beer instead.

'We were both due a vacation,' Hunter continued. 'We'd been working on the case for too long. It'd taken over our lives and we were literally losing our minds. The pressure had gotten to everyone. It was affecting our logical thought process. We were doubting our abilities and depression was setting in fast. When Mike confessed to the crucifix killings we were ordered to take some time off. For our own sanity.' Hunter toyed with his empty beer bottle, scraping off the label.

'I think I'll take that single malt now, do you want one?' Garcia said making a head movement towards the bar.

'Sure, why not, if they have any.'

A couple of minutes later Garcia came back with two single shots. 'The best they could manage was Arran eight years, and the prices in here are a joke.' He placed a glass in front of Hunter and sat down.

'Thanks . . . to good health,' Hunter said raising his glass. He had a sip of the brownish liquid and let its strong taste engulf his entire mouth. 'Much better than beer I'd say.'

Garcia agreed with a smile.

'I live alone, I always have, but Scott had a wife . . . Amanda. They'd been married for only three and a half years.' Hunter's eyes were fixed on his glass.

Garcia could tell this wasn't easy for Hunter.

'The case had put a lot of pressure on their marriage. Sometimes he'd go for days without going home. It was hard for Amanda. They started arguing a lot. Scott had become obsessed with the case and so had I,' Hunter said having another sip of his single malt. 'We were sure there had to be some sort of bond, something that would link all the victims together. We were waiting for the killer to slip up. Sooner or later they all do, no one could be that thorough.'

'Did you check with the FBI?'

'Yeah, we were given clearance to their database and library. We spent days . . . weeks looking for something that could help us.' Hunter paused for a few seconds. 'There's always something. It doesn't matter how evil or crazy someone is, there's always a reason for murder. Most of the time it's an illogical one, but a reason nevertheless. We were going crazy; we were checking the most absurd possibilities.'

'Like what?' Garcia asked curiously.

'Oh, we checked things like if they all had the same childhood diseases, holiday destinations, allergies – anything really, and then . . .'

'And then you got your break.'

'And then we got our break – we arrested Mike Farloe. For Scott, that was a blessing.'

'I can see why.'

'I'm sure if the case had gone on for a few more months, Amanda would've walked out on him and Scott would've ended up in a crazy house.'

'So what happened after the arrest?'

'We were ordered to go on a vacation, not that we needed any persuasion,' Hunter said with a shy smile.

'I bet you didn't.'

'Scott's big passion was this boat of his. He'd saved for years to be able to afford it.' Another sip. 'He needed to spend time with Amanda, you know, just the two of them to try and patch things up. A sailing vacation sounded like a great idea.'

'It was a sailboat?' Garcia's interest grew.

'Yeah, something like . . . Catarina 30.'

Garcia laughed. 'Catalina 30, you mean.'

Hunter's eyes met Garcia's. 'Yeah, that's it, how do you know?'

'I grew up with sailboats. My father was obsessed with them.'

'Huh! How about that? Anyway, there was some sort of fuel leak on board. Something ignited it causing it to blow. They died in their sleep.'

'A fuel leak?' Garcia sounded surprised.

'That's right,' Hunter replied, noticing Garcia's skeptical look. 'I know what you're thinking.'

Garcia raised his eyebrows.

'Sailboats don't carry that much fuel. Why would they, right? They are sailboats. And it would've had to have been a massive leak to cause the boat to explode.'

Garcia nodded.

'Yeah, that didn't sit right with me either so I tried carrying out my own private investigation. I don't believe someone as thorough as Scott would've overlooked any sort of problem with his most prized possession, no matter how small. Scott was a very proud man.' Hunter had another sip of his whisky. 'The leak didn't come from the engine. It came from the fuel barrows.'

'Fuel barrows?'

'For some reason that I'll never find out, Scott took more fuel onboard than usual. A few barrows.'

'Was he planning a longer trip?'

'I don't know, and as I've said, I'll never find out.'

Garcia looked pensive for a long minute and watched Hunter drink the rest of his whisky in silence. 'Did Scott smoke?'

'Both of them did, but I don't buy it. That's what the official report tried to blame it on.' Hunter shook his head. 'There's no way I'll ever believe that some sort of cigarette accident caused the boat to blow. Not with Scott on board. He wouldn't make that sort of mistake.'

They stared at each other without saying a word.

'I was only told about it two weeks after it'd happened, when I got back to the RHD.'

Garcia could sense real pain in his partner. 'I take it that the case's been closed.'

Hunter nodded. 'They saw no reason to investigate it any further.'

'I'm sorry.'

'If I'd lost a partner to the job, then maybe . . .' Hunter paused, moving his index finger around the rim of his now empty glass. 'But that just felt wrong – a freak accident and suddenly I'd lost two very important people in my life.'

'Two?'

Hunter rubbed his eyes, taking his time to respond. 'Amanda was my only cousin. I had introduced them to each other.' His voice was sad. It was obvious Hunter was battling with his emotions. This was the first time he'd talked about what had happened to anyone, and in a way, it made him feel better. Hunter noticed that Garcia looked like he wanted to say something. Maybe something to try and comfort him, but he knew that in situations like these words would make no difference.

Garcia bit his lip and said nothing.

It took Hunter a few more seconds to gather himself again. 'We better get going,' he finally said then got up.

'Yeah, sure.' Garcia finished his whisky in one big gulp.

Outside the warm air felt a little uncomfortable.

'Maybe we should just call police rescue,' Garcia said as they reached Hunter's car once again.

'No need.' Hunter turned the key in the ignition and the engine started straight away.

'I'll be damned!'

'I told you, great car, just a little temperamental.' Hunter had a proud smile on his lips as he drove away.

Twenty

Hunter's shirt was drenched in sweat when he woke up from another vivid and disturbing dream at five in the morning.

He sat in bed, breathing heavily, his forehead wet with perspiration, his whole body shaking. When would these dreams leave him? Since Scott's death they'd become a constant part of his nights. He knew he wouldn't be able to go back to sleep now. He walked into the bathroom and splashed some icy-cold water on his face. His breathing had slowed down but his hands were still shaking. The reflection in the mirror disturbed him. The bags under his eyes seemed heavier, his complexion too pale.

He moved to the kitchen and sat in the dark for a few minutes nursing his anxiety. His eyes grazed the kitchen's noticeboard and he saw the note he'd pinned up a few days ago – Isabella.

Hunter had forgotten about her. He unpinned the note from the board and read it. A pleasing grin found its way to his lips without him even noticing it. For a quick second he forgot all about the Crucifix Killer's case and remembered how she made him smile. He remembered how he had to fight the urge to jump back in bed with her after her invitation.

Hunter retrieved his cell phone from his jacket pocket, keyed in her number and created an alarm entry to remind him at 12:30 p.m.

*

Hunter arrived at the RHD building at eight o'clock to find Garcia already sitting at his desk. They spent the morning faxing photos to model and acting agencies and trying to gather all the information they could about D-King. Hunter knew from experience never to interrogate anyone unprepared, especially if that someone was a self-proclaimed crime lord.

'Yeah, it looks like we're gonna be dealing with one tough sonofabitch here,' Garcia said, holding the fax he'd just received.

'I knew that, but what do you have?'

'As you've said before it seems like our guy deals in just about anything you'd like, drugs, guns, prostitution, stolen goods . . .' Garcia made a movement with his hand indicating that the list went on and on. 'And you were right when you said he was very slick. He's been taken to court a few times . . .'

'Let me guess, walked every time.'

'Free as a bird.'

'That figures. Where did that information come from?'

'The District Attorney's office.'

'And that's all they sent us?' Hunter arched his eyebrows.

'Uh-huh.'

'Get back onto them and see if they can send us the whole file. They usually do a very good job of gathering information on the people they're after.'

'I'm on it.' Garcia started searching his desk for the DA's office number. He knew he had it just a minute ago.

Hunter felt the vibration of the cell phone in his pocket before he heard its sound alert – '12:30 call Isabella'.

'I'll be right back, gotta make a quick personal call.' He stepped into the empty corridor and closed the door behind him, leaving Garcia still looking for the DA's phone number.

He selected Isabella's number from his phone's address book, pressed the dial button and heard it ring three times.

'Hello!'

'Hi . . . Isabella?'

'Yes, this is Isabella.'

'Hi, this is Robert Hunter.' He couldn't remember if he'd told her his name or not. 'We met over the weekend at the Hideout bar.'

'This past weekend?' she sounded uncertain.

'Yeah, I ended up in your apartment. Had to rush out at three in the morning, remember?'

She laughed. 'Yes, I remember you – teddy-bear underwear man who thought I was a prostitute right?'

Hunter contorted his face as if he'd been punched in the stomach. 'Yep, that'd be me.'

'Did you call to apologize again?' she asked half laughing.

'Actually I called to ask if you'd like to get together again sometime, maybe lunch . . . or dinner.' Hunter found it easier to get straight to the point.

'Well, that's a big leap. From thinking I was a hooker and rushing off in the middle of the night to asking me out on a date. Surprising.'

'I guess I'm full of surprises,' Hunter joked.

'Aren't you just?'

'Look, I acted like a jerk before and I'm sorry. I was half drunk, half asleep and you looked too good to be true.' Hunter bit his bottom lip and hoped the flattering worked.

'Was that a compliment or are you telling me that the only attractive women you go to bed with are hookers?'

'Noooo. Wow, this conversation has gone all wrong.' Hunter heard her laugh. 'What do you say we completely erase that first night?'

Several silent seconds went by. 'OK,' she finally replied. 'Give me just a second.' Hunter heard the faint sound of pages turning. 'I've got a few things coming up, but I could do a quick lunch tomorrow if that's OK with you.'

'Lunch tomorrow sounds fine,' Hunter answered casually. 'One o'clock OK?'

'Yeah, that's perfect.'

'Since it sounds like you're on a tight schedule maybe we could meet closer to where you work.'

'Sure. I work at the University. Do you like Italian food?'

'Yeah, Italian is tasty.'

'I guess that's one way of putting it.' She giggled. 'There's a great little Italian restaurant called Pancetta in Weyburn Avenue, just a block away from the University. How about I meet you there at one o'clock?'

'Looking forward to it.' Hunter placed his cell phone back in his pocket. 'Italian is tasty?' he said out loud shaking his head. 'What the hell was I thinking?'

Twenty-One

'They do have a file on D-King and they said they'd be glad to share it with us on one condition,' Garcia said as Hunter walked back into the office.

'And what condition is that?'

'That we do the same. We tell them whatever we find out about him.'

'Well, that sounds easy enough.'

'That's what I thought, so I told them they had a deal and we'll be dropping by to collect the file this afternoon.'

'That's fine.'

Hunter felt his cell phone vibrate once again followed by its ringtone.

'Hello, Detective Hunter speaking.'

'*Hello Robert.*' Hunter's throat knotted and he immediately snapped his fingers twice at his partner to get his attention. Garcia knew exactly who was on the other end of the line.

'*I'm gonna give you a chance to make a difference today.*'

'I'm listening.'

'*I'm sure you are. Are you a gambling man, Robert?*'

'Not if I can avoid it.' Hunter sounded calm.

'*Well, I'm sure you'll find someone to help you. Maybe your new partner.*'

Hunter frowned. 'How do you know I have a . . .'

The metallic voice cut Hunter short. *'In about four minutes there will be a greyhound race starting at the Jefferson County Kennel Club. I want you to pick me the winner.'*

'Greyhounds?'

'That's right, Robert. I'm putting someone's life in your hands. You pick the wrong dog and he dies.'

Hunter exchanged a tense and confused look with Garcia.

'I will call you back twenty seconds before the race starts to get your selection . . . be ready.'

'Wait!' but the line had already gone dead.

'What did he say?' Garcia demanded anxiously even before Hunter had a chance to close his phone.

'Do you understand anything about greyhound racing?' There was a desperate tone in Hunter's voice.

'What?'

'Dog racing . . . do you know anything about it, do you bet?' he shouted nervously.

'No, never have.'

'Shit!' Hunter scratched his forehead in thought for a moment. 'We've gotta go downstairs.' Hunter raced to the door, not a second to spare. Garcia followed him. They made it down the six flights of stairs that took them to the main detective floor in record time. The floor was almost empty, only Detective Lucas and Detective Maurice were at their desks.

'Do you guys know anything about greyhound racing?' Hunter shouted as soon as he was through the door. The puzzled look on the detectives' faces was uniform.

No response.

'Dog racing, does anyone in here bet on it?' The desperation in Hunter's voice was alarming.

'Dog racing is illegal in California,' Detective Lucas said calmly.

'I don't give a damn, I just wanna know if any of you two know anything about it. Do any of you two bet?'

'What the hell is going on in here, Hunter?' Captain Bolter had come out of his office to check what the yelling was all about.

'No time to explain it now, Captain. I need to know if anyone bets on the dogs in here.' Hunter noticed a slight uneasiness about Detective Lucas. 'Lucas c'mon, talk to me,' Hunter pressed.

'I bet every now and then,' Lucas said shyly.

All eyes were now on him. Hunter checked his watch. 'In two and a half minutes there's a dog race starting at the Jefferson County Kennel Club. I need you to pick me the winner.'

The puzzled look that had graced the detectives' faces turned into laughter. 'Well, if it was that simple I wouldn't be working here, would I?' Lucas replied.

'You'd better do your best or else someone is gonna get murdered.' Hunter's urgency sent a cold shiver around the room.

Captain Bolter immediately realized what Hunter's impatience was all about. 'How do you get the race card?' he shot the question at Lucas.

'Over the internet.'

'Do it, now,' the captain ordered, moving towards the detective's desk.

Lucas turned to his PC and fired up his browser. He enjoyed gambling, mainly dog and horse racing and he had several racing links saved into his favorites. Hunter, Garcia and Captain Bolter were already by Lucas's side. Detective Maurice was the last one to join them.

'Let's see, you said Jefferson County Kennel Club right?'

'Yes.'

'That's in Florida.'

'Do I look like I give a shit where the hell it is? Just get the race card will you?' Captain Bolter's irritation was exploding.

'OK, here we go.' With a few more clicks he had the race card in front of him.

'What does all that mean?' Garcia had never seen a dog-racing card before.

'Well, these are the dog-trap numbers, these here are the dog names and these are the betting odds,' Lucas replied pointing to different sections of the card on his screen.

'How about all these other numbers?' Hunter this time.

'Sectionals and number of wins, but that's too complicated to explain now.'

'Fine, how do you usually make your selection?'

'I analyze the form but in this case I just don't have the time.'

'So what's the second option?'

'I don't know, maybe go with the market.'

'And that means what?' Captain Bolter asked annoyed.

'In short, wait for the odds on the dogs to start moving and bet on the favorite. The market is usually a very good indication of the probable outcome of the race.'

'It wouldn't be that easy,' Hunter said, knowing the killer would never set him off on an easy task.

'That's the thing, it's not easy at all, look at these odds.' Lucas pointed to his computer screen. 'We have co-favorites of four, traps 1, 2, 4 and 5 all with the exact same odds, three-to-one, and the other dogs aren't that far behind. This is a very hard race to predict. If I had the choice I would never place a bet on a race like this.'

'You don't have the choice,' Garcia said.

'Your guess is as good as mine then.'

'You're supposed to be the gambler here.' The conversation

was starting to turn into yelling. By now everyone realized the gravity of the situation and nerves were starting to get the better of everyone.

'OK, everyone calm the fuck down,' Hunter ordered. 'Lucas, just do your best.'

He turned his attention back to his computer screen. 'At first glance, the sectionals of the dog in trap five look better, but by no means is that a confident guess.'

'I like the name of the dog in trap seven,' Detective Maurice offered.

Captain Bolter's look was enough to shut him up.

'What do we do?' Garcia asked nervously.

'Maybe we should go with the five dog then,' Hunter said, quickly analyzing the numbers on the race card.

'The sectionals from the dog in trap two look pretty good too.'

'I don't understand what you are talking about . . . sectionals? Just pick a goddamn dog,' Captain Bolter demanded.

'Captain, this is gambling, if it were that easy we'd all be making a living out of it.'

'We are running out of time here,' Hunter snapped.

'Just pick the one you think has got the best chance of winning.' Garcia this time.

Hunter's cell phone rang, making everyone in the room jump. He looked at the caller display – *withheld*. 'It's him.'

'Him who?' Lucas asked curiously.

Garcia placed his index finger over his lips telling everyone to keep quiet.

'Detective Hunter speaking.'

'*What's your selection?*'

Hunter locked eyes with Lucas's, raising his eyebrows as if asking 'Which one?'

Lucas thought about it for a quick second and then raised his right hand, all five fingers spread apart. Hunter could see no conviction in his eyes.

'*Three seconds, Robert.*'

'Five, the dog in trap five.' The line went dead.

Silence took over the room. Hunter knew nothing about greyhound racing and he was sure the killer was aware of that.

'The result, how do we know which dog won? Can we watch the race?' Garcia's voice broke the silence.

'It depends if the track has its own website and if they do live broadcasting.'

'Can we find out?'

Lucas turned to his computer to search for the Jefferson County Kennel Club website. He found it within seconds and just a moment later he had it up on his screen. He checked the links on the home page and clicked on the *Program & Results* one. 'Shit.'

'What?' Captain Bolter asked.

'We can't watch it. They don't have live broadcasting. But they will display the result about a minute after the race has ended.'

'How long does the race take?'

'Only about thirty or forty seconds.'

'So that's it? We just wait here like idiots?'

'There's nothing else we can do,' Hunter said, taking a deep breath.

Twenty-Two

Lucas refreshed the web page on his screen. 'That's it, they are racing.'

'How do you know?' Garcia asked.

Lucas pointed to the top of the page '*Race status: racing*'.

Everyone stood motionless; all eyes fixed on Lucas's computer screen as if they could all see the race track. For an instant it felt like no one was breathing. Garcia shifted his weight to his left leg, but no position was a comfortable one. The tension inside the office was palpable.

Hunter was starting to get restless. He didn't like this. Why was the killer playing games now? Did the killer know that one of the detectives was a gambler?

The silence in the room was broken by Detective Maurice's voice. 'Refresh it,' he said excitedly.

'It's only been about ten seconds since they started racing.'

'Refresh it anyway.'

'OK, OK.' Lucas clicked the button on his browser. The webpage refreshed in less than a second. *Race status: racing*. 'See? No result yet.'

The anxiety was making everyone uncomfortable. People were starting to get fidgety, but all eyes were still on Lucas's computer screen. The seconds went by like hours. Garcia started massaging his forehead and temples. Maurice was done biting his nail on one thumb and had now moved to the other one. Hunter hadn't said a word since the race started.

'Can't we call the track and explain that someone is gonna die if dog five doesn't win,' Detective Maurice offered.

Garcia laughed. 'Yeah, of course we can, they won't just think you're some crazy gambler who has bet all your life savings on that race. Think about it.'

Maurice realized how stupid his suggestion sounded.

Lucas refreshed the webpage once again. Still no result.

'This is taking quite a long time, isn't it? It's been about two minutes since the race started,' Garcia said with a worried look.

'I know, and I don't like that,' Lucas replied.

'Why not, why not?' Maurice asked, unable to contain his concern.

'Usually when it takes too long it means the result went to the judges, two or more dogs crossed the finish line together so they have to look at a photograph to decide who the winner is. If they can't tell the dogs apart, they might call a dead heat.'

'What the hell is a dead heat?'

'You know nothing about races do you, Garcia? It's like a draw, two or more dogs are declared winners.'

'What happens then?' Garcia's question was directed at Hunter who had no answer.

The room fell silent again and everyone turned back to the computer screen. Maurice had stopped biting his nails and had placed both of his hands in his pockets in an attempt to stop them from shaking.

'Let me try one more time.' Lucas clicked his mouse and waited. The page reappeared on the screen and this time they finally had a result.

Twenty-Three

Darkness – that was all that surrounded George Slater as he regained consciousness. An unbearable pain shot up from his groin. His head was throbbing, making him dizzy. Everything was unsteady. His legs. His body. His memory. He tried to remember what had happened, but his brain wasn't cooperating.

Where the hell am I?

How long have I been unconscious?

How did I get here?

Very slowly his memories started to form. The knock on the door. The excitement of seeing Rafael again. The strange intruder that had shown up at his rented apartment. The one-sided struggle, the confusion, the pain and then – the syringe.

He felt dizzy, weak, hungry, thirsty and scared. His hands were resting over his chest, but they weren't tied. He tried to move them, but there simply wasn't enough space. They touched what felt like unplaned wooden planks, his fingers feeling the splintery texture. He made an effort to scream but the gag in his mouth kept him from making a sound.

George tried moving his legs, but he could only manage one inch or so before they hit another wall in front of him.

A box, I'm inside a wooden box, he thought as panic started to take over.

I've gotta get out of here.

He jerked his body violently from side to side, his legs trying to kick out, his hands scraping away on the wood until all his nails were broken, but his efforts were not rewarded. He started to feel claustrophobic, making him more desperate.

He knew panicking wouldn't help. He needed to work with whatever little knowledge of the situation he had. He took a moment to calm himself down. Concentrating on his heartbeat he took deep breaths. After a minute it started to work. George urged his brain to think. He tried to gather all the information he had so far. He'd been attacked, drugged, taken hostage and placed inside some sort of wooden box. He could feel the blood flowing normally through his body, and that told him the box was in an upright position instead of lying down. That brought him some relief. If the box had been in a horizontal position it could mean he was underground – buried alive inside some kind of coffin, and that petrified him. From a very young age George had been terrified of confined spaces. He was only ten when his mother beat him senseless and locked him inside a wardrobe for twelve hours with no food and no water. His crime – falling off his bike and tearing his brand-new pair of trousers at the knee.

He kicked his legs against the wooden walls again. They felt solid, as if the box had been nailed shut.

'Would you stop making all that noise?'

The voice took George by surprise. Someone else was there. George's heart started beating faster. He tried to scream once again, but the gag in his mouth was too tight and he produced only a muffled grunt.

'It won't be very long now.'

George could feel the panic coming back. What wouldn't be long? Until he was freed or until he was dead? He needed to get rid of the gag in his mouth. He knew that if he could speak he would be able to reason with whoever else was there. That's what he knew how to do – talk to people. As a lawyer he had negotiated million-dollar deals. He had convinced juries and judges that his side of an argument was the correct one. If he was given the chance he was sure he could reason with his captor. If only he could speak.

He jerked his body once again, making even more noise, hysteria starting to take over.

'That won't help you.'

Suddenly George froze. He knew that voice, he was sure he'd heard it before, but where? He made more noise.

'Suit yourself, if you wanna make noise, go right ahead.'

There was no doubt in George's mind anymore. He knew that person. He closed his eyes in an effort to search his memory. Where had they met before? In the office? In a court of law? Where? George implored his memory to help him.

'Jesus!' he said, shivering and reopening his eyes. It had been at a party, a BDSM party. It all came back to him. He could clearly picture the person's face in his mind.

'I know you . . . I know who you are . . .'

Twenty-Four

Lucas stared at the race result on his computer screen. Garcia was trying his best to look over everyone's shoulders and get a glimpse of it. Hunter kept his eyes shut, too nervous to look.

'We lost,' Lucas's voice croaked. 'Trap two won it, trap five got second.' He had to force himself to look at Hunter.

'No,' Garcia said, his voice barely audible. He made an effort not to be sick and tasted his breakfast rise in his throat.

Captain Bolter pushed Lucas aside so he could get a better look at the screen.

'Shit! I should've picked trap two, I was between two and five – I should've gone for two,' Lucas said, collapsing onto his chair.

Captain Bolter's eyes were still on the screen. The result read: *1st trap two, 2nd trap five, 3rd trap eight*. 'It's not your fault,' he finally said, placing a friendly hand on Lucas's shoulder.

Hunter was still silent. His eyes closed, his hands tucked inside his pockets. After a few more seconds he looked at Garcia and mouthed the words 'I can't believe this.'

Everyone stood motionless. No one knew what to say. Hunter wanted to scream and punch Lucas's computer screen, but he kept his anger locked inside.

Hunter's cell phone rang once again startling everyone. He snapped it out of his pocket and checked the display. A gentle nod towards Captain Bolter indicated that the caller was who they expected it to be.

'Yes,' Hunter said in a defeated tone of voice.

'*Unlucky.*'

'Wait . . .' Hunter pleaded but it was too late, the line went dead.

'Turn it off,' Captain Bolter pointed to Lucas's computer screen. 'There's no need for any more dog racing today.'

Lucas closed his browser and glanced at Hunter. 'I'm sorry, man, if I'd had some more time . . .'

Hunter knew Lucas had done his best. As he'd said, if it were that easy, everyone would be making money out of gambling.

'Hunter, Garcia, we need to talk,' Captain Bolter's voice was firm. This was not going to plan, at least not to the plan he had in mind. He walked back to his office, his heavy footsteps echoing throughout the silent room. Hunter and Garcia followed him in silence.

'What the hell's going on?' Captain Bolter said, even before Garcia had closed the door behind him.

'What do you think, Captain? The killer's at it again, only this time he made me choose. If I picked the correct dog the victim would live.'

'That last phone call, did he tell you where the new victim is?'

'No, not yet.'

'He's playing games now?'

'It sure as hell seems like it.'

Captain Bolter turned and faced the window. Fifteen long silent seconds followed before he spoke again. 'Why? He's never done it before. He's never given you a chance to save a victim. Why now? Why dog racing?'

'I couldn't tell you why now or why he's chosen dog racing, but the logical conclusion for why he's playing games is that he wants to share the guilt.'

'What? Are you for real?' the captain asked incredulously.

'It's a psychological game, Captain. He wants to share the guilt with someone, in this case, me. He wants me to feel like I played a hand on the victim's death by not picking the winner – I'm just as guilty as he is.'

Captain Bolter turned to face both detectives. 'Are you telling me that all of a sudden this guy's feeling too guilty? He's feeling remorseful?' His irritation was carrying through to his voice.

'I'm not sure.'

'Well, you're the one with the big brain.'

'It's a possibility, who knows?' Hunter said after a small pause. 'In all the previous killings it was only the two of them, the killer against the victim. There was nothing anybody could do. It was the killer's decision to kill. By making me pick a dog the killer has brought me into the equation. In the killer's mind the decision to kill doesn't belong to him anymore. It belongs to me.'

'As if you had told him to do it?' Garcia asked.

'Yes,' Hunter said with a nod. 'And because he feels the decision to kill isn't his anymore . . .'

'He feels he's not as guilty,' Captain Bolter concluded.

'He might also be hoping to increase the frustration and consequently slow the investigation down,' Hunter confirmed.

'Well, it's definitely adding to my frustration,' Captain Bolter shot back.

'Or he may just be playing games for the hell of it.'

Captain Bolter shook his head. 'He's fucking with us, that's what he's doing.'

'It looks like he's been doing that for a while, Captain,' Garcia said, immediately regretting his words.

The captain looked at him like a hungry Rottweiler ready to attack. 'Have you identified the first victim yet?'

'Not yet, Captain, but we're meeting someone on Friday that might give us a lead.'

'We're not moving very fast on this, are we?'

'We're moving as fast as we can.' Hunter's turn to sound irritated.

'Let's hope that this lead of yours turns out to be something real. This is starting to turn into a goddamn circus, and I hate circuses.'

Hunter understood the anger in the captain's voice – it was the same anger he had bottled up inside. They knew the killer was about to claim a new victim, but they didn't know when, they didn't know where and they didn't know who. They were playing a losing game. There was nothing they could do but wait for the next phone call.

Twenty-Five

Hunter arrived at Weyburn Avenue at exactly one o'clock. The street was buzzing with university students on their lunch break looking for the cheapest meal deal they could find. Burger bars and pizza parlors seemed to be the preferred choice. It didn't take him long to find the Pancetta restaurant tucked away between a Pizza Hut Express and a stationery store.

The restaurant entrance was pleasantly decorated with colorful flowers and plants, all in a red, green and white theme. The place was small and it resembled a typical Italian cantina. Its squared wooden tables were covered with red and white checked tablecloths. A strong but pleasant smell of provolone cheese mixed with bresaola and salami greeted customers.

Hunter waited at the restaurant entrance for a moment, observing the waiters moving in between tables. His eyes browsed the entire room. Isabella hadn't arrived yet. The maître d' showed him to a corner table next to an open window. As he made his way through the restaurant floor, two women, no older than twenty-five, followed him with their eyes. Hunter couldn't help noticing it and returned the compliment with a confident smile, which in turn was met with a shy giggle and a sexy wink from the dark-haired one.

He placed his jacket over the back of his chair and sat facing the entrance door. Out of habit he checked his cell phone for any missed messages or calls – there weren't any. He ordered a Diet Coke and had a quick look at the menu. He wondered if he'd recognize Isabella. His memory of the weekend was pretty hazy.

The events of yesterday still played in his mind. Why greyhound racing? If the killer wanted to gamble, why not horse racing or roulette or something more common? Was there some hidden meaning behind it all? And as the captain had said, why has the killer started playing games now? Guilt? Repentance? Hunter didn't buy that. His thoughts were disrupted by the waiter who had just finished pouring his drink into an icy glass. As he had his first sip his attention was drawn to the restaurant door.

Dressed casually in a thin, white, cotton blouse tucked into tight, faded, blue jeans with black cowboy boots and belt to match, Isabella looked prettier than he remembered. Her long dark hair fell loose over her shoulders and her olive-green eyes carried an intriguing sparkle.

Hunter raised his hand to catch her attention, but Isabella had already noticed him sitting by the window. With a pleasant smile she made her way towards his table. Hunter stood up and was about to extend his hand for the conventional handshake when she leaned forward and kissed him twice, once on each cheek. Her perfume was citrusy and subtle. He held out the chair opposite his offering her a seat, a gentleman-like gesture that was very much unlike him. He waited for her to sit down before going back to his chair.

'So you found it OK?' she asked in a cheerful voice.

'Yeah, no problem. It looks like a very nice restaurant,' he said, looking around.

'Oh it is, trust me.' She renewed her smile. 'The food here is very *tasty*.'

'*Touché*,' he thought. 'I'm sorry about that. That sentence came out all wrong yesterday. Sometimes my brain works faster than my lips and words don't come out quite as I'd like them to.'

'It's OK. It made me laugh.'

'So, you work at the University?' Hunter changed the subject.

'Yes.'

'Medical or biological department?'

Isabella looked baffled for an instant. 'Biomedical research actually. Wait, how did you know? Oh God! Please tell me I don't smell of formaldehyde.' She subtly brought her right wrist to her nose.

Hunter laughed. 'No, you don't. You smell terrific to be honest.'

'Thank you, that's quite sweet. But tell me, how did you know?'

'Observation really.' Hunter played it down.

'Observation? Please tell me more.'

'I just pick up on silly things that most people don't.'

'Like what?'

'Just above your wrist line there's a slight depression,' he said, tilting his head towards her hands. 'As if you've been wearing tight rubber bands around both of your wrists. The white powder residue around your cuticles is consistent with cornstarch powder, which you know is used in surgical gloves. My guess is that you've been wearing gloves all morning.'

'Wow. That's quite impressive.' She looked at her hands for a couple of seconds. 'But the powder on my fingers could be from chalk. That means that I could be a professor at the University. And I could teach any subject, not just biomedical,' she challenged Hunter.

'Different kind of powder,' he shot back with conviction. 'Cornstarch is much finer and a lot harder to wash off, that's why you have it only around your cuticles and not your fingers. Plus you have it on both of your hands. So unless you're an ambidextrous professor, I'll stick with my surgical gloves theory.'

She stared at him in silence. A nervous smile played on her lips.

'The other giveaway is that UCLA Medical School is just around the corner,' he said with a new tilt of the head.

Isabella hesitated for a second. 'Wow, you *are* good. I have been wearing gloves all morning.'

'As I've said, just observation, really.' Hunter smiled, secretly glad that he'd impressed her.

'You said you teach? You don't look like the professor type.'

'I said I *could* be a professor, but now I'm curious. What does the professor type look like?' she asked with a chuckle.

'Well, you know . . .' he chose his words carefully. 'Older, balder, thick glasses . . .'

Isabella laughed and ran her fingers through her hair, pulling it to one side but letting her fringe fall partially over her left eye. 'Here at UCLA you'll find even the surfer-type professor. Long hair, tattoos, piercings. Some even come to class wearing flip-flops and shorts.'

Hunter laughed.

The waiter came back to check on their orders.

'Sig.na Isabella, come sta?'

'Va bene, grazie, Luigi.'

'What can I get for you today?' he asked in a very strong Italian accent.

Isabella didn't need to look at the menu to decide, she knew exactly what she wanted.

'What do you recommend?' Hunter asked, struggling to make a selection of his own.

'Do you like olives, pepperoni and pine nuts?'

'Yeah, very much.'

'OK, then have the penne Pazze, it's gorgeous,' she said, pointing down at her menu.

Hunter accepted her suggestion and complemented it with a small rucola and parmesan salad. He thought about having some garlic bread, but decided against it – not the best of dishes when you're out on a date. They both opted for no wine as they still had to go back to work after lunch.

'How about you? How's work going?' she asked.

'Same old, same old, just a different day,' he said playing with his bread knife.

'I bet being a detective in a city like LA isn't easy?'

Hunter looked up and stared at Isabella, intrigued. 'How do you know I'm a detective?'

It was Isabella's turn to fix him down with a stare. 'Huh?' She paused and worked her fingers through her fringe. 'Are you kidding?'

His expression told her he wasn't.

'This past weekend? In my apartment?'

She got no reaction from him.

'Do you remember anything about that night? We went back to my place from the bar, you took off your jacket and the first thing I saw was a gun. I freaked out and you showed me your badge saying that everything was OK, you were a detective for the city of Los Angeles.'

Hunter looked down in embarrassment. 'I'm sorry . . . I actually don't remember much about that night . . . little memory flashes, but that's all. How much did I have to drink?'

'Quite a lot,' she said giggling to herself.

'Was I on Scotch?'

'Yep,' she nodded. 'So you don't remember much about that night at all?'

'Very little.'

'Do you remember sleeping with me?'

The embarrassment was now complete. A slight shake of the head was all he could muster.

'Oh God! So I wasn't memorable?'

'Oh no, it's not like that. I'm sure you're incredible in bed . . .' Hunter realized he'd said those words louder than he intended. Their conversation had suddenly attracted the attention of some of the neighboring tables. 'Wow, that sentence came out all wrong,' he said in a much lower tone of voice.

Isabella smiled. 'Your brain working faster than your lips again?' she teased.

Luigi came back with a bottle of still mineral water and poured it into the wine glass in front of her. Hunter declined signaling that he was alright with his Diet Coke.

'Grazie, Luigi,' she said softly.

'Si figuri, sig.na,' he replied with a jovial smile.

Isabella waited until Luigi was gone. 'I must admit that your phone call yesterday came as a surprise.'

'Surprising people is one of the things I do best,' Hunter replied, sitting back on his chair.

'I was unsure of what to make of it. I didn't know if you really wanted to see me or just get into my pants again.'

Hunter smiled. He admired her forwardness. 'And that's why you opted for a quick lunch. Dinner dates are easier to escalate into something else.'

'Lunch dates are safer,' Isabella confirmed.

'Plus you wanted to check me out.'

'What do you mean?' She played dumb.

'We both had a few more drinks than we intended on the night we met. Our perceptions probably got somewhat . . . distorted. You were probably unsure of what I look like and if I was worth going on a second date with. A quick lunch date would clear all that up.'

Isabella bit her lip.

Hunter knew he was right.

'I'm sure I remember more than you do,' she said, playing with her hair again.

'True,' Hunter admitted. 'But that night was atypical. I usually don't drink to the point of passing out and not remembering what happened.' He had a sip of his Diet Coke. 'So, did I pass the lunch-date test?'

Isabella nodded. 'With flying colors. Did I?'

Hunter frowned.

'C'mon. You were checking me out just as much as I was checking you out. You said it yourself. You don't remember much.'

Hunter enjoyed her company. She was certainly different from most women he'd met. He liked her sense of humor, her sharp answers and her irreverent way. They both stared at each other for a little while. Hunter felt just as comfortable being silent with her as he did in conversation.

Luigi arrived with their pasta and Hunter watched as Isabella placed her serviette around the collar of her blouse like a true Italian. He did the same.

'Wow, this is absolutely beautiful,' he said after his first mouthful.

'I told you, this is authentic Italian food, that's why they are always busy.'

'I bet you eat in here all the time. I would.'

'Not as much as I'd like. I have to keep an eye on my figure you know.' She looked down at her waist.

'Well, whatever you are doing, it's working out fine for you,' he said with a smile.

Before she was able to thank him for his compliment Hunter's phone rang. He knew it was impolite to leave his phone on inside a restaurant, but he had no choice.

'Sorry about this,' he said semi-embarrassed, bringing his phone to his ear. Isabella didn't seem to mind.

'Detective Hunter speaking.' He heard a faint click.

'*Go down Camp Road in Griffith Park. Before you get to the end of it you'll reach a sharp right elbow turn, don't go right, take the tiny dirt road on the south end of it and follow it all the way around until you reach the high trees. There you'll find an M-Class Mercedes-Benz. I left the result of yesterday's gamble inside it.*' Before Hunter had a chance to say anything the robotic voice hung up.

Hunter looked up at Isabella's staring eyes. She didn't need to be psychic to know something wasn't right. 'What's wrong?' she asked concerned.

Hunter took a deep breath before answering. 'I gotta go . . . I'm so sorry.'

Isabella watched as Hunter stood up and grabbed his jacket from the back of his chair.

'I'm really sorry for having to run out on you again.'

'It's OK, trust me, I understand.' She stood up, took a step forward and kissed him on both cheeks.

Hunter pulled two twenty-dollar bills out of his wallet and placed the money on the table. 'Is it OK if I call you sometime?'

'Of course.' With an insecure smile Isabella watched as he raced out of the restaurant.

Twenty-Six

Hunter called Garcia on the way to Griffith Park, asking him to inform the forensics department together with the LAPD Special Tactics Unit. He was sure the killer wouldn't be at the location, but he had to follow protocol, the STU team needed to clear the area first.

Encompassing over 4,107 acres, Griffith Park is the United States' largest municipal park of natural terrain covered with California oak trees, wild sage and manzanita. It is also home to the famous Hollywood sign, which stands on Mount Lee.

It didn't take the STU long to find the abandoned Mercedes-Benz. The area was hidden away from any members of the public that might've been strolling around the park. High and bushy white oak trees surrounded the car, blocking most of the two o'clock sunlight. The air felt uncomfortably humid and hot, soaking everyone's shirt in sweat. It could be worse, it could be raining, Hunter thought. Garcia was already busy faxing the vehicle details through.

The car seemed intact, the heat making its rooftop shimmer like water, but its dark-green tinted windows prevented anyone from seeing inside properly. A perimeter had been rapidly delimited around the car. After deliberating over their plan of action, four STU agents approached the car in two by two formation, with their MP5 sub-machine guns at eye level; the powerful flashlights attached to the bottom part of their barrels cast light circles over the abandoned car. With every cautious step dried leaves and sticks crunched under their feet.

They carefully checked the immediate area. Gradually inching their way towards the vehicle. Searching for any trip wires or booby traps.

'We've got someone in the driver's seat,' the agent at the front announced in a firm voice.

Suddenly all the light circles illuminated a figure slumped in the front seat. His head was tilted back resting against the headrest with his eyes shut. His mouth was semi-open and his lips looked a dark shade of purple. Droplets of blood had run down his cheeks from his eyes like blood tears. He'd been stripped of his shirt and his body was covered in hematomas.

'Backseat, what have I got?' Tim Thornton, the STU leader, called out. His voice demanding.

One of the agents broke off from the four-strong group and approached the right-side back window, his powerful flashlight illuminating the car's interior. Nothing on the backseat, nothing on the floor. 'Backseat is clear.'

'Show me your hands,' Tim shouted, his machine gun pointed directly at the driver's head.

No movement.

Tim tried again, his words coming out slower this time. 'Can you hear me? Show me your hands.'

No movement.

'He looks dead, Tim,' another agent offered.

Tim approached the driver's door while the other agents kept their aim locked on the man at the wheel. Tim cautiously dropped down to his knees and checked underneath the car – no explosives, no wires. It all looked clear. He got up and slowly reached for the handle.

Still no movement from the driver.

Tim could feel the sweat rolling down his forehead. He took a deep breath to steady his hands. He knew what he needed to do. In one clean movement he pulled the door open. A split second later he had his MP5 aimed back at the driver's head.

'Jesus Christ!' he gasped, turning his face away from the car before taking a step back and quickly lifting his left hand to protect his nose.

'Talk to me, Tim, what's wrong?' Troy, the second in command, shouted, approaching the passenger's door.

'The smell goddammit, it's like putrid meat.' Tim paused for a moment fighting nausea, coughing violently. The warm, fetid breath that shot out of the car quickly intoxicated the air. It took Tim several seconds to collect himself. He needed to check for the victim's vital signs.

Hunter, Garcia, Captain Bolter and Doctor Winston were avidly observing the action from the perimeter mark. Their standard-issue headset allowed them to listen in as the STU communicated with each other. Standing just behind them were an ambulance and a paramedic team.

Tim had another look at the victim. His hands had been tied to the steering wheel and the only piece of clothing he had on was a pair of pin-striped boxer shorts saturated in blood. His entire body was covered in large, dark, boil-like blisters and a sunburn-type rash. Some of the blisters had burst open, secreting thick, yellow mucus.

'Is that pus?' Troy asked, standing by the passenger's door. The comment brought a worried look to Doctor Winston's face.

'How the hell would I know? I'm not a doctor,' Tim fired back, and with shaky hands reached for the victim's neck feeling for the carotid artery.

'I've got no pulse,' he shouted after a few seconds.

Cough ... Without warning, the victim's head jolted forward, spitting blood onto the steering wheel, dashboard and windscreen. Tim stumbled back in a hurry falling to the ground after losing his balance.

'Holy shit! He's alive.' His voice filled with horror.

Troy, who had come close to shooting the driver after his sudden burst of life, rushed to the driver's side. 'Medic!'

A shocked look came over everyone's faces. Hunter and Garcia dashed towards the car, closely followed by Captain Bolter and Doctor Winston.

'We need that ambulance in here now.' Tim was back on his feet and had joined Troy by the driver's door, his breathing still emphatic.

'We need to cut him loose,' Tim said, pulling his MOD knife from his belt.

'Sir, can you hear me?' he called but the car occupant had already lost consciousness once again.

'Don't move, I'm gonna free your hands from the wheel and we're gonna get you to a hospital, you'll be OK, stay with me, pal.'

Tim carefully sliced through the bloody rope that kept the victim's left hand tied to the wheel and it slumped down lifelessly to his lap. Tim moved to the next hand and repeated the procedure. Seconds later the driver was free.

Troy searched for the paramedic team who still hadn't reached the car. Unexpectedly, the victim coughed once again spitting out more blood, this time onto Tim's STU uniform.

'Where the fuck is the ambulance?' Tim shouted in an angry voice.

'We're here,' one of the paramedics said, pushing his way through to reach the driver's door. Within a few seconds the rest of the ambulance team had reached the car.

Hunter, Garcia, Captain Bolter and Doctor Winston all watched in silence as the team carefully moved the victim from the driver's seat to the stretcher and into the ambulance. The smell causing a group gagging frenzy as they came closer to the car.

'Where's he being taken to?' Hunter asked the paramedic nearest to him.

'The Good Samaritan Hospital. It's the closest one with an emergency ward.'

'The victim's alive . . .?' Captain Bolter asked in a skeptical voice. 'First he plays games with us and then he gives us a live victim? What the hell is he up to? Is he getting sloppy?'

Hunter shook his head. 'I don't know, but I'm sure he's not getting sloppy. This could be part of his game.'

'Do you think the killer was interrupted? Surprised by a member of the public or something?' the captain asked, looking around as if searching for something, or someone.

'No,' Hunter replied firmly. 'The killer wouldn't have called if this wasn't exactly what he wanted us to find. He made no mistake here.'

'Don't tell me you think he's having guilt trips and decided to let this one live after that whole drama yesterday.'

'I don't know, Captain,' Hunter shot back with irritation. 'But we'll find out soon enough.' He turned and faced Garcia. 'What do we have on the car?'

'It belongs to a . . . George Slater, thirty-three years old, attorney at law with Tale & Josh, a law firm in central Los Angeles,' Garcia read from a faxed report. 'He's been reported missing by his wife, Catherine Slater. Apparently he never came home from his weekly Tuesday-night poker game.'

'Do we have a photo?'

'Yes, the one his wife used when reporting him as missing.' Garcia produced a black and white printout.

'Let me see that.'

The man in the photograph was dressed in an expensive-looking suit with his hair slickly combed back. It wasn't hard to see the resemblance between the man in the printout and the half-dead body they saw being dragged from the car a few minutes ago. 'It's him,' Hunter said after analyzing the photo for a few seconds. 'The facial features are all there.'

'I think so too,' Garcia agreed.

'I'll follow the ambulance back to the hospital. If there's any chance this guy can survive, I wanna be there.'

'I'm coming with you,' Garcia said.

'I'll get the forensic team to start here, though after the events of the last five minutes, this whole scene has been contaminated to high heaven,' Doctor Winston said worryingly. 'And judging by the vegetation surrounding the car, this could take a hell of a long time,' he said and pointed to the thick shrubs and high grass.

'Just ask them to do their best,' Hunter said, looking around the area.

'Don't they always?'

They all walked away as the forensic team moved in.

Twenty-Seven

The Good Samaritan Hospital building stands imposingly on Wilshire Boulevard, in downtown LA. Its main entrance is through a circular driveway on the east side of Witmer Street. On a normal day, the trip from Griffith Park would've taken Hunter around thirty minutes; this time he made it in less than twenty, almost giving Garcia a heart attack in the process.

They rushed through the spotlessly clean glass doors of the entrance lobby, towards the admissions desk. Two middle-aged nurses were busy shuffling through piles of paper, answering telephones and dealing with the demanding crowd of patients surrounding the desk. Hunter disregarded the line of people and pushed his way to the front.

'Where's your emergency ward?' he asked with his badge in hand.

One of the nurses looked up from her computer screen through the top of the thick-rimmed pair of glasses she had balancing on the tip of her nose and merely studied the two men in front of her. 'Are you two blind? There's a line of people in front of you.' Her voice was calm as if she had all the time in the world.

'Yeah, that's right, we're all waiting here, get in line,' came a protest from an elderly man with his arm in a cast, igniting shouts from the other patients.

'This is official business sir!' Hunter said. 'The emergency ward, where is it?' The urgency in his voice made the nurse look up again. This time she checked both of their badges.

'Through there, take a left at the end,' she said reluctantly, pointing to the hall on her right.

'Damn cops, not even a thank you,' she murmured as Hunter and Garcia disappeared down the corridor.

The emergency ward was a busy shuffle of doctors, nurses, orderlies and patients all running around as if the end of the world was about to take place. The area was large, but with the chaotic movement of people and wheel stretchers it appeared crowded.

'How can anyone work in a place like this? It's like Carnival in Brazil,' Garcia said, looking around with a worried expression.

Hunter surveyed the messy scene looking for someone who could offer them any information. He spotted a small, semi-circular counter against the north wall. A sole nurse sat behind it, her face flushed. They wasted no time in getting to her.

'An emergency patient came in about five or ten minutes ago. We need to know where he's been taken to,' Hunter said in a frustrated tone of voice as he approached the large woman.

'This is the emergency ward, sweetie, all the patients that come through here are emergency patients,' she said in a tender voice with a very strong southern accent.

'A crime victim, Griffith Park, about thirty-something years of age, completely covered in blisters,' Hunter shot back impatiently.

She pulled a brand-new Kleenex tissue from a super-sized box on the counter and wiped the sweat from her forehead, finally gazing at the detectives with her black pearl eyes. Realizing the urgency in Hunter's voice, she quickly checked a few documents behind the counter.

'Yeah, I remember him being brought in not that long ago' –

she paused to take a deep breath – 'if I remember correctly . . .
he was DOA.'

'What?'

'Dead on arrival,' she explained.

'We know what it means. Are you sure?' Garcia asked.

'Not one hundred percent, but Doctor Phillips admitted the
patient. He'll be able to confirm it.'

'And where can we find him?'

She stood up to survey the room. 'Right over there . . .
Doctor Phillips,' she called waving her hand.

A short, bald-headed man turned, his stethoscope swinging
around his neck; his white overall looked old and wrinkly, and
judging by the dark circles under his eyes, he hadn't had any
sleep in at least thirty-six hours. He was busy in conversation
with another man who Hunter immediately recognized as one
of the paramedics who had pushed his way through to get to
the victim's car in Griffith Park.

Both detectives went over to the two men before they had a
chance to come to the small counter. They quickly went
through the customary introductions.

'The victim from the park, where's he? What happened?'
Hunter asked.

The paramedic's eyes avoided Hunter's, using the floor as
refuge. The short doctor shifted his stare from Hunter to Garcia
a couple of times. 'He didn't make it. They had to turn off the
sirens five minutes away from the hospital. He was DOA –
dead on arrival.'

'We know what it means.' Hunter sounded annoyed.

The short silence that followed was broken by Garcia. 'Shit!
I knew it was too good to be true.'

'I'm sorry,' the paramedic said with a distressed look. 'We tried
everything we could. He couldn't breathe. He was choking on his

own blood. We were about to perform an emergency tra-
cheotomy, but before we had the chance . . .' his voice trailed off
as Doctor Phillips took over.

'By the time the ambulance reached the hospital there was
nothing more anyone could do. He was pronounced dead at
three-eighteen this afternoon.'

'What was the cause of death?'

Doctor Phillips gave Hunter a quick nervous laugh. 'The
body just came in, but take your pick, suffocation, cardiac
arrest, general organ failure, internal hemorrhage, your guess is
as good as mine. You'll have to wait for the official autopsy
report to find out.'

An announcement came through the loudspeakers and
Doctor Phillips paused and waited for it to be over. 'At the
moment the body is isolated.'

'Isolated? Why?' Garcia sounded concerned.

'Have you seen the body? It's covered in blisters and sores.'

'Yes, we've seen it. We thought they were burn marks or
something like that.'

Doctor Phillips shook his head. 'I can't tell you what they are
without a biopsy, but they certainly aren't burn marks.'

'Definitely not,' the paramedic agreed.

'Viral?' Hunter asked.

Doctor Phillips looked at him intrigued. 'At first glance, yes.
Like a disease.'

'A disease?' The astonished question came from Garcia.
'There must be some kind of mistake, doc, he's a murder victim.'

'Murder?' Doctor Phillips looked perplexed. 'Those blisters
weren't inflicted on him by anyone. His own body produced
them as a reaction to something, like an illness or an allergy.
Trust me, what killed that man was some sort of terrible disease.'

Hunter had already figured out what the killer had done.

He'd infected the victim with some sort of deadly virus. But it had only been a day since the dog race – how could the reaction have come so quickly? What disease could kill a man in a day? Once again he would depend on Doctor Winston's autopsy examination to give him any sort of clue to what had happened.

'We need to determine what this disease is, if it is indeed a disease, and if it's contagious or not.' The doctor's eyes wandered over to the paramedic. 'That's what we were talking about, first-hand contact with the patient. Have any of you two . . .'

'No,' the answer came in unison.

'Do you know of anyone who did come in contact with him?'

'Two agents from the Special Tactics Unit,' Hunter snapped back.

'They'll probably have to come in for some tests, depending on the biopsy result.'

'And when are you expecting the results?'

'As I've said, the body just came in. I'm gonna send a tissue sample to the lab as soon as possible with an urgent request. If we're lucky we might get a result sometime today.'

'How about the body and the autopsy?'

'The body will be sent to the Department of Coroner today, but its condition and the fact that it has to be kept in isolation make things more difficult, so I can't tell you exactly when. Look, detective, I'm not gonna lie to you, I'm very concerned about this. Whatever killed that man did it very fast and in a very painful manner. If it's some sort of contagious disease, judging solely by his state when he came in, we could be facing some very horrific epidemic here. The whole city could be in danger.'

Twenty-Eight

The rest of the day passed in a state of limbo. There was very little Hunter or Garcia could do but wait. Wait for the forensic team to finish processing the crime scene, wait for the biopsy result to come through, wait for the body to be sent to Doctor Winston and wait for his autopsy report.

Both detectives went back to Griffith Park just before darkness set in. If the crime lab team came across anything, no matter how small, they wanted to know, but the search was laborious and slow. The high grass, heat and humidity made things even more difficult, and by one in the morning the team had found nothing.

The loneliness of Hunter's apartment was overwhelming. As he opened the door and turned on the lights he wondered what it would be like to be coming home to someone who cared, someone that could give him some hope that the world wasn't on the road to hell.

He tried to fight the destructive guilt that had gradually crept in since the dog race, but even his experience and knowledge couldn't keep his mind from wondering. *If only I'd picked dog number two.* At this point in time the killer was also winning the psychological battle.

He poured himself a double dose from the twelve-year-old

bottle of Laphroaig, dropped in his usual single cube, dimmed the lights and collapsed onto his old, stiff sofa. He felt physically and mentally exhausted, but he knew he wouldn't be able to fall asleep. His mind kept playing back everything that had happened in the past few hours and it intensified his pounding headache.

'Why couldn't I have chosen a simple profession, why couldn't I have been a chef or a carpenter?' he thought out loud. The reason was simple. Cliché or not, he wanted to make a difference, and every time his investigations and hard work caught a killer, he knew he'd made that difference. It was a high unlike any other – the self gratification, the exhilaration, knowing how many lives he saved by following the evidence, staying calm and piecing together a scene that seemed lost and diluted in time. Hunter was good at what he did and he knew it.

He had another sip of his single malt and swirled it around in his mouth before swallowing it down and welcoming the burning sensation. He closed his eyes and dropped his head back, trying his best to clear his mind of all the day's events, but they were hammering his memory with a thunderous force.

The message alert from his cell phone made him jump. He felt his pockets for it but found they were empty.

'Shit!'

The phone was on the small glass bar. He'd left it there together with his wallet and keys.

Placing his glass on the floor Hunter slowly stood up and glanced at his watch.

'Who the hell would be sending me a message at this godforsaken hour anyway?' He checked the phone.

I hope you are OK. It was very nice seeing you again this afternoon, even if it was just for a few minutes – Isabella.

Hunter had forgotten all about their quick lunch in the

afternoon. He grinned and at the same time felt guilty for having to run out on her for the second time. He quickly typed a reply message.

Can I call you? He pressed the 'send' button and went back to the sofa.

A minute later the phone vibrated and played its message alert, breaking the silence in the room.

Yes.

Hunter had another sip of his single malt and pressed the 'call' button.

'Hello . . . I thought you'd be asleep by now,' she said softly.

'I thought the same about you. Isn't this a little late for a researcher? Don't you have to be in the lab early tomorrow?' Hunter asked with a little smile.

'I never sleep much. Usually five to six hours max every night. My brain is always busy. Research work does that to you.'

'Five to six hours only. That really isn't much.'

'Look who's talking. Why aren't you asleep?'

'Insomnia is part of the package. It comes with the job.'

'You need to learn how to unwind.'

'I know. I'm working on it,' he lied.

'Talking about the job – is everything OK? You looked a little distressed after that phone call this afternoon.'

Hunter paused for a minute and rubbed his tired eyes. He thought of how innocent the majority of the people were, not knowing the evil that awaits just a stone's-throw away. Part of his job is to make sure these people stay innocent.

'Everything is alright. It's just the job. It always carries that sort of pressure.'

'I'm sure . . . more pressure than I can imagine. Anyway I'm really glad you called.'

'I'm sorry I had to leave in such a hurry again. Maybe I can make it up to you.' He could swear he heard her smile.

'I'd like that . . . and that's what I was thinking about. How would you like to have dinner with me at my place on Saturday evening?'

'A dinner date?' Hunter teased.

'Well, now that the *check out* lunch date is out of the way, I thought dinner would be nice. Are you busy this Saturday?'

'No, no, I'm free. Saturday is fine. What time shall I come over?'

'How about six o'clock?'

'That sounds great. I'll bring a bottle.'

'Fantastic. Do you remember the address?'

'You'd better give it to me again, just in case. I was pretty drunk that night.'

'Don't I know it?'

They both laughed.

Twenty-Nine

The next morning Hunter and Garcia went back to the County Department of Coroner. Doctor Winston had called them at around ten o'clock, after he'd completed the autopsy on the new victim. He wanted both detectives to be the first ones to hear the results.

George Slater's body rested on the metal autopsy table near the far wall. A white sheet covered him from the waist down. Most of his internal organs had been remo`ved, weighed, and placed over the organ tray. Doctor Winston had buzzed the two detectives into the basement autopsy room and left them waiting by the door as he finished analyzing a small piece of human tissue.

'Well, one thing is for certain, our killer is very inventive,' the doctor said, lifting his eyes from the dissecting microscope. Only then Hunter realized how tired Doctor Winston looked. His thin hair was messy, his complexion heavy and his eyes exhausted.

'So he's a murder victim?' Hunter asked, pointing to the ghostly white body on the table.

'No doubt about that.'

'From our killer?'

'Oh yes, unless someone else knows about this,' the doctor said walking over to the body followed by both men. He lifted the victim's head about four inches off the autopsy table surface. Hunter and Garcia bent over at the same time, almost hitting head against head. Their eyes met the unmistakable symbol.

'It's the same killer alright,' Garcia said getting back to an upright position. 'So what was all that crap about him dying from some sort of disease?'

'That was no crap. A disease is exactly what killed him.' The confusion and frustration intensified in Garcia's face. 'Have you ever heard of *streptococcus pyogenes*?'

'What?'

'I guess not. How about *staphylococcus aureus*?'

'Yes, doc, Latin is a constant part of my everyday vocabulary.' Garcia's sarcastic tone brought a quick smile to Hunter's lips. 'What the hell is it?'

'It sounds like a bacterium,' Hunter said.

'And you're right on the money, Robert. Come here, let me show you.' Doctor Winston took a` moment to search for a slide from a small portable archive and then walked back to the microscope desk. 'Have a look,' he said after placing the slide over the stage.

Hunter moved closer, bent over and positioned his eyes over the eyepiece. He rotated the coarse-focus knob and analyzed the slide for a moment.

'What the hell am I looking for here, doc? All I can see is a whole bunch of . . . little worm-like things moving around like headless chickens.'

'Let me have a look,' Garcia said like an excited college student and gesturing for Hunter to move out of the way. 'Yep, I see the same thing,' he commented after looking through the viewer.

'Those little worm-like things are *streptococcus pyogenes*, my dear students,' Doctor Winston said assuming a professor's tone. 'Now, have a look at this one.' He retrieved another slide from the portable archive and replaced the one on the microscope stage.

This time Hunter saw green circular shapes that moved at a much slower pace than the previous worm-like ones. Garcia had a quick look right after Hunter.

'Yes so? Green round things this time.'

'OK, those are *staphylococcus aureus.*'

'Do we look like biology students to you, doc? Give it to us in English.' Garcia wasn't in the mood for playing games.

Doctor Winston rubbed his eyes with the back of his right hand. He pulled a chair and sat down resting his right elbow on the microscope desk.

'The first slide that you looked at – *streptococcus pyogenes*, the worm-like bacteria, once inside the human body it releases several destructive toxins. One of these toxins is the one responsible for scarlet fever.'

'He didn't die of scarlet fever, doc. The symptoms are all wrong,' Hunter shot back.

'Patience, Robert.'

Hunter threw both hands up in an 'I give up' gesture.

'Another toxin that can be released by the bacteria causes necrotizing fasciitis.'

'And that is?' Garcia now.

'That's the disease from hell,' Hunter said as his brow creased with worry. 'Flesh-eating disease.'

'That's what it's commonly known as,' Doctor Winston agreed.

'Wait, wait, wait,' Garcia said making a 'T' sign using both of his hands. 'Did I hear you guys right? Did you just say flesh-eating disease?'

The doctor nodded, but before he was able to say anything Hunter started to explain.

'The term is widely used but not actually correct as the bacterium that causes it doesn't really eat the flesh. It's a rare infection of the deeper layers of the skin and subcutaneous tissues. It causes the destruction of skin and muscle by releasing toxins, but the overall effect makes it seem as if the victim is being eaten from the inside out.'

Garcia shivered and stepped away from the microscope. 'How do you know that?' he asked Hunter.

'I read a lot.' The answer came with a shrug.

'Very good, Robert,' Doctor Winston said with a smile before picking up from where Hunter left off. 'The victim starts to show flu-like symptoms, quickly moving to very strong headaches, a drop in blood pressure and tachycardia. The skin then starts to develop extremely painful, large, mucus-filled blisters and sunburn-type rashes. The victim will then go into toxic shock losing and regaining consciousness periodically. Health deteriorates lightning fast and then . . . death.'

Garcia and Hunter both looked at the corpse. The blisters had all burst, revealing dried and scabby flesh sores.

'In 2004 a rare but even more serious form of the disease started to appear with increasing frequency, and the majority of those cases were found here, in California,' the doctor continued. 'In those cases, it was discovered that the bacterium causing the disease was a strain of the *staphylococcus aureus* – a much stronger strain of it.'

'That's the second slide we looked at, the green round things?'

Doctor Winston nodded.

'I remember that story,' Hunter said. 'It didn't really get the attention of the media. Just a sideline in the papers.'

Doctor Winston stood up and walked over to the autopsy table. Garcia and Hunter followed him with their eyes.

'The way the disease works is as follows – the bacterium enters the body and reproduces itself. The more bacteria there are, the more toxins they release. The more toxins they release, the quicker and more painful the death. Unfortunately for our victim, these little bastards reproduce like crazed rabbits. They can double their number in the space of a few hours.'

'Can it be treated?' Garcia this time.

'Yes, if found early enough, but that rarely happens due to how fast the bacteria spread.'

'And how do you get it? How does the bacterium enter the body?'

'Funnily enough, the bacterium is frequently found living on the skin or inside the nose of a healthy person.'

Garcia placed both of his hands over his nose as if he was about to blow it. Hunter couldn't help but laugh.

'It's in a dormant state,' Doctor Winston said with a smile. 'But the bacterium can easily infect an open flesh wound. Sometimes it's picked up in hospitals from infected surgery incisions.'

'Wow, that's reassuring,' Garcia joked.

'Necrotizing fasciitis is one of the fastest-spreading infections known to man. In regular cases it takes only three to five days for a patient to go from early symptoms to death. In the case of our victim, and I'm sure you both have probably guessed it, the killer has injected him with the *staphylococcus aureus* bacterium.'

A morbid silence took over the room. What else could this killer come up with?

'But the dog race was only two days ago, how can a disease have such a quick reaction time?' Garcia asked shaking his head.

'Dog race?' Doctor Winston frowned.

Garcia waved his hand in a dismissive gesture. 'Too complicated to explain it now, doc.'

'Anyway, as I've said, the bacterium multiplies fast and the more there is the more damage it causes. Our victim was injected with a phenomenal amount of it and straight into the bloodstream. Within ten to twelve hours he would've gone from healthy to knocking on death's door.'

Doctor Winston approached the organ tray. 'His liver and kidneys were thirty-five percent destroyed. There was also great deterioration of the heart, the intestines and esophagus, and that would explain the blood when he coughed, he was hemorrhaging internally very badly when we got to him at the park. It was probably his body's last struggle before death.'

Garcia contorted his face remembering the images from the park.

'And there's one more thing,' the doctor continued.

'And what's that?'

'The victim's nails on both hands are all broken, as if he'd tried to scrape his way out of somewhere. A wooden box probably.'

'Wood splinters under the nails?' Hunter concluded.

'Yep. Under what's left of them and on his fingertips.'

'Wood analysis?' Garcia asked excitedly.

'Common pine wood. Very easy to come across. The killer could've nailed him shut inside a regular wardrobe.'

'Why would the killer do that if he'd already injected the victim with the bacteria and death was a certainty?' Garcia asked intrigued.

'To speed up the process as much as possible,' Hunter answered first.

Garcia frowned.

'The heart speeds up when a person panics. Blood is pumped faster, so the bacteria spread faster.'

'Correct,' Doctor Winston said with a nod.

'And what easier way to make someone panic than nailing him shut inside a wooden coffin.'

'This killer knows the business of killing better than anyone I've ever encountered,' the doctor said staring back at the body.

'So if we'd gotten to the park earlier?' Garcia asked.

'It would've made no difference. Our victim's fate was sealed the moment the killer injected him with the bacteria,' Hunter said. 'It was all part of his plan. Nothing was left to chance.'

'How can someone come across this bacterium? Where could the killer have gotten it from?'

Doctor Winston and Hunter both understood where Garcia was coming from. The killer had to have had access to the bacteria from somewhere, a hospital, a laboratory perhaps. They could check visiting and employees' records and maybe come out with a lead.

'Our problem is that every hospital and lab in California will probably have a sample of the bacterium,' the doctor explained. 'As I've said, it reproduces itself extremely fast and the killer would've only needed a few drops of infected blood. No one would've missed it. No one would've reported it. Cultivating it and transforming the few drops of infected blood into the deadly amount that was injected into our victim is also very easily done. This was a very clever death. Not very difficult to achieve if you know what you're doing, but very, very hard to trace the source.'

'So it would be like looking for a needle in a haystack?'

Doctor Winston nodded.

'We'll look into it anyway,' Hunter said. 'At this point I'm not discarding anything.'

'Why didn't the killer wait for the victim to die like all the previous ones before calling in?' Garcia asked.

'The shocking effect,' Hunter shot back in a calm voice. 'A person dying of flesh-eating disease is a very disturbing and powerful image. Blisters bursting open to release pus and mucus, the victim hemorrhaging from the eyes, nose, ears, gums ... the putrid smell, the certain and imminent death. This is his show. He's showing off. And it all adds to my guilty feeling. He wanted me to see what I'd done when I picked the wrong dog.'

'What's this dog thing you keep on talking about?' the doctor asked looking puzzled.

Hunter gave him a quick explanation of what had happened, how they'd come so close to saving the victim.

'Do you think the killer would've really let him go if you had picked the winner?'

'I'm not sure,' Hunter said shaking his head. An uneasy silence followed.

'What did he take?' Garcia asked rubbing his chin.

'What do you mean?' Doctor Winston looked hesitant.

'You said the killer always removes a body part from the victim, like a trophy.'

'Ah yes.' He lifted the small white sheet, revealing the victim's groin region.

'Oh God!' Garcia brought both hands to his mouth. He knew that had been done while the victim was still alive.

Half a minute went by before Hunter spoke. 'Let me guess, the forensic team found nothing inside the car, right?'

'Ah-ha!' the doctor replied, lifting his right index finger with an enthusiastic smile. 'They found a hair. And it isn't the victim's.'

Thirty

As they approached the Vanguard Club entrance on Friday night, Garcia was surprised to see such a big crowd waiting in line to get in.

'I can't believe this club is full, this is supposed to be a massive club.'

'The club ain't full,' Hunter replied confidently.

'How do you know?'

'It's a psychology trick,' Hunter continued. 'If they make you wait in line it increases your expectations of the club. You'll be more eager to get in. A busy club usually means a good club.'

'That's true.'

'But the trick is to make you wait in line just long enough. Get the timing wrong and it'll put punters in a bad mood. No one likes standing in line for too long.'

'That's also true.'

They ignored the line of people and walked straight up to the two muscle-bound bouncers at the club's entrance.

'Sorry, gentlemen, you gonna have to join the line like everyone else,' one of the bouncers said, placing a hand on Garcia's shoulder.

'Oh no, you see we've got special VIP passes,' Hunter said in a funny voice and producing his detective badge.

The bouncer checked Hunter's police credentials and removed his hand from Garcia. 'Is there some sort of a problem, Detective Hunter?'

'No, we're just looking for someone.'

The two bouncers exchanged a worried look. 'We don't want no trouble here.'

'Neither do we, so if you get out of our way, we'll be off to a good start,' Hunter said, pinning the bouncer down with a firm gaze. Without losing eye contact, the bouncer took one step to his right and opened the door.

'Enjoy your evening, gentlemen.'

The two detectives stepped into the luxurious lobby entrance. The thumping music instantly caused an impact. It was loud, very loud. There were a handful of people standing around in this first room, some dancing, some just chatting. Hunter and Garcia made their way through the small mob and into the main dance floor area.

The music in there was twice as loud as in the entrance hall and out of instinct Hunter placed a finger in each ear.

'What's the problem, old man, can't handle the younger generation's music?' Garcia said with a cynical grin.

'Music? This is just . . . loud repetitive thumping noise. Give me heavy metal any day.'

'This place is enormous!' Garcia said as the giant dance floor inside the 20,000-square-feet venue stood majestically in front of them. Hunter widened his eyes to try and take in the enormity of the place. The dance floor was busy with a colorful and vibrant crowd moving to the beat of the latest 'drum 'n' bass' and dirty-funk sounds. The club lights and lasers cast different shapes on the crowd as they danced. The atmosphere in the Vanguard was contagious. People came in here to have fun and it showed. Hunter and Garcia weren't in the Vanguard to appreciate it or to take part in the fun, they needed to find D-King.

To the left of the dance floor they saw a small, cordoned-off flight of steps that led to a separate upper level.

'Over there,' Hunter said, pointing to the stairs. 'That's gotta be the VIP area.'

Garcia nodded and frowned as he noticed the two pro-wrestler look-alike bouncers standing guard at the bottom of the stairs. Hunter's eyes searched the upper level for D-King. The file they'd picked up from the District Attorney's office had everything they needed to know about the famous dealer, including several photographs. It didn't take long for Hunter to spot him seated comfortably accompanied by four women.

'I got him, last table on the right,' Hunter said, pointing to the VIP area.

They negotiated their way through the dancing crowd fighting off bumps and pushes from the mobbed floor. An attractive brunette placed both of her arms around Hunter's neck as he walked past her.

'Umm, I love a man with muscles,' she said, pulling him closer. 'And you've got beautiful blue eyes. Dance with me, gorgeous.' Her lips found his and she kissed him passionately, spinning him around in a half-moon twist.

It took Hunter a few seconds to pull his lips free from hers. Even through the flashing lights Hunter noticed her dilated pupils.

'I'll dance with you in a sec, babe. I have to go find the bathroom.' He gave her the first excuse he could think of.

'Bathroom? Would you like some company?' Her eyes had moved down to his groin.

Hunter gave the brunette a confident smile. 'Not this time, babe.'

'Faggot,' she hissed as he walked away leaving her to look for her next prey.

'She looks nice . . . classy,' Garcia commented. 'Maybe you could come back later and share a Slow Comfortable Screw Up Against the Wall with her.'

Hunter ignored his partner's sarcasm as they approached the steps that led to the exclusive upper level and the two bouncers standing guard.

'Sorry, gentlemen, this is for VIPs only, out of bounds,' one of them said, looking down at the two detectives.

'It's OK, we're VIPs,' Garcia said producing his badge and waiting for Hunter to do the same.

'Gentlemen, you can't just use your badges to push your way into places,' the taller of the two musclemen said, keeping his eyes fixed on Garcia.

'Do we look like we're here for our own entertainment?' Hunter cut in. Both bouncers shifted their stare in his direction. 'We're here to see someone,' he continued.

'And who would that be?'

'We're here to see Mister NoneOfYourDamnBusiness. Now step aside or I'll have you for obstruction of justice.' Hunter's voice was threatening and firm. Without waiting for the bouncers to move out of his way, Hunter stepped in-between them and muscled his way through, Garcia following his lead.

Jerome had been watching the whole scene from the table closest to the top of the stairs. As the two detectives stepped onto the VIP upper level Jerome got up to obstruct their path.

'Can I help you?'

'What the fuck? This guy has more security than the President of the United States,' Hunter said, turning to face Garcia before locking eyes with Jerome. 'No, you can't help me, gigantore, I need to talk to your boss,' Hunter said, pointing to D-King's table.

Without moving, Jerome studied both men in front of him.

'OK, we can do this here in the cosiness of this VIP lounge or we can take this damn circus all the way back to the station and have a real party. Your call, big man.'

Jerome kept his eyes on both men for a few more seconds before turning to face D-King who was beginning to show interest. He gave Jerome a quick nod.

'Excuse me, girls, it looks like I have some business to attend to – why don't you go dance for a little bit?' D-King said to the four stunning girls that shared his table. They got up, each one giving Hunter and Garcia a sexy wink followed by an inviting smile as they walked past them. Garcia's face seemed to light up with each smile, his eyes following the girls.

'If you like any of them, maybe I can put in a good word for you,' D-King said with a broad smile, showing gleaming white teeth. Hunter noticed he had a small diamond inserted into his top left incisor.

'What? Oh no, no. It's not like that,' Garcia said, looking uncomfortable.

'Of course not. Please have a seat. Champagne?' D-King offered, pointing to the bottle resting inside the ice bucket.

'Not for us, thank you.'

'OK, how may I help you then?'

D-King was a very handsome African American man. Only thirty-one years of age, five foot nine with a carefully shaved head. His hazel eyes were striking and his face was formed by strong, but well-defined lines. He was wearing a dark-colored viscose suit with a white silk shirt, its two top buttons undone, revealing a couple of thick gold chains.

'I'm Detective Hunter and this is Detective Garcia,' Hunter said with his badge in hand.

D-King didn't get up and made no attempt to shake their hands. Jerome had moved to his boss's side.

Hunter and Garcia sat facing D-King with their backs to the dance floor. There was no need for small talk. Hunter retrieved the computer portrait from his pocket and placed it on the table in front of them.

'Do you know who this woman is?'

D-King lowered his eyes to the picture and studied it for a few seconds without picking it up. 'Not a man for preliminaries are you, Detective Hunter? I like that.'

Hunter's steady expression remained unchanged.

'This is a computer image,' D-King said a little surprised.

'Yeah!'

'And why is that?'

'I'm afraid I can't disclose that information.'

'I'm afraid I can't help you.' The reply came almost immediately.

The two detectives exchanged a quick look. 'Look Mr Preston, this is extremely important . . .'

'Sister Joan used to call me Mr Preston in lower school' – D-King raised his right hand interrupting Hunter before he had a chance to finish his sentence – 'you can call me D-King.'

Hunter didn't like being interrupted. 'As I was saying, this is a very important matter.'

'I'm sure it is, but let me tell you how this works. If you want me to help you, you've gotta give me something, baby. I'm a businessman, I have no time for bullshit and you won't get no freebies here.'

Hunter didn't like negotiating, especially not with people like D-King, but he knew he didn't have much of a choice. He'd observed D-King and Jerome's reaction while their eyes analyzed the picture on the table. He knew they'd recognized her. If he wanted them to help him, he needed to play ball.

'She's dead. She's been killed in a very horrific way and her face . . .' Hunter searched for the appropriate word. 'Is unrecognizable. We had to use a special program to hypothesize what she looked like.'

D-King kept his stare on Hunter for a while longer before reaching for the picture. He considered it for a few more seconds. Hunter had no doubt D-King had recognized the woman in the picture, but there was something else. Some hidden emotion.

'What makes you think I'd know this woman?'

Hunter knew what he was trying to do. 'Listen, P-Diddy . . .'

'D-King . . .'

'Whatever. I'm not interested in you or in what you do. Whatever illegal business you conduct, I'm sure the law will catch up with you soon enough, but today is not that day. You might not believe this, but you aren't a suspect in this investigation. The person who killed her killed again yesterday, and he'll keep on killing until we stop him. Her identity could give us a clue as to who this monster is. If she is one of your girls . . .'

'One of my girls?' D-King interrupted Hunter once again. He wasn't about to admit to being a sex merchant.

'You wanna play dumb, go right ahead, but at this point in time I couldn't give a shit if you were the biggest pimp in the world, I'm not after you. We're Homicide, not Narc.'

D-King placed the picture back on the table. 'Nice speech, Detective.'

Hunter took a deep breath. His stare was still fixed on the man sitting in front of him.

D-King quickly saw an opportunity opening its doors. 'If you need my help, maybe we can get into some sort of agreement.'

'Agreement?' Hunter knew what was coming.

'Every once in a while I need some help from the boys in

black and white. I help you, you help me and everyone's happy. It can be a very profitable partnership for both sides.'

Only then Garcia realized what D-King meant. Unlike Hunter he was unable to contain himself.

'Fuck you! Someone has tortured and killed one of your girls and you couldn't give a damn? I thought you were supposed to protect them, to be their guardian. Isn't that what pimps do?' Garcia's face flared red. His voice angry and loud, causing the occupants of most of the neighboring tables to turn their way. 'Now you're using her death to try and get us into your dirty-cop pay list? Some kinda king you are. Maybe you should think about changing your name to D-Loser.' Garcia got up and waited for Hunter to do the same. He didn't follow.

Garcia's antics made D-King laugh. 'Oh c'mon now, you're not gonna play the old "good cop, bad cop" crap on me, are you? Do you take me for a fool? That shit only works in movies, and this ain't fucking it?'

'We're not playing games here,' Hunter said calmly, 'but the killer is. Detective Garcia is right. This killer took one of your girls from you and left you a big "fuck you" as a souvenir.' Hunter leaned forward placing both of his elbows on the table. 'We don't think you're a fool but the killer certainly does. He's laughing at you and I'm not surprised. He waltzed into your turf, snatched one of your girls and you didn't even know. Did you think she was on vacation? What'll happen if he decides to take another one of your girls? Maybe one of the girls who were sitting with you just a few minutes ago.'

D-King kept his steady eyes on Hunter.

'So,' Hunter continued, 'you just gonna sit there and pretend you're still cool, you're still in command, you're still the King? We're only asking you for her name, if only to let her family know what's happened to her.'

Hunter waited for a reaction but it never came. He knew D-King had recognized the girl on the computer-generated portrait and that had been a huge step in the right direction. He could easily find out who she was now that he knew where to look. D-King's cooperation wasn't that important anymore. Hunter got up and joined Garcia.

'Detective,' D-King called as both men reached the staircase. Hunter turned and faced him once again. D-King made a hand gesture towards Jerome who quickly produced a picture from his jacket pocket and placed it on the table next to the computer-generated one. Both detectives sat back down and compared the pictures. The resemblance was uncanny.

'Her name is Jenny Farnborough. I've been looking for her since last Friday.'

Hunter felt his blood warming. 'Was that the last time you saw her?'

'That's correct. Last Friday, in here.'

'Here?' Garcia asked excitedly.

'Yeah, we were sitting at this same table. She excused herself and said she needed to go to the ladies' room to retouch her make-up or something. She never came back.'

'What time was that?'

D-King raised his eyebrows at Jerome.

'Late, around two or a quarter past two in the morning,' Jerome said.

'So you think she was abducted from this club?' Hunter asked calmly.

'It looks that way.'

'Maybe she knew her abductor, someone that she'd been with before.'

D-King shook his head. 'Even if she had bumped into someone she knew, she wouldn't have just walked out of the club, she would've come back here to talk to me first. Jenny was a good girl.'

Hunter paused for a second, measuring how much he wanted to reveal about the victim. 'She was drugged. GHB, have you ever heard of it?'

D-King gave Hunter a car-salesman smile. He knew Hunter couldn't be that naive. 'Yes, I know of it. Is that what was used?'

'Yes.'

'You said she was tortured?' Jerome asked.

'Yes.'

'What exactly does that mean?'

Hunter's gaze dropped to the pictures on the table. The image of her naked, mutilated body tied to the wooden posts flashed in his mind.

'Whoever killed her wanted her to suffer as much as possible. There was no mercy kill, no shot to the head, no knife through the heart. The killer wanted her to die slowly.' Hunter saw no point in hiding the truth. 'She was skinned alive and left to die.'

'She what?' Jerome's voice went up half an octave.

There was no response from either detective.

D-King tried to conceal his rage, but his eyes burned with it. His mind immediately created a grotesque picture of Jenny, alone, tortured, pleading for mercy, crying for help. He tried in vain to shake the image from his head. When he spoke, there was inimitable anger in his voice. 'Are you a religious man, Detective?'

The question surprised both Hunter and Garcia. 'Why?'

'Because if you are, you better pray to God you find whoever killed Jenny before I do.'

Hunter understood D-King's anger. While Hunter had to do things by the book and follow protocol, D-King didn't. The idea of D-King getting to the killer before him was somehow appealing.

'We'll need to see a list of all her . . . clients, all the people she'd been with in the past six months. The killer could be someone she knew.'

D-King gave Hunter another cheesy smile. 'I like you, Detective Hunter, you amuse me,' he paused. 'I have no idea what you're talking about. Clients . . .?'

There was no way Hunter would be able to force a list of Jenny's clients out of D-King and he knew it.

'You said you needed her name, you've got it now. I'm afraid there is nothing more I can do for you,' D-King said gesturing towards the stairs. Both detectives got up without saying a word. Hunter grabbed both pictures from the table. 'One more thing,' Hunter said, retrieving a piece of paper from his pocket.

D-King looked up at him with a 'what now' expression.

'Have you ever seen this symbol before?'

D-King and Jerome both stared at the strange-looking drawing. Jerome shook his head.

'No, never,' D-King confirmed. 'What does it have to do with Jenny's death?'

'It was found close to her body,' Hunter lied.

'Just one more thing . . .' Garcia this time. 'Do you know where Jenny came from? We'll need to contact her parents.'

D-King looked at Jerome who shrugged. 'I don't really do background checks, but I think she said she came from somewhere like Idaho or Utah or something like that.'

Garcia nodded and followed Hunter. As they reached the stairs, Hunter turned and faced D-King once again. 'If you get to him before we do . . .'

D-King locked eyes with Hunter.

'Make him suffer.'

D-King uttered no reply and watched as both men left the VIP area and disappeared into the dancing crowd.

Thirty-One

'What did that idiot Culhane tell you over the phone about Jenny?' D-King asked, turning his attention to Jerome as soon as both detectives were out of sight.

'He said he'd checked the morgue, the hospitals and the missing persons' files and didn't find a thing.'

'What a useless piece of shit he is. And we paid him for that?'

Jerome agreed with a nod.

'Tell the girls we'll be leaving soon, but before that get me that barman, the one Jenny used to talk to every once in a while, the long-haired one.'

'Sure.' Jerome watched D-King finish half a bottle of champagne in one swig. 'Are you OK, boss?'

He threw the empty champagne bottle onto the table knocking over several glasses and attracting unwanted attention. 'What the fuck are you looking at?' he yelled at the table closest to his. Its four occupants quickly turned away to mind their own business.

'No, I'm not OK,' D-King said, turning to face Jerome. 'As a matter of fact I'm pretty damn far from OK, Jerome. Someone snatched one of my girls right from under my nose. If what the detectives said is true she was tortured and killed.' He looked disgusted. 'Skinned alive, Jerome. Now you tell me, what sort of stupid motherfucker would be crazy enough to do that to one of my girls?'

Jerome could offer no answer but a shrug of his shoulders.

'I'll tell you who . . . a fucking dead one. I want this guy, do you feel me? I want him alive so I can show him what torture really is.' He put his right arm around Jerome's neck and pulled his face within an inch of his own. 'Whatever it takes, nigga, do you understand me? Whatever it fucking takes.'

Thirty-Two

The realization that the killer had been in the Vanguard Club only a few days ago made Hunter's blood boil. He decided they should stick around for a while longer. The killer had been here, he had touched things, allowed other people to look at him, maybe even talk to him. Somehow he'd managed to drug Jenny between the VIP area and the ladies' room and then drag her out of the club without looking suspicious – or did he?

Hunter touched Garcia's arm to get his attention and pointed to the low ceiling. 'Do you see what I see?'

Garcia looked up, following Hunter's extended index finger. 'CCTV!'

'Bingo.'

'Excuse me!' Hunter said, approaching the bouncer standing next to the fire exit. 'Where is your CCTV control room?' he asked, showing the muscle man his badge.

'Upstairs, next to the manager's office.'

'Can you show me where it is? I need to take a look at some of your tapes.'

The two detectives followed the bouncer back through the dancing crowd to the western side of the club. A narrow staircase led them up to the next level and into a small corridor. They approached the second door on the right where the sign read 'CONTROL ROOM'. Inside a solitary guard sat surrounded by small TV screens. He was holding a newspaper neatly folded in four with the crossword section showing. Hunter noticed he had yet to complete a single word.

'Hi there, Stu,' the bouncer said.

The guard didn't look up. 'Emotional shock, six letters beginning with T, do you have any idea what it could be?' The top of the ballpoint pen he was holding in his right hand had been completely chewed off.

'Trauma.' The answer came from Hunter.

The guard finally lifted his eyes from the paper with a surprised look, only then realizing Tarik wasn't alone. He put down the newspaper and straightened himself in his chair. Hunter took care of the introductions and badge-displaying ritual.

'I need to clear it with the manager first,' Stu said reaching for the phone after Hunter had explained the reason for their unannounced visit. Hunter made no objection and listened as the guard quickly explained the situation over the phone to one of his superiors.

'OK, sir. We'll wait,' he said, putting the phone down.

'So?' Hunter asked.

'He's coming over.'

Hunter scanned the small TV monitors in front of Stu's desk. 'How many cameras in total?'

'One over each bar, one over the dance floor entrance, one above the fire exit, two out on the patio, one over the club entrance, one in each of the two corridors that lead to the bathrooms, three over the dance floor and two over the VIP area,' Stu said, pointing to a different monitor with each new camera he mentioned.

The door opened and a short man dressed in an immaculately pressed pin-striped suit walked in. He was about five-foot five and the bad acne from his youth had left his pale face pitted like a sponge. His thick bushy eyebrows made him look like a cartoon character. He introduced himself as Tevez Lopez, the security manager.

'We need to see all your CCTV footage from last Friday,' Hunter said wasting no time with frivolous explanations.

'What exactly are we looking for?'

'A young woman was abducted last Friday. We have reason to believe she might've been abducted from this club. We need to check those tapes.'

Tevez and Stu looked worried for a moment. 'We might have a problem here, Detective,' Tevez said.

'Why?'

'We only keep our recordings for two, maybe three days; last Friday has been erased.'

'What? Why?' Garcia asked with frustration.

'We have no need to keep it,' Tevez offered casually. 'If we had no problems on the night, no fights, no money's gone missing from the tills, no drug-related incident, we see no point in holding on to the recordings. You see, Detective, everything is digital in this day and age. We have about thirteen cameras recording something like twelve to fifteen hours every night and that uses a hell of a lot of hard-drive space. Once we're satisfied the night has gone on without a problem, we erase it to make room for the new recordings.'

Both detectives were stunned by Tevez's statement. Probably the only ever footage of the killer, erased to save disk space. Hunter knew an opportunity like this would never come up again. He turned and faced the monitors.

'You have no hard copy?' Garcia questioned.

'No, as I've said, there's no need.'

'Wait, can you zoom in on this camera,' Hunter pointed to the top left monitor.

'Sure.' Stu twisted a knob on his desk and the monitor image zoomed in to three times its original size.

'Who is this?' Hunter pointed to a long-haired man seated in the VIP area. D-King and Jerome were sitting in front of him.

'That's Pietro, one of our barmen, but he's not supposed to be in the VIP area,' Tevez replied.

'We'll need to talk to him.'

'Sure, would you like me to call him up here now?'

Hunter looked around the control room. It was hardly an appropriate place for an interview. 'Do you have another room we could use?'

'You could use my office, it's just down the corridor.'

'Wait until he's finished talking to whoever it is he's talking to and then call him up. We'll wait in your office.' Hunter didn't want Tevez to know he'd already made D-King's acquaintance.

Tevez's office was small but well decorated. A square mahogany desk sat towards the back of the room. To its right, a neon-illuminated fish tank gave the office a nice personal touch. An array of shelves filled with photographs and books covered the entirety of the east wall. The loud music from the dance floor was muffled but still audible, making the floor under their feet tremble slightly but constantly. They'd been waiting for about five minutes when Pietro came in to greet them.

'Mr Lopez said you'd like to talk to me,' Pietro said after the usual introductions.

'That's right. Your conversation with Bobby Preston, what was it about?' Hunter saw no need for beating around the bush.

The look on Pietro's face told them that he didn't recognize the name.

'D-King, your conversation with D-King,' Garcia clarified.

'Was it about this girl?' Hunter showed him Jenny's picture.

Pietro was visibly nervous. All of a sudden he'd had D-King and the cops asking him questions about Jenny. 'Yes, he wanted to know if I'd talked to her last Friday.'

'And did you?'

'Yes, briefly.'

'Can you remember what time?'

'It was around two in the morning.'

'What did you talk about?'

Pietro felt as if he were in an episode of *The Twilight Zone*. D-King had just asked him exactly the same questions.

'Nothing important. She looked tired so I asked her if she wanted a drink. We only chatted for about a minute. I had to get back to serving customers.'

'Did she have a drink?'

'Not from me, she had a glass of champagne with her already.'

'Did she leave after you guys talked?'

'Not straight away, she hung out by the bar for a while. She said she needed a break from the party. As I said she looked tired.'

'Did you notice if she talked to anyone else?'

Again, the same questions as D-King's. 'Jenny is a very attractive girl. A woman like that hanging by the bar alone on a Friday night is like a magnet for men, so guys always approach her, but there was this one guy . . .'

'What about him?'

'He looked a little different. For starters he was wearing a pretty expensive-looking suit. No one really wears suits in here, except the bosses and some of the VIP guests, especially on Friday and Saturday nights. It looked like he was trying to pick her up, but he had no joy.'

'How do you know?'

'Not Jenny's style. She'll chat and flirt with everyone, guys and girls, but she's not the kind of girl you can simply pick up in a nightclub. He chatted to her for a few minutes and then left.'

'What did this guy look like?'

'I couldn't really tell you. I just remember he was tall and very well dressed, but other than that . . .' Pietro shook his head. 'I'm not very good with faces.'

'Did you see her talking to anyone else?'

'Not that I can remember, but then again, it was Friday night, I was too busy to really notice.'

'Can you remember if you've ever seen this tall, well-dressed man in here . . . before or since Friday?'

'Sorry.' Another shake of the head. 'If I have, he didn't stick out. The only reason I remember him from Friday is because I saw him chatting to Jenny.'

'Do you know if they left together?'

'I didn't see. But as I've said before, it's not Jenny's style.'

'Did she seem high or drunk?'

'Not at all, just tired really.'

Hunter grabbed a card from his beat-up leather wallet. 'If you ever see the tall guy in here again, stop whatever it is that you're doing and you call me, do you understand?'

'Yeah, sure.' D-King had asked for exactly the same thing.

'My cell phone number is on the back.'

Pietro examined both sides of Hunter's card and placed it in his back pocket. 'She's not OK, is she?' he asked with tenderness in his voice.

Hunter hesitated for a moment, but revealing the truth would probably make Pietro keener to help. 'She's dead.'

Pietro closed his eyes for an instant. It was hard for him to believe that he would never again see Jenny's smile or her warm eyes. He would never again hear her soft voice. 'And you think this tall guy did it?'

'We don't know, but it looks like he was the last one to have talked to her.'

Pietro nodded as if he understood what he had to do.

Thirty-Three

The next day started with Hunter and Garcia taking a drive up to George Slater's house in Brentwood.

'Wow, this looks nice,' Garcia said, admiring the striking building. Even by the lofty standards of Hollywood the house was impressive. It was positioned at the end of a narrow lane, shadowed by oak trees. The carved lintels and immaculate white front made the house stand out on a street of distinguished residences. On the east side of the house, overlooking a gorgeous garden was a detached double garage.

'Being a lawyer has its advantages I guess,' Hunter replied as he parked his car on the driveway. They made their way along the cobblestone walkway, up the small flight of stairs to the front door and pressed the 'call' button on the video-entry system.

'Yes,' the reply came just a few seconds later.

Both detectives lifted their badges to the small camera on the wall and introduced themselves.

'Can you give me just a minute?' The voice was soft and feminine, but Hunter detected the slight quiver that came from having cried for hours.

'Of course, ma'am.'

They waited patiently for almost a minute before they heard the sound of approaching footsteps. The door opened to reveal a very attractive woman with golden blond hair that she had up in a slicked-back bun. Her lipstick was a pale shade of red and her make-up subtle, just not enough to disguise the dark circles under her sad hazel eyes. Hunter put her age at around thirty-two. She was wearing a light black chiffon dress that suited her body perfectly. Her grief made her looked tired and frazzled.

'Hello!' She had a stunning presence about her, with a sort of delicate superiority. Her posture was perfect.

'Thank you for seeing us, Mrs Slater, I hope this is not too much of an inconvenient time.'

Catherine forced a shy smile and stepped aside. 'Please come in.'

The house had a hint of scented candles, jasmine perhaps, but the air inside felt cold and impersonal. The walls were white and Hunter noticed the even whiter squares revealing where pictures had once hung.

She showed them into what looked to have been an office. The book shelves were now empty and the sofa and armchair were covered with large white dustsheets. The room was brightly lit as the curtain that once protected it from the sunlight had been taken down. Cardboard boxes scattered around the room completed the 'moving away' decoration.

'I'm sorry about the mess,' she said, pulling the dustsheets from over the sofa and placing them behind the large hard-wood desk that stood just a few feet from the window. 'Please have a seat.'

Hunter and Garcia took the sofa while Catherine sat in the armchair opposite them. She noticed the inquisitive look on Hunter's face and offered an answer even before the question.

'I'm moving back to Alabama. I'll stay with my parents for a little while until I decide what to do. I have no business here anymore, the only reason I came to LA was so George could take a position with Tale & Josh,' she said in a sad and fragile voice. 'Can I get you anything to drink? Coffee, tea?'

'No thank you. We're OK.'

Catherine tried to renew her smile but her lips simply faded into a thin line. 'George loved a cup of tea in the afternoon,' she whispered.

'How long have you lived in LA, Mrs Slater?'

'We moved here two and a half years ago, and please, call me Catherine.'

'And your husband had a job with Tale & Josh from the start?'

'Yes,' she replied with a slight nod.

'Did he follow a common routine? I mean other than work, did he regularly go to any other places like sports clubs, bars, nightclubs?'

'George never had much time for anything, he was always working. He would stay late in the office at least three times a week. He didn't go to any sports club or gym. He'd never been a very physically active person.' Catherine's gaze wandered towards the window and she seemed to stare at nothing for a while. 'The only social engagement he liked to keep was his Tuesday-night poker game.' Her eyes started to get tearful and she reached for the box of tissues on the desk.

Hunter and Garcia exchanged a quick, tense look. 'Do you know who he played poker with? Was it work friends or . . .?'

'Yes, other lawyers from his firm. Maybe some other people, but I can't be sure.'

'Have you ever met any of them?'

'I've met other lawyers from Tale & Josh, yes.'

'I mean, have you ever met any of your husband's poker buddies?'

'I've never been to any poker night if that's what you're asking.'

Hunter detected a tone of arrogance in her voice. 'Do you know where they played? Was it a club, someone's house?'

'George told me that every week they played in a different house. They took turns hosting it.'

'Really? How about here? Did you ever host it?'

'No. I wouldn't let him.'

'And why is that?' Garcia asked surprised.

Catherine's eyes still showed the signs of fought-back tears. She looked dazed and still in shock. 'I'm a Christian, Detective Garcia, and I don't approve of gambling. Even though George had sworn there was no money involved, I just wouldn't have it in my house.'

'No money?'

'No. He said they did it for the social aspect of it.' She pulled a new tissue from the box and softly brought it to the corner of her eyes. 'He hasn't gambled for many years.'

Garcia raised his eyebrows in surprise. 'Did he used to gamble?' he asked.

'Years ago. But he gave it up after we met. I asked him to.'

'Casinos?'

She hesitated for a moment as if what she was about to say embarrassed her. 'No, dog-racing . . . greyhounds.'

Hunter swallowed dry. 'Greyhounds? Are you sure?' The surprise in his voice more than evident.

'Yes, I'm sure.'

Garcia shivered.

'And are you sure he'd given it up? I mean, are you sure he hadn't been to any greyhound tracks lately?'

Catherine looked staggered by the question. 'Yes, I'm sure. He promised me. Why would he break his promise?' Her voice full of conviction.

'Maybe he was betting over the internet instead of going to

this poker game,' Garcia suggested, and immediately bit his lower lip realizing the sort of accusation he'd just made.

'What? Why would he do that?' Catherine sounded deeply offended by Garcia's insinuation.

'Catherine . . .' This time there was real concern in Hunter's voice. 'We spent most of yesterday at Tale & Josh, talking to everyone who had ever met George. From the partners themselves to the mail boy. No one knows anything about a Tuesday-night poker game.'

'What? Of course they do, they must . . .' The tremor in her voice gave away how shocked she was by Hunter's statement.

'Can you think of a name? Someone you think would be part of his poker group of friends?'

'I don't know,' she said, visibly shaking.

'According to everyone we talked to, no one has ever played poker with your husband and they never even knew he played on Tuesday evenings.'

'They're lying, they must be.' She buried her face in her hands unable to fight the tears. When Catherine looked up again, her mascara had just started to run giving her a Gothic look. 'Why would he lie?'

'As Garcia said, he could've been gambling again and he was too embarrassed to admit it.'

'No, I know he wouldn't do that. He wasn't gambling. That's all in the past.' Catherine was adamant.

Hunter scratched his head, uncomfortable with what he was about to ask. 'How was your relationship with George? Could he be seeing someone?'

The shock of Hunter's allusion made Catherine gag. 'What are you saying? That George was having an affair? That he was lying to me so he could spend Tuesday nights with another woman?'

'I'm sorry, but we have to look at every possibility, Catherine, and affairs are a very common thing in LA.'

'But George wasn't from LA. He was a good man, a good husband. He respected me. We had a good marriage.' She had to pause for another tissue as the tears were now streaming down her face. 'Why are you doing this to me? You should be out there looking for the monster who did that to my husband, not accusing him of being unfaithful.'

'I'm . . . I'm really sorry,' Hunter said, feeling terrible for what he'd just said. 'I assure you, we're doing everything we can.'

'And then some . . .' Garcia complemented Hunter's assertion. They both sat in silence staring at Catherine. Her pain so contagious it made the room feel small and dark.

'They told me he was murdered, that someone did that to him, but how can it be?' she said with a hysterical edge to her voice. 'George wasn't shot, he wasn't stabbed, he was infected with a deadly virus. Who kills someone like that? And why?' Catherine broke down. Her head was back in-between her hands, her body shaking.

Hunter wished there was something he could say that would bring her some comfort. How could he tell her that he'd been after this killer for over two years and yet he had come no closer to catching him?

'I'm truly sorry.' Hunter could think of nothing else to say.

'Catherine,' Garcia took over. 'We're not gonna pretend we know all the answers, but I give you my word that we won't rest until we catch this guy.'

'I'm sorry, this has all been too much for me, I loved him very much,' Catherine said in-between sobs.

'We understand and we won't take any more of your time. Just one last question,' Hunter said, walking over to her. 'Have you ever seen this symbol?' He showed her a sketch of the double-crucifix.

She stared at it for a few seconds.

'No . . . never . . . what is it?'

'Nothing really, we found it around the park so I wondered if it meant anything to you . . . or George. Look, if you need anything, or if you just feel like talking, please don't hesitate to call me.' He handed her one of his cards.

'Thank you,' she whispered.

'We'll see ourselves out.'

Thirty-Four

Hunter poured himself another cup of coffee from the machine in his office. Garcia had brought in a special blend of Brazilian coffee imported direct from the state of Minas Gerais. It was grounded finer than most well-known blends and roasted at a lower initial temperature preventing it from over-roasting and giving it a stronger but smoother taste. Hunter had been instantly converted.

He had a sip of the dark liquid and joined Garcia, who was facing the photograph-covered corkboard. George Slater's picture was the last in line.

'What was he hiding?' Garcia asked, pinching his lower lip with his thumb and index finger.

'One thing is for sure, there was no Tuesday-night poker game,' Hunter commented.

'Uh-huh, but what was he doing? My initial hunch was that he'd been cheating on his wife, but . . .'

'But since she mentioned greyhound racing . . .'

'Exactly, and that was no coincidence. The killer knew.'

'I know. So was he gambling again or did the killer know about his past?'

'I don't know, but we really need to find out.'

'As Lucas had said, dog racing is illegal in California, right?' Hunter asked.

'Yes, why?'

'Can we find out which is the nearest state that allows it?'

'Yes, easy, give me a minute.' Garcia walked back to his desk and sat in front of his computer. After a few clicks and some typing he shouted out his search result. 'Arizona.'

Hunter chewed his lower lip in thought. 'That's way too far. If George had been going to a racing track, it had to be within driving distance so he could make it there and back in the same evening. Arizona is totally out of the question.'

'So if he was gambling again he was doing it over the internet or over the phone.'

'Which means the killer did not single him out from a dog track.'

'We have to find out where he was the night he was abducted. We know Jenny was in a nightclub,' Garcia said, getting up once again.

'We've gotta re-interview that tall, skinny, receding hair guy we talked to at Tale & Josh – what was his name?'

'Peterson, something Peterson,' Garcia recalled. 'Why him?'

'Because he knows more than he told us.'

'How do you know?'

Hunter gave Garcia a confident smile. 'He showed all the signs of being too nervous. Avoided eye contact, sweaty palms, uneasiness with all his answers and he kept on biting his bottom lip whenever we pressed him for a straight answer. Trust me, he knows more than what he told us.'

'Surprise home call then?'

Hunter nodded with a devious smile. 'Let's do it tomorrow, Sunday. People always get caught off guard on Sundays.'

Garcia's eyes were back on the photographs. Something else had been nagging him. 'Do you think they knew each other?'

The question came unexpectedly and Hunter took a moment to think about it. 'Maybe. She was a high-class hooker. If he was cheating on his wife, and that's still a major possibility, he certainly had enough money to afford her.'

'That's exactly what I was thinking.'

'So we'd better find that out as well, and I know just who to ask.'

'Who? D-King won't give us Jenny's client list and I'm sure you're not thinking about that mound of muscle bodyguard.'

'No, we ask one of D-King's girls.'

Garcia hadn't thought of that.

'Anyway, what do we have on our first victim so far – did we manage to get a file on her?' Hunter asked.

'Not exactly.' Garcia walked back to his desk. Hunter had never seen a better-organized desk. Three very neatly arranged piles of paper stood to the left of Garcia's computer screen. All pencils and pens had been placed into color-coded can-like containers. The phone was precisely aligned with the fax machine and there wasn't a speck of dust anywhere. Nothing looked out of place. Everything about Hunter's partner suggested organization and efficiency.

'Farnborough isn't a very common name, but it's common enough to make things difficult,' Garcia carried on. 'D-King couldn't tell us for certain where she was from. He mentioned Idaho and Utah, so I used that as the starting point. My initial check has returned thirty-six Farnboroughs in both states. I'm getting in touch with the sheriffs in every town I found a Farnborough, but so far, no luck.'

'And if D-King was wrong about Idaho or Utah?' Hunter asked.

'Well, then we're in for a very long search. She probably ran away from wherever she came from looking to become the newest Hollywood star.'

'Don't they all?' Hunter said matter-of-factly.

'That didn't work out, so she ended up becoming a pro, working for our scumbag friend D-King.'

'Welcome to the Hollywood dream.'

Garcia nodded.

'No easy identification via DNA then?'

'Not until we locate her family.'

'And we'll obviously have no joy with dental records.'

'Not after the job the killer's done on her.'

They spent a minute in silence. Their eyes back on the photographs. Hunter finished the rest of his coffee before glancing
at his watch – 5:15 p.m. He grabbed his jacket from the back of
his chair and checked the pockets as always.

'You're leaving?' Garcia asked half surprised.

'I'm already late for a dinner appointment, and anyway I
think we need to try and disconnect from this case even if just
for a few hours. You should go home to your wife, have some
dinner, take her out, get laid . . . poor woman.'

Garcia laughed. 'I will, I just wanna go over a few more
things before I leave. Dinner plans huh? Is she nice?'

'She's pretty. Very sexy,' Hunter said with a matter-of-fact
shrug.

'Well, have a good time, I'll see you tomorrow.' Garcia
started flipping through some files. Hunter stopped by the
door, turned and watched Garcia. Hunter had seen that same
scene before. It was like looking back in time, the only difference was he'd be sitting in Garcia's seat and Scott would be by
the door. He sensed in Garcia the same passion for success, the
same hunger for the truth that still burned inside him, the same
desire that had almost driven him to the brink of madness but
unlike Garcia, he'd learned to control it.

'Go home, rookie, it's not worth it, we'll carry on tomorrow.'

'Ten minutes, that's all.' Garcia gave Hunter a friendly wink
before turning his attention back to the computer.

Thirty-Five

Hunter hated being late, but he knew he wouldn't make it in time from the moment he left his RHD office. He'd never been the type to pay much attention to his clothes, but today he tried all seven of his 'going out' shirts on at least twice and his indecision had cost him almost an hour. In the end he'd decided to go with a dark-blue cotton shirt, black Levi's jeans and his new leather blazer jacket. His main problem was choosing a pair of shoes. He had three and all of them were at least ten years old. He couldn't believe he'd spent so much time choosing what to wear. After splashing a handful of cologne on his face and neck he was ready to leave.

On the way to Isabella's apartment he stopped at a liquor store to pick up a bottle of wine. Hunter's alcohol knowledge was restricted to single malt whisky, so he accepted the salesman's advice and bought a 1992 bottle of Mas de Daumas Gassac, and hoped it would go with whatever she was cooking. For the price he paid, it'd better.

The entrance hall to her Glendale apartment block was pleasantly decorated. Authentic oil paintings adorned the walls. A beautifully arranged bouquet of colored flowers sat on a squared glass table in the center of the room. Hunter caught a glimpse of his reflection in a full-length mirror positioned to the right of the door and made sure his hair was all in place. He rearranged his blazer collar before making his way up to the second floor via the stairs. He paused in front of number 214 and stood still for a moment. There was music coming from inside. A suave beat with strong bass lines and softly played tenor sax – contemporary jazz. She had good taste. Hunter liked that. He reached for the doorbell.

Isabella's hair was tied back in a loose style with several strands falling over her shoulders fully exposing her face. Her light-red lipstick and subtle eye make-up perfectly contrasted with her olive tanned skin and emphasized her European features. She was wearing a tight, red charmeuse satin top, a black pair of jeans and no shoes. Hunter didn't need X-ray vision to notice she was wearing no bra.

'Hi there, you're fashionably late,' she said as she leant forward to give Hunter a peck on the lips.

'I'm sorry about that. I had a bad hair day.'

'You too?' She laughed, pointing to her own hair. 'Come in.' She pulled him by the hand and led him into the living room. There was a pleasant and exotic smell in the apartment. The living room was illuminated by soft light courtesy of a table lamp in the corner next to a comfortable-looking leather armchair.

'I hope this goes with dinner, I'm not a wine expert so I followed a recommendation,' he said, handing her the wine bottle.

Isabella held it with both hands and tilted it towards the dim light so she could read the label. 'Ooh! Mas de Daumas Gassac . . . and a 1992 bottle, I'm impressed. I'm sure this goes well with anything. How about a small glass now?'

'That sounds good to me.'

'Great, the glasses are on the table and the corkscrew is just over there.' She pointed to a small drinks cabinet next to the window. 'Dinner will be ready soon. Make yourself comfortable.' She turned and walked back into the kitchen leaving Hunter to do the honors.

He took his jacket off, remembering to remove his Wildey pistol as well. He picked up the corkscrew from the drinks cabinet and opened the wine bottle, pouring the dense red liquid into two glasses on the table. Next to the drinks cabinet an elegant glass rack held a considerable number of CDs. Hunter couldn't help browsing through them. Her jazz collection was impressive, most of it contemporary with a few old school classics thrown in. Everything immaculately arranged in alphabetical order. A handful of autographed Rock albums disrupted the remarkable jazz compilation. Hunter quickly had a look at them. So she secretly listens to rock music, he thought with a smile. My kinda woman.

'Whatever it is that you're cooking smells great,' he said, walking into the kitchen with both glasses in hand. He handed one to Isabella who slowly swirled it around and brought it to her nose before having a small sip.

'Wow, as I expected . . . delicious.'

Hunter had no idea what difference it made but he copied Isabella's moves, swirling, sniffing and sipping.

'Yeah, not bad.' They both laughed.

She lifted her glass in Hunter's direction. 'To . . . a nice evening together. Hopefully with no phone interruptions.'

Hunter nodded and softly touched his glass against hers.

The evening proceeded better than Hunter could've hoped for. Isabella cooked veal parmesan with prosciutto and Mediterranean roasted vegetables, which came as a surprise. He was expecting some traditional Italian pasta dish. Most of the conversation over dinner revolved around her life, with Hunter revealing very little about his own.

She grew up in New York. Her parents were first-generation

Italian immigrants who had come to the United States during
the early seventies. They owned a restaurant in Little Italy
where she spent most of her childhood and teenage years
together with her brother. She'd moved to LA only five years
ago when she accepted a research job with the University of
California in Los Angeles. She still flew back to New York at
least three times a year to visit her folks.

'Do you keep in touch with your brother?' Hunter asked.

Isabella took her time before pulling her stare away from her
wine glass. 'My brother passed away,' she said with sadness in
her eyes.

'Oh! I'm so sorry.'

'It's OK,' she replied with a slight shake of the head. 'It was
a while ago.'

'Were you still kids?'

Her stare went back to her wine glass. Hunter could tell she
was searching for the right words. 'He was a Marine, sent to a
war we didn't belong. In a country most Americans can't even
spell the name of.'

Hunter wondered if he should ask any more about it, but
Isabella made the decision for him. 'You know, this ain't fair,'
she said, clearing the table and taking the dishes into the
kitchen.

'What ain't fair?' Hunter followed her, carrying both glasses
with what was left of the wine.

'You. I've basically told you my whole life story and every
time I ask you about yours you give me some evasive answer. Is
that a common thing among detectives?' She turned on the
sink tap placing the plates under the running water.

'We're very good at asking questions, but not so hot at
answering them.' Hunter had another sip of his wine and
watched Isabella wash the first plate and place it on the dish

rack. 'Wait. Let me do that for you.' He placed his hand on her shoulder and gently led her away from the sink. She smiled and picked up her wine glass.

'So you'll tell me nothing of your life.' She tried again.

Hunter finished washing the remainder of the dishes and turned to face her. 'I'm a detective for the Los Angeles Robbery-Homicide Division, assigned to a section called Homicide Special 1. We only deal with serial killers, high-profile and other homicide cases that require extensive time. In other words, I'm assigned mainly sick, overly brutal cases. The people I deal with on a day-to-day basis are either very evil or very dead. The things I see every day would make most people sick to the stomach. Talking about my life is, without a doubt, the biggest conversation killer anyone could come up with.' He paused for another sip of wine. 'Trust me, you don't really wanna know about my days or my job.'

'OK then. Don't tell me about your job. Tell me about your childhood, your family.'

'Not much to tell,' he said shortly.

She understood and decided not to push it. 'OK. I like mystery.' His boyish charm excited her. She stepped closer and took the glass from his hand placing it on the kitchen worktop. She slowly moved her face nearer until her mouth was less than an inch from Hunter's left ear.

'So what do you do to relax?' Her sexy voice was now just a tender whisper. Her warm breath against his neck made him rigid. Hunter lent his face back just enough so they were looking into each other's eyes.

'Can I suggest something?' At that moment their lips touched. Hunter immediately felt her soft tongue against his and they exploded into a passionate kiss. He pulled her closer and felt the stiffness of her nipples against his chest. He pushed her against the worktop and lifted her onto it. In an instant she'd lost her blouse, Hunter's mouth exploring every inch of her breasts. Isabella threw her head back and moaned with pleasure. Before Hunter had a chance to unbutton his shirt she grabbed it with both hands and ripped it from his body, the buttons bouncing over the worktop and floor. They embraced once again, leading to another ferocious kiss; this time Isabella plunged her long red nails into Hunter's back, her grip tight and tender at the same time.

They made love over the worktop, on the kitchen floor and then moved into the bedroom. By the time their sexual desires were satisfied the first rays of sunlight had started to grace the sky.

'I'm exhausted,' she said, rolling over towards Hunter and resting her hand on his chest. 'You were good the first time we met, but boy, what an improvement.' A smile played around at the corners of her mouth.

'I really hope so.' Hunter turned to face her and gently moved a strand of hair away from her eyes.

She kissed him again. 'I'm starving, how about some food? It's almost breakfast time anyway.'

'Great idea.' They both got out of bed. Isabella searched one of her drawers for some clean clothes while Hunter went back into the kitchen where all of his were scattered around the floor.

'What happened to teddy-bear underwear?' Isabella had just walked back into the kitchen wearing nothing but a pair of white lace panties.

'You better put something else on or we're gonna go through everything we did last night all over again.' His eyes never leaving her body.

'Is that a promise?' she said, picking Hunter's shirt from the floor and putting it on. There were no buttons left so she simply tied a knot around her waist. 'Is this better?' She gave him a quick wink.

Hunter swallowed dry. 'It actually turns me on even more.'

'Great, but let's have breakfast first.' She opened the fridge door and retrieved a few eggs, a carton of milk, a small bottle of orange juice and from the freezer some hash browns.

'Do you need any help?' Hunter asked.

'No, I'll be OK, besides, last time you offered to help in the kitchen you know what happened.' She poured two glasses of orange juice and handed him one.

'Yeah, you've gotta point. I'll just wait in the living room then,' he said, giving her a quick kiss.

'How do you like your eggs?'

'Umm . . . scrambled, I guess.'

'Scrambled it is.'

Hunter walked back into the living room and sat at the table. For the first time since the new killings began he'd managed to disconnect.

'You forgot these in the kitchen,' Isabella said, coming into the living room and handing him his very old-looking pair of shoes. 'How long have you had these?'

'Too long.'

'Yeah, it shows.'

'I've been meaning to get a new pair,' he lied.

'You should. In Italy it is a known fact that you can tell a man from the shoes he wears.'

'Damn. So I'm old and . . . dirty?'

She laughed a contagious laugh. 'Anyway, breakfast will be just a couple of minutes.'

Hunter had just finished his orange juice when Isabella walked back into the living room carrying a breakfast tray.

Scrambled eggs, hash browns, brown toast and freshly made coffee.

'Coffee? I thought you'd said you only had tea.'

'I did, last week, but somehow I had a feeling you'd stay the night, so I bought some yesterday. I hope it's OK, I'm not really a coffee person. I'm not sure if this is a good brand or not.'

'I'm sure it will be just fine . . . it smells great,' he reassured her.

'What's that?' she said, pointing to the piece of paper in front of him.

Hunter had unconsciously started fiddling with a pen and paper while waiting for breakfast. Amongst the several meaningless doodles he'd drawn, he'd reflexively sketched the double-crucifix symbol.

'Oh, nothing really.'

'That's funny.'

'What's funny?'

'That thing you've drawn. I've seen it before, I thought it meant something.'

Thirty-Six

Los Angeles is a great party town. Rock stars, movie stars, celebrities, politicians, super rich, it doesn't matter, one thing they all have in common is their love for parties, their desire to be seen.

Martin Young was a thirty-six-year-old entrepreneur who made all his millions in the property business. His company, Young Estates, specialized in properties for the super rich – Beverly Hills, Bel Air, Malibu and Venice Beach mostly. He'd rubbed shoulders with famous people from all walks of life. Madonna had sold one of her LA properties through Martin's company before moving to London. It took Young Estates only six months to bring its owner his first million in profit. Two years after he started his company, Martin could've retired if he wanted to, but he'd been bitten by the money bug and the more he had, the more he wanted. He became a ruthless businessman with most of his life revolving around his company, except for the weekends. To Martin weekends were for partying, and he liked to party hard. Once a month he'd hire some extravagant-looking house on the outskirts of town, invite a few close friends, pay several prostitutes and fill the place up with every kind of drug imaginable – just like last night.

As Martin opened his eyes, it took him a while to realize where he was. The effect of whatever he'd taken the night before hadn't

properly worn off yet and he still felt dazed. He looked around
the room taking his time to absorb the strange medieval decoration. He blinked a few times trying to clear his vision and slowly
his focus started to come back. Over on the far wall, above a
magnificent marble fireplace he could see a knight's shield positioned over two crossed swords. To the right of the fireplace a
full-size suit of armor. The floor had been lined with Persian rugs
and the walls plastered with tapestries and paintings of English
Dukes, Lords, Kings and Queens.

With great effort he sat up. His head felt heavy and a bitter
taste lingered in his mouth. Only then he realized he'd been
sleeping in a four-poster bed surrounded by silk sheets and pil-
lows. Damn, I fell asleep on the set of King Arthur, he thought
to himself with a little chuckle. Over on the bedside table, several pills lay scattered together with a small cellophane bag –
some sort of white powder inside it.

That's what I need before the comedown hits me, he
thought. Without knowing or caring what they were, Martin
picked up a couple of pills from the table and popped them into
his mouth. He looked around searching for something to wash
them down with. A half-full bottle of champagne was on the
floor next to the bed. He took a large swig of it and shook his
head, allowing the stale liquid to run down his throat. He
waited a few minutes for the pills to start taking effect before
getting up and slowly making his way out of the room.

From the landing Martin had a clear view of the living room
downstairs. He could see another nine or ten people spread over
the ancient-looking furniture and rug. One lonely body had
fallen asleep over the grand piano. Two naked hookers on the
floor next to it. Everyone seemed down and out. Martin stumbled over to the staircase passing another empty room to his
right. This is definitely the entertainment room, he thought as he

peeked inside. Holding on to the balustrade, he made his way down to the room below, one slow step at a time. As he reached the bottom of the stairs he realized how hungry he was.

'Where the hell is the kitchen in this horrible place?' he said out loud, scanning the exotically decorated lounge. He heard noises coming from a room at the end of a small corridor to the left of the staircase. 'Someone is up.'

Staggering as if drunk, Martin made it to the door. He tried to push it open but it barely moved. He wasn't sure if it was stuck or his effort just hadn't been enough. He took a step back and tried again, this time throwing his right shoulder against the door and putting every last ounce of energy into it. The door swung open and Martin was catapulted onto the floor.

'Hey, man, are you OK?' Duane, Martin's best friend, was sitting at the kitchen table with a two-liter bottle of water in front of him.

Slowly Martin picked himself off the floor. The kitchen was very spacious, and unlike the rest of the house, decorated in a pleasant modern style. The black Italian marble worktop contrasted beautifully with the gleaming, polished, stainless-steel double-door fridge positioned at the north end of the room. An overwhelming collection of pots and pans hung grandly above the table where Duane was sitting.

'Are you the only one up?' Duane asked, sounding a little too animated.

'I haven't seen anyone awake apart from you, but then again I only surfaced a little more than ten minutes ago.'

'Have you looked around this place? It's awesome. It's more like a museum than a house, except for this kitchen. Whoever owns this place is totally obsessed with medieval England, it's everywhere like a rash.' Duane's words came out fast and in a steady rhythm like a machine gun.

'And you think that's awesome?' Martin's expression clearly indicated that he didn't share Duane's thoughts.

'Well, it's very different.'

Martin wasn't very interested in Duane's house review. His eyes roamed the kitchen looking for something. 'Is there any food around?' he asked.

'Yeah, man, truck loads of it, just check the fridge.'

As Martin opened the fridge door he was greeted by an enormous variety of junk food. From donuts to marshmallows, hot dogs to fried chicken – a hungry man's paradise. He quickly grabbed a jar of peanut butter and one of jelly together with two cans of soda and a bag of marshmallows. 'How about bread?' he asked, facing his friend once again.

'Right over there.' Duane pointed to a bread dispenser on the kitchen worktop.

Martin wasted no time in retrieving a couple of bread slices. Using a knife he found in the sink he smothered the bread with enormous amounts of peanut butter and jelly.

'Damn, man, easy on the jelly,' Duane giggled. 'What are you on, hash?'

'I have no idea. I took a couple of pills that were on a table upstairs,' Martin said in-between huge bites. A blob of jelly ran down the left side of his mouth.

'Tripping?'

'Hell yeah. How about you?'

'No, man, I'm on dust. Haven't slept since we got here, I'm still buzzing like hell, man.'

'When did we get here?' Martin asked, looking confused.

'Shit, dude, you *are* tripping. On Friday night,' Duane responded with a laugh.

'And what day is it?'

Duane's laughter grew louder. 'Early hours of Sunday morning.'

'Damn, you've been awake for two nights and a day.'

'Hell yeah.' Duane looked proud.

Martin shook his head in disapproval, grabbed a handful of marshmallows and walked back to the bread dispenser. 'Would you like a peanut butter and jelly sandwich?' he offered.

'No man, I've got no appetite, but knock yourself out.'

Martin made himself another sandwich, this time with even more jelly.

'Hey, Mart, remember I said I had a surprise for you?'

Martin looked at his friend curiously. 'No, I actually don't remember that at all.'

'Well I did. Would you like to see it now?' Duane sounded excited and Martin couldn't tell if it were the drugs talking or his friend was really happy to be able to show him some sort of surprise.

'Sure, what is it?' he said casually.

'It's a DVD. I'll go get it while you finish that jar of jelly,' Duane said, pointing to the almost empty jar on the worktop.

'A DVD?' Martin questioned unimpressed.

'Trust me, you'll like this one.' He dashed out of the kitchen leaving Martin to finish his sandwich. A few moments later Duane stormed back in holding a slim DVD case. 'Here it is.'

Martin checked the case. There was no front or back cover. The disk inside it had no printing on it either.

'Where can we watch it?' Duane asked, sounding even more animated.

'I seem to remember a room with a huge flat-screen TV and surround sound system upstairs.' He drank the last of his soda down in huge gulps. 'But what the hell is this DVD all about, Duane?'

'This is gonna be cool, man. I know you're into bondage, right?' He sounded like a character out of *Wayne's World*.

To his closest friends it was no secret that Martin enjoyed bondage and rough sex.

'This is a bondage DVD?' A tingle of interest in his voice now.

'This, my friend, will probably freak you out. This is supposed to be some extreme bondage shit.'

Martin stared at a hyper Duane. 'I'm game, the rougher the better.' He stuffed the last of the marshmallows into his mouth.

'So where's this room with the flat screen?'

'Upstairs somewhere. We'll find it, don't worry. Let me just grab a donut.'

Martin went back to the fridge and grabbed a box with three chocolate donuts and another can of soda. They both left the kitchen.

It didn't take them long to find the entertainment room with several spacious and very comfortable-looking leather chairs facing the biggest flat-screen TV they'd ever seen. The surround sound system together with the DVD equipment was state of the art.

'Now this is cool,' Duane said, jumping onto one of the leather chairs like a little kid in a bouncing castle. 'And that's sweet.' His eyes had rested on the impressive TV set.

'Give me that DVD, and stop acting like a stupid kid,' Martin ordered. Duane handed the disk over and made himself comfortable.

The first thing Martin noticed was the amateurish quality of the images; this was definitely not a professionally made film. The opening scene showed a young woman, no older than twenty-five, already tied to a metal chair. Her long blond hair disheveled as if she'd just woken up. Her white blouse looked dirty and drenched in sweat. Her denim skirt had been ripped to expose well-toned and tanned legs. She'd been blindfolded and gagged and her running mascara was a clear indication she'd been crying. Her lipstick had been smudged off her lips and she seemed scared and exhausted. The room she was in was about thirty feet by twenty-two with holes in the walls as if someone had used a sledgehammer on it. Besides the chair she'd been tied to, the only other piece of furniture in the room was a small metallic table.

There were two other people in the room, both male, but the camera never focused on them. In fact, they were only seen from the torso down. Martin was instantly intrigued and his grogginess started to subside.

'This is different,' he commented. 'Forget about having a plot, they just go straight into the action here, don't they?'

'I knew you'd like it, man.'

One of the two males approached the scared-looking woman with an erection bulging in his black trousers. He tried running his fingers through her hair, but when she felt his touch her head jerked back violently, her frightened scream muffled by the gag in her mouth. Her reaction angered him. His blow landed on her left cheek, the impact so powerful it lifted her off the chair.

'Don't fight it, bitch,' he said in a menacing voice.

The man turned and faced the other person in the room who handed him a switchblade. He slowly ran it over the girl's right cheek. As she felt the cold metal against her skin she gave a petrified cry, tears running down her face through the blindfold. He turned the blade towards her blouse. In a quick movement he tore it off her body. A small speck of blood formed in between her breasts where the tip of the blade had scraped her skin. She emitted a frightened moan and was instantly slapped across the face once again.

'Shut up, whore!' he commanded.

The second male approached the terrified woman and forced her legs apart before slashing through her miniskirt revealing a pair of see-through red panties. They seemed moist and that aroused Martin who shifted his position on his seat in an attempt to get more comfortable.

The film proceeded with both males touching her, rubbing their visible erections against her body and getting more and more abusive. The violence at times seeming to get out of hand. Martin, nevertheless, was enjoying every second of it, until the last scene.

One of the two males had positioned himself behind the young woman, who by then had been freed from the chair, stripped naked and raped by both men several times. Her blindfold was suddenly torn from her face forcing her into a blinking frenzy as her eyes struggled to get used to the light. As they did, they focused on the second man standing directly in front of her. First a look of recognition, then terror took over. Her horrified expression was reproduced in Martin's face.

'Jesus Christ!' he breathed, quickly jumping to his feet. His body now shivering with fear.

With no warning her head was pulled back exposing her neck. The gleaming knife came out of nowhere. Her eyes saddened as she realized what was about to happen, there was no point in fighting anymore.

'You've gotta be shitting me!' Martin's eyes widened in horror. His excitement evaporating into repulsion.

The knife slash was clean and swift, ripping her neck open from left to right. Her dark and warm blood first gushed out and then streamed down onto her body. Martin and Duane had never seen so much blood. The man behind held her head back while the camera zoomed in on her dying eyes. Laughs were the only sound track.

'Holy shit . . . What the hell?' Martin yelled hysterically.

Duane had now jumped to his feet as well. His horrified eyes were glued to the screen.

'It's a snuff movie? You got me a fucking snuff movie?' Martin turned to face Duane.

'I didn't know,' he replied, taking a step back. 'They told me it was extreme BDSM, man,' he said, feeling faint, his voice unsteady.

'Extreme?' Martin shouted. 'She's dead, Duane. Murdered right in front of our eyes. Yeah I'd say that qualifies as fucking extreme.' Martin brought his shivering hands up to his face rubbing it as if trying to wipe away what he'd just seen. 'Who are they?'

'What?' Duane looked confused.

'You just said *they* told you it was extreme BDSM, who the hell are *they*? Who did you get this from?'

'Just some contacts I have. You know the kind of people you can score drugs or girls from.'

'Not my kind of people,' Martin shouted nervously and walked over to the DVD player and retrieved the disk. His hands still shaking.

'Why are you so fucking messed up about it anyway, man, it's got nothing to do with us. Let's just get rid of the disk and forget about it.'

'I can't, Duane.'

'Why not?'

'Because I know who she is.'

Thirty-Seven

'What? What do you mean you've seen it before? Where? When?' Hunter's voice rose a few decibels above normal.

'I'm not sure, maybe three, four months ago,' Isabella said casually. 'Aren't you gonna eat your breakfast?'

Hunter's appetite had vanished. 'Forget the breakfast. I need to know where you've seen this symbol before. I need to know when and I need to know now.' He held her by the arms.

Isabella stared at him with fear in her eyes. 'Robert, you're scaring me. What the hell's going on?' She shifted her body trying to free herself from his grip.

Hunter let go of her realizing how crazy his actions looked. 'I'm sorry,' he said, lifting his hands.

She stepped away from him as if moving away from a stranger. 'What's this all about? What the hell's gotten into you?' she asked scared.

Hunter paused and ran his fingers through his hair, taking his time to calm down. Isabella stood waiting for a reasonable explanation.

'Please have a seat and I'll explain it to you.'

'I'm fine standing, thanks.'

Hunter took a deep breath. 'I lied about the symbol meaning nothing at all.'

'Yeah, I guessed that.'

Hunter proceeded to tell Isabella about the significance of the double-crucifix, being very careful to reveal only what he deemed necessary. He told her about the two latest killings, but none of the previous murders were mentioned. The symbol, according to Hunter, had been drawn into a piece of paper found at the scene of both crimes. There was no mention of it being carved into the victim's flesh.

Isabella stood quiet and motionless for a minute, her eyes fixed on Hunter. When she spoke, her voice was unsteady.

'So you're talking about a serial killer? I could've been face to face with a serial killer?'

'Not necessarily,' he tried to calm her down. 'The textbook definition of a serial killer is – "someone that kills three or more people in three or more separate events." We've only had two murders so far,' he lied again.

'That doesn't make him less of a psychopath.'

Hunter agreed but said nothing. 'Isabella, I need you to tell me about that symbol. Where did you see it?' He gently held her shaking hands.

'I'm not sure. I'm too nervous to remember now.'

'Please try.'

She let go of his hands and massaged her closed eyelids for a moment. 'About two or three months ago,' she finally said. 'I was having a drink with a friend of mine in some bar.' She reopened her eyes.

'Can you remember which bar?' Hunter asked.

A shake of the head.

'It's OK. We can come back to it later. What happened next?'

'We were sitting at the bar and my friend had to go to the ladies' room.'

'So you were by yourself?'

'For a minute or two, yes.'

'Carry on.'

'This guy approached me and asked me if he could buy me a drink.'

'What did he look like, can you remember?'

She looked at the floor for a few seconds. 'He was very tall, maybe six two, six three. Shaved head, looked quite strong and fit and his eyes . . .' She paused for an instant.

'What about his eyes?'

'They seemed different.'

'Different how?'

'Cold . . . no emotion . . . scary even, like he hated me from the moment he saw me.'

'What color were they?'

'Green. I remember that very well.'

'Contact lenses maybe?'

'No, I don't think so. They looked natural.'

'OK, what did you say after he offered to buy you a drink?'

'I said no thanks, I already had a drink.'

'How about the symbol?'

'He leant forward placing both of his arms on the bar and asked me if I was sure. He said something about it being just a friendly drink. Anyway, both of his sleeves hitched up revealing his wrists, and that's when I saw them, he had it tattooed on both of them.'

'On both of his wrists?'

'Yes.'

'Are you sure it was the same symbol?' Hunter showed her his rough sketch again.

'Yeah, it was just like that. I even asked him about it.'

'What did you ask him?'

'I asked if the tattoos had something to do with the military. You know, sometimes Marines or army people like to brand themselves with special emblems, as if reaffirming their devotion.'

'What did he say?'

'He was very evasive. He quickly pulled his sleeves back down and said they were nothing, just something personal.'

'Can you remember anything else?'

'The tattoos didn't look like they were done by a professional. They looked rough, like the ones you do yourself using a needle and some ink.'

'Are you sure?'

'That's how it looked to me.'

'Did he say anything else? Did he give you a name or something?' Hunter knew he wouldn't have given her his real name, but it could be a start.

'No. After I asked him about the tattoos he seemed a little irritated. He said "Sorry to have bothered you" or something like that and left.'

'When you say he left, do you mean he left the bar or he just left you alone?'

'I'm not sure. I think he left the bar, I don't really remember.'

'It's OK, you're doing really well. The tattoos, where exactly were they?'

Isabella pointed to the inside of her wrist, just below the base of her palm. 'Right about here.'

'And how big were they?'

'Not that big, maybe just about an inch, in dark ink.'

'Have you ever seen him again since then?'

'No.'

'How about his voice, was there anything particular about it?'

'Not that I remember.'

'Let's go back to the bar, Isabella. Can you try and remember the name?'

She closed her eyes and took a deep breath.

'Was there anything specific about the bar, like a neon sign, a wall decoration or maybe its location?'

'It was a while ago. Just give me a minute and I'll remember it.'

Hunter sat silently for a few seconds.

'I'm pretty sure it was by the beach somewhere,' she said squinting.

'OK, let's try this. Instead of trying to think about the bar, try to think about the friend you were out with that evening. Your brain will have a better recollection of your night out with your friend than it will of the bar itself. And one thing will trigger the other,' Hunter explained.

'I was out with Pat that night. We haven't been out together for a while,' she said staring at the floor. A few seconds later she gave Hunter a warm smile. 'You're right. Thinking of Pat made me remember. We were at the Venice Whaler Bar and Grill in Venice Beach.'

'I know that bar. Been there a few times,' Hunter said with excitement. 'Can I ask you one more thing?'

'Sure,' she said with an unanimated nod.

'Do you think you could give our sketch artist a description of what this man looked like? That could really help us.'

'Yes, I'll do my best,' she said with a shy shrug.

Hunter moved closer and kissed her lips. 'I'm sorry for losing it earlier. You caught me by surprise when you said that you'd seen that symbol before, and this really is the first break we've had in this case.'

'It's OK,' she said, kissing him back. Hunter reached for the loose knot she had tied around her waist and the button-less shirt dropped to the floor. They still hadn't had any breakfast.

Thirty-Eight

It was another hot day in Los Angeles with the temperature getting up to 90 degrees. The streets were full of life with people walking their dogs, strolling, jogging or simply hanging out.

Hunter left Isabella's apartment around lunchtime, after finally having some breakfast. She was still a little shaken up, but she'd assured him she'd be fine.

'Jesus, if that's our guy, she could've been a victim,' Garcia commented after Hunter told him the news.

'I know and I'll get the police artist to her apartment this afternoon, right after we're done talking to this Peterson character from Tale & Josh. By the way, did you get his address?' Hunter asked.

'Yep, Via Linda Street in Malibu,' Garcia replied, checking a note he'd stuck to his computer monitor.

'Malibu huh?' Hunter cocked both eyebrows.

Garcia nodded. 'I guess some lawyers do live the high life.'

'I guess they do. How about one of D-King's girls? Any news on that?'

Since his conversation with D-King on Friday, Hunter had worked hard to convince Captain Bolter to have him under twenty-four-hour surveillance.

'Yes, our tail followed one of them home after the club last night,' Garcia said, pulling a piece of paper out of his pocket.

'Great, we can drop in on her right after Peterson. Let's go, you drive.'

Malibu is a twenty-seven-mile strip of spectacular coastline northwest of Los Angeles. It's a retreat for people like Barbra Streisand, Tom Hanks, Dustin Hoffman, Pierce Brosnan and scores of other rich and famous Hollywood stars.

Most of the long drive to Peterson's house was made in silence. Hunter's thoughts were divided between the amazing night he'd had with Isabella and the astonishing breakthrough she might've brought into the investigation. Had she really stood face to face with the killer? If so, was he wearing no disguise? Had she scared him off by noticing the tattoos on his wrists? Hunter knew this killer never left anything to chance, but there was a minute possibility that his meeting with Isabella had been accidental. Hunter felt his luck was changing.

'This is his road,' Garcia said as he turned into Via Linda Street.

'Number four, that's his house right over there,' Hunter said, pointing to a pale-blue-fronted house with three cars parked on the driveway, one of them a brand-new-looking Chevy Explorer van.

By Malibu standards Peterson's house wasn't anything spectacular, but by Hunter and Garcia's standards it was simply huge. The house itself was a three-story modern development and the generous lawn in front of it had been mowed to perfection. A curved cobblestone walkway led from the street to the enormous front door, its landing decorated by beautifully arranged flowers producing a riot of color. Whoever took care of this house was a perfectionist.

Hunter loved the element of surprise. Forewarning gave people the chance to prepare their lies, get them organized in their heads. If he could get away with it, he preferred not to make interview appointments, just show up. A homicide cop with a bag full of questions tended to make the regular citizen nervous.

On the front door they found a brass lion's head with a knocker coming out of its mouth.

'Eccentric,' Garcia commented and knocked three times. 'I bet they have a swimming pool in their backyard.'

'This is Malibu, rookie, all the houses around here come with a swimming pool, whether you want it or not.'

A few seconds later the door opened to reveal a fair-haired, brown-eyed little girl no older than ten. Not who they were expecting.

'Hi there, is your daddy home?' Garcia said with a broad smile and bending over to draw level with the little girl.

She took a step back and studied the two men in front of her for a short moment. 'May I ask who I should announce?'

Garcia was taken aback by the little girl's eloquence. 'Of course you may,' he replied trying to match her pompousness. 'I'm Detective Garcia and this is Detective Hunter,' he said, pointing to Hunter.

'May I see some identification please?' she asked with a skeptical look.

Garcia couldn't help laughing. 'Sure.' Both detectives produced their badges and watched in amusement as the little girl checked their credentials.

'Is there some sort of problem, detective?'

'No. But we do need to speak to your daddy if you don't mind.'

'I'm not to call my father "daddy." "Daddy" is for little kids. Please wait here,' she said dryly and closed the door on them.

'What just happened?' Garcia asked turning to face Hunter

who shrugged. 'She's what? Around ten years old? Can you imagine what she'll be like when she's fifty?'

'It's not her fault,' Hunter said with a head tilt. 'Her parents probably force her to behave like an older child, not allowing her to come out and play, not allowing her to have many friends, pushing her to become an exemplary student. Without knowing they are doing more harm than good.'

They heard heavier footsteps approaching. An adult finally. The door opened and this time the same tall, skinny man they'd talked to at Tale & Josh stood in front of them.

'Mr Peterson, we talked on Friday. Detectives Garcia and Hunter,' Garcia said first.

'Yes, of course I remember. What's this about, gentlemen? I've told you everything I know.'

'It's just a follow-up call, sir,' Hunter this time. 'We just wanna tie up some loose ends.'

'And you wanna do this in my home?' Peterson asked in an irritated tone.

'If we could have only ten minutes of your time . . .'

'It's Sunday, gentlemen,' he cut in. 'I like to spend Sundays with my family . . . uninterrupted. If you wanna tie anything up, my secretary would gladly arrange an appointment. Now if you'd excuse me.' He started to close the door but Hunter pushed his foot forward stopping it.

'Mr Peterson,' Hunter said before Peterson had a chance to voice his discontentment. 'Your colleague, your friend, was murdered by a total maniac who respects nothing. That wasn't a vengeance killing, and it sure as hell wasn't a chance one either. We're not sure who will be next, but what we do know is if we don't stop him, there will be another victim.' Hunter paused, staring Peterson straight in the eye. 'I'd love to have Sunday off, to spend it with my family and I'm sure so would Detective Garcia.'

Garcia raised an eyebrow at Hunter.

'But we're trying to save lives. Ten minutes, that's all we ask.'

Peterson compressed his lips still looking annoyed. 'OK, let's talk out there, not in here.' He made a head movement towards the road where Garcia's car was parked. 'Honey, I'll be back in ten minutes,' he called to the inside of the house before closing the door behind him.

As they reached Garcia's car Hunter stole a peek back at the house. The little girl was looking down at them from a window on the second floor with sad eyes.

'Great kid you've got there,' Hunter commented.

'Yes, she's adorable,' Peterson replied uninterested.

'It's a beautiful day. Doesn't she like playing by the pool?'

'She has schoolwork to do,' he said firmly.

Hunter moved on. 'Is that a new Chevy van?' He pointed to the car.

'I've had it for a couple of months.'

'What kind of mileage do you get per gallon?'

'Detective, you're not here to talk about my daughter or my new van, so how about you cut to the chase.'

Hunter nodded. 'We need to find out a little more about George's Tuesday nights. We know he wasn't playing poker. If you have any information, we need to know.'

Peterson retrieved a cigarette from a pack in his pocket and placed it on his lips letting it hang loosely. 'Do you mind?' he asked, lighting it up.

Hunter and Garcia both shrugged at the same time.

'George was a quiet person, kept himself to himself,' he said, taking a long drag.

'Anything out of the ordinary?'

'Well . . .' Peterson paused.

'Yes?' Hunter pressed.

'He might've been having an affair.'

Hunter studied Peterson for a few silent seconds. 'With someone in the office?'

'No, no. Definitely not.'

'How can you be so sure?'

'We have no women lawyers in the firm. All the secretaries and assistants are senior women.'

'So? A lot of men like older women,' Garcia offered.

'Still too risky, it could've cost him his job. George wasn't stupid,' Peterson replied, shaking his head.

'So why do you say you think he was having an affair?' Hunter asked.

'By chance I've overheard him on the phone a few times.' Peterson made sure he emphasized the words 'by chance.'

'And what did you hear?'

'Lover's talk – "I miss you and I'll see you tonight." That kinda thing.'

'He could've been speaking to his wife,' Garcia suggested.

'I doubt it,' Peterson shot back, twisting his mouth to the left and blowing a thin cloud of smoke.

'Why do you doubt it?' Hunter asked.

'I've heard him speaking to his wife before. He didn't talk to her like that, you know, all sweet and all, like newlyweds do. It was somebody else, I'm sure of it.' He paused for another drag. 'Most of the secret calls came on Tuesdays.'

'Are you sure?'

'Yes I am. So when you guys came around the firm asking about George's Tuesday-night poker game, I figured it must've been some sort of lie he'd told his wife. I didn't wanna be the one to rat him out, so I kept my mouth shut. His wife already has a lot on her plate as it is . . . poor woman.'

'Have you ever met her?'

'Yes, once. She's a very nice woman . . . pleasant. I'm a family man, Detective, I also believe in God and I don't approve of cheating, but George didn't deserve what he got. Even if he was cheating on his marriage.'

'How about gambling? Did you know he used to gamble?'

'No!' Peterson replied surprised.

'Have you ever heard him say anything about going to dog races, greyhounds?'

Another shake of the head.

'Internet gambling?'

'If he was gambling he would've kept it really quiet from everyone in the office. The senior partners wouldn't approve of it.'

'How about friends from outside the firm? He must've known other people. Have you ever met any of them, you know, at a party or something?'

'No, I can't say I have. His wife was the only person he's ever taken to any of the firm's social engagements.'

'How about his clients?'

'As far as I know, strictly professional relationships. He didn't mingle.'

Hunter started to feel like he was trying to force blood out of a stone.

'Is there anything else you can tell us about him, anything peculiar you've noticed?'

'Other than the sweet-talk phone calls . . . no. As I've said, he was a quiet man, kept himself to himself.'

'Was there anyone else in the firm who was closer to him, like a buddy?'

'Not that I know of. George never hung around. He never came out for a drink with any of us. He did what he needed to do in the office and that was that.'

'Did he stay late?'

'We all do when the case demands it, but not for fun.'

'So the only reason why you believe he was having an affair is because you, *by chance*, overheard him sweet-talking on the phone?'

Peterson nodded and blew another thin cloud of smoke to his right.

Hunter scratched his chin wondering if there was any point in continuing the interview. 'Thanks for your help. If you can think of anything else, please let us know.' He handed him a card.

Peterson took one last drag of his cigarette and dropped it onto the floor. He nodded to both detectives and started walking back up to his house.

'Mr Peterson,' Hunter called.

'Yes,' he replied with irritation.

'It's a really nice day. Why don't you spend a few hours outside with your daughter? Maybe play a few games. Take her out for some ice cream or donuts. Just enjoy the day together.'

The little girl was still staring at them from the second-floor window.

'I told you, she's got schoolwork to do.'

'It's Sunday. Don't you think she deserves a break?'

'Are you trying to tell me how to raise my daughter, Detective?'

'Not at all. Just a suggestion so you don't lose her. So she doesn't grow up hating her parents like so many nowadays.' Hunter waved goodbye at the little girl who replied with a bashful smile. 'As you've said, she's adorable.' He turned his attention to Peterson once again. 'Don't take that for granted.'

Thirty-Nine

The address they were looking for was number 535 Ocean Boulevard in Santa Monica. Garcia decided to take the scenic route along the Pacific Coast Highway.

The PCH is where most American car commercials are filmed. The highway follows the Pacific coast from the sandy beaches of Southern California to the rugged coastline of the Pacific Northwest. Along the way, it passes through quaint coastal towns, numerous national parks and wildlife refuges.

With the sun high in the sky and the temperature now soaring to 95 degrees, Santa Monica Beach was jammed. If it were up to them, both detectives would just grab a cold beer at one of the many ocean front bars and lazily watch the day go by, but it was never up to them.

Her name was Rachel Blate, but to her clients she was known as Crystal. Hunter knew the renowned drug dealer would be going after whoever had killed Jenny with everything he had. He knew the streets better than Hunter. He had contacts under every dirty rock and inside every filthy hole. If D-King came up with anything, Hunter wanted to know.

As Garcia parked the car, Hunter quickly checked all the information they had on Rachel Blate.

'Is this it? Is this everything we have on her?' he asked as he studied the single-page document Garcia had given him.

'Yeah, she's clean, no prior convictions, no arrests. Her prints aren't even in the database. A model citizen.'

Hunter screwed up his face in disappointment. That meant he couldn't use a little police blackmail to persuade her to cooperate.

Both detectives were impressed by number 535. A glassy, twelve-floor apartment block that stood imposingly on Ocean Boulevard. Every apartment had its own balcony, every balcony at least twenty feet by fifteen. At the entrance lobby they were greeted by marble floors, leather sofas and a chandelier that belonged more in Buckingham Palace than in Santa Monica.

Rachel's apartment was number 44C, but as they approached the building's concierge, Garcia gently touched Hunter's arm making a quick head movement towards the lift. An impressive-looking African American woman had just walked out of it. Her straight black hair fell matter-of-factly over her shoulders. She was wearing skintight shorts cut from a pair of ice-blue jeans, with a light yellow T-shirt tucked in at her narrow waist. Her figure was worthy of a *Playboy* centerfold. A pair of Gucci sunglasses hid her eyes from the bright daylight. Hunter immediately recognized her as one of the girls sitting at D-King's table on Friday night.

They waited as she obliviously walked past them and onto the street. It took them just a few strides to catch up with her.

'Miss Blate?' Hunter called now coming up to her side.

She stopped and turned to face both detectives. 'Hello, do I know you?' she said cheerfully.

Hunter quickly displayed his badge – Garcia did the same. 'Can we have a few minutes of your time?'

'Am I in some kind of trouble?' she asked unconcerned.

'Not at all. We actually wanna talk to you about one of your friends.'

'And which one would that be?'

'Jenny Farnborough.'

She threw them a quick look of assessment, her eyes resting on each detective for no more than a couple of seconds. 'Don't know who you're talking about, sorry,' she said facetiously.

'Yes, you do.' Hunter was in no mood to play games. 'She worked for D-King, just like you.' His stare was cold and firm.

'D-King?' She frowned and very slightly shook her head as if she had no idea who they were referring to.

'Look, we've all had a long week and just like you, we'd rather be enjoying the sun than doing this. So the quicker we disperse with the bullshit the faster we can get back to doing whatever it is that we do. We were at the Vanguard Club on Friday night, you were sitting with him, so don't play dumb, it doesn't suit you, and as I've said, you're in no trouble, we just need your help.'

Now she remembered where she'd seen them before. She also remembered finding the blue-eyed, muscular detective quite attractive. She removed her sunglasses and placed them on her head using it to hold her fringe back. She realized there was no point in trying to deny she knew D-King or Jenny. If they wanted to arrest her, they would've done so already.

'OK, but I haven't seen Jenny since she decided to quit. I'm not sure how much help I can be.'

'Quit?' Garcia's baffled look giving away his surprise.

'Yes, I think she decided to go back home.'

'How do you know that?'

'That's what we were told.'

'By D-King?'

Rachel took a deep breath and held it for a second or two. 'Yes.'

Hunter knew why D-King had lied to Rachel and the other girls. They would've panicked if they found out Jenny had been kidnapped, tortured and killed. He was supposed to be their protector, their guardian as well as their boss. Hunter debated how much he was willing to reveal. If he told her what had really happened, he'd be the one starting the panic in D-King's camp. He decided not to stir anything up – for now.

'Have you ever seen this man?' Hunter showed her a picture of George Slater.

Rachel analyzed it for a few seconds. 'Umm . . . I'm not sure.'

'Look again.' Hunter was sure she had recognized him but on instinct she'd lied.

'Maybe . . . in a club or party.'

'Private party?'

'Yeah, maybe one of the extreme parties if I'm not mistaken.' She bit her bottom lip as if trying to recall something. 'Yes, I'm pretty sure of it, he liked the extreme parties. I don't know his name if that's your next question.'

'That's not my next question,' Hunter said with a quick shake of the head. 'Extreme parties? What are those?'

'That's what we like to call them. Some people like to party, some people like to party hard and everyone has a fantasy, something that turns them on. Extreme parties are basically fantasy, fetish parties.'

'Like what for example?' Garcia looked more interested now.

Rachel faced him and took a step closer. 'Anything that gets you excited, honey.' She softly ran a finger over his left cheek. 'Rubber clothing, PVC, bondage, pain . . . or maybe you just like it rough.' She gave him a sexy wink. Garcia stepped away from her touch half blushing, half embarrassed.

'I'm sorry to have to break up this beautiful moment, but what exactly goes on at these parties?'

Rachel leant back against a parked car. 'Anything and everything. Why? Are you interested?'

Hunter disregarded her question. 'And you've attended some of these parties?'

'A few,' she said casually.

'How about Jenny?'

'Yeah, she's been to some.'

'How many girls at a party?' Garcia asked.

'Depends on how many guests there are, but it's usually somewhere between ten to fifteen of us, plus some others.'

'Some others?'

'If it's a big party, twenty or thirty guests, they'll need at least fifteen to twenty girls, plus guys.'

'Guys?'

Garcia's naivety made Rachel laugh. 'Yeah, honey, male models. As I've said, people have all kinds of fantasies, including bisexualism and homosexualism. If that's what they like, that's what they get. Does that turn you on, hun?'

Garcia's shocked look amused Hunter. 'No, of course not,' he replied in a firm voice.

'I'm glad.' Another sexy wink.

'Do you remember ever seeing Jenny and this man together at any of the parties?' Hunter cut in.

'Probably, it's very hard to say. At these parties everyone plays with everyone if you know what I mean, but I do remember seeing him playing with other guys.'

Both Hunter and Garcia's eyes widened in surprise.

'I guess you weren't expecting him to be into men, right?'

Garcia shook his head.

'Are you sure?' Hunter asked.

'Oh yeah. He puts on quite a show too.'

'How can we get into one of these parties?'

'You can't. Unless you're invited. They aren't paid parties. The host, usually some rich jerk, hires the models and invites whoever he wants. You ain't friends with him, you ain't getting invited,' she explained.

Hunter feared that was the case. 'Do these parties happen on Tuesday nights?'

'There isn't a specific day for them. Whatever day the rich jerk decides to throw them I guess.'

'Was there one last Tuesday?'

Rachel thought about it for a few seconds. 'If there was, I wasn't one of the girls.'

'Did you ever notice anyone strange in these parties?' Hunter asked.

Rachel laughed. 'Other than the people who like to be peed on, stepped on, tied down and spanked, burnt with hot wax or have things shoved up their ass?'

'Yes, other than them,' Hunter answered.

'No, nobody stranger than them.'

'Do other women apart from the models attend these parties?'

'Sometimes. I've seen guests bring their wives or girlfriends to them. I guess some couples are very liberal,' she replied with a chuckle.

'So no one in particular caught your attention?'

'I don't pay much attention to the people in the parties. I'm just there to do a job. People's looks play no part in my job. If it did, I wouldn't be doing it.'

Hunter could easily understand why.

'Did Jenny live in your building?' Garcia asked.

'No. I don't know where she lived. I don't know where any of the other girls live. D-King prefers it this way. Anyway, her old place would be cleared out by now.'

'What do you mean?'

'All the apartments belong to him. When one girl goes, another comes in. He takes good care of us.'

'I can see that,' Garcia said, tilting his head towards the glassy building. 'What happens to her stuff? If she left any-thing behind I mean.'

'Most of the stuff also belongs to D-King. He decorates the place, gives us clothes, perfume, make-up, you name it. He knows how to pamper us girls.'

The three of them fell silent for a few seconds.

'Can I go now?' Rachel asked with an impatient tone.

'Yeah, thanks for your help. Oh, just one more thing,' Hunter called out as she'd started to move away from them. She stopped and with a loud sigh turned to face both men. Her sunglasses back over her eyes.

'Do you remember seeing anyone with a tattoo that looked something like this?' He showed her a small drawing of the double-crucifix.

She looked at it, frowned and shook her head. 'No, never seen it before.'

'Are you sure?'

'Very.'

'OK, thanks again.' Hunter folded the paper and placed it back in his pocket before handing her one of his cards. 'If you ever see anyone sporting a tattoo that resembles this one or if you see this symbol anywhere, please get in touch.'

She took Hunter's card and regarded it with a smile. 'I might just call you anyway.'

'I think she likes you,' Hunter said, giving Garcia a pat on the back as soon as Rachel was out of earshot.

'Me? You're the one she wants to call. Maybe you guys can get together and who knows, she might even take you to one of those extreme parties,' Garcia teased.

Forty

Hunter lay awake in darkness staring at the ceiling, his mind too full of thoughts to fall asleep.

Was that how the killer chose his victims? From bars, clubs and parties?

This killer wasn't one to stick to any routine and Hunter had a feeling he was missing something, but he couldn't put his finger on it. He felt exhausted and drained of energy. No matter how hard he tried, his brain would never disconnect for more than just a few seconds. He knew he was starting to fall into the same abyss as before, and his partner was following on the same path. He couldn't allow that to happen.

The room was silent except for the tender breathing sound of the brunette sleeping next to him. Her hair soft and shiny, her skin beautifully smooth. Her presence calmed him.

After their quick interview with Rachel Blate, Hunter and Garcia had gone back to their office. There, Hunter met up with Patricia Phelps, the RHD sketch artist, and they both went back to Isabella's apartment. Garcia had decided to stay behind, saying he wanted to check up on a few things. Isabella had done her best to remember everything she could about the tattooed man she met a few months ago. It had taken her fifty-five minutes and three cups of tea, but in the end Patricia had sketched an image that Isabella agreed was pretty close to the man she'd seen.

After Patricia was done, Isabella asked Hunter to spend the night with her. Hunter's revelation that she may have met the killer had scared her too much. She felt alone and vulnerable and Hunter was the only person she could think of, the only person she wanted next to her. Hunter was itching to get on with the case. To start processing the new information he got today, but he couldn't leave Isabella alone. Not tonight.

'Can't sleep?' Hunter hadn't noticed that Isabella was also awake. He shifted his body to face her.

'Not really, but I never sleep much anyway, I've told you that.'

'Aren't you tired?'

'My body is tired. My brain's wide awake. My brain always wins that argument.'

She moved closer and kissed his lips softly. 'I'm glad you decided to stay.'

Hunter smiled and watched as she struggled to keep her eyes open, her head resting against his bare chest. Hunter hadn't spent two consecutive nights with the same woman in a very long time. He had no time for romance, no interest in sharing his life with anyone at the moment. And he preferred it that way.

He carefully moved her head back to her pillow and skill-fully eased himself out of bed leaving her undisturbed. In the kitchen he found the jar of instant coffee she'd bought espe-cially for him and a smile danced on his lips. Hunter made himself a strong cup before walking into the living room and dumping himself on the comfortable sofa, his mind rummaging through both interviews from the day before. Once again it looked like they'd established some sort of link between two of the victims. Jenny and George knew each other, he was sure of it. Sex parties, he thought. Did the killings have a sexual meaning behind them? Was the killer after promiscuous people? Still more questions than answers, but Hunter could feel they were inching closer. For the first time he felt excited about this case. For the first time they had something to go on – a face – maybe.

He had another sip of his strong coffee and wondered how many cups he'd need to get through the day. He checked his watch – 6:00 a.m., time to get ready.

He slowly opened the door to Isabella's room to check on her. She looked peaceful. She was still asleep when he left.

Forty-One

Getting to the RHD before eight in the morning was something Hunter rarely did, but the developments of the past two days had injected new life into him and the investigation. Today he felt as eager as he did on his first day as a detective.

'Do you ever go home or have you moved into the office?' he asked, surprised to find Garcia already sitting at his desk.

'The captain wants to see you straight away,' Garcia replied, paying no attention to his partner's comment.

Hunter glanced at his watch. 'It's seven-thirty in the morning, are you serious?'

'I know. He called up here around seven. I'd just got in.'

'You got here at seven? Do you guys ever sleep?' Hunter asked, taking his jacket off. 'Did he say what it was about?'

'Not to me.'

'Did we not hand in a report yesterday?'

'I did. A little later than ten in the morning as he'd requested, but he got it.'

Hunter could smell freshly made Brazilian coffee and that was exactly what he needed before facing the captain.

The detectives' floor was almost deserted except for Detective Maurice who was standing by a window. Pieces of paper were scattered all over his desk and on the floor. He looked like he hadn't gone home in days. Hunter said hi with a simple nod but Maurice didn't even seem to notice his presence. Hunter reached the captain's office and knocked twice.

'Come in!' the captain shouted from inside.

Even though it was still early, the room felt hot. There was no air conditioning, none of the windows were open and the two pedestal fans in the room were switched off. The captain was sitting behind his desk reading a copy of the morning paper.

'You're in early,' Hunter commented.

'I'm always in early,' the captain said, lifting his eyes to greet Hunter.

'So you wanted to see me?'

'Yep.' Captain Bolter opened his top drawer and retrieved a copy of the facial sketch Patricia had drawn. 'Come take a look at these.' He pointed to his computer screen. Hunter maneuvered past the two large armchairs and positioned himself to the captain's right. On the screen he could see several permutations of the sketch – long hair, cropped hair, beard, mustache, glasses – twenty different drawings in all.

'We've tried every combination we could think of and these have been sent to every station in LA. If this guy is still around, we'll pick him up sooner or later.'

'Oh he's still around, I'm very sure of it,' Hunter said with undeniable conviction. 'We'll be checking the bars and clubs as well, starting tonight with the ones in Santa Monica. If we're lucky maybe someone has seen him recently.'

'That's good . . .'

Hunter noticed the captain's uneasiness. 'That's good but there's something bothering you.'

Captain Bolter walked over to his coffee machine. 'Coffee?'

Hunter shook his head. Only once he'd been naive enough to taste the captain's coffee and he swore never to do it again. He watched as the captain poured himself a cup and dropped four sugars in it.

'The woman that gave you this . . . are you involved with her? Are you involved with a potential witness?'

'Wait a second, Captain. Don't even go there,' Hunter replied, immediately going into defensive mode. 'We got together a couple of times, but I met her before I even knew she'd had an encounter with a possible suspect. She's just someone I met in a bar and . . . she's not a potential witness. She hasn't witnessed anything.'

'You know what I mean. Getting involved with anyone that, in one way or another, is part of an ongoing investigation is at the best of times risky, not to mention against protocol and dumb.'

'We slept together, Captain. That doesn't really qualify as being involved. Especially in LA. And she ain't part of this investigation. She's not a witness and she's not a suspect, she's a lucky break, and to tell you the truth it was about fucking time we got one.'

'Have you gone stupid all of a sudden?' The captain's voice firm and dry. 'You know how serial killers work. More to the point you know how this one works. He profiles people just as much as we're trying to profile him. He studies his selected victims, sometimes for months because he knows if he picks the wrong person his game is over. If this is our guy, I know you don't think he just happened to bump into your lady friend in a bar?'

That same thought had been playing in the back of Hunter's mind ever since Isabella told him about the man she'd met at the Venice Whaler. Hunter knew this killer was very methodical, no mistakes, no slip-ups. He stalked his victims, studying their habits, their schedules, waiting for the best time to make his move.

'Yes, Captain. I know there's a possibility that that's how the killer chooses his victims. He first approaches them with some sort of frivolous conversation just to size them up in a bar or a nightclub.'

'And that doesn't bother you?'

'Everything about this case bothers me, Captain, but this particular incident gives me some hope.'

'Hope? Have you gone mental?' the captain enquired wide-eyed.

'Their meeting was over two months ago, Captain, before he started killing again. As you remember the first killing happened just over a week ago. Maybe he did size Isabella up and he didn't like her, she didn't fit his victim's profile, so he passed her up and looked for someone else.'

'The faceless woman?'

Hunter nodded.

Captain Bolter had a sip of his coffee and immediately made a bitter face. 'But why would that be? What made him not like her? She lives alone, doesn't she?'

'Yeah, she does.'

'That makes her an easy target. What made him discard her?' He walked back to the coffee machine and dropped two more sugars into his cup.

'I'm not sure yet, but that's one of the reasons I have to be close to her. I need to find out why she didn't fit. Maybe she's just too strong-willed. Isabella is not the kind of woman that would take crap from anyone. Maybe the fact that she'd noticed his tattoos straight away scared him off. Maybe he realized she wasn't such an easy target after all.' Hunter paused and looked uncomfortable for a moment. 'Or maybe she's still a possible target and the killer has simply moved her further down the list.'

Captain Bolter hadn't thought of that possibility. 'Do you think?'

'With this killer anything is possible, Captain. You know it and I know it. Anyone could be his next victim,' Hunter replied skeptically. The heat inside the office was starting to make him feel uncomfortable. 'Can I open one of these windows?'

'And let the city smog into my office? Hell no.'

'Aren't you hot?'

'No, I'm fine.'

'How about one of these fans, can I turn one on?'

The captain leaned back on his chair placing both hands behind his head with his fingers interlaced. 'If you must.'

'Thank you.' Hunter set one of the fans to full speed.

'What do you think? Could this be our guy?' the captain asked.

'It's hard to say, but he's definitely a person of interest.'

'So if he's our guy you're saying he made his first mistake in three years?'

'As far as he's concerned, he made no mistake.'

Captain Bolter gave Hunter a puzzled look.

'You see, Captain, he simply approached someone at a bar, and as we've said that could be how he makes first contact with his victims.'

'But he wasn't counting on the woman he'd approached becoming your girlfriend.' A half malicious grin had formed on the captain's lips

'She ain't my girlfriend,' Hunter replied firmly. 'But yes, he wasn't counting on us knowing each other. And we'd never have known they'd met if not for the fact that I unconsciously drew the double-crucifix on a piece of paper while waiting in the living room. That's why I said it's a lucky break.'

'We're not gonna be able to keep this out of the papers for

much longer you know. If he kills again the press will pick up on it and then it'll be just a matter of time before some smart-ass reporter links these murders to the old crucifix killings. When that happens, we're finished.'

'I can tell we're getting closer, Captain. You have to trust me this time.'

Captain Bolter ran his hand over his mustache and stared at Hunter with a laser-sharp gaze. 'I turned a deaf ear on your opinion about a case before and it cost me dearly. It cost the entire division and I know you've never forgiven yourself for it. That big-shot record producer. John Spencer was his name, right?'

Hunter nodded in silence.

'You told me and Wilson that we had the wrong guy. That he couldn't have murdered his wife. He didn't have what it took to be a murderer. We didn't wanna hear it. You wanted to carry on with the investigation even after the case had been officially closed and I told you not to, I remember that. Hell, I almost suspended you.' Captain Bolter leaned forward placing both elbows on his desk and resting his chin on his closed fists. 'I'm not making that mistake again. Do whatever you need to do, Robert. Just catch this goddamn Crucifix Killer.'

Forty-Two

'We've got some news from Doctor Winston,' Garcia said as Hunter walked back into the office.

'Go ahead,' Hunter said after refilling his coffee cup.

'As we expected, Catherine has identified the body of our second victim as her husband's, George Slater.' Hunter showed no reaction. Garcia continued. 'It will be about five days before we get a result on the DNA test done on the hair found inside George's car, but they've confirmed it isn't his.'

'It doesn't matter,' Hunter said. 'We don't have a suspect yet for a DNA comparison.'

'That's true.'

Hunter noticed that Garcia looked overly tired. Even his desk seemed a little messier. 'Are you OK, rookie? You look hammered.'

It took Garcia a few seconds to register Hunter's question. 'Yeah, I'm fine. Haven't had much sleep in the past few days, that's all.' He paused to rub his eyes. 'I've been studying the files on all the past victims, trying to find some sort of connection between them or with one of our two new ones.'

'And have you found anything?'

'Not yet,' Garcia replied in a half-defeated tone. 'Maybe it's not in the files. Maybe it's something that was missed during the initial investigation.'

'Missed? What was missed?'

'Some link . . . something that would connect all the victims. There's gotta be something, there always is. The killer can't just be picking them at random.' Garcia sounded annoyed.

'Why, because the books say so?' Hunter pointed to the forensic psychology books on his desk. 'Let me explain something to you about this link, this connection between the victims that you so blindly keep looking for. I searched for it just like you're doing now, like an eagle searching for food, and it ate me inside just like it's doing to you. What you have to understand is that this link may only exist in the killer's head. It doesn't have to make sense to us or to anyone else for that matter. To us it could be the most superfluous of things like . . . all the victims' last names contain three out of the five vowels, or they all sat at the same park bench on a particular day of the week. It doesn't matter what it is. To the killer it's something that enrages him. Something that makes him wanna kill. Finding the link is just a small part of what we have to do. OK, I admit it, it can help us, but I don't want you to burn out on it . . . like I did.'

Garcia detected a paternal tone in Hunter's voice.

'There's only so much we can do, rookie, and you know we're doing everything we can. Don't ever forget, we're dealing with a social psychopath who takes immense pleasure in kidnapping, torturing and killing people. The human values that to us come as second nature are completely distorted in the killer's mind.'

Garcia pinched the bridge of his nose as if trying to fight off an oncoming headache. 'Every night when I go to bed and close my eyes I see them. I see Jenny Farnborough staring at me with those unhuman eyes. She tries to say something but she's got no voice. I see George Slater tied to that steering wheel, his skin popping open like bubble wrap, coughing blood onto me. His last breath, his last cry for help and there's nothing I can do,' Garcia said, looking away from Hunter for an instant. 'I can smell the death smell from the wooden house, the putrid odor from George's car.'

Hunter knew what Garcia was going through.

'I'm starting to scare Anna. I keep her up at night with my tossing and turning. Apparently I've started talking in my sleep . . . on the rare occasions that I manage to fall asleep that is.'

'Have you told her about the case?'

'No, I know better than that, but she's scared. She's very intelligent and she knows me too well. I can't get anything past her.' He gave Hunter a pale smile. 'You gotta meet her sometime, you'd like her.'

'I'm sure I would.'

'We met in high school. She broke my nose.'

'What? You're joking?'

Garcia gave Hunter a sincere smile while shaking his head. 'My gang in school . . . we were jerks, no doubt about it. Always making rude comments to all the nice girls. I even made her best friend cry once. One day, I was down at the library studying for a final exam. Anna was at the table just in front of mine. We kept swapping looks and smiles until she got up and walked to where I was. Without saying a word, she swung the heavy 500-page hardcover she had in her hands. It hit me squared in the face. Blood everywhere. After that, I was hooked. Wouldn't leave her alone until she agreed to go out with me.'

'I like her already,' Hunter laughed.

'I'll arrange dinner at my place sometime.'

Hunter could sense his partner's anguish. 'When I got to the sight of the first-ever Crucifix killing, it took me just thirty seconds to be sick,' Hunter said in a low voice. 'After so many years as a detective I thought I could handle anything this city could throw at me . . . I was wrong. The nightmares started almost immediately, and they've never stopped.'

'Not even when you thought you had the killer?'

Hunter shook his head. 'Catching the killer will soothe the pain, but it won't erase what you've seen.'

An uncomfortable silence came between them.

'On that first killing, one of the first officers to arrive at the scene was a rookie, brand new into the police force, no more than two months,' Hunter recalled. 'He didn't handle it. After months with the police psychologist he ended up quitting the force.'

'How do you handle it?' Garcia asked.

'Day by day, nightmare by nightmare. I fight a day at a time,' he replied with sad eyes.

Forty-Three

She had to confess she was nervous. Maybe more nervous than she thought she'd be. Becky had spent most of the day with one eye on her computer screen and the other on the clock. She wasn't sure if it was apprehension or excitement, but the butterflies in her stomach had been flying around since she'd got out of bed this morning. She'd barely been able to concentrate on her work, taking more breaks today than any other day, but today wasn't like any other day, at least not for Becky.

She'd left her office at the main branch of The Union Bank of California in South Figueroa Street at around 5:30 p.m., not her usual leaving time. As a financial adviser, her job had always demanded a lot from her. It wasn't unusual for Becky to stay behind until seven or eight in the evening. Today, even her boss had given her some advice in what she should and shouldn't do, and he was happy to see her leave a little earlier than normal.

Even with traffic as bad as it was, Becky still had enough time to drop by her apartment and grab a quick shower. She also wanted to try out the little black number she'd bought this afternoon during her lunch hour especially for tonight's occasion. As she thought about her new dress and how she should wear her hair, she found herself feeling anxious again. She turned on the radio and hoped the music would help calm her down.

How difficult could this be? She was sure things hadn't changed that much since the last time she had a date, but that had been almost five years ago. She could remember it vividly. How could she forget it? The man she'd dated that night had become her husband.

Becky met Ian Tasker through the bank. A charming six-foot-one, curly blond-haired playboy who had just inherited a considerable amount of money after the death of his property millionaire father. An only child, and with his mother having passed away when he was only five years old, he'd become the sole beneficiary of his father's estate.

Ian had never been very good with money, and if it was up to him, he would've probably lost it all in Las Vegas or Atlantic City to the blackjack and roulette tables, but for some reason he'd decided to take his best friend's advice and invest part of the money.

Ian was completely clueless about finances. He'd never saved a penny, never mind invested it, but his best friend came to his rescue once again and suggested he had a look at The Union Bank of California's 'wealth planning service'.

Given the amount of money he intended to invest, the bank was more than happy to assign Rebecca Morris as Ian's personal financial adviser.

Their relationship had begun in a strictly professional way, but Ian's financial naivety and charming light-blue eyes had struck a weak spot with Becky. The initial, somewhat subdued attraction was mutual. Ian found the sweet, five-foot-six brunette fascinating. She was funny, attractive, lively, very intelligent and her sense of humor was laser sharp. After only one week, Ian's main interest had flipped from Becky's financial expertise to Becky herself. He'd be on the phone to her daily, asking for market tips, financial suggestions, anything really, just for the pleasure of hearing her voice.

Despite Ian Tasker being an undeniable playboy and a self-proclaimed ladies' man, his arrogance and self-confidence would disappear when Becky was around. She was different from all the other blood-sucking women he'd met. Her interest in his money seemed to be purely professional. It had taken him almost two weeks to gather enough courage to ask her out on their first date.

Becky had been asked out by bank clients many times before, most of them married men, and politely she'd rejected all their invitations. Even though Ian's playboy ways were far from what she'd envisaged as dating material, she decided to break her own rule – 'never date a client'.

That night had been as close to perfect as anyone could've dreamed of. Ian had chosen a small restaurant by the sea in Venice Beach, and, at first, Becky was unsure what to make of the fact that he'd hired out the entire place for the night. Was that just a trick to impress her or was it a sincere attempt at romanticism? As the night progressed she found herself sucked in, first by his boyish and lively personality, then by the surprising pleasure of his company. There was no doubt Ian loved himself, but he was also very witty, kind and entertaining.

Their first romantic night consequently ignited a string of new ones, and their relationship flourished with every new date. His irreverent manner swept her off her feet and when Ian popped the question live on national television during the interval of a Lakers game, Becky became the happiest woman in Los Angeles.

Against his will, she'd insisted on a prenuptial agreement saying she was in love with him, not his money.

Their marriage picked up from where their dating left off.

Everything seemed perfect. Ian was a very attentive and caring husband and to Becky it all felt like a fairy-tale story. For two years Becky did live a dream. The dream of being happy, the dream of being with someone who cares, the dream of being loved. But things were about to take a drastic turn.

Just over two and a half years ago, by sheer bad luck, Ian had found himself in the proverbial wrong place at the wrong time. On his way home from his usual Friday afternoon golf game, Becky had called and asked him to drop by a liquor store to pick up a bottle of red wine.

As he looked through the unimpressive selection he failed to notice the two new customers that had just come in wearing ice-hockey masks. The store he was in had been burgled several times – twice in the last month alone. Its owner had had enough of what he called 'police incompetence' and if the police couldn't protect his store, then he would.

Ian had finally chosen a bottle of Australian Shiraz when he heard loud shouts coming from the front of the store. At first he discarded it as a complaining customer having an argument with the store owner, but the argument heated up faster than usual. Sneakily he peeked around the aisle. The scene he saw was comically tragic. Both masked men were standing in front of the counter, guns drawn and aimed at the store owner who in turn had his double-barreled shotgun in hand and his aim moving back and forth from one masked man to another.

Instinctively Ian stepped backwards, trying to hide behind a brandy and whisky stand. Not able to contain his nervousness he stepped back too quickly, tripping, colliding with the stand and sending two bottles crashing to the floor. The unexpected noise caught everyone by surprise, spooking the two masked men who opened fire in Ian's direction.

With both masked men's attention diverted for a split

second, the store owner saw his opportunity and quickly discharged his first shot at the man standing closer to the door. The powerful blast from the shotgun propelled its victim into the air, his head obliterated. Shards of glass from the now-demolished front door flew up like hailstones. Panic took over the second masked man as he saw the decapitated body of his partner hit the floor. Before the store owner had a chance to turn his weapon towards the second masked man, the man squeezed two quick shots in succession, both hitting their target in the stomach.

The store owner stumbled backwards, but he still had enough time and strength to pull his trigger.

The bullets that were fired earlier had somehow missed Ian completely smashing into brandy and whisky bottles behind him. In his panic he'd tripped, lost his balance and instinctively tried to grab on to something before falling to the ground. The only thing he was able to reach was the bottle stand itself. He came crashing down like a ton of bricks, the stand smashing against his legs, bottles exploding onto the floor. That would've been a very lucky escape for Ian if not for the fact that the bottle stand crashed into an insect repellent light on the wall, blowing it to pieces and producing a sparkle rain. The alcoholic cocktail bath that Ian found himself in lit up like gasoline.

The traffic light turned green and Becky drove on, trying desperately to keep herself from crying.

For almost two and a half years Becky had avoided dating, and she was still unsure if she could go ahead with it. The pain of losing Ian was still there.

Becky met Jeff in her local supermarket. The same supermarket she stopped by twice a week for groceries and wine after leaving her office. It had been a chance meeting. Becky had been struggling to choose a ripe melon for a new salad recipe. She'd been moving from fruit to fruit, holding it with both hands, giving it a tight squeeze and then shaking it close to her ear.

'Are you searching for the one with the surprise gift inside?' Those were the first words Jeff had said to her.

She smiled. 'I'm a percussionist. Melons make great maracas.'

Jeff frowned. 'Really?'

She laughed. 'Sorry. It's my sense of humor. Dry as a desert. I'm just trying to find a good melon . . . a ripe one.'

'Well, shaking them won't do the trick.' Somehow his voice didn't sound condescending. 'The secret here is in the smell. You'll notice that some will have a sweeter, more mature smell, those are the ripe ones,' he said, bringing a melon to his nose and giving it a good sniff. 'But you don't want them to smell too sweet, those would be past their best.' He extended his hand, offering her the melon he was holding. She tried his technique. A warm, sweet smell exuded as she brought the melon to her nose. Jeff gave her a quick wink and carried on with his shopping.

In the weeks that followed, they ended up bumping into each other several times. Becky was always very talkative and funny, while Jeff was content to listen and laugh. Her sense of humor shining through in every conversation.

Jeff finally gathered enough courage to ask Becky out for dinner after a few months of supermarket meetings. She was hesitant at first, but she'd decided to accept.

They'd arranged to meet the next Monday at the Belvedere restaurant in Santa Monica, at 8:30 p.m.

Forty-Four

Washington Square is located at the beach end of Washington Boulevard, just across the road from Venice Beach. It's home to several well-known bars and restaurants, including the Venice Whaler. Monday nights aren't their busiest night, but the place looked full of activity with a colorful young crowd in shorts and beach shirts surrounding the large bar. The atmosphere was relaxed and pleasant. It was easy to see why Isabella would've enjoyed a drink or two at this bar.

Hunter and Garcia arrived at the Venice Whaler at five-thirty and by six-thirty they'd talked to every member of staff, including the two chefs and the kitchen porter, but the more people they talked to, the more frustrated they became. Long or short hair, beard or no beard, it didn't matter. No one seemed to have ever laid eyes on anyone that resembled any of the computer-generated sketches.

After talking to the entire staff, Hunter and Garcia decided to ask a few of the customers, but their luck didn't change and Hunter wasn't surprised. This killer was too careful, too prepared, took no risks and Hunter had a strong suspicion that picking potential victims out of busy and popular bars wasn't really his style – it was too dangerous – too exposed – there were too many factors he couldn't control.

After leaving a copy of the sketches with the manager they

moved on to the next bar on their list – Big Dean's Café. The outcome was a carbon copy of what had happened at the Venice Whaler. No one remembered seeing anyone that looked like any of the images.

'This is turning out to be another wild goose chase,' Garcia commented, visibly bothered.

'Welcome to the world of chasing psychopaths,' Hunter said with a cheesy smile. 'This is what it's like. Frustration is a major part of the game. You're gonna have to learn to deal with it.'

It had just gone eight o'clock when they came to the third and final bar on their list for the night – Rusty's Surf Ranch where beech-colored wood was the main theme. Behind the small bar a single barman was happily serving the loud crowd of customers.

Hunter and Garcia approached the bar, grabbing the attention of the barman. Half an hour later and the entire staff had been asked the same questions and shown the same pictures – nothing. Garcia couldn't hide his disappointment.

'I was really hoping for some sort of a break tonight . . .' He thought better of what he'd just said. 'OK, maybe not a break, but some kind of development,' he said, rubbing his tired eyes.

Hunter surveyed the restaurant floor for some seating space. Luckily a party of four were just leaving, vacating a table.

'Are you hungry? I could do with some food – let's grab a seat.' He pointed to the empty table and they both made their way towards it.

They checked the menu in silence, Hunter struggling to make a decision. 'I'm actually starving. I could have half of this menu.'

'I bet you could. I'm not that hungry, I'll just have a Caesar salad,' Garcia said indifferently.

'Salad!' Surprise in Hunter's voice. 'You're like a big girl. Order some proper food, will you?' he demanded dryly.

Reluctantly, Garcia reopened the menu. 'OK, I'll have a chicken Caesar salad. Is that better, Mom?'

'And some BBQ back ribs to go with it.'

'Are you trying to make me fat? That's way too much food.'

'Trying to make you fat? You *are* a big girl,' Hunter said laughing.

The waitress came up to take their order. Apart from the Caesar salad and the back ribs, Hunter also ordered a California burger and some fried calamari for himself together with two bottles of beer. They sat without saying a word, Hunter's observant eyes moving from table to table, resting on each occupant for only a few seconds. Garcia regarded his partner for a minute and then placed both of his elbows on the table leaning forward, his voice low as if whispering a secret.

'Is there anything wrong?'

Hunter moved his stare back to Garcia. 'No, everything is fine,' he said calmly.

'You're looking around like you've seen something or somebody.'

'Oh that. I do that a lot when I'm in public places, it's like an exercise that has carried on from my criminal psychology days.'

'Really . . . like what?'

'We used to play this game. We'd go out to restaurants, bars, clubs, places like that and we'd take turns picking a subject in the crowd, watching him or her for a few minutes and trying to profile them as best as we could.'

'What, just by watching them for a minute or so?'

'Yeah, that's right.'

'Show me.'

'What? Why?'

'I just wanna see how it works.'

Hunter hesitated for a moment. 'OK, pick someone.'

Garcia looked around the busy restaurant but his eyes were drawn to the bar. Two attractive women, one blond, one brunette, were having a drink together. The blond one was by far the more talkative of the two. Garcia had made his choice. 'Right there, over at the bar. See the two girls by themselves? The blond one.'

Hunter's gaze fell on his new subject. He observed her, her eye and body movements, her quirks, the way she spoke to her friend, the way she laughed. It took him only about a minute to start his assessment.

'OK, she knows she's attractive. She's very confident and she loves the attention she gets, she works hard for it.'

Garcia lifted his right hand. 'Wait up, how would you know that?'

'She's wearing very revealing clothes compared to her friend's. So far she's run her hand through her hair four times, the most common "notice me" gesture, and every so often she furtively checks herself against the mirror behind the bottle shelves at the bar.'

Garcia observed the blond girl for a while. 'You're right. She just checked herself again.'

Hunter smiled before carrying on. 'Her parents are rich and she's proud of that. She makes no effort to hide it from anyone and she knows how to spend their money.'

'Why do you say that?'

'She's drinking champagne in a bar where ninety-five percent of the customers order beer.'

'She could be celebrating.'

'She isn't,' Hunter said confidently.

'How do you know?'

'Because she's drinking champagne and her friend is drinking beer. If they were celebrating her friend would be sharing the bottle with her. And there was no toast. You always toast when you celebrate.'

Garcia smiled. Hunter continued. 'Her clothes and handbag are all designer. She's never placed her car keys back into her handbag, preferring to leave them on the bar in plain view, and the reason for that is probably because her key ring shows some prestigious car emblem, like a BMW or something. She's got no wedding ring and anyway she's too young to be married or have a well-paid job, so the money has to come from somewhere else.'

'Please go on.' Garcia was starting to enjoy the exercise.

'She's got a diamond-encrusted W on her necklace. I'd say her name would be either Wendy or Whitney, those being the two favorite names beginning with W of rich parents in Los Angeles. She loves flirting, it boosts her ego even more, but she prefers more mature men.'

'OK, now you're pushing it?'

'No I'm not. She only returns eye contact from more mature men, ignoring the flirtation of younger guys.'

'That's not true. She keeps on checking out the guy standing next to her and he looks quite young to me.'

'She's not looking at him. She's looking at his cigarette pack in his shirt pocket. She probably gave up smoking not so long ago.'

Garcia had a peculiar grin on his face when he got up.

'Where are you going?'

'Check out how good you really are.' Hunter looked on as Garcia started towards the bar.

'Excuse me, you don't happen to have an extra cigarette do you?' he said, approaching the two women but directing his question to the blond one.

She gave him a charming and pleasant smile. 'I'm sorry, but I quit smoking two months ago.'

'Really? I'm trying to myself. It's not easy,' Garcia said, returning the smile. His eyes moved to the bar and onto her key ring. 'You drive a Merc?'

'Yeah, just got it a few weeks ago.' Her excitement was almost contagious.

'Very nice, is it a C-Class?'

'SLK convertible,' she replied proudly.

'That's a very good choice.'

'I know. I love my car.'

'By the way, I'm Carlos,' he said, extending his hand.

'I'm Wendy, and this is Barbara.' She pointed to her brunette friend.

'It's been very nice meeting you both. Enjoy the rest of your evening,' he said with a smile before returning to Hunter's table.

'OK, I'm even more impressed now than I was before,' he commented as he sat down. 'One thing is for sure. I ain't never playing poker against you,' he said, laughing.

While Garcia was testing Hunter's profiling skills, the waitress had come back with their dinner. 'Wow, I was hungrier than I thought,' Garcia said after having finished his BBQ ribs together with the Caesar salad. Hunter was still munching on his burger. Garcia waited until he was done. 'How come you decided to be a cop? I mean, you could've been a profiler, you know . . . gone and worked for the FBI or something like that.'

Hunter had another sip of his beer and used the napkin on his mouth. 'And you think that working for the FBI is better than working as a Homicide detective?'

'I didn't say that,' Garcia protested. 'What I meant is that you had a choice and you picked being a Homicide detective. I know a lot of cops who'd kill for the chance to work for the feds.'

'Would you?'

Garcia's eyes didn't shy away from Hunter's. 'Not me, I don't really much care for the feds.'

'And why is that?'

'To me they're just a whole bunch of glorified cops who think they are better than everyone else simply because they wear cheap black suits, sunglasses and earpieces.'

'First day I met you I thought you wanted to be an FBI agent. You were wearing a cheap suit.' A smirk on Hunter's face.

'Hey, that suit wasn't cheap at all. I like that suit, it's my only suit.'

'Yeah, I could've guessed that.' The smirk turned into a sarcastic smile. 'At first I thought I would become a criminal profiler. That would've been the logical move after my PhD.'

'Yeah. I've heard you were some kind of child prodigy, a genius in what you did.'

'I moved through school faster than usual,' Hunter said, playing it down.

'And is it true that you've written a book that's used as a study guide by the FBI?'

'It wasn't a book. It was my PhD thesis paper. But yes, it was made into a book and the last I heard it was still used by the FBI.'

'Now that's impressive,' Garcia said, pushing his plate away. 'So what made you choose not to become an FBI profiler?'

'I spent all of my childhood immersed in books. That's all I did when I was young. I read. I guess I was starting to get bored of the academic life. I needed something with a little more excitement,' Hunter said, revealing only half the truth.

'And the FBI wouldn't be exciting enough?' Garcia asked with a mocking smile.

'FBI profilers aren't field agents. They work behind desks and inside offices. Not the kind of excitement I was looking for. Plus I wasn't ready to lose the little sanity I had.'

'What do you mean?'

'I don't think most human brains are strong enough to go through the journey of becoming a criminal profiler in today's society and come out on the other side unscathed. Anyone who decides to put themselves through that sort of pressure inevitably will pay the price, and that price is too high.'

Garcia looked a little confused.

'Look, there are basically two schools, two main theories where criminal profiling is concerned. Some psychologists believe that evil is something inherent to certain individuals, they believe it's something people are born with, like a brain dysfunction that leads them to commit obscene acts of cruelty.'

'Meaning some believe it's like a disease, a sickness?' Garcia asked.

'That's right,' Hunter continued. 'Others believe that what causes a person to go from being a civilized individual to becoming a sociopath are the series of events and circumstances that have affected that person's life so far. In other words, if you were surrounded by violence when young, if you were abused or mistreated as a child, chances are you'll reflect that in your adult life by becoming a violent person. Are you with me so far?'

Garcia nodded, leaning back on his chair.

'OK, so quick and dirty, the profiler's job is to try and understand why a criminal is acting the way he is, what makes him tick, what drives him. Profilers try to think and act just like the offender would.'

'Well, I figured that much out.'

'OK. So if the profiler can manage to think like a criminal, then he might have a chance of predicting the criminal's next move, but the only way he can do that is by deeply immersing himself in what he thinks the criminal's life is like.' He paused for a swig of his beer. 'Disregarding the first theory because if being evil is something like a disease, there's nothing we can do about that. There's no way we can go back in time to reproduce an offender's aggressive or abusive childhood either, so the only thing left is the offender's present life, and here comes step one of profiling. We take a guess at what his life might be like. Where he'd live, places he'd go, things he'd do.'

'A guess?' Garcia looked incredulous.

'That's all profiling is, nothing but our best guess based on the facts and evidence found at the crime scene. The problem is that when we walk in the footsteps of such deranged criminals for long enough, acting like they do, thinking like they do, immersing ourselves so deep in such dark minds, that unavoidably leaves scars . . . mental scars, and sometimes the profiler loses track of the line.'

'What line?'

'The line that keeps us from becoming like them.' Hunter looked away for a moment. When he spoke again his voice was sad. 'There have been cases . . . profilers that have worked in investigations of sadistic sexual offenders becoming obsessed with sadistic sex themselves, or going the opposite way, becoming sexually inadequate. The simple thought of sex being enough to make them sick. Others that have worked brutal murder cases have become violent and abusive. Some have gone as far as committing brutal crimes themselves. The human brain is still pretty much a mystery, and if we abuse it for long enough . . .' Hunter didn't need to finish the sentence. 'So I chose to abuse my brain in a different way, by becoming a Homicide detective.' He smiled and finished the rest of his beer.

'Yeah, and that is some abuse.' They both laughed.

A mile from Rusty's Surf Ranch a well-dressed man checked his reflection against the full-size mirror in the entrance lobby of the Belvedere restaurant. He was wearing a tailored Italian suit, freshly polished shoes, and his blond wig suited him perfectly. His contact lenses gave his eyes an unusual shade of green.

From where he was standing he could see her sitting at the bar, a glass of red wine in her hand. She looked beautiful in her little black dress.

Was she nervous or excited? He couldn't really tell.

All that time at the supermarket, all those months he'd been working her, feeding her lies, getting her to trust him. Tonight his lies would pay off. They always did.

'Hello, sir, are you here to meet someone or will you be having dinner by yourself this evening?'

In silence he stared at the maître d' for a few seconds.

'Sir?'

He glanced at her once again. He knew she'd be perfect.

'Sir?'

'Yes, I'm meeting a friend. That lady by the bar,' he finally replied with a pleasant smile.

'Very well, sir, please follow me.'

Forty-Five

Friday night at the Vanguard Club produced a lively mix of people, but tonight the place was busier than usual. Tonight the club was hosting the only Los Angeles appearance of the renowned Dutch DJ – Tiësto.

The club was full to capacity and the main show was due to start at midnight, but everyone was already having a great time. It was a perfect place for what he had in mind. The more people around, the less anyone would notice him.

He'd been growing his beard for six days, just enough to make him look different. He completed his disguise by wearing a trendy cotton baseball cap, a professional-quality wig of pitch-black hair, together with a very colorful designer shirt. His youngish-looking outfit was a far cry from his usual businessman attire with his Italian designer suit and his leather briefcase. But tonight he was no businessman.

Tonight he had only one thing in mind, he had to deliver something. He'd had it for six days and for six days he'd been debating what he should do with it. Businessmen are not best known for being honest, and God only knew he hadn't been the most honest of businessmen, but some things are just plain wrong, even for him. He had to do something about it.

He stood in a corner on the opposite side of the VIP area observing the vibrant crowd, his eyes sailing the dance floor, searching for anyone that could recognize him – he saw no one. He placed his hand inside his trouser pocket and ran his fingers over the object inside. Immediately a cold tingle started at the base of his back and ran up through his spine all the way to the back of his neck. He quickly moved his hand away.

'Hey, man, do you need something?'

A young, dark-haired kid, no older than twenty-three, stood in front of him. He squinted his eyes as if trying to see better. 'What?'

'You know, man, it's a rave . . . are you looking for a trip?'

'Oh no, I'm good,' he replied, finally understanding what the kid meant.

'You better get it now, man, before the show starts,' the kid said, flicking his head towards the stage, his dark hair flipping around just like in a shampoo commercial.

'No . . . really, I'm fine.'

'If you change your mind, I'll be around.' The kid made a small circular movement with his finger before moving away.

He had another sip of his Jack Daniel's and Coke and scratched his itchy beard.

The music came to a halt and the lights and lasers went into overdrive on the dance floor. Gusts of smoke coming from the high ceiling filled the place up with a colorful haze. The crowd jumped and screamed and applauded. They were ready to welcome tonight's special guest.

This was his chance. Everyone's attention would be on the stage, no one would notice a person dropping a small packet over at the bar. He left his drink behind and quickly squeezed his way through the thirsty customers to position himself against the wall on the far right end of the nearest bar. Even the barmen had stopped serving for a few seconds.

'Ladies and gentlemen, this is what you've been waiting for.

Get your dancing shoes on and prepare to party. The Vanguard Club is proud to present, on his only appearance in Los Angeles, one of the biggest names in house music in the world . . . Tiësto.'

The crowd went berserk. The colored lasers switched their aim towards the stage.

He quickly pulled the small squared packet out of his pocket, leaned forward and dropped it. As the packet hit the floor, he rapidly moved away glad to have finally disposed of it. He was sure no one had seen him do it.

Fifteen minutes later, the second barman finally came across the package. As he rushed to one end of the bar to serve a very loud customer he felt something uneven under his feet. Looking down he noticed the square wrap. He bent over and picked it up.

'Yo, Pietro!' the barman called.

Pietro finished serving two attractive young girls and walked over to the other end of the bar.

'Is this yours?'

Pietro took the small packet from Todd's hands and stared at it with intrigued eyes. 'Where did you get this?'

'I found it on the floor, just there.' He pointed to a spot at the far end of the bar.

'Did you see who dropped it?'

'No, man. It could've been there for a while. I only saw it because I stepped on it.'

Pietro analyzed the tightly wrapped pack in his hand. He couldn't tell what it was, but the inscription on it left no doubt who the owner should be – 'TO D-KING.'

Forty-Six

He climbed up the steps to the VIP area wondering why it was left up to him to play mailman. The area was swarming with B-list celebrities. Pietro maneuvered his way around the noisy crowd towards the last table on the right – D-King's table. Jerome, who was standing just a few feet in front of his boss, had already spotted the long-haired barman.

'Is there a problem?'

'Somebody left this at the bar,' Pietro said, handing the squared packet to the ex-boxer who looked it over with questioning eyes.

'Wait here.'

Pietro watched as the muscle-bound man walked over to the table behind him, bent over and whispered something to his boss while handing him the small packet. A few seconds later he was given a signal to come closer. He knew he had no reason to feel nervous, but he could feel his chest tightening around his heart.

'Where did you get this?' D-King asked without getting up.

'At the bar. Somebody left it there.'

'So somebody just left this over at the bar and walked away or did he hand it to you?'

'Neither, somebody dropped it over the counter onto the bar floor. Todd, the other barman, found it.'

'And he didn't see who dropped it?'

'He said he didn't.'

'When was that, when did he find this?'

'About five minutes ago. He gave it to me and I brought it straight over, but it could've been there for a while. We're really busy over at the bar and Todd said he'd only noticed it because he'd stepped on it.'

D-King studied the man in front of him for a few seconds. 'OK,' he said and made a hand movement dismissing the barman.

'Can I open it, babe, I love opening presents?' asked one of the three girls sitting at the table.

'Sure, here you go.'

She quickly ripped the packet open, her excited smile rapidly fading away as the contents were revealed. 'It's a disk?' she said unimpressed.

'What the hell?' D-King took the case from her hands, flipped it over and studied it for a few more seconds. 'It's a DVD,' he said, uninterested.

'Too bad, I was hoping for diamonds,' another one of the girls commented.

'There's something inside the wrapper,' Jerome said, noticing a small, white note stuck to the discarded wrapping paper. D-King reached for it and read it in silence.

I'm sorry.

'What does it say, babe?'

'Why don't you three go dance,' D-King commanded. 'Come back in twenty minutes or something.'

They knew that wasn't a request. Silently, all three stunning-looking girls left the VIP area quickly disappearing into the dancing crowd.

'We have a DVD player in the limo, don't we?' D-King asked, now sounding a little more curious.

'Uh-huh,' Jerome nodded.

'Let's go take a look at this now.'

'Sure boss.' Jerome immediately retrieved his cell phone from his dark Tallia suit. 'Warren, bring the car around back . . . No, we're not leaving just yet, we just need to check something out.'

Cars were something D-King enjoyed and he made no secret of it. His extensive private collection included models such as a Ford GT, a Ferrari 430 spider, an Aston Martin Vanquish S and his newest addition – a twelve-passenger Hummer limousine.

Within five minutes they'd met Warren around the back of the Vanguard Club.

'Is anything the matter, boss?' Warren asked, standing next to the open back door of the thirty-eight-feet-long vehicle.

'No, everything is cool. We just gotta have a look at something.' D-King and Jerome jumped into the back of the limo and waited until Warren had closed the door on them.

A small panel next to the main seat hosted an array of buttons and faders giving its occupant total control over everything: different light settings and colors, sound and speaker configuration, access to the state-of-the-art high-definition DVD system and to the hidden compartment containing a small arsenal of weapons.

D-King placed himself comfortably on the main seat and quickly pressed a button. To his right, the front of a wooden cabinet slid open revealing a slimline DVD player. Without hesitation he placed the disk in it. The front panel that divided the driver's cabin from the rest of the car glided shut and a colossal screen extending the width of the vehicle rolled down from its ceiling. The entire operation took less than ten seconds.

Low-quality images filled the screen and for a minute Jerome struggled to understand what was going on.

In a dirty and derelict square room a blindfolded and gagged young woman had been tied to a metal chair. Her body half exposed through her ripped clothes.

'What the fuck's this?' Jerome asked, still looking confused.

'Hold on, nigga,' D-King replied as he reached for the fast-forward button. The images danced frantically on the screen for a few seconds before he released the button allowing the film to resume play. They both watched in silence for a while longer as the frightened young girl was being physically, verbally and sexually abused.

'This is sick, boss. Somebody's playing a practical joke on you,' Jerome said, turning his face away from the screen and getting ready to leave the luxurious car.

'Wait a second.' D-King stopped his bodyguard before he had a chance to open the door. Something wasn't right, D-King could feel it. He reached for the fast-forward button once again allowing the disk to skip ahead several minutes. When he resumed play the movie carried on showing more violence and abuse.

'Ah damn. Turn it off, boss, it's making me feel ill,' Jerome pleaded.

D-King raised his hand signaling Jerome to be quiet for a second. He advanced the film one more time stopping it just short of the last scene.

As the two other mysterious characters in the film positioned themselves for the film's climax, D-King realized what was about to happen. Jerome still looked clueless to what was really going on, but his attention was still on the screen. They both watched as her blindfold was torn away from her face.

'What the fuck!' Jerome yelled, jerking backwards. The camera focused on the girl's face. 'That's Jenny.' His voice half stating the obvious, half asking a question.

D-King had realized who the girl was a full minute before Jerome did. His anger oozed through every pore in his body. They observed in morbid silence as the knife sliced through her neck like a Bushido sword through rice paper. The camera zoomed in on her helpless and dying eyes and then on the blood spilling from the fatal wound on her neck.

'What the hell is going on, boss?' Jerome's voice was an excited shout.

D-King remained silent until the DVD reached its end. When he spoke, his voice was ice cold. 'What do you think is going on, Jerome? We just saw how they tortured and killed Jenny.'

'But that's wrong. The detectives said that she had no bullet or knife wounds, that she'd been skinned alive. We just saw someone slice her neck open.'

'The detectives said the girl on the picture they showed us had been skinned alive. We thought that girl was Jenny. We were wrong.'

Jerome brought both hands to his face. 'This is fucked up, boss.'

'Listen to me.' D-King snapped his fingers twice to get Jerome's attention back to him. 'The fucking gloves are off. I want those two in the video,' he said with so much rage it made Jerome shiver. 'I want the sonofabitch behind the camera, I want whoever owns that shithole of a place and I want the person responsible for that whole motherfucking operation, do you hear me?'

'I hear you, boss,' Jerome said regaining his composure.

'Don't get the word out on the streets. I don't want to scare these fucks away. Use only reliable people. I want them fast and I want them alive if possible. It doesn't matter who you pay. It doesn't matter how much you pay. It doesn't matter what it takes.'

'How about the cops?' Jerome asked. 'I think we should tell them that the girl on the photo is not Jenny.'

D-King pondered the idea for an instant. 'You're right, but I wanna get these guys first. After that, I'll get in touch with them.'

Forty-Seven

It'd been several days and their bar and club search hadn't produced any results yet. They'd covered Santa Monica in its entirety and had moved to the bars and clubs in Long Beach, but the response had been the same everywhere. The rest of their investigation was also moving at no pace. Just like the original Crucifix killings they were yet to establish any definite links between the victims. There was the possibility Jenny and George knew each other from one of the sex parties they'd attended, but they still hadn't managed to positively identify their first victim. No one could confirm the faceless woman's body was indeed Jenny Farnborough's. Carlos was yet to find her family in Idaho or Utah. Assumption was the only thing they had to go on and Captain Bolter hated assumptions. He wanted facts.

With every resultless day that went by they knew they were a day closer to receiving another phone call – another victim. Everybody's patience was wearing thin, including the Chief of Police. He demanded results from Captain Bolter who, in turn, demanded results from his two detectives.

The investigation was slowly consuming everyone. Garcia had barely seen Anna in the past few days. Hunter had spoken to Isabella over the phone a couple of times, but he had no time for romantic meetings. Time was wearing thin and they knew it.

Hunter arrived early at the RHD to once again find Garcia already at his desk.

'We've got some news,' Garcia said the instant Hunter walked through the door.

'Make me smile, tell me that someone has recognized our sketched suspect.'

'Well, it's good news, but not that good,' Garcia said a little less excited.

'OK then, tell me?'

'Doctor Winston just sent me the result of the DNA test from the hair strand found in George Slater's car.'

'Finally, and?'

'No DNA could be obtained from the hair as it had no skin follicles.'

'So the hair didn't fall naturally. It's been cut instead of being pulled out.'

'That's correct.'

'So we've got nothing?' Hunter's asked, unimpressed.

'No, no, there were chemicals on the hair and that allowed the lab to find out where it came from.'

'And?'

'It's European hair.'

'From a wig?' Hunter's eyes widened in surprise.

'How do you know European hair is wig hair?'

'I read a lot.'

'Oh that's right. I forgot about that,' Garcia said with a cynical nod. 'So disregarding synthetic hair wigs, the three best types of wigs you can buy are: real hair, human hair and European hair. In the wig-making industry, real hair and human hair refer to Asian hair which has been processed, bleached from its original color and then dyed to match European hair colors. This process damages the hair, but it's very readily available and inexpensive. But European hair . . .' Garcia shook his head '. . . is almost unprocessed hair. It comes mainly from Eastern Europe. No hair dyeing is used although it's coated with a high-grade conditioner for longevity. It's the closest to naturally grown hair you can get.'

'But that comes at a price,' Hunter concluded.

'Get a load of this – prices start at a mere four thousand dollars.'

'Phew,' Hunter whistled as he sat down.

'Exactly. These wigs are made to order. It can take anywhere between one to two months for them to be ready and that means that whoever ordered it has to leave an address or a contact number.' Garcia smiled enthusiastically. 'There can't be that many places in Los Angeles that sell European hair wigs.'

'Catherine?'

'What?'

'Have you checked with Catherine Slater? Maybe she wears wigs. A lot of women do these days. She could definitely afford them.'

'No, not yet.' Garcia's enthusiasm was half damped. 'I'll get on it straight away, but if she doesn't wear wigs, don't you think it's worth getting in touch with all wigmakers in LA that sell European hair wigs?'

Hunter scratched his chin. 'Yeah, we can give it a try. I just think our killer is too smart for that.'

'Too smart for what?'

'You said these wigs are made to order?'

'Correct.'

'But I bet if you walk into a wigmaker they would have one or two on display, like a showcase. Our killer wouldn't be stupid enough to order a wig and leave behind a paper trail. He would simply take whatever the wigmaker had on display, pay cash for it and that would be that. Remember, the killer isn't buying the wig for its looks, so any one would do.' Hunter got up and walked over to the coffee machine. 'There's one more thing.'

'What's that?'

'The internet,' Hunter said.

Garcia frowned.

'The internet can help us and hinder us at the same time,' Hunter explained. 'Maybe a few years ago it would've been a case of us checking the wigmakers and with just a little luck we would've come across something that could lead us to our killer, but today . . .' He poured himself a cup of coffee. 'Today the killer could order it over the internet from any country in the world and the wig would be with him in less than a week. He could've bought it from Japan or Australia or directly from Eastern Europe.' He paused, another thought entering his mind. 'And then we have eBay, where the killer could've bought it from a private owner and no one would ever know. This guy is too smart to leave a paper trail behind.'

Garcia had to admit Hunter had a point. Any half-clever person could buy almost anything over the internet these days and leave such a minuscule trail it would be almost impossible to trace it. It's just a case of knowing where to shop.

'We might get lucky, he might've taken us for granted and ordered a wig from a shop,' Garcia said positively.

'Maybe. I'm not discarding any possibilities. We'll check with all wigmakers just in case.'

'I just wanted to get at least one step closer to him before he adds another photograph to that damn board,' Garcia said, pointing to the corkboard and drawing Hunter's attention to it.

Hunter stood motionless for a while, his eyes fixed on the photographs.

'Are you OK?' Garcia asked after a minute of silence. 'You're not blinking.'

Hunter lifted his hand asking Garcia to wait a second. 'We're missing something there,' he finally said.

Garcia turned and faced the board. All the pictures were there. Nothing had been moved, he was sure of it.

'What are we missing?'

'Another victim.'

Forty-Eight

'What the hell are you talking about? What do you mean, we're missing a victim? They are all there, seven from the first killing spree and two since he started killing again.' Garcia's eyes moved from the photograph board to Hunter.

'We have a victim he didn't mark, no double-crucifix on the back of the neck, no phone call to me. We have a victim he didn't kill.'

'A victim he didn't kill? Are you high? That doesn't even make sense.'

'Of course it does. He didn't kill him as he's done with all his other victims . . . he got him killed.'

'Are you listening to yourself, crazy man? Who didn't he kill?'

Hunter's gaze fell on Garcia. 'Mike Farloe.'

'Mike Farloe?' Garcia looked mystified.

'The real killer framed him as the Crucifix Killer, remember? I've even mentioned it before, over the phone when the killer called me right after we found the faceless woman, but for some reason it didn't click.'

'I remember you saying it, yes. I was standing right next to you.'

'Framing him makes Mike Farloe a victim.'

'By default,' Garcia accepted it.

'That doesn't matter, he's still a victim.' Hunter walked back to his desk and started shuffling through pieces of paper. 'OK, what do we know about our killer?'

'Nothing,' Garcia replied with a half chuckle.

'That's not true. We know he's very methodical, intelligent, pragmatic and he chooses his victims very, very carefully.'

'OK,' Garcia said still unsure.

'The killer didn't just pick Mike Farloe out of the blue. Just like his victims, the subject had to fit a specific profile. The difference here is that the subject had to fit the profile of a killer. To be precise, the profile of a sadistic, religious serial killer.'

Garcia started to pick up on Hunter's theory. 'Meaning that if you had arrested someone who didn't fit that profile you would've discarded him as the killer?'

'Correct. The killer is smart but he also knows we're not stupid. We wouldn't just fall for the first person he decided to frame. It had to be the right person. Someone believable. Someone that we'd buy. Mike Farloe was the perfect choice.'

Garcia ran both of his hands through his hair pulling it back and making a small ponytail. 'Did Mike have a criminal record?'

'Fuck yeah. In and out of Juvi halls . . . Three county convictions for public nudity. He loved exposing himself to schoolkids.'

'Pedophile?' Garcia asked with a twist of his mouth.

'With a capital P. He did twenty-eight months for fondling a twelve-year-old boy in a lavatory downtown.'

Garcia shook his head.

'And where do you find a person like Mike Farloe?' Hunter proceeded.

'Maybe the killer knew him from before,' Garcia offered.

'Possible, but I doubt it. Mike was a loner, lived alone, no wife, no girlfriend, no kids. He worked as a garbage collector and spent most of his free time locked inside his little dirty apartment reading the Bible. The guy didn't have much of a life.'

'How about a medical record? Our killer could have access to medical records. One thing we do know is that he has medical knowledge, even Doctor Winston said he wouldn't be surprised if the killer turned out to be a surgeon.'

Hunter nodded. 'I was thinking exactly that.'

'Religious cults, churches? If Mike attended any, the killer could've singled him out there.'

'We'll check that out too.'

'What else do we know about Mike Farloe?' Garcia asked.

'Not much. There was no reason to investigate him any further, he confessed remember.'

'Yes I do, and that brings me to my first why. Why the hell did he confess? Why would he confess to such heinous crimes if he didn't commit them and he knew he'd get death?'

'To end his life with something,' Hunter said decisively.

'Excuse me?'

'You've heard about people that don't have the guts to commit suicide, so instead they buy a gun and walk down the street waving it about. The police arrive, tell the person to put the gun down, the person waves it about a little more and the police shoot him dead.'

'Yes, I've heard of suicide by cop.'

'Correct. This follows the same theory. As I've said Mike was a loner, no friends, not much of a life and no prospect of getting a better one either. He obviously knew about the Crucifix Killer.'

'Everyone knew about the Crucifix Killer, the press made sure of it.'

'Right, so you won't be surprised to know that there were some religiously fanatical people out there that actually thought the Crucifix Killer was doing the right thing. Killing sinners.'

'And Mike was one of them,' Garcia completed Hunter's sentence.

'He probably ran the fan club.'

Garcia laughed.

'Anyway, to these people the Crucifix Killer was a hero, someone doing God's work, and suddenly Mike was handed the opportunity to become his hero.'

'You mean take the rap for his hero?'

'It makes no difference. To the rest of the world Mike Farloe's name would become synonymous with the Crucifix Killer. He'd leave his life of obscurity behind. His name would be mentioned in books and studied in criminology classes. He would in death have the fame he never had when living.'

'But you said Mike knew certain things about the victims that probably only the killer would know . . . like the reasons for killing them. He'd mentioned things like one of the victims fucking her way to the top of her company. How would he know that?'

'Because the killer told him,' Hunter concluded.

'What?'

'Just think about it. You're the killer right, and you want to frame someone for what you've done. You finally find the right person. You befriend him.'

'Something that wouldn't be very hard to do since Mike had no friends.'

'That's right. Most of your conversations would revolve around the Crucifix Killings. How great a job the killer is doing in ridding the world of sinners or what have you. Now you start filling Mike's head up with rumors. "*I've heard that one of the victims was a diseased prostitute . . . another had sex with everyone in her company just to get to the top.*" Hunter put on a different voice pretending to be the killer.

'Preparing him for when he got caught,' Garcia cut in.

Hunter bit his bottom lip and nodded.

'But why not tell him about the real Crucifix Killer's carvings to the back of the neck.'

'Because no one knew about it except the real killer and a handful of people that were working the case. Telling Mike Farloe about the real symbol would've made him instantly suspicious. Mike was fucked up, not stupid.'

'Meaning he would've thought the person telling him about it was the real killer?'

'Possible but not probable. Mike would've thought the guy was full of shit.'

'Why?'

'How do you think Mike got to know about the Crucifix Killer in the first place?'

'Through the papers and the press.'

'Exactly. Mike probably read and watched everything about the Crucifix Killer the media threw at him. And he believed every word of it. People are very impressionable. Telling Mike that what he read and believed was a load of crap would've pushed him away, not gain his confidence. Who do you think your normal street man would believe, the papers and TV or a complete stranger?'

Garcia thought about it for a moment. 'You've got a point.'

Hunter nodded. 'The killer knew what he needed to do to gain Mike's confidence.'

'Do you think the killer was counting on Mike confessing?'

'Maybe, I'm not sure.'

'He had nothing to lose,' Garcia concluded, but still looked bothered by something. 'But why?'

Hunter threw him an alarmed look. 'Have you been listening to what I've said? I've just explained to you why.'

'No, why frame Mike?'

Hunter paused and stared at his cup of coffee. 'That was about to be my next question. What are the reasons for framing somebody?'

'Revenge?'

'Not in real life.'

'Huh?'

'Framing someone for revenge only happens in Hollywood movies. In real life people skip through all the bullshit, go directly to the source and pop them a head hole. Why go through all the trouble of planning a frame? Plus Mike died by lethal injection, not a lot of suffering. If our killer wanted him to suffer, he would've taken care of Mike himself.'

Garcia nodded in agreement. 'That's true.'

'So why else would you frame someone?'

'Maybe he wanted the police investigation to end.'

'Possible.'

'Perhaps his initial intention was to commit only seven murders.' Garcia turned to pour himself a glass of water. 'After the killer achieved what he set out to achieve, why keep the investigation open and risk some cop bumping into some evidence that could lead to him a few years down the line? Frame somebody, the case gets closed and he's scot-free.'

'So now the killer changed his mind and is back to commit another seven?'

Garcia cocked an eyebrow. 'He could be.'

'I don't buy that. This killer had an agenda set from the word go and I'm sure he's sticking to it. Whenever he's finished doing what he's set out to do, if we haven't caught up with him by then, he'll disappear and we'll never hear from him again.' Hunter's voice sounded somber.

'When Mike was arrested, did you have another suspect, someone you were investigating?' Garcia said, breaking the silence.

Hunter shook his head.

'You weren't getting closer to anyone or anything?'

'I've told you this before, we had nothing, no suspects, no leads – but I know what you're getting at. If we were getting closer to someone, especially if we were getting closer to the right someone, framing Mike would've thrown us off course.'

'Uh-huh! It would've put a stop to the investigation. Why carry on investigating when you have a suspect with such overwhelming incriminating evidence?'

'Well, we didn't have any suspects.'

'But the killer didn't know that. Unless he had some inside information from the police.'

'Very few people had that information and they're all trustworthy.'

'OK, so maybe you did dig into something that hit pretty close to home with the killer.'

A muscle flexed on Hunter's jaw. 'We weren't digging anything. The only thing we had was seven victims and a lot of frustration,' Hunter said, staring out the window, his gaze distant. 'But we'll go though the files again . . . two months prior to Mike's arrest. Let's check what we had then.'

'There's one more possibility,' Garcia said, flipping through some papers on his desk.

'And what's that?'

'How long between Mike Farloe's arrest and the first victim this time around?'

'About a year and a half?'

'What if the killer framed Mike because he knew he'd be out of action for a certain amount of time? Like if the killer had been in prison for some other minor charge.'

Hunter sat back on his chair and crossed his arms in front of his chest. 'The problem here is that he had to know in advance he'd be out of action for so long. Framing someone takes time and as we've said before, he had to find the right person first. You don't get that much warning before being arrested. But . . .' Hunter shook his right index finger in Garcia's direction.

'What?'

'An operation,' Hunter said cocking both eyebrows. 'The killer could've had some sort of operation scheduled. He would've known that well in advance.'

'But the killer was out of action for over a year. What sort of operation puts you on the sidelines for that long?'

'That's easy. Back operation, hip operation, any operation that would require the patient to go through physiotherapy to regain movement and strength. Our killer needs all his strength to commit these murders. He wouldn't have struck again if he wasn't one hundred percent fit. We'd better make a list of hospitals and physiotherapy clinics.'

Garcia was already typing his first search into his keyboard.

Forty-Nine

They spent the rest of the day digging into Mike Farloe's life. His criminal record was long, but not vicious: convictions for indecent exposure, non-violent sexual assault and pedophilia. He was a scumbag, Hunter thought, but not a violent scumbag. In his last spell in prison he found God and upon his release he started wandering the streets preaching the gospel to those who'd listen and those who wouldn't.

Mike's medical records showed nothing out of the ordinary. A few treatments for venereal disease and broken bones from street beatings but that was all. He had no psychological history and nothing stood out. They concluded the killer couldn't have picked Mike based on his medical or criminal record. They were still looking into any religious cults that Mike might've been involved with, but by eleven-thirty in the evening they still hadn't come up with anything.

Garcia quickly checked his watch as he parked his car in front of his apartment building. 'Past midnight once again.' In the past two weeks not once had he managed to get home before the early hours of the morning. He knew there was nothing he could do. That's what the job demanded and he was certainly prepared to give it. The same couldn't be said about Anna.

He sat in the darkness of the parking lot for a while. From his car he stared at the window of his first-floor apartment. The lights were still on in his living room. Anna was still awake.

He'd told her not to worry, that the case they'd been working on was a complex one and he had to put a lot of extra hours into it, but he knew she wouldn't listen. He knew she'd rather he'd been a lawyer or a doctor; anything really but a Homicide detective in Los Angeles.

He slowly made his way past the other cars on the lot, to the building and up to his apartment. Even though he was sure Anna wouldn't be asleep, he opened his front door as carefully as he could. Anna was lying on the blue fabric sofa that faced the TV set on the east wall. She was wearing a thin, white nightgown and her hair was flattened on one side. Her eyes were closed, but she opened them as Garcia took his first steps into the apartment.

'Hi there, honey,' he said in a tired voice.

She sat up, crossing her legs underneath her. Her husband looked different. Every night when he came back home to her he looked a little older, more tired. He'd only been with the RHD less than a month, but in Anna's eyes it seemed like years.

'How are you, babe?' she said softly.

'I'm OK . . . tired though.'

'Are you hungry? Did you eat? There's food in the fridge. You've gotta eat something,' she insisted.

Garcia didn't feel hungry. In fact his appetite had been non-existent since he walked into that old wooden house a few weeks ago, but he didn't want to say no to Anna. 'Yeah, I could eat a little.'

They both walked into the kitchen. Garcia took a seat at the small breakfast table while Anna retrieved a plate from the fridge and placed it into the microwave.

'Do you wanna beer?' she asked, going back to the fridge.

'Actually, a single malt would do me better.'

'It won't go with the food. Have a beer now and if you still want one later . . .'

She passed him an open bottle of Bud and sat across from him. The silence was broken by the microwave bell announcing his late supper was ready.

Anna had cooked one of Garcia's favorite dishes – rice, Brazilian beans, chicken and vegetables, but Garcia had only managed about three spoonfuls before he started rearranging the food around on the plate without ever bringing it to his mouth again.

'Is there something wrong with the chicken?'

'No, babe. You know I love your cooking. I'm just not as hungry as I thought I was.'

Without any warning Anna buried her head in her hands and started crying.

Garcia quickly moved towards her and kneeled in front of her chair. 'Anna, what's wrong?' He tried lifting her head from her hands.

It took her a few more seconds before she finally looked at him with eyes full of tears and sadness. 'I'm scared.'

'Scared? Scared of what?' he asked concerned.

'Of what this new job of yours is doing to you . . . what it's doing to us.'

'What do you mean?'

'Look at you. You haven't slept properly in weeks. On the rare occasions when you do fall asleep it's only a matter of minutes before you wake up in a cold sweat almost screaming. You haven't been eating. You've lost so much weight you look ill, and me . . . you don't even look at me anymore, never mind talk to me.'

'I'm sorry, babe. You know I can't talk to you about the cases I work on.' He tried to hug her, but she pulled away.

'I don't want you to tell me the details of your investigation, but you have become a ghost around here. I never see you anymore. We never do anything together anymore. Even little things like having a meal together have become a luxury. You leave before the sun is out and you only come back at this godforsaken time. Every day I watch you come through that door looking like you've left a little bit of your life out there. We're becoming strangers to each other. What will happen six months or a year down the line?' she asked, wiping the tears from her cheeks.

An overwhelming sense of protectiveness rushed through Garcia. He wanted to take her in his arms and reassure her, but the truth was he also felt scared. Not for himself, but for everyone else. There was a killer out there that took pleasure in inflicting as much pain as the victim could possibly take. A killer that made no distinction of race, religion, social class or anything else for that matter. Anyone could be the next victim, anyone including Anna. He felt helpless.

'Please don't cry babe, everything will be OK,' he said, softly touching Anna's hair. 'We're making progress on the investigation and with just a bit of luck we'll be closing the case very soon.' Garcia wasn't sure if he believed it himself.

'I'm sorry,' she said still tearful. 'But no other case you've worked on has affected you this way.'

Garcia didn't know what to say.

'I'm scared of what this job may do to you. I don't wanna lose you.' Tears filled her eyes once again.

'You're not gonna lose me, babe. I love you.' He kissed her cheek and wiped away the rest of her tears. 'I promise you everything will be fine.'

Anna wanted to believe him, but she saw no conviction in his eyes.

'C'mon, let's go to bed,' he said helping her up.

They both stood up slowly. She hugged him and they kissed. 'Let me get the lights in the living room,' she said.

'OK, I'll get the dishes into the dishwasher.' Garcia cleared his plate and quickly ran it under the tap.

'Jesus Christ!' Anna's cry came from the living room.

Garcia left his plate on top of the dishwasher and dashed out of the kitchen. 'What's wrong?' he said, approaching Anna who was standing by the window.

'There was somebody down there staring at me.'

'What? Where?' Garcia said, staring out the window at an empty street and parking lot.

'Down there, just between those two cars,' she pointed at two vehicles parked halfway down the street.

Garcia looked out the window again. 'I can't see anything, plus it's quite dark down there. Are you sure you saw someone?'

'Yes. I saw someone staring straight at me.'

'Are you sure?'

'Yes. He was looking up at me.'

'He? It was a he?'

'I'm not sure. I think so.'

'Maybe it was a cat or something.'

'It was no cat, Carlos. Someone was staring into our apartment.' Anna's voice was less steady now.

'Into our apartment? Maybe the person was just looking up at the building.'

'He was looking straight at me, I know it, I felt it, it scared me.'

'Maybe it was just one of the neighborhood kids. You know they're always out and about until the early hours.'

'The neighborhood kids don't freak me out like that.' Her eyes became tearful once again.

'OK, do you want me to go downstairs and have a look around?'

'No . . . please stay with me.'

Garcia hugged her and felt her body shivering against his. 'I'm here, babe. You're just tired and upset, I'm sure it was nothing. C'mon, let's go to bed.'

From the parking lot, hidden in the shadows, the stranger watched with an evil smile as they hugged and moved away from the window.

Fifty

They had divided their tasks. Garcia was to go over Hunter and Scott's initial investigation files, going back three months prior to Mike Farloe's arrest. He was also in charge of checking with the wigmakers and physiotherapy clinics.

Hunter took over the hospital search. He thought about contacting them and requesting a list of patients who'd had an operation anywhere up to two months after Mike Farloe's arrest. An operation that would've required a long recuperation period, especially physiotherapy. Through experience he knew that putting in a request, no matter how urgent it was, would still take weeks. To speed up the process he decided to check the hospitals in the downtown Los Angeles area himself and place a request for the remaining ones.

The task was laborious and slow. They first needed to narrow it down to what sort of operation would require such a lengthy recovery period and then go back almost a year and a half to find the records.

Hunter wasn't surprised to find that the archiving of records in hospitals was bordering on comical. Part stored in drawers in some stuffy and crammed archive room. Part stored in disorganized spreadsheets and part stored in databases that very few people knew how to access. Not that far away from the archiving of files by the RHD, he thought.

He'd been at it since eight-thirty that morning. At midday the temperature hit 98 degrees and the badly ventilated rooms made Hunter's task seem like penitence. By the end of the afternoon his shirt was drenched and he'd only managed to cover three hospitals.

'Have you been swimming?' Garcia asked, frowning at Hunter's wet shirt as he got back to the office.

'Try being locked in stuffy, pathetically small rooms in the basement of hospitals for a few hours and see how you like it,' Hunter shot back unamused.

'If you got rid of that jacket it would probably help. How did you get along anyway?'

Hunter waved a brown envelope at Garcia. 'Patients' lists for three hospitals. Not much but it's a start.'

'And what's that?' Garcia pointed to the box Hunter had under his left arm.

'Oh, it's just a pair of shoes,' he said matter-of-factly.

'Big spender, are we?'

'That's the thing. I saw these in the window of a shop close to one of the hospitals. They are closing down in a week so everything is at *giveaway* prices. I got them for a bargain.'

'Really? Can I have a look?' Garcia asked, being curious.

'Sure.' Hunter handed him the box.

'Wow, they are nice,' Garcia said, after taking both black-leather shoes from the box and looking at them from every angle. 'And God knows you need new ones,' he said, pointing to Hunter's old shoes.

'I've gotta wear them in though. The leather is quite stiff.'

'With the amount of walking we've been doing lately you'll have no problem.' Garcia placed both shoes back inside the box and handed it to Hunter.

'Anyway, how did you get on?' Hunter brought the subject back to the investigation.

'I've managed to contact Catherine Slater. She doesn't wear wigs.'

'Great. Any luck with the wigmakers then?'

Garcia twisted his mouth and frowned, shaking his head. 'If we wanna get a list of clients that have ordered European hair wigs from any of the wigmakers in LA we're gonna need a warrant.'

'A warrant?'

'They won't disclose their list of clients. The excuse is always the same . . . clients' privacy. Their clients wouldn't appreciate the fact that they wear wigs being advertised to the world.'

'Advertised to the world? We are conducting a murder investigation here, we're not the press. It's not like we're gonna sell the information to the tabloid papers.' Hunter snapped.

'It doesn't matter. If we don't get a warrant we'll get no clients' list.'

Hunter dropped the envelope on his desk, placed his jacket on the back of his chair and walked over to one of the fans.

'I can't believe these people. We're trying to help them, we're trying to catch a sadistic killer whose next victim could be someone in their family or themselves, but instead of cooperation what do we get? Fucking hostility and reluctance. It's like we're the bad guys. As soon as we say we're cops it's like we just punched them in the stomach. All the doors slam shut and on come the security locks,' Hunter said, walking back to his desk. 'I'll talk to Captain Bolter. We'll get this fucking warrant and the list as soon as . . .' Hunter detected an air of doubt about Garcia. 'Something's bothering you.'

'The hair found inside George Slater's car bothers me.'

'Go on,' Hunter urged him.

'Nothing else was found inside the car, right? No finger-prints, no fibers, only a hair strand from a wig?'

'And you're thinking this doesn't sound like our guy, right?' Hunter concluded. 'The killer cleans the entire car as he's done with every crime scene, but leaves a hair behind?'

'He's never screwed up before, why would he screw up now?'

'Maybe it isn't a screw-up.'

Garcia stared at Hunter with uncertainty. 'What are you saying? He wants to be caught now?'

'Not at all. He might just be playing games like he's always done.'

Garcia still looked unsure.

'He knows we can't afford to overlook this. He knows we'll be following this up, checking with every wigmaker in LA, spending time and resources.'

'So you think he might've left the hair behind on purpose?'

Hunter nodded. 'To slow us down. To buy him time to plan his next kill. He's getting closer to his final act,' he said in a quiet voice.

'What do you mean, final act?'

'These killings have some sort of meaning to the killer,' Hunter explained. 'As I've said before, I'm sure this killer has an agenda, and something tells me he's about to complete it.'

'And you believe if we don't catch him before he completes his psycho agenda, we'll never catch him. He'll simply disappear.'

Hunter nodded slowly.

'So let's catch him,' Garcia said, pointing to the brown envelope Hunter had obtained from the hospitals.

Hunter smiled. 'The first thing we gotta do is eliminate anyone under twenty or over fifty years of age from the list.

After that let's try and get a picture of everyone that's left. We might just come up with something.'

'Sure, pass me one of the lists.'

'Have you been through the old investigation files?'

'I'm still on them.'

Hunter looked pensive for a moment.

'What's up?' Garcia asked.

'Something's been bothering me. Maybe the Crucifix Killer did frame Mike Farloe to throw us off course. Maybe he made a mistake and he had to cover it.'

'A mistake?'

'Maybe. It could be something to do with the last victim. The one just before we caught up with Mike Farloe. A young lawyer, I remember that. Do you have her file?'

'It should be here.' Garcia started searching through the files on his desk.

Their conversation was interrupted by Garcia's fax machine's ringtone. He pulled himself closer to his desk and waited for the printout to come through.

'Você tá de sacanagem!' Garcia suddenly said after staring at the received fax for half a minute.

Hunter didn't understand Portuguese but he knew that whatever it meant, it wasn't good.

Fifty-One

Hunter stared at his partner and waited, but Garcia kept his eyes on the fax, still mumbling something in Portuguese. 'What the hell is it?' Hunter shouted impatiently.

Garcia extended his hand displaying a black and white picture of a woman. It took Hunter a few seconds to realize what he was looking at. 'Is that Jenny Farnborough?'

Garcia shook his head. 'No this is Vicki Baker.'

'Who?

'Victoria Baker, age twenty-four, works as a manageress for a gym called 24 Hour Fitness in Santa Monica Boulevard,' Garcia read from the foot of the picture.

'I know that gym,' Hunter cut in.

'Apparently she was supposed to have gone to Canada on the second of July.'

'And did she?'

'It doesn't say.'

'Who sent us this?'

'Logan from the Missing Persons' Department. We still have a flag up on anyone that looks like the computer-generated image we got from Doctor Winston remember?'

Hunter nodded.

Because the first victim hadn't been positively identified yet all protocol measures were still in place and that included constant checks against new entries to the MUPU database.

'When was she reported missing?'

Garcia checked the fax's second page. 'Two days ago.'

'By who?'

Another check. 'Joe Bowman, the head manager of the gym.'

Hunter grabbed the fax from Garcia's hand and studied it for a minute. The resemblance was there, but then again attractive, tall blonds seemed to grow on trees in Los Angeles. Hunter could clearly see how easily Vicki Baker and Jenny Farnborough could both be matched to the original computer-generated image. On their rush to identify the first victim they'd simply assumed Jenny Farnborough was their girl.

'When did Jenny go missing from the Vanguard Club?' Hunter asked.

Garcia flipped through a few pieces of paper he'd taken from his top drawer. 'On the first of July. Vicki went missing one day later.'

'This girl might not have gone missing on the sixth. She might've taken the plane to Canada and gone missing there, or when she got back, we don't know yet. Let's call the gym and check if this Joe Bowman is on duty today. If he is we'll be on our way. The head of Customs at LAX is an old buddy of mine. I'll get him to check if she boarded the plane on the sixth.'

Garcia quickly went back to his computer and with just a few clicks he had the gym's information in front of him. He dialed the number and sat back on his chair waiting impatiently for someone to pick it up at the other end. It took only three rings for Garcia to get an answer. The conversation was restricted to about five sentences.

'He's on now until eleven-thirty tonight,' Garcia said as he replaced the receiver.

'Let's go, you drive. Let me just call Trevor first.'

Trevor Grizbeck was the head of Customs and Immigration for the Los Angeles International Airport – LAX. Hunter knew there was no way he'd get an airline to disclose passengers' information without a warrant, and he didn't have time for one. It was time to call in some favors.

The sun had already set, but the heat seemed almost as intense as in the afternoon. Hunter sat in silence and read Victoria Baker's fax sheets over and over again, but it still looked too surreal. Just as they were arriving at the gym in Santa Monica his thoughts were disrupted by his cell phone.

'Trevor. What have you got for me?'

'Well, as you know I have no access to airline records, but I do have access to Immigration records. Just to be on the safe side I checked from the 1st to the 12th of July. Victoria Baker never cleared passport control.'

'She never boarded the plane.'

'It looks that way.'

'Thanks, bud.'

'Sure, man. Don't be a stranger.'

With his badge in hand Hunter forced his way through the small crowd at the gym's entrance lobby to reach the reception desk.

'Is Joe Bowman the manager here?' he asked even before one of the two receptionists had a chance to check his credentials.

'Yes.' The reply sounded a little shy.

'We need to speak to him.' His voice was demanding.

Both detectives watched as the blond receptionist quickly picked up the phone and dialed the manager's direct line. A quick murmured conversation followed.

'Trish, can you handle it out here by yourself for five minutes?' the blond girl asked, putting the phone down and turning to the other receptionist, a short, red-haired girl with a handful of freckles under each ocean-blue eye.

'Yeah, I'll be alright,' Trish replied with a slight Texan accent.

The blond receptionist pressed a button behind the counter and the light on one of the turnstiles went green. 'Please come through, gentlemen,' she said to both detectives before joining them on the other side. 'Please follow me.'

The manager's office was at the far end of the packed main gym floor. The receptionist knocked three times and as the door opened they were greeted by a striking-looking African American man, about two inches taller than Hunter and at least twenty pounds heavier, all of it muscle. He was wearing a black, skintight T-shirt that seemed to be two sizes smaller than he needed and his crew-cut hairstyle made him look like an army sergeant. He introduced himself as Joe Bowman.

'This is about Vicki I presume,' he said, showing both detectives into the room.

'That's correct,' Hunter said as they occupied the two leather chairs facing an attractive black and white desk. Joe sat behind it.

Hunter studied the man behind the desk for a quick second. 'You look familiar, have we met before?' he asked, squinting as if searching his memory.

Bowman stared at Hunter for a moment. 'I don't think so, not that I can remember anyway.'

Hunter dismissed the thought after a few seconds with a quick shrug of his shoulders. 'You were the one who reported Victoria Baker missing, is that right?' he asked.

'Yes.'

'And why was that?'

Bowman looked up from his hands with a dubious smile.

'Because she's gone missing.' He pronounced every word slower than normal.

Wise-ass, Hunter thought. 'What I mean is why you? Are you her husband, boyfriend, lover?'

Bowman's eyes moved to the receptionist who was still standing by the door. 'That will be all, Carey. I'll take it from here.'

In silence she stepped out of the room and closed the door behind her.

His attention came back to the detectives. 'I'm not her husband, boyfriend or lover. I'm married.' He made a head movement towards a picture on his desk of a woman with short black hair and a contagious smile.

Hunter acknowledged the photograph but the sorrow in Bowman's eyes betrayed him.

'She was supposed to be back at work on the twenty-sixth, but she never showed up. That's very unlike her. She's a very responsible person, very professional, never takes sick days or time off, always on time.'

'But why you and not her family, husband or boyfriend?'

'Vicki isn't married and she's not in a relationship at the moment. Her family is from Canada. She was flying back there to see them. She lives alone in a small rented apartment a few miles from here.'

'Has her family contacted you?' Hunter asked. 'If they were expecting her and she didn't turn up, wouldn't they be worried?'

Bowman looked at Hunter nervously. 'They didn't know she was going up there. Sort of a surprise you see? What do you mean, she didn't turn up?'

'We checked with the airline, she never boarded the plane.'

'Oh my God!' Bowman said, running his hands through his hair. 'She's been missing for all this time?'

'You said she was supposed to be back here on the twenty-sixth of last month, still you only reported her missing two days ago – the thirty-first. Why did you wait five days?'

'I just got back from Europe on the thirty-first. I was in a bodybuilding competition.'

'When did you leave for Europe?' Garcia asked.

'Two days after Vicky left.' He stared down at his trembling hands. 'I should've tried calling her when I was in Europe; we spoke on the day she was supposed to go to Canada,' he murmured in a sad tone.

'Why would you call her? She's just an employee, right?' Hunter pushed him.

Joe Bowman looked uncomfortable. He tried giving Hunter a pale smile but failed.

Hunter pulled his chair closer to his desk and leaned forward, resting both elbows on it. 'C'mon Joe, it's time to come clean now, she was more than just an employee, right?'

Silence.

'Look Mr Bowman, we're not the marriage police. We're not here to question you about your relationship with your wife,' he pointed to the framed picture over the desk. 'But Victoria Baker might be in some serious trouble and all we wanna do is help, but for that we need your cooperation. Whatever you tell us, will stay between us. If she means anything to you, please help us.' Hunter gave him a confident smile.

Bowman hesitated for a moment, staring at his wife's picture. 'We are in love,' he finally gave in.

Hunter kept his eyes on Bowman, waiting for him to carry on.

'We're thinking about moving in together.'

Garcia's eyes widened in surprise. 'How about your marriage?' he asked.

Bowman massaged his eyes with his right hand taking his time to answer. 'My marriage died a couple of years ago.' His eyes were back on the picture over the desk. 'The love is gone . . . the conversation is gone . . . it's like we're total strangers to each other. We tried patching things up a year ago, but there's nothing there to patch up.' His tone was firm with a hint of sadness.

'When did you and Vicki start seeing each other?'

'About eight months ago. She has this thing about her, this contagious happiness . . . she made me happy again. So a couple of months ago I decided I would ask my wife for a divorce and do what makes me happy, and that is being with Vicki.'

'Did Vicki know? Did you tell her about your plans?'

'Yes, that's why she was going back to Canada.'

Hunter gave him a puzzled look.

'She wanted to let her parents know that she was thinking about getting a place together with me. She wanted their blessing.'

Hunter's confused look didn't go away.

'She comes from a very traditional family,' Bowman explained. 'She wanted them to accept me.'

'Accept the idea that their daughter was moving in with a married man?' Garcia asked intrigued.

'No,' Hunter answered first. 'Accept the idea of their daughter moving in with an African American man,' he concluded.

'Black,' Bowman corrected him. 'We like to be called black. That's what we are and black is not an offensive word. This political correctness thing is all bullshit if you ask me, but you're right. You can say her family would disapprove of our relationship.'

'And you didn't keep in touch with her while you were in Europe?'

'No . . . I should have . . .' his voice trailed off.

'Why not?'

'She wanted it that way. She said she needed time to get the idea through to them. I knew she was supposed to be back here on the thirty-first, so I tried calling her from Europe then, but I never got a reply. There was nothing I could do from where I was. When I got back I panicked when I couldn't find her, so I called the police.'

'You said she lives just a few miles from here?' Hunter asked.

'Yes, in North Croft Avenue.'

'Do you have the keys to her apartment?'

'No, I don't,' Bowman's eyes were unable to meet Hunter's. 'But I've already been through all this with the other officers.'

'From the Missing Persons' Department?'

'That's right.'

'We're not Missing Persons. We're Homicide.'

Bowman glared in surprise and fear. 'Homicide?'

Hunter took out a copy of the sketch Isabella had given them together with the twenty different permutations of it and placed it on Joe's desk.

'Have you ever seen this man?'

Bowman picked the sketches up with shaking hands and looked at them attentively.

'No, I can't say I have. Who's he supposed to be?'

Without saying a word, Hunter produced the computer-generated portrait of the first victim and placed it on the desk. Joe stared at it confused. His eyes pleaded for an explanation. 'Why do you have a digital image of Vicki?' he offered in an unsteady voice with watery eyes before Hunter had a chance to ask the question.

'What does this have to do with Vicki going missing? Why do I have Homicide detectives in my office? Why do you have a digital image of Vicki?'

'There might be a connection to a different investigation we're conducting,' Garcia explained.

'A Homicide investigation? Do you think she might be dead?' His voice croaked with dread.

'We don't know yet.'

'Oh my God! Who would ever want to harm Vicki? She is the sweetest person you could ever meet.'

'Let's not jump to conclusions yet, Mr Bowman,' Hunter tried calming him down. 'About this person,' he pointed to the sketches. 'Are you sure you haven't seen him in your gym?'

'If he's been in this gym, the receptionists are the ones to ask.'

'Don't worry, we'll ask them. We'll also need Vicki's address.'

In silence Joe wrote her address down and handed it to Hunter.

'Were you guys into clubbing, partying, going out, you know, that sort of thing?' Hunter carried on.

Bowman looked at Hunter confused. 'No, not at all. Because of my situation we couldn't really advertise our relationship to the world.'

Hunter nodded. 'Did she like going out by herself or with friends to places like that?'

'Not that I know,' Bowman answered hesitantly.

'Do you know if she took part in unorthodox parties?' Garcia cut in.

Bowman and Hunter looked at Garcia with the same mystified look. Neither of them really certain of what he meant by *unorthodox parties*.

'I'm not sure I know what you're asking me,' Bowman replied.

Hunter was as interested in Garcia's explanation as Bowman was.

No point in beating around the bush, Garcia thought. 'Was she into sex parties, BDSM, fetish . . . things of that nature?'

'What sort of question is that?' Bowman asked wide-eyed.

'The sort of question that pertains to this investigation.'

'Are you asking me if Vicki was a pervert?' Bowman blasted in an offended tone.

'No, just if you know if she was into that sort of thing.'

'No, she wasn't.'

Hunter decided to cut in. 'Is she well off? I mean is she well paid?'

Bowman turned his attention to Hunter with a 'what does that have to do with anything?' expression.

'Can she afford expensive stuff?' Hunter tried to clarify.

'What kind of stuff? Drugs?' Bowman's expression was even more puzzled now.

'No. Beauty stuff – moisturizers, creams, make-up, you know, women stuff.'

'Well, she ain't rich, not by LA standards anyway, but I'd say she earns enough. Now, where beauty stuff is concerned she spends a fortune. I've seen her pay over 300 dollars for an anti-wrinkle night cream and the bottle was the size of a pack of gum.'

Hunter cocked both eyebrows in surprise.

'That's not all,' Bowman continued. 'Four hundred dollars on an eye cream from Switzerland, 150 dollars on a bottle of nail varnish, not counting what she spends on manicures, pedicures, moisturizers, beauty treatments and spas. She can go without food, but not without her beauty creams and serums. Vicki's very vain. Maybe too vain.'

'Does Vicki have a locker or a place where she keeps her stuff?' Hunter asked.

'Yes. All members of staff do. We encourage everyone to exercise. We all have assigned lockers.'

'That's great. Can we see hers?'

'It's got an electronic lock and it needs a four-digit combination code. She's the only one who knows hers.'

'Yes, but I'm sure there's an override code,' Garcia said.

Bowman twisted his mouth wondering if that was the right thing to do. 'Don't you need a warrant to look through her things?'

'We are trying to find her, not put her in prison. A warrant could take a day or so, meanwhile we are losing precious time,' Hunter shot back.

'It's inside the women's changing room.'

'We only need five minutes, just tell whoever is inside the changing room to cover up,' Garcia said.

A short silence followed.

'We're losing time here,' Hunter pressed.

'OK,' Bowman finally gave in. 'Give me a few minutes. I'll ask one of the receptionists to make an announcement.'

Hunter studied Bowman as he quickly spoke on the phone to the front desk. 'Are you sure we haven't met before? You really do look familiar,' Hunter asked once he had put the phone down.

'I've appeared in several bodybuilding magazines. I'm a pro competitor. You look pretty fit yourself. Do you ever buy any fitness magazines?' Bowman replied.

Hunter snapped his fingers. 'Once or twice, yes. That's probably where I've seen you before then.'

Bowman gave Hunter an unenthusiastic smile.

Ten minutes later they were standing in front of locker number 365 inside the ladies' dressing room. Bowman punched in a six-digit code that bypassed Vicki's original one. The small light on the locking mechanism went from red to green and the door clicked open. Garcia had fetched some latex gloves from his car and Hunter was the one with the task of going through her things.

There wasn't much in there. A pair of running shoes, two pairs of socks, training shorts, a woman's top and a pair of fingerless weightlifting gloves. On the top shelf he found what he needed. A spray can of deodorant and a hairbrush. He picked them both up and placed them inside separate plastic bags.

Bowman watched in silence wondering why they were taking only two items and leaving the rest behind.

Fifty-Two

At eight o'clock that evening Doctor Winston was getting ready to finish for the day and go home when he received the call from Hunter. The deodorant spray can and the hairbrush needed testing for prints and DNA.

Hunter knew the results from the DNA test would take around five days to come through, maybe three if they put in a super-urgent request, but the fingerprint analysis could be done tonight. Doctor Winston said he'd wait for them.

Hunter was glad they weren't inside the basement room where both victims' bodies were kept. The Coroner's building made him feel uneasy, but the basement room gave him the creeps. The forensics lab was located on the first floor and Doctor Winston had asked Ricardo Pinheiro, one of the forensic analysts, to stay behind and help him with the fingerprint job. Hunter handed Ricardo the deodorant can and watched while he applied a fingerprint powder made of titanium dioxide to it. The high-reflexive index of the powder against the smooth metal surface of the can reacted almost immediately, revealing several latent fingerprints.

Ricardo dusted the excess powder from the can and proceeded to transfer the prints to several clear cellophane slides.

'On a fast naked-eye first look I'd say we probably have three sets of prints here.' Ricardo was rarely wrong. He took the cellophane slides to the nearest microscope and carried on analyzing them.

'Yep, three different sets, but there's a predominant one,' he said after a minute at the microscope.

'Let's check the predominant set of prints first then,' Doctor Winston said. 'Can you transfer them to the computer?'

'Sure,' Ricardo said, taking the slides and moving on to one of the video microscopes, which were already linked to the lab computers. He took a snapshot of each fingerprint and with each shot the photo-analysis software displayed an enhanced image on the computer screen.

'Do you want me to run the prints against the police criminal fingerprint database?' Ricardo enquired.

'No, check it against this one.' Doctor Winston handed him a small pen drive with the digital image of the first victim's fingerprint on it.

Ricardo loaded the image into the computer's hard drive and with just a few clicks he had both images side by side on the analysis software. He clicked the 'compare' button.

Several comparison point red dots appeared over both fingerprint shots. It took the software less than five seconds to display the words *Positive Match* at the bottom of the screen.

'Yep, they're the same person,' Ricardo confirmed.

'It's official, we finally have a match for our victim,' Doctor Winston said. 'Who was she again?'

'Her name was Victoria Baker. Canadian . . . had been living in LA for four years,' Garcia replied.

Hunter kept his eyes on the fingerprint images on the computer. 'We'll run the other two prints against the police database just in case,' he finally said, obviously bothered about something. It wasn't until they were back in Garcia's car that he spoke again.

'We're back to square one where links between victims are concerned. This screws up our "sex party" theory. George Slater probably never heard of Victoria Baker.'

Garcia ran both hands over his face and rubbed his eyes in the process. 'I know.'

'We have to find out where she was abducted from. Her place might give us some clues, but we won't get a warrant until tomorrow.'

Garcia agreed. 'We also have to contact her family in Canada and let them know.'

Hunter nodded slowly. That was one task they both could do without.

'I'll do it tonight,' Hunter said.

As Garcia parked his car back by the RHD building Hunter wondered if he looked as tired and defeated as his partner did.

'I'll talk to Captain Bolter about the warrant and hopefully we'll have it first thing tomorrow morning,' Hunter said. 'I'll meet you here at around ten-thirty, first I'll try and get another list of patients from one more hospital.'

Garcia rested his head against the headrest and took a deep breath.

'Go home, rookie,' Hunter said stealing a peek at his watch. 'It's not even nine o'clock yet. Spend the night with your wife. You need it and so does she. There's nothing more for us to do tonight.'

There was always something to do in the office, but Hunter was right. There was nothing else they could accomplish tonight. Garcia thought of what had happened the night before with Anna and he could do with being home before she'd gone to bed at least once this week. They'd been working on casino time for weeks, never knowing what time it was. Even a tiny break would be welcome.

'Yeah, Anna will appreciate me being home tonight.'

'That's right,' Hunter agreed. 'Get her some flowers on the way home. Not some cheap bouquet, something nice. Remember, buying somebody a present indicates your knowledge of that somebody's personality, so get her something that you know she'll like,' he said with a reassuring smile.

Fifty-Three

Garcia took Hunter's advice and dropped by Markey's, a small convenience store on North Rampant Boulevard. It stocked just about everything, from flowers to booze, and their meatball sandwich and freshly brewed coffee weren't bad either. Garcia had stopped there plenty of times back when he used to be a detective for the LAPD. It was a small detour from his way home, but he was sure Anna would appreciate his effort.

The tall, very attractive blond behind the counter greeted Garcia with a wide smile showing beautifully formed teeth. Garcia smiled back and ran his hand through his hair in an attempt to look a little more presentable.

Garcia decided to take a nice bottle of red wine home as well as the flowers. It'd been some time since he and Anna shared a bottle and she loved a nice bottle of Rioja. The flowers were displayed right at the store entrance, but Garcia ignored them for the moment.

'Excuse me, where do you keep your bottles of wine?'

'Right at the back,' the blond girl replied with a new smile.

Their selection wasn't exactly impressive, but then again Garcia wasn't exactly a connoisseur. He chose a bottle by price. The more it costs, the better it should taste, he thought. He went back to where the flowers were and chose a nicely arranged bouquet of red roses.

'I guess this will be all,' he said placing everything on the counter.

'That will be 40.95 please!'

Garcia handed her three twenty-dollar bills.

'She's a very lucky lady,' the blond girl said, handing back his change.

'Excuse me!'

'The lady those flowers are for . . . very lucky lady.' She smiled again and Garcia noticed how young and pretty she was.

'Oh! Thank you,' he blushed.

'Do you live around here?'

'Umm . . . no, I just needed to get a few things. This is on my way home,' he lied.

'Oh . . . that's a pity, but maybe you can stop back here again some time?'

Garcia had no reply but a timid smile.

Outside, as he approached his car, Garcia couldn't believe the store attendant had come on to him. That hadn't happened in a very long time.

Other than a brand-new-looking Chevy van there was no other car on the parking lot. He opened his passenger door and carefully placed the roses on the seat. His thoughts going back to the day's developments. He still found it hard to come to terms with how alike Jenny Farnborough and Victoria Baker looked. Garcia didn't believe in coincidences, but he also didn't believe that both women going missing at the same time had been planned. This killer didn't keep his victims for long. Once they were abducted, they would turn up tortured and dead within a few days. Vicki Baker had been the victim. Jenny Farnborough had probably just gone missing, he thought.

Suddenly Garcia remembered they still had a police tail on

D-King. With the events of the past few hours happening so fast he'd completely forgotten about it. He'd have to call them off as there was no need for them now. He grabbed his cell phone and searched its address book for the correct number. He'd been so absorbed in his thoughts that he didn't notice the presence behind him. The reflection of the dark figure against his shiny car came too late. Before Garcia had a chance to turn around and face his attacker he felt a sharp prick against the right side of his neck.

The drug reacted almost instantly. Garcia's vision blurred and he felt his knees buckle. He dropped his cell phone and heard it smash as it hit the ground. He tried holding on to the car door for balance but it was all too late, the stranger was already dragging him to the nearby van.

Fifty-Four

Jerome had one more stop, one more person to see before he went back home to face another nightmarish night. D-King had given him one job and one job only – find the people who'd taken Jenny.

He'd seen many people die in many different ways, a good number of them by his own hands and it had never bothered him. Their dying faces had never lingered in his memory, but the scenes from the DVD he'd watched inside D-King's limo had never left him. He found it hard to sleep, to eat. He missed her. Jenny had been his favorite girl. She was always smiling, always positive about everything. No matter how bad any situation might've looked, she'd always find the good, the funny side to it.

Jerome had been at it for almost two weeks. He'd called favors from every dirty underground contact he had on the streets. All information leading to another scumbag. The newest one on his list was a low-life junkie named Daryl.

The web of filth that surrounded the snuff-movie business was weaved tight. No one seemed to know anything, or if anyone did they weren't talking. The information Jerome was given was that Daryl wasn't involved with snuff movies, but he might've come across something that could give him a lead.

Daryl lived on the streets, sleeping in any hole that would

offer him a shelter for the night. Tonight he was sharing the luxury ruins of a semi-demolished building in South Los Angeles with a few other homeless junkies. All Jerome had to do was find him.

He'd been waiting patiently, observing the building from a safe distance. He'd been given a good enough description of Daryl, but it seemed that everyone around there looked pretty much the same. Jerome's advantage was that Daryl was supposed to be six-foot four and that would make him an easy target to spot.

It wasn't until just past one in the morning when Jerome noticed a tall, awkward figure crossing the street and moving towards the ruined building. Jerome quickly doubled his step to catch up with him.

'Daryl!'

The man stopped and turned around to face Jerome. His clothes were dirty and torn. His shaved head was covered in scars and scabs. It was obvious he hadn't shaved or showered in a few days. He looked frightened.

'Who wants to know?'

'A friend.'

The man looked Jerome over from head to toe. Jerome had dressed down, swapping his usual thousand-dollar suit for a regular T-shirt and blue jeans, but he still looked too well dressed for that part of town.

'What sort of friend?' the tall man asked, taking a step back.

'One that can help you,' Jerome said, pulling a small cellophane bag from his pocket containing some brown powder inside. He watched as the man's eyes lit up with excitement.

'What do you want man?' he asked, still looking skeptical.

'I want to know if you are Daryl or not.'

'And if I am, am I gonna get that bag?'

'Depends if you can tell me what I need to know.'

The tall man stepped closer and Jerome noticed how weak he looked. It was obvious Jerome could simply beat the information out of him at any time.

'Are you a cop, man?'

'Do I look like a cop?' Jerome had always wondered why people would ask that question – as if an undercover cop would just come clean and say 'Yes, you got me, I'm a cop.'

'Cops can look like anything these days.'

'Well, I'm not one. Are you Daryl or not?'

The tall man hesitated for a few more seconds, his eyes fixed on the brown powder bag. 'Yes, that's me.'

Oh! The power of bribing, Jerome thought. 'Good, so now we can talk,' he said, placing the cellophane bag back in his pocket.

Daryl's eyes saddened just like a little boy who'd lost his candy. 'What do you wanna talk about?'

'Something you know.'

A new doubtful look came over Daryl. 'And what is it that I'm supposed to know?'

Jerome sensed a hint of hostility in Daryl's voice. More bribing was needed. 'Are you hungry? I could certainly use some food and a cup of coffee. There's a twenty-four-hour cafe just around the corner. How about we go talk in there, I'm buying.'

Daryl hesitated for a second before nodding. 'Yeah, coffee and food would be nice.'

They walked in silence, Daryl always two steps in front of Jerome. They reached the empty cafe and sat at a table at the back. Jerome ordered some coffee and pancakes and Daryl a double cheeseburger with fries. Jerome took his time with his food, but Daryl devoured his.

'Would you like another one?' Jerome asked as soon as

Daryl was done. Daryl finished the last of his root beer and let out a loud burp.

'No thanks. That hit the spot just right. So what is it that you'd like to know?'

Jerome leaned back on his seat looking relaxed. 'I need information about some people.'

'People? What kinda people?'

'The not very nice kind.'

Daryl scratched his bushy beard and then his crooked nose. 'Everyone I know fits into that category,' he said with a half smile.

'From what I heard you don't really know these people, you just know where I can find them.'

Daryl raised his eyebrows. 'You gotta tell me more than that, man.'

Jerome leaned forward and placed both hands over the small table. He waited for Daryl to do the same. 'Do you know what a snuff movie is?' he whispered.

Daryl jumped back, almost knocking Jerome's coffee off the table. 'Fuck that, man. I knew this was bullshit. I know nothing about that.'

'I've heard differently.'

'Well, you heard wrong. Who the hell told you that?'

'That's not important. What is important is that I need to know what you know.'

'I don't know nothing, man,' he said gesticulating aggressively while avoiding Jerome's eyes.

'Look, there are two ways we can do this.' Jerome paused for a second and took out the same cellophane bag he'd shown Daryl earlier. 'You can tell me what you know and I'll give you ten of these.'

Daryl shifted his weight on his seat. 'Ten?'

'That's right.'

That was more heroin than he'd ever had. He could even sell some of it and make a small profit. He ran his tongue over his cracked lips nervously. 'I'm not involved in it, man.'

'I never said you were. I just need to know what you know.'

Daryl started to sweat. He needed a hit.

'The people that deal with that shit . . . they are bad motherfuckers, man. If they find out I said something, I'm dead.'

'Not if I get to them first. You'd never have to worry about them again.'

Daryl ran both hands tensely over his mouth as if wiping something off. 'I guess the other way we can do this is a painful one, right?'

'For you . . . yes.'

Daryl took a deep breath and let it out slowly. 'OK, but I don't know names or nothing.'

'I don't need names.'

'You know, I've been down on my luck for a little while now.' Daryl's voice was low and sad. 'It's not every day I have a meal that hasn't been someone else's leftovers. If I could manage to have a shower every day I would, but it's not that easy when you're really broke. Most of the time I have to sleep rough, so any place would do, but a sheltered place if I can find one, is much better.'

Jerome listened.

'A few months ago I was high, drunk and I ended up in some abandoned old factory or something like that in Gardena.'

'Gardena? That's way out of town,' Jerome interrupted.

'Well, I move around a lot, one of the perks of being homeless.' Daryl forced a cheesy smile. 'Towards the back of the main building you can still find part of a roof covering a room, so that's where I crashed. I was woken up by the sound of a car approaching. I have no idea what time it was, late I guess, it was still dark. Anyway, out of curiosity I peeked through a hole in the wall to see what was going on.'

'What did you see?'

'Four guys dragging a tied-up woman out of a big van.'

'Where did they take her?'

'Around the back, down a little dirt track. I got curious, so I followed them. I never knew there was an underground area to that building, but there is. A heavy iron door hidden behind some high grass at the end of the dirt track. I waited about five minutes before following them down.'

'And?'

'The place was filthy, full of rats and shit and it smelled like a sewer.'

Coming from Daryl, Jerome thought that was priceless.

'They have this whole thing set up down there, man. Lights and cameras and things like that. The room is all fucked up, full of holes in the walls, it was easy to watch everything without being noticed.'

'What were they doing?'

'Well, I thought they were filming a porn movie, man. They tied this girl to a chair. She was kicking and screaming, putting up a real good fight, but they kept on slapping her about. Two of the guys were working the camera and the other two went to work on the girl. But it wasn't a porn film, man.' Daryl's voice weakened. 'After they were done beating and fucking her they sliced her man. They carved her up like a Halloween pumpkin, and that was no special effect either.' His gaze was distant as if he could still see the images of that night. 'They were all laughing afterwards, man, like as if they had just finished a game of b-ball. It was sick.'

'What did you do?'

'I panicked, but I knew that if I made any noise, I'd be next. So while they were cleaning up their mess I sneaked back up and hid in the old factory until daybreak. I never went back there again, man.'

'But can you remember where it is?'

'Hell yeah,' he said, nodding slowly.

'C'mon, let's go.' Jerome got a twenty-dollar bill from his wallet and left it on the table.

'Let's go where?'

'To Gardena. To this old factory.'

'Wow, man, you never said anything about going back there.'

'I'm saying it now.'

'I don't know about that man. I told you what I know, that was the deal. That's worth the bags right?'

'If you want the bags, you've gotta take me there.'

'That ain't fair, man, that wasn't the deal.'

'I'm changing the deal,' Jerome said firmly.

Daryl knew he had no choice. He needed a hit – badly. 'OK, man, but if those motherfuckers are there, I'm staying the fuck in the car.'

'I just wanna see where it is.'

Fifty-Five

Darkness was absolute and wakening had come very slowly. The residue effect from the drug still lingered in his aching body. A throbbing invaded his head, reaching down into his neck and shoulder blades and even the smallest of movements felt like agony. He was trying to come to terms with what had happened and where he was, but his memory was still fuzzy.

Confusion reigned for several minutes before details started to emerge.

He remembered the store, the attractive blond shop assistant, choosing a bottle of wine and a bouquet of roses for Anna. Anna . . . he hadn't called her to let her know he'd be coming home earlier than usual. She wouldn't be expecting him.

He remembered someone's dark reflection on his car window, but not being able to turn around quick enough, the sharp pain on his neck and then nothing.

Squinting in the darkness he tried to understand where he was but nothing made any sense. The air was humid and foul with a fetid odor.

He had no idea how long he'd been unconscious. He tried looking at his watch, but he couldn't make out its hands.

'Hello!' He tried calling out. His voice was too feeble. 'Hello!' He tried once again and heard the sound reverberate off the walls. As he struggled to sit up he felt something grab at his right ankle. He tried to pull clear, but whatever it was it just snapped taut. He ran his fingers over it.

A chain.

A very thick chain attached to an iron ring on a brick wall. He tried pulling it as hard as he could to no avail.

'Hello, is anyone there?'

Silence.

He took a deep breath trying to contain his nervousness. He needed to stay calm and think clearly.

What'd happened? Someone had attacked me, but why?

His gun was gone, but his wallet and detective badge were still with him. Suddenly the realization of who could've taken him made him shiver.

The killer – the Crucifix Killer.

If he was right, he knew he was as good as dead. No one would ever find him until the killer was done with him.

He closed his eyes and thought of Anna.

He'd never be able to tell her how much he really loved her, how much he would miss her. He wished he'd given her a better life. A life of not having to wait up wondering if her husband would come home or not. A life that wouldn't have required her to play second best to his job.

'Get a grip Carlos, you ain't dead yet,' he whispered to himself.

He needed to identify his surroundings, to understand where he was. He reached for the chain around his ankle once again and ran his finger over it to find out how much movement he had. Standing up for the first time he realized how weak his legs felt. He quickly grabbed hold of the wall closest to him. His legs ached with thousands of pinpricks. He stood there for a long moment waiting for the blood to resume its normal flow.

With his hands against the wall he started moving to his left. The wall bricks felt moist but solid. He managed to move only about five feet before he reached the next wall. He carried on moving left, but before he reached the end the chain on his ankle held him to a stop. He extended his arm and touched the third wall. Garcia turned and walked in the opposite direction. He reached what felt like a heavy wooden door. He pounded on it with his clenched fists but it produced nothing but muffled thuds. Wherever he was, it was certainly a very solid prison.

He started walking back to his starting point when his foot kicked something. He stumbled back on instinct and waited, but nothing else happened. He crouched down and felt for the object cautiously. He touched it with his fingers – a plastic bottle full of liquid.

He undid the lid and brought the bottle up to his nose. It smelled of nothing. He dipped his right index finger into it. The liquid felt light like water and that brought on the realization of how thirsty he felt. Warily he brought his finger up to his mouth and touched the tip of his tongue – no taste, just like water.

Maybe the killer didn't want him dead, at least not yet. It wasn't unheard of, killers keeping their victims alive for a period of time before killing them. If Garcia was to stand a chance in any kind of struggle against this killer, he needed all the strength he could muster. He dipped his finger into the bottle one more time and brought it back to his mouth. He was certain – it was water. Slowly he moved the bottle up to his lips and had a sip. He kept the liquid moving around in his mouth without swallowing it for a while, testing for any abnormal taste. He got none. Finally he let the liquid run down to his throat and it felt like heaven.

He waited about two minutes for any kind of stomach reaction but he got nothing. He quickly gulped down three or four mouthfuls. The water wasn't cold, but it filled him with life.

He replaced the lid and sat facing the wooden door with the water bottle between his legs. That door was the only way in or out of the room and he hoped that sooner rather than later it would open. He needed a plan, but he had no time to hatch one.

Fifteen minutes later he started feeling drowsy. He slapped his face vigorously with both hands trying to keep himself awake, but it made no difference. Feeling faint, he reached for the water bottle and threw it against the wooden door. He knew what he'd done. He had willingly drugged himself.

Fifty-Six

Hunter got up at five o'clock after another troublesome night. He'd dozed off in uneven intervals and never for more than twenty minutes at a time. The double Scotch had helped but not enough. He sat in the kitchen nursing his early morning headache with a glass of orange juice and a couple of strong painkillers.

He was hoping for an early start, but not 5 a.m. He wanted to obtain at least one more patients' list before meeting up with Garcia back at the RHD. The cross-referencing and picture search from last night had yielded no results, but there were still several hospitals and physiotherapy clinics to go and Hunter was trying to stay positive.

He'd figured he'd be doing a fair amount of walking today and that gave him the perfect opportunity to wear his new shoes in. They did feel a little on the tight side as he walked around in his living room, but he knew that one or two days walking around LA would definitely do the trick.

The visit to the next hospital on his list went as slowly as the ones from the day before. Another cramped little room, another filing system that seemed to need a cryptographer to get through it. 'Why do hospitals have computers if no one knows how to use them?' he cursed under his breath as he finally managed to get the list of patients he needed just in time to make it back to the RHD.

Hunter didn't pay much attention to the fact that Garcia wasn't at his desk when he walked in at a quarter past ten. He gathered his partner was probably downstairs running through the daily report with Captain Bolter.

He dropped the envelope with the new patients' list on his desk and stared at the picture-covered corkboard for a minute. What he needed was a cup of Brazilian coffee before going downstairs. He noticed that Garcia hadn't prepared it yet. Strange, he thought as it was always one of the first things his partner would do as soon as he walked through the door.

Hunter brewed the coffee himself.

'Are those new shoes?' Detective Lucas said as Hunter walked onto the detectives' floor.

Hunter paid no attention to Lucas's sarcasm.

Most of the other detectives lifted their eyes from their computer screens to have a look.

'They are new, aren't they, you big spender?' Lucas insisted.

'I buy a new pair of shoes every ten years and you're giving me heat?' Hunter answered with disdain.

Before Lucas could hit back, Hunter's cell phone rang.

'Hello, Detective Hunter speaking.'

'*Hello, Robert, I have a surprise for you. Have you heard from your partner lately?*'

Fifty-Seven

59, 58, 57 . . . Hunter's eyes were fixed on the digital display just above Garcia's head. His heart pounded against his chest like a sledgehammer. Despite the basement room feeling like a sauna, Hunter felt cold. A freezing cold that came from inside making him shiver.

Choose a color . . . any color, he thought. Black, white, blue or red. The colors flashed in front of his eyes like a psychedelic film. He looked at Garcia nailed to the cross. Blood dripping down his face from the barbed-wire crown that had been rammed into his head.

'*This is a simple game,*' as the metallic voice from the tape recorder had explained. Pick the correct color and the door on the bulletproof Perspex cage will open. Hunter would be able to get to Garcia and get the hell out of that place. Pick the wrong color and an uninterrupted high-voltage current will be sent directly to the crown on Garcia's head. If that wasn't sadistic enough, explosives placed behind the cage would detonate, blowing the whole room to high heaven if the monitor reading Garcia's heartbeat displayed a flatline.

Garcia seemed to have passed out again.

'Rookie, stay with me,' Hunter shouted, hammering his fists against the cage's door.

No movement – no response.

'Carlos . . .' The loud shout echoed across the basement room. A slight head movement this time.

Hunter checked the heart monitor once again. The small ball of light was still peaking.

43, 42, 41 . . .

'C'mon, rookie, stay with me,' he pleaded before looking around the room for any clues, anything that could point him to a specific button. He found nothing.

Less than two months. Garcia had joined the RHD less than two months ago. Why did he have to be paired up with me? Hunter cursed. This shouldn't have been his first case.

Garcia's body convulsed slightly, forcing Hunter's thoughts back to the basement room.

32, 31, 30 . . .

How much blood has he lost? Even if I get him out of here he might not make it. He hoped Garcia was stronger than he looked.

Just a few seconds to death. Hunter's brain was working as fast as it could, but he knew he needed a miracle to figure out which button to go for. A guess was all he was left with. He felt mentally exhausted. He was sick and tired of playing these games. Games he knew he could never win because the killer had too much of an upper hand. Even now, he had no guarantees that the Crucifix Killer was telling the truth. Maybe none of the buttons would unlock the cage door. Maybe he was walking into certain death.

Hunter turned and faced the basement door. He could still get out of there alive.

'If I stay here I'm as good as dead,' he whispered.

For a split second he forgot everything he'd ever believed in and considered running for his life. The thought made him sick and ashamed.

'What the fuck am I thinking? We ain't dead yet.'

15, 14, 13 . . .

'Shit!' He pinched the bridge of his nose and squeezed his eyes as tight as he could. 'This is it, pick a fucking button, Robert!' he told himself. 'Color coded, why color coded? The killer could've used numbers, why give them colors?'

He knew he was running out of time.

'He's playing a fucking game again, just like the dog race . . .' He suddenly stopped in a fright. 'The dog race . . . the winner, what color was it?' He tried to think. He knew it was dog number two, but what color was its jacket?

'Shit, what color was the winner?' he shouted out loud.

His eyes lifted from the buttons and met Garcia's who had regained consciousness again.

6, 5, 4 . . .

'I'm sorry,' Hunter said with sadness in his eyes. He was about to reach for one of the buttons when he saw Garcia's lips move. They emitted no sound but Hunter could easily read them.

'Blue . . .'

Hunter didn't have time to hesitate. He pressed the blue button.

2 . . .

The digital display froze. The Perspex cage door emitted a humming sound and clicked open. Hunter's face transformed into one huge smile. 'I'll be damned!' He ran inside and lifted Garcia's chin from his bloody chest. 'Hang in there, buddy.'

Hunter quickly assessed the inside of the cage. Garcia's hands had been nailed to the wooden cross. There was no way he'd be able to free him. He had to call for help.

'C'mon, give me a fucking signal,' he shouted as he tried his cell phone. It was no good, he had to go back up to ground level.

'Hold on, rookie, I'm gonna go call for help. I'll be right back.' But Garcia had already drifted back into unconsciousness. Hunter stepped out of the cage and started towards the door but a beeping sound made him stop and turn back. His eyes widened in horror.

'You're fucking kidding me!'

Fifty-Eight

The red digital display was active once again.

59, 58, 57 . . .

'I pressed the right button . . . that was the fucking deal,' Hunter yelled at the top of his voice. He ran back to the cage and double-checked the wooden cross. He had no way of freeing Garcia from it. The nails that pierced his hands were deeply embedded in the wood. Hunter noticed that the main body of the cross was slotted into a separate wooden foundation.

42, 41, 40 . . .

His only hope was to lift it off its base and drag it out of the room in time.

33, 32, 31 . . .

He had no more time to think. He quickly placed his right shoulder under Garcia and the cross's left arm. From his weight-training experience he knew he had to use his legs and not his arms and back to lift it up. He steadied himself on his feet; bent his knees and in one quick push used all his power to shove his shoulder against the wooden cross. It surprised him how easily it all came apart.

The cage door stayed open but Hunter wouldn't be able to get the cross through it without tilting it. He twisted his body, rotating his waist to the left as far as he could go. Garcia emitted a muffled grunt of pain, but Hunter's acrobatics did the trick. They were out of the cage. Now he had to make it to the door.

20, 19, 18 . . .

His feet were in agony and he was starting to feel the double weight on his back. 'A few more steps,' he whispered to himself, but suddenly his left knee buckled under the weight and he came crashing down, slamming it against the concrete floor. A searing pain shot up his leg, making him dizzy for a couple of seconds – precious seconds. Somehow he still managed the cross on his back.

Hunter wasn't sure how much longer he had. He was scared to turn around and check the clock, but he knew he needed to get back on his feet. He firmed his right foot on the ground and with a scream pushed himself back up.

9, 8, 7 . . .

He finally made it to the door. He needed to use the twisting trick once again, but this time he couldn't rely on his left knee to support the weight. Using his right leg as his main balance point he repeated the same movement of seconds ago. He screamed out in pain, praying he could hold on for just a few more steps. He tasted sick in his mouth as his body felt faint and struggled to cope with the unbearable pain. Hunter felt his grip weakening – he was losing the cross.

One more step.

He used his last ounce of strength to push himself and the cross through the doorframe.

No more time.

He let the heavy iron door slam behind him hoping it'd be strong enough to withhold the blast. Hunter let go of the cross and fell over his partner using his own body as a human blanket. He closed his eyes and waited for the explosion.

Fifty-Nine

The ambulance came screeching to a halt in front of the emergency ward entrance. Three nurses were waiting to retrieve its patients. They watched in horror as the first stretcher was wheeled out. A half-naked man with a barbed-wire crown on his head had been nailed to a life-size wooden cross. Blood was pouring out of his opened wounds.

'Jesus Christ . . .' gasped the first nurse to reach the patient.

The second man was covered in a thin gray powder, as if he'd been dug out from under a collapsed building.

'I'm alright, get off me. Take care of him,' came the loud shouts from the second patient. Hunter was trying to sit up, but being restrained by the ambulance paramedics. 'Get your hands off me,' he demanded.

'Sir, we're already taking care of your friend. Please calm down and let the doctors have a look at you. Everything will be OK.'

Hunter observed in silence as the nurses hurried Garcia through the double doors at the end of the busy corridor.

As he opened his eyes he struggled to understand what was happening. For a few seconds everything was blurred, then he noticed the white walls. He felt dizzy and desperately thirsty.

'Good, you're awake.' The woman's voice was soft and sweet.

With great effort he turned his head in her direction. A petite, short dark-haired nurse was staring down at him.

'How're you feeling?'

'Thirsty.'

'Here . . .' She poured some water from the aluminum jug next to his bed into a plastic cup. Hunter drank greedily, but as the water hit his throat it burned. A look of pain washed over his face.

'Are you OK?' the nurse asked worried.

'My throat hurts,' he whispered in a weak breath.

'That's normal. Here, let me take your temperature,' she said, offering him a thin glass thermometer.

'I don't have a fever,' Hunter protested, pushing the thermometer away from his mouth. He finally remembered where he was and what had happened. He tried to sit up but the room did a back flip somersault on him.

'Wow!'

'Easy there, mister,' she said, putting her hand over his chest. 'You need the rest.'

'I need to get the hell out of here.'

'Maybe later. First you need to let me take care of you.'

'No, you need to listen to me. My friend . . . how is he?'

'Which friend?'

'The one who came in nailed to a fucking cross. I don't think you could've missed him. He looked like Jesus Christ. Do you remember him? Supposed to have died for our sins.' Hunter tried sitting up once again. His head pounding.

The door opened and Captain Bolter stuck his head through. 'Is he giving you attitude?'

The nurse gave the captain an ivory smile.

'Captain, where's Carlos? How's he doing?'

'Can you give us a moment?' the captain asked the nurse as he stepped into the room.

Hunter waited until she was gone. 'Did he make it? I gotta go see him,' he said, trying to stand up but collapsing back into bed.

'You ain't going anywhere,' the captain said firmly.

'Talk to me, Captain, is he alive?'

'Yes.'

'How is he?' Hunter demanded.

'Carlos lost a lot of blood, what the doctors call a class-four hemorrhage. In consequence, his heart, liver and kidneys have weakened considerably. He was given a blood transfusion, but other than that there isn't much else anyone can do. We have to wait for him to fight back.'

'Fight back?' Hunter's voice now showing a slight quiver.

'He's stable, but still unconscious. They are not calling it a coma just yet. His vital signs are weak . . . very weak. He's in the ICU.'

Hunter buried his head in his hands.

'Carlos is a strong man – he'll come out of it,' the captain reassured him.

'I've gotta go see him.'

'You ain't going nowhere for now. What the fuck happened, Robert? I almost lost two detectives in one go and I didn't even know what the hell was going on.'

'What the fuck do you think, Captain? The killer went after Carlos,' Hunter shot back angrily.

'But why? Are you telling me the killer suddenly decided to up his game and become a cop killer? That's not what he's about.'

'Is that so? So please tell me, Captain, what is the killer about?'

Captain Bolter avoided Hunter's eyes.

'I've been after him for over three years and the only thing I know he's about is torturing and killing. Who he kills seems to make no fucking difference. It's all a game to him and Carlos was supposed to be just another pawn,' Hunter said, trying to raise his voice.

'Run me through what happened,' the captain ordered in a calm voice.

Hunter went over every detail, from the time he'd received the phone call to when he'd closed his eyes waiting for the explosion.

'Why didn't you call me? Why didn't you call for back-up?'

'Because the killer had said no back-up. I wasn't about to gamble with Carlos's life.'

'It doesn't make sense. If you'd beaten him at his own game, why set the detonator again?'

Hunter shook his head, staring at the floor.

'He wanted you both dead. No matter what,' Captain Bolter concluded.

'I don't think so.'

'If he didn't want you killed, why reset the bomb?'

'Evidence.'

'What?'

'That room was full of evidence, Captain. The tape recorder, the cage, the explosives, the door-lock mechanism, the wheelchair. If we were to get our hands on all of that, something was bound to give us a lead. Blow it all to hell and we've got nothing.'

The captain made a face as if he wasn't very convinced.

'The cross came off its base as if it had been greased,' Hunter continued. 'It was too easy. The amount of explosives the killer used was exactly enough to destroy only the laundry room. We were just about two feet from the door. The killer could've arranged for a stronger explosion, one that would've obliterated the entire basement floor giving us no chance of escaping. The primary objective of the explosion wasn't to kill.'

'So the killer has knowledge of explosives?'

'At least some,' Hunter said nodding.

'What do you mean "At least some"?'

'I don't believe the bomb was anything spectacular. Definitely not state of the art or terrorist style. Yes, the killer would need some knowledge of explosives to put it together and build the detonating mechanism, but he wouldn't need to be an expert.'

'And where the fuck would he get explosives from?'

'This is America, Captain,' Hunter answered with a sarcastic chuckle. 'The land where money buys you anything you want. With the right contacts and cash you could get an anti-aircraft gun never mind a small amount of explosives to blow up a basement room. If the killer has enough understanding of chemistry he could've built it himself using easy-to-purchase chemicals.'

The captain shook his head in silence for a few seconds. 'We're gonna have to come clean about this case you know that, right? The press is all over this now. Explosives, a detective being crucified alive. It's a goddamn circus out there, and we're the clowns.'

Hunter had nothing to say. The room had almost stopped spinning and he tried standing up once again. As his feet touched the floor Hunter let out an agonizing grunt. His new shoes had done a good job of rubbing his feet raw.

'Where the hell do you think you're going?' the captain asked.

'I gotta go see Carlos – where is he?'

The captain ran his hand over his mustache and regarded Hunter with a sharp gaze. 'I told you, in the ICU. C'mon, I'll show you.'

As he walked past the small mirror to the left of the room door, Hunter stopped and peered critically at his outline. He looked like death. Hundreds of small cuts covered his tired and pale face. His eyes were bloodshot. His lower lip was swollen and disfigured. A blob of dried blood decorated the right corner of his mouth. He'd aged ten years in one afternoon.

'You must be Anna,' Hunter said as he entered the L-shaped ICU room.

A short dark-haired woman was sitting next to Garcia's bed. Her complexion heavy, her hazel eyes swollen from crying.

'And you must be Robert.' She sounded weak and shattered.

Hunter attempted to give her a smile, but his cheeks gave way. 'I'm sorry we're meeting this way.' He extended a shivering hand.

She shook his hand with the most gentle of touches, her eyes filling up with tears. In silence all three of them stared at an unconscious Garcia. He lay flat under a thin coverlet. Tubes came out of his mouth, nose and arms looping away through the bed frame and connecting to two separate machines. His hands and head were heavily bandaged and his face bruised and cut. A heart monitor beeped steadily at the corner of the room and at the sight of it Hunter shuddered.

Garcia looked peaceful but fragile. Hunter stepped closer and placed a soft hand on his right arm.

'C'mon, rookie, you can fight this, this is easy,' he whispered tenderly. 'The difficult part is over. We got out of there, rookie. We beat him. We beat him at his own game . . . you and I.'

Hunter kept his hand on Garcia's arm for a while longer

before turning to face Anna. 'He's very strong, he's gonna come out of this easy. He's probably just sleeping it off.'

Anna had no reply. Tears rolled down her face. Hunter returned his attention to Garcia and bent over to draw level with him. He seemed to be searching for something.

'Is something wrong?' the captain asked.

Hunter shook his head and pressed down on Garcia's pillow around neck height being careful not to disturb his head. Very gently he ran his finger around the back of his partner's neck.

'C'mon, he needs the rest and so do you,' the captain said, moving towards the door. Hunter wanted to say something to Anna, but words simply evaded him. He merely followed the captain and no one said a word until they were back in Hunter's room.

'He had no mark,' Hunter spoke first.

'What?'

'On the back of Carlos's neck . . . no carving. The killer didn't mark him.'

'And what does that mean?'

'It means he wasn't supposed to die.'

'He wasn't supposed to die? But you could've pressed the wrong button.'

Hunter had no answer. He tried to think but the thumping inside his head prevented him. He sat down on the bed as the room started spinning again.

'You're gonna have to brief Matt and Doyle on the case,' the captain said, breaking the silence.

'What? What are you talking about?'

'I have to pull you off the investigation, Robert, you know the protocol. Matt and Doyle will take over. I want you to share everything you know, everything you have with them.'

'Fuck protocol, Captain! That's bullshit . . .'

'You know I can't let you carry on with this case. For some freaky reason this killer has gotten attached to you. Phone calls. Calling you by your first name. Killing games. Next thing you know you're gonna be having drinks with him. It's like he knows you too well now.'

'Exactly, and if you pull me from the case it might enrage him further. Hell knows what he'll do then.'

'Hell knows what he does now, Robert. We have nothing on him and you know it. Three years of investigation and we have jack-shit to show for it. Maybe two fresh brains is what this investigation needs.'

'What this investigation needs is for me to carry on from where I've left off. We are edging closer, Captain. Carlos and I were on the trail of something that we're sure is gonna lead us to him.'

'Good, so you can fill Matt and Doyle in on this trail of yours.'

'This is my investigation, mine and Carlos's.'

'Are you concussed? Has the explosion affected your brain? Let me give you a quick reality check,' the captain shot back aggressively. 'Carlos is lying in intensive care in a half coma. He was crucified alive, Robert. A barbed-wire crown shoved so hard into his head that the thorns were scratching his cranium. Two six-inch nails driven through the palms of his hands. It'll be some time before he's able to hold a pen, never mind a gun. You are a psychologist, so you can probably guess what sort of traumas he'll have to overcome to be able to get back to the job, if he gets back to the job. It was his first case.'

'You think I don't know that, Captain?'

'At the moment you have no partner. I don't have anyone else to assign to you and even if I did . . . I wouldn't, not now.'

Hunter pointed a finger at Captain Bolter. 'You said, just a few days ago that you wouldn't make the same mistake you made with John Spencer's case. You said you should've listened to me when I told everyone that he didn't kill his wife. You said that you should've allowed me to carry on with the investigation . . .'

'This isn't John Spencer's case, Robert,' the captain cut him short. 'We don't have an innocent man in custody. We have no one in custody and that's the problem. All we have are bodies. And they keep on fucking piling up.'

'You're making another mistake, Captain. Don't pull me from this case.'

Captain Bolter took a deep breath. His stare finding refuge on the floor.

'What the hell's going on, Captain?'

'Look, Robert. You know I trust your instincts. And I wish I'd trusted them more in the past. You've got some sort of sixth sense when it comes to that, but it's out of my hands now.'

'What do you mean?'

'I'm having my ass chewed by everyone above me, from the Mayor to the Chief of Police. They want answers and I don't have any. They are controlling this game now, I don't have much of a say anymore. It's gotten out of hand. They are talking about bringing the FBI into this. I'll be lucky if I manage to keep my job.'

Hunter rubbed his face with both hands. 'Taking me off the case is a mistake.'

'Well, it won't be the first mistake we made in this investigation, will it?'

The door opened and the petite, dark-haired nurse entered the room once again. 'Gentlemen, this is a hospital, not a Lakers' game. Maybe I should sedate you again,' she turned to Hunter.

'I don't think so,' Hunter said, jumping to his feet. 'Where the hell are my clothes?'

'You're supposed to stay here for at least twenty-four hours under observation,' the nurse said, stepping closer to him.

'Well, that just ain't gonna happen, honey, so back off, and show me where my clothes are.'

She looked at Captain Bolter hoping for some support which wasn't forthcoming. Hesitantly she pointed to the small wardrobe to the right of the door. 'In there.'

'We'll keep it down,' the captain said, gesturing to the door. He waited until the irritated nurse had left.

'Take some time off, Robert.'

'What?'

'You need a break. I want you to take some time off after you've briefed Matt and Doyle.'

'Are you suspending me?'

'No, I'm just telling you to take some time off.'

'You need me on this investigation, Captain.'

'I need you to brief the two new detectives on the case and then for you to take a vacation. It's not a request, Robert. Take a break, get yourself fit and forget about this case. You did everything you could. When you get back we can talk about what to do next.' Captain Bolter paused at the door. 'If I were you I'd listen to the nurse. Maybe it is a good idea to stay here overnight.'

'Is that another order?' Hunter said, giving the captain a sarcastic military salute.

'No, just a suggestion, but I'm worried.'

'About what?'

'You. The killer came after Carlos, you could be next.'

'If the killer wanted me dead, I'd be dead already.'

'Maybe he wants you dead now, which could be the reason

for the explosives in the room. The killer could be through with playing games and now he wants you.'

'Let him come then,' Hunter said defiantly.

'Oh yeah. You're the man, not scared of dying, real tough guy.'

Hunter eye's avoided the captain's.

'You're not a superhero, Robert. What would you do if the killer decided to come after you tonight? Pull something out of your super Hunter belt?'

'Why would he do that?'

'To finish the job he started.'

Hunter had no reply. He stared down at his bare, blistered feet.

'Look, Robert, I know you're fit. God knows my money would be on you on a hand to hand combat against just about anybody, but right now you're not one hundred percent . . . physically and mentally. If the killer comes after you in the next few days he'd have too much of an advantage.'

Hunter had to admit the captain had a point. An uncomfortable chill came over him.

'Think, Robert, don't be a fool, you're not superhuman. Spend the night in here where someone can keep an eye on you.'

'I don't need a babysitter, Captain,' he said, walking over to the window.

Captain Bolter knew how pointless it was to try and reason with Robert Hunter. He'd tried it many times before.

Hunter stared out at a busy hospital car park. 'My car, what happened to my car?'

'It's been towed back to the RHD. If you want, I can bring it over tomorrow,' he tried one last time.

Hunter turned and faced the captain. 'I ain't staying here

overnight, Captain. I'll pick it up on my way home,' he said, his voice firm.

'Suit yourself, I'm through arguing with you. Take tomorrow and the day after off, then I need you to bring Matt and Doyle up to speed.' He let the door slam behind him as he left the room.

Sixty

Hunter stepped out of the cab and looked up at the RHD building. His whole body ached. He needed a rest, but he knew there was no way he could've spent the night in that hospital room.

A guilty feeling started to torment him. He should've stayed with Garcia, he should've stayed with his partner, but what good would that have done? His wife was with him – he was in good hands. He would be back there first thing in the morning.

The dizziness had subsided but not enough to allow him to drive home just yet. Maybe what he needed was a strong cup of coffee.

He allowed the door to close slowly behind him and stared at an empty office. His gaze fell on the photo-covered board. Nine victims staring back at him. Nine victims that he couldn't help and he'd been a button push away from making it eleven.

Memories of the old laundry room came back and all of a sudden the room felt cold. The realization of how close to death he and Garcia had been made him shiver. A dry knot formed in his throat.

Slowly he prepared a pot of coffee just the way Garcia had taught him, triggering a new barrage of memories.

Why Carlos? Why go for a cop? Why go for his partner and not him? And no carving, no trademark double-crucifix on the back of the neck. Why? Maybe Garcia wasn't really supposed to die or maybe there was no point in marking the victim if the explosion would've disintegrated the room anyway. Hunter was sure this killer had an agenda set from the beginning and maybe the captain was right, the killer had achieved whatever he'd set out to achieve and Hunter was the last piece of the puzzle.

He poured himself a large coffee and sat back at his desk maybe for the last time. The new patients' list that he'd acquired from the hospital only that morning was still sitting on his desk. On any other day he'd fire up his computer and start looking for a match against the police database, but today wasn't any other day, he'd been defeated. The killer had won. No matter what happened from here on, even if the two new detectives managed to catch the killer, Robert Hunter had lost. The killer had been too good for him.

He touched his lower lip and felt it pulsating against the tips of his fingers. He leaned back and rested his head on the back of his chair closing his eyes. He needed some rest but he wasn't sure if he'd be able to sleep. Maybe tonight was the night to get hammered drunk, he thought, that would definitely help the pain.

He massaged his temples wondering what to do next. He needed some fresh air, he needed to get out of the office. Maybe going back into the RHD building hadn't been such a great idea after all – not tonight.

His thoughts were disrupted by his mobile ringtone.

'Detective Hunter speaking,' he said unenthusiastically.

'Hunter, it's Steven.'

Hunter had forgotten about the tail they'd placed on D-King. Steven was one of the three-man team that had D-King under twenty-four-hour surveillance.

'Oh God, Steven!' Hunter said, closing his eyes. 'I forgot to call off the team. You can drop the surveillance. It was a cold lead.'

'Thanks for telling me now,' Steven replied a little irritated.

'Sorry, man, but it's been a fairly eventful day, haven't had a lot of time to do much.'

'So you don't wanna know about what's happening tonight?'

'What's happening tonight?' Hunter asked with renewed interest.

'I'm not sure, but whatever it is, is something big.'

Sixty-One

Hunter followed Steven's directions and met him outside the disused factory in Gardena.

'Jesus! What the hell happened to you?' Steven asked as he caught sight of Hunter's battered face.

'Long story. What have we got here?'

Steven handed Hunter a pair of binoculars. 'Down there, towards the back of the building.'

Hunter looked in the direction Steven had indicated.

'It's too dark. What the hell am I supposed to be looking at?'

'Close to the north wall. Right over there,' Steven said, pointing at the main building again.

'Wait . . . Is that a van?' Hunter asked, a little more excited now.

'That's D-King's van. He and four of his men parked down there about half an hour ago and went into an underground entrance further towards the rear of the building. They were carrying a small arsenal with them.'

Hunter's interest grew. 'What's this all about?'

'I don't know, but we split the surveillance team in two. One team kept an eye on D-King and the other tailed his right-hand man, the giant muscle guy.'

'Yeah, and?'

'Well, in the past few days something's happened. They've

been going crazy searching for something or someone. Whatever it is that they've been after, I think this is it.'

Hunter had another quick look at the rear of the main building. D-King doesn't know the first victim isn't Jenny, he thought. He's been after the killer and he might've found something, some sort of lead. 'Where's the rest of the surveillance team?'

'I pulled them. You said we didn't need to keep an eye on your drug-dealer friend anymore. I'm just showing you this because I thought it could be of some interest. I'm out of here myself.'

'Before you go, where exactly did they go?'

'See that little trail at the back of the main building?' He pointed down to the factory once again. 'Follow it. That's where they went, but you're crazy if you're thinking about going down there alone. Where the hell is your new partner?'

Hunter hesitated for a few seconds. 'He's coming,' he said in a not very convincing tone.

'Do you want me to call for back-up?'

'No. We'll be OK.' Hunter knew Captain Bolter would throw a fit if he called for back-up after their conversation earlier.

'Suit yourself.'

Hunter watched as Steven jumped back into his unmarked vehicle and drove off.

'What the fuck am I doing?' he said out loud while checking his weapon. 'Haven't you had enough action for one day, Robert?' He retrieved a small flashlight from his glovebox and started down towards the little path Steven had indicated.

Sixty-Two

Hunter made his way down the dirt track at the back of the old factory, until he came to an iron door concealed by some over-grown vegetation. Behind the door, he found stone steps leading to an underground area. He waited a few seconds listening for any sounds.

Silence.

Cautiously he started down the dark tunnel.

A heavy moldy, damp smell made him gag. He hoped nobody heard him cough.

'What the hell, Robert?' he whispered. 'Another old building, another dark basement . . .'

The tunnel at the bottom of the stairs was narrow, lined in concrete and filled with debris. As he moved deeper underground, voices started to materialize – several voices – angry voices. The foul smell now mixed with some sort of raw sewage. Rats meandered everywhere.

'I fucking hate rats,' Hunter murmured through clenched teeth.

He reached a large circular area with a half-demolished square structure at the center of it. Its walls were full of holes. The voices were coming from inside the makeshift structure.

He turned off his flashlight and edged closer, being careful not to disrupt any of the loose bricks that littered the entire underground floor. He went around to the left of the squared structure and positioned himself behind some old cement bags, just a few feet away from the wall. Hunter bent down trying to level his eyes with one of the holes. He could see some movement inside but his angle kept him from having a clear picture.

The voices got louder. He could clearly recognize D-King's voice.

'We're not gonna hurt you. We're here to get you away from these fucks. You're free, it's over. I'm gonna undo your blindfold and gag OK, don't be afraid, I'm not gonna hurt you.'

What the fuck is going on in there? Hunter thought. He needed to get closer. He inched his way nearer to the wall and quickly found a better position leveling his eyes with one of the larger holes. Three men were standing facing the opposite wall with their hands on their heads. One of them was completely naked, his back entirely covered with what seemed like a tattoo of Jesus on a cross. D-King was kneeling down in the center of the room in front of a petrified-looking brunette woman no older than thirty. She'd been blindfolded, gagged and tied to a metal chair. What was left of her black dress was dirty and torn. Her bra had been ripped off her body. Freshly made cigarette burns surrounded both of her nipples with water blisters already starting to form. Her legs had been spread apart and tied to the sides of the chair. Her dress had been hitched up exposing her vagina with more cigarette burns around it. Parts of her hair were stuck together with what seemed like dried blood. Her bottom lip was swollen and cut.

Hunter watched as D-King reached behind the woman's head to untie both of her restraints. As the blindfold came off she blinked rapidly several times. The strong light burning her eyes. Her gag had been tied so tightly it had cut into the corners of her mouth. She coughed violently as her mouth was set free.

D-King pulled a paper tissue out of his pocket and wiped her face clean of the mascara and bloodstains on her face. One of D-King's men had already freed her hands and legs and she'd started crying again. Her body was shaking with every new sob, but this time the tears were a combination of fear and relief.

'What's your name?' Hunter heard D-King ask.

'Becky,' she replied in-between sobs.

'You'll be OK, Becky. We'll get you out of here,' D-King said, trying to help her up, but her knees buckled under her. Quickly he grabbed hold of her waist before she collapsed back onto the chair.

'Easy now . . . your legs are still weak. We gotta do this slowly.' He turned his attention back to one of his men. 'Find something to cover her up.'

The man's eyes searched the room for a piece of cloth or something suitable but found nothing.

'Here, take this.' Hunter recognized Jerome from the night-club. He took off his shirt and handed it to D-King. The massive shirt over the woman's petite frame looked almost like a long dress.

'You'll be OK, Becky. It's all over now.'

D-King's voice took a different tone altogether. 'Take her upstairs, put her in the car and don't leave her side,' D-King barked at someone.

Hunter quickly ducked behind some cement bags as best and as quietly as he could, the shadows helping to conceal him. Through an opening between the bags Hunter saw another huge man exiting the room. On his arms the petrified-looking Becky.

'You'll be safe with me, Becky,' the man reassured her in a caring voice.

Hunter waited until they'd disappeared down the corridor and inched closer once again.

'So you believe in Jesus, do you?' D-King asked in an angry voice as he approached the naked tattooed man.

No reply.

Hunter saw D-King slam the wooden butt of his double-barreled shotgun into the man's lower back, who collapsed to the ground. Instinctively, the shortest of the three captured men turned in a reaction, but before he was able to make a move Jerome struck him across the face with an Uzi sub-machinegun. Blood splattered against the wall. Two of his teeth bounced onto the floor.

'Who the fuck told you to move?' Jerome's voice was an angry shout.

Damn, Steven wasn't joking when he said they had a small arsenal in here, Hunter thought.

'That girl was what, twenty-eight, twenty-nine?' D-King hit the man on the floor once again, this time a hard kick to the stomach. 'Get up and turn around, you sack o' shit.' D-King paced in front of the now scared men.

'Do you know who I am?' The question hung in the air before the shortest of the three nodded.

D-King looked on in amazement. With a calm voice he continued. 'So you know who I am and still you took one of my girls from me, raped her, tortured her and killed her?'

No answer.

'Boy, you've just taken the word stupid to new heights. You two . . . strip,' he ordered, pointing at the two men who were dressed.

They looked back at him with a puzzled expression.

'Are you fuckers deaf? He said strip,' Jerome commanded, striking the one who was wearing glasses in the stomach.

'Wow, she would've needed magnifying glasses, boys,' D-King said, staring at their naked bodies. 'No wonder you have problems getting women. Tie them to the chairs, just like they do to their victims.'

Click, Hunter heard the unmistakable sound of a semi-automatic pistol being cocked behind him. A split second later he felt its cold barrel being pressed against the back of his head.

'Don't even think about moving,' the voice commanded.

Sixty-Three

The door opened and Hunter was pushed into the room, the gun still pressed hard against the back of his head.

'I found this piece of shit sneaking around outside. He was packing this,' the man said, throwing the gun he'd retrieved from Hunter onto the floor. D-King turned to face the new arrival.

'Detective Hunter? This is a surprise.'

'Detective?' Warren, who had discovered and captured Hunter, said in astonishment.

'What the hell happened to you?' D-King asked, staring at Hunter's bruised and cut face.

'Don't look at me, boss,' Warren said, lifting his hands up. 'He was already this ugly when I found him.'

Hunter's eyes quickly scanned his surroundings. The room was illuminated by battery-powered professional filming lights and the entire floor had been covered with plastic sheets. The metal chair Becky had been tied to stood in the center of the room. Next to the wall, behind D-King, a selection of knives had been placed on a small table. On one of the corners a semi-professional video camera had been mounted onto a tripod and just behind it, two extra chairs. It took Hunter less than three seconds to realize where he was.

'A snuff movie joint? Very classy.' His eyes fixed on D-King.

'Oh you're quick,' D-King said, before noticing Hunter's derisive look. 'Wait a second. You think I run this fucked-up operation? Oh hell no.'

Hunter's eyes moved over to the three naked men standing against the south wall and then to a shirtless Jerome. 'So you folks having a little party? *Getting down with it?*' He teased, putting on a silly, nasal voice.

'Oh, you're in the mood to be funny?' D-King asked, cocking his shotgun. 'What the fuck are you doing here, Detective?'

'I was in the neighborhood. This is one of my favorite hangouts.'

'You're in a pretty fucked-up position to be cracking jokes,' Jerome warned him.

Hunter's eyes shifted to the three men.

'My question still stands, Detective,' D-King said. 'What the fuck are you doing here?'

Hunter kept silent.

'Wait a second,' D-King said, squinting his eyes. 'You slick motherfucker. You wanted me to do your job for you, ain't that right?'

Jerome looked confused. 'What?'

'He knew I'd be going after whoever hurt Jenny with everything I had, so he sat still with his eye on me waiting for me to do all the hard work, waiting for me to scan the streets for him so he could turn up at the last minute and take the glory.'

'Not quite like that,' Hunter replied.

'Well, I've got some bad news for you, Detective. The girl in your computer picture isn't Jenny. Your maniac killer didn't get to her. These three cocksuckers did.' He pointed to the three naked men. 'They raped, tortured and sodomized her before ripping her neck open. I've got it all on film.' The anger was back in D-King's voice and he exploded in a new violent rage

slamming his shotgun barrel into the lower abdomen of the tattooed man for a second time. Hunter watched.

'Tie them to the chairs,' D-King commanded, tilting his head
towards Warren.

'You're a policeman, do something,' the one with glasses
pleaded.

'Shut the fuck up,' Warren shot back, punching the man in
the mouth.

'He's right,' Hunter intervened. 'I can't just allow you to
take your vengeance any way you want to.'

'Stay the fuck out of this, Detective. This ain't your show.'

'I'm making it my show.'

D-King looked around the room with a sarcastic smile on his
lips. 'I think you'll find you're outnumbered, Detective. What
do you think you can do?'

'And if he's got back-up boss?' Jerome asked.

'He doesn't. If he did they'd be down here already,' D-King
said, throwing Hunter a defiant look.

'Tie them up,' D-King commanded again.

A couple of minutes later the three naked men sat tied to
metal chairs in the center of the room.

'Look, you're not in the wrong yet,' Hunter said, taking a
step closer to D-King. 'This still hasn't gotten out of hand. Let
me take them in. Let the law deal with them. They'll rot in jail.'

'If I were you I'd stand still,' Warren said, lifting his gun and
aiming at Hunter's head.

'If you were me you'd be good-looking,' Hunter shot back.
'D-King, I know you're upset by what they did to Jenny, but we
can solve this the right way.'

D-King let out a loud laugh. 'Somehow "upset" doesn't quite
say it. And this *is* the right way. Let me bring it to you real,
Detective Hunter. The law will allow them to walk and you

know it. They'll turn this thing around using some bullshit technicality as they always do. If you take them in, you've gotta take us in and that ain't happening, baby. Sorry, Hunter, we've gotta deal with them our way.'

'I can't just stand here and watch you kill them.'

'Close your eyes then. You're not even supposed to be here. These people kidnap, rape, and kill women for profit.'

Hunter gave D-King a nervous laugh. 'Coming from you that's grand.'

'Oh hell no. You ain't comparing me to these fucks? I don't force any of my girls to do the job they do. I also don't force anyone to hire them. What these guys do, whatever way you look at it, is just fucking sick. Look at this place. How does this compare to what I do?'

Suddenly, catching everyone by surprise, the wall behind D-King swung open. A tall, shaven-headed man holding a Desert Eagle .50 pistol in each hand emerged, his eyes wide open, his pupils dilated, his nostrils inflamed. There was a murderous and deranged look on his face.

No one had any time to react. As gunshots showered the room Hunter sensed his opportunity and jumped to the floor searching for his pistol.

The onslaught of bullets had neither aim nor specific direction. One of the filming lights exploded with a deafening blast. The sudden change in light blinded everyone for a split second and on instinct D-King ducked down – bullets hitting the wall behind him, missing his head by a fraction. He heard Warren's agonized cry as his colossal body crumpled to the floor, both of his hands covering his face, blood dripping through his fingers.

Jerome stood his ground like a fearless soldier ready to face death. He squeezed the trigger on his machinegun and the wave of bullets found its target with military precision. The intruder's body shook violently with every blow and he tumbled back. The total impact was so powerful it almost separated his legs from his torso. His limp body fell to the floor. The entire gunfight lasted less than ten seconds.

As the shots died down, their echoes were replaced by the terrified screams of the three helpless naked men. Miraculously they were still alive.

'Shut the fuck up!' Jerome blasted in a heated voice, turning his Uzi towards them.

'Chill, nigga!' D-King shouted, aiming his shotgun at the newly revealed door. 'They're no threat to us. Check him,' he gestured towards the semi-mutilated intruder.

Warren was still on the floor, his hands and shirt covered in blood.

Hunter was also up on his feet with his gun in hand. 'OK everyone, put your guns down.'

D-King's aim moved from the door to Hunter as did Jerome's. 'This ain't the time for this kind of crap, Detective, there could still be more people hiding in that room. I ain't got no beef with you, not yet, but if I have to I will gun you down like a dirty dawg. Remember, you're still outnumbered and outgunned.'

Hunter's aim stayed on D-King. The trigger mechanism on Hunter's Wildey Survivor pistol had been modified to lighter than normal. That, coupled with the knowledge that the average trigger resistance on a double-barreled shotgun is about half a pound heavier than most pistols, meant Hunter knew he could squeeze a shot out at least a second faster than D-King could. On the other hand, Jerome with his Uzi would pose a bigger problem. But they weren't the enemy. Hunter wasn't about to start another gunfight. And he sure wasn't about to risk getting shot on behalf of the three naked scumbags in the room. He moved his aim away from D-King.

'OK, let's secure this place.'

'Warren, talk to me, how're you doing, buddy? Are you hit?' D-King called out without diverting his attention from his primary target.

Like a wounded animal Warren emitted a loud growl indicating he was still alive.

'This one is dead,' Jerome announced, standing over the lifeless body by the new door.

D-King turned his attention back to the three tied-up men. 'Anyone else where that motherfucker came from?'

No reply.

'Anyone else in that room?' he asked, pressing the barrels of his shotgun against the tattooed man's head.

'No.' The answer finally came from the shortest of the three.

D-King nodded at Jerome who slotted a new clip onto his Uzi and very cautiously stepped into the new room. 'We're clear here,' he called out after a few seconds.

'I've gotta check on Warren. Jerome, keep your gun on Hunter.'

Jerome turned and aimed the Uzi at Hunter who returned the favor.

D-King placed his shotgun on the floor and rushed to Warren's side.

'OK, let me take a look. Move your hands.'

Warily Warren removed his bloody hands from his face. D-King wiped some of the blood away with his shirt in an attempt to get a better look. He saw two large cuts – one on Warren's forehead and the other on his left cheek.

'No bullets,' D-King said after a quick examination. 'You weren't hit by bullets. It looks like shrapnel from the walls.

You'll live.' He took off his shirt and placed it in Warren's hands. 'Here, just keep pressure over the wounds.'

'Boss, you gotta come and have a look at this.'

Something in Jerome's voice worried D-King.

'What is it?'

'You have to see it for yourself.'

Sixty-Four

D-King picked up his shotgun and approached Jerome by the open door. He stood rigid. His eyes carefully scanning the new room. 'What the fuck?' he whispered,. 'Hunter, come and have a look at this.'

Hunter cautiously joined them.

The new room was in much better shape than the one they were in. The ceiling had been painted blue and decorated with what looked like a million fluorescent stars. The walls were even more colorful, displaying a tremendous variety of drawings – dragons, wizards, horses, leprechauns ... On the far wall a series of wooden shelves held an impressive collection of toys – dolls, cars, action figures with even more toys scattered all over the floor. A large rocking horse sat to the left of the door. Against the west wall a video camera had been placed on a tripod.

Hunter felt his chest knot around his heart. His eyes left the room and rested on D-King's baffled face.

'Kids,' Hunter whispered. The anger in his voice as clear as a loud shout.

D-King's eyes seemed glued to the room's decoration. It took him another thirty seconds to face Hunter. 'Kids?' D-King's voice trailed off. 'Kids?' This time a powerful cry as he stormed back into the first room. The sadness inside him had been replaced by pure rage.

'This is fucked up, man,' Jerome said, shaking his head.

'You do this to kids? What kind of sick fucks are you?' D-King demanded standing before the three bound men. His bravado met with silence, his eyes met by no one.

Hunter's stare rested on the three naked men. He simply didn't care anymore.

'Let me tell you something, Detective Hunter.' D-King's voice quivered with anger. 'I grew up on the streets. I've dealt with scum my whole life. If there's one thing I've learnt is that out here we have our own way of dealing with things. Most moth-erfuckers aren't scared of getting caught. Prison is like holiday camp. It's their home away from home. In there they've got their gangs, their drugs and their bitches. It ain't much different from outside. But they'd shit a brick if they thought street-law was knocking on their fucking door. Out here we're the jury, the judge and the executioner. This doesn't concern you or your law. They'll pay for what they've done to Jenny and you ain't coming between me and them.'

There was more to it than rage. Hunter knew he'd been right. To D-King Jenny had been a lot more than just one of the girls.

Hunter turned to face the three men tied to the metal chairs. They stared back at him with insolent smiles, like they knew he had to take them in, it was protocol, it was what cops had to do.

Hunter felt tired. He'd had enough. He wasn't even sup-posed to be there. This had nothing to do with the Crucifix Killer. This was D-King's problem.

'Fuck protocol,' Hunter whispered. 'I was never here.'

D-King gave him a quick nod and watched as Hunter hol-stered his weapon and silently made for the door.

'Wait!' the tattooed man shouted. 'You can't just walk away. You're a fucking cop. How about our human rights?'

Hunter didn't stop. He didn't even look back as he closed the door behind him.

'Rights?' D-King asked with an animated laugh. 'We'll give you your rights . . . your last rites.'

'What do we do about this place . . . and them,' Jerome tilted his head towards the men in the first room.

'Torch the place, but we'll take them with us. We still gotta get the name of their ringleader out of them.'

'Do you think they'll talk?'

'Oh they'll talk, I promise you. If it's sodomizing pain they're into, we'll give it to them . . . over a ten-day period.' The evil smile on D-King's lips made even Jerome shudder.

Back in his car Hunter stared at his shaking hands, struggling with an agonizing and uneasy feeling. He was a detective. He was supposed to uphold the law and he'd just disregarded it. His heart told him he'd done the right thing, but his conscience didn't agree. D-King's words still echoed in his ears. *Out here we're the jury, the judge and the executioner.* Suddenly Hunter stopped breathing.

'That's it,' he said in a trembling voice. 'That's where I know him from.'

Sixty-Five

With his heart thumping violently against his chest, Hunter made his way back to the RHD as fast as he could. He needed to check some old records.

As he entered his office he was glad it was on a separate floor to all the other detectives. He needed to do this alone, no disturbances. He locked the door behind him and fired up his computer.

'Be right . . . be right . . .' he said to himself as he accessed the California Department of Justice databank. Hunter quickly typed in the name he wanted to search for, selected the criteria and hit the 'search' button. As the Department of Justice data server went to work, he sat still staring anxiously at the little dot moving back and forth on the screen. The seconds seemed like minutes.

'C'mon . . .' he urged the computer to work faster as he paced nervously in front of his desk. Two minutes later the dot stopped moving and the message *No Results Found* appeared on the screen.

'Shit!'

He tried again. This time going back a few more years. He knew he was right, he knew this had to be it.

The familiar dot started moving on the screen again and Hunter went back to pacing the room. His anxiety at boiling point. He stopped in front of the picture-covered corkboard and stared at all the photographs. He knew it was there, the answer was there.

The searching dot stopped moving and this time the screen filled up with data.

'Yes . . .' he said triumphantly, moving back to his desk and quickly scanning the information on the screen. As he found what he was looking for he frowned.

'You gotta be shitting me!'

Hunter sat in silence thinking about what to do next. 'The family trees,' he said. 'The victims' family trees.'

On the initial investigation Hunter and Scott had tried everything they could think of to establish a link between the victims. They'd even traced the family trees for some of them. Hunter knew he had it somewhere. He started flipping through the mountain of paper on his desk that constituted the old case files.

'Here it is,' he said, as he finally came across the lists. He analyzed them for a few moments. 'This is it.' Hunter moved back to his computer and typed in a new name. The result came back almost instantly now that the search criteria had been narrowed down to exactly what he wanted.

Another match . . . and then another.

Hunter massaged his tired eyes. His whole body ached, but his new discovery had injected new life into his veins. He wasn't able to establish links between all the victims, but he already knew why.

'How could I've missed this before?' he asked himself, as he knocked on his forehead with his clenched fist. But he knew exactly how. This was an old case, going back several years. A case where he'd been the arresting officer. The obscured victims' links sometimes spanned three generations according to the family trees. Some of them not family at all. Without a hint he would've never found it. Without D-King he would've never thought of it.

Robert started pacing the room once again and stopped in front of Garcia's desk. A sudden overwhelming sadness brought a tight knot to his throat. His partner was lying in hospital in a semi-coma and there was nothing he could do. He remembered Anna's sad eyes. How she sat next to her husband's bed waiting for a sign of life. She loved him more than anything. There's no love stronger than family love, Hunter thought and then stopped dead. The hair on the back of his neck standing on end.

'Holy shit!'

He rushed back to his computer and for the next hour he devoured every result page he came across with astounding eagerness and surprise. Slowly, everything was falling into place.

The arrest files . . . the tattoos, he remembered. A few minutes later, after searching the RHD's own database, he was staring at the arrest records from the old case.

'This can't be . . .' he stuttered the words catatonically. A mixture of excitement and fear sucked the heat out of his body. Suddenly, he remembered what he'd seen just a few weeks ago and his stomach knotted. 'How blind have I been?' he murmured before turning to his computer for one last search. A name that could bring everything together. It took him less than a minute to find it.

'I had it right in front of me,' he whispered, staring blankly at his computer screen. 'I had the answer right in front of me.'

He needed one final confirmation and it had to come from the San Francisco Police Department. After speaking to Lieutenant Morris from the SFPD over the phone he waited impatiently for Morris to fax him an arrest file. When the file came through half an hour later Hunter stared at it soundless. His mind battling reality. It was an old photograph, but there was no doubt in his mind – he knew who that person was.

Proof. That's what every investigation comes down to and Hunter had none. There was no way he could link the person on that photograph to any of the Crucifix Killings and he knew it. No matter how sure he was, without proof he had nothing. He checked his watch one more time before reaching for the phone and placing one last call.

Sixty-Six

Hunter drove slowly, taking no notice as the other drivers sped past him shouting profanities out of their windows.

He parked in front of his apartment building and rested his head on the steering wheel for a moment. His headache, if anything, had worsened and he knew tablets would have no effect. Before leaving the car he checked his cell phone for missed calls or messages. A futile exercise as he was sure he didn't have any. He'd left instructions with everyone at the hospital that he should be informed the second Garcia regained consciousness, but something told him that wouldn't happen tonight.

He stepped into his empty apartment and closed the door behind him, resting his throbbing body against it. The devastating solitude of his living room saddened him even further.

With his brain half numb he slowly walked into the kitchen, opened the fridge and stared at it blankly for a few seconds. His body should be screaming for food as he hadn't eaten anything all day, but he didn't feel at all hungry. In reality he was dying for a shower. It would help relax his tense muscles, but that would have to come second. His primary need was for a double Scotch.

He struggled to make a decision, staring at the bottles in his small bar for a few seconds. He smiled as he decided to go for something strong – Aberlour thirty years. He filled his glass halfway and opted for no ice this time. 'The stronger the better,' he told himself, collapsing into his beat-up sofa. The effect of the strong liquid as it touched his lips was invigorating. It burned against the small cuts that surrounded his mouth, but he welcomed the sensation – enjoyable pain.

He rested his head against the sofa backrest, but forced himself not to close his eyes. He feared the images that hid behind his eyelids. He spent a couple of minutes staring at the ceiling, allowing the sturdy taste of his single malt to numb his tongue and mouth. Soon he knew it would numb his entire body.

He got up and walked to the window. Outside, the street looked quiet. He turned to face the empty living room once again. His body was slowly relaxing. He had another sip of his whisky and checked his cell phone once again pressing a few keys to make sure it was working OK.

In the kitchen he placed his glass on the table and sat down. Leaning back on the uncomfortable wooden chair he rubbed his face vigorously with both hands. As he did so, he heard a faint creaking sound coming from the corridor that led to his room. A shiver of fear raced through his body with extraordinary speed. Someone was there.

Hunter jumped to his feet and immediately felt the kitchen spinning around him. His legs started losing their strength and he held on to the worktop for balance. As confusion set in, his eyes rested on the empty whisky glass on the table. *Drugged.*

Before he collapsed onto the kitchen floor his unfocused eyes registered a dark figure moving towards him.

Sixty-Seven

Slowly he opened his eyes, but it made no difference. The darkness was unconditional. He felt dizzy and very light-headed. Whatever drug he'd taken with his whisky had knocked him out in minutes. The first thing he realized was that he was sitting down, bound to some sort of uncomfortable chair. His hands were tied behind his back, his ankles tied to the chair's legs. He tried breaking free but his efforts were in vain. His body hurt even more now but he was sure he had no broken bones – at least not yet. He felt thirsty – very thirsty.

Hunter had no idea how long he'd been out. Slowly and painfully his memory began to fill him in on what had happened. He tried to calm himself down and a familiar feeling came over him. He looked around in darkness and even though he couldn't see, he knew where he was. He'd never left his apartment. He was sitting in his living room.

He tried moving again, but his hands and legs had been bound too tight. He made an effort to scream but his voice barely made a sound. It surprised him how weak he felt. Suddenly he sensed a chilling presence behind him.

'*I can hear you're awake.*'

The same robotic voice that had tormented him for over three years echoed through the room, catching him by surprise and startling him stiff. It came from behind him, some sort of speaker set up. Hunter felt a strange sensation run through him. He was finally in the presence of the killer. The Crucifix Killer.

Hunter tried turning, rotating his neck as far as it would go, but darkness prevented him from seeing his assailant.

'*Don't rush it, Robert. This is the final chapter. For you at least. It'll all end tonight. Right here. You're the last one.*'

The last one. Hunter's findings in his office were now confirmed. This had all been about revenge.

He suddenly heard the sound of metal against metal. Surgical instruments he presumed. Instinctively his body went rigid with fear, but consciously he forced himself to stay calm. Hunter understood the psychology of killers, especially serial killers. The one thing they want more than anything else is to be understood. To them their killings have meaning, they serve a purpose and they want their victims to know they aren't dying in vain. Before the kill, there's always the explanation.

'*Tonight you'll pay for what you've done.*'

Those last words sent a judder of recognition through Hunter's body. The voice that came from behind him was loud and clear – not robotic – not metallic – no distortion box. Hunter didn't need to search his memory, he didn't need to think about it. He knew that voice and he knew it well. All of a sudden the darkness disappeared. Hunter squeezed his eyes as uneven circles of light blurred his vision. His pupils contracted trying to get used to the brightness. As the blurriness dissipated a familiar shape took form in front of his eyes.

Sixty-Eight

The blurriness seemed to have taken forever to subside, but once his eyes regained focus he knew he'd been right. Strangely enough he didn't want to believe it. His eyes fixed on the person standing before him.

'By the look on your face I can see you're surprised,' she said, her voice as sweet as it'd always been.

Hunter had hoped he'd been wrong. But now, staring at her, it all fell into place. He managed to whisper only one word. 'Isabella.'

She smiled at him. The same smile he'd seen so many times, but this time her smile carried something else, something it'd never carried before. A hidden evil.

'I thought you'd be happy to see me.' Her Italian accent was gone. In fact, everything about her was different. As if the Isabella he knew had vanished, replaced by a total stranger.

Hunter's expression remained immutable. His brain was finally piecing together the last of the puzzle.

'You deserve an Oscar. Your Italian accent was perfect.'

She bowed down acknowledging the compliment.

'Very clever trick with that phone call at the restaurant too. A perfect alibi,' Hunter said, remembering the call he'd received from the killer when he was having lunch with her for the first time. 'A recorded message with a timer. Simple, but very effective.'

A hint of a smile creased her lips. 'Allow me to introduce myself . . .' she said steadily.

'Brenda . . .' Hunter interrupted in a hoarse and weak voice. 'Brenda Spencer . . . John Spencer's sister. The record producer.'

She shot him a surprised and uncomfortable look. 'Doctor Brenda Spencer if you don't mind,' she corrected him.

'A medical doctor,' Hunter asserted.

'If you must know . . . a surgeon.' A new malevolent smile.

'This has all been about revenge for your brother's death?' Hunter asked, already knowing the answer.

'Very good, Robert,' she said overenthusiastically clapping her hands together like a child who'd just been given another unexpected present.

The ghostly silence that followed seemed to go on forever.

'He committed suicide in his cell,' Hunter finally offered.

'He committed suicide because you failed to do your fucking job.' The anger in her voice was undeniable. 'To protect and to serve, what a joke. He was innocent and you knew it.' She paused, letting her words float through the room. 'He'd told you many times that he would've never hurt Linda. He loved her, the sort of love you'd never understand.' She took a moment to collect herself again. 'You interviewed him. You knew he was innocent and still you let them sentence him. You could've done something, but instead you let them sentence an innocent man to death.'

Hunter remembered the dinner he had at Isabella's. She'd lied about everything to do with her life, but she did mention a dead brother. That had been a mistake, a slip-up. She was fast to cover it up with the Marine story, saying her brother died serving his country. A bullshit story, but Hunter didn't pick it up. What he saw in her eyes that night wasn't sadness. It was rage.

'It was out of my hands.' He thought about telling her how he'd tried to convince others of his opinion about her brother's case, but there was no point now. It wouldn't make a difference.

'If you had run the investigation how it should've been run you would've found the real killer sooner, before my brother lost his mind, before he hanged himself. But you stopped searching.'

'You can't blame the police for your brother's suicide.'

'I'm not blaming the police. I'm blaming you.'

'We would've found the real killer eventually and your brother would've walked free.'

'No, you wouldn't have.' Her voice was angry once again. 'How would you have found the real killer if you weren't looking? You'd given up on the investigation because the initial, superficial evidence pointed to John and that was good enough for you and your partner. No need to find the truth. One more successful conviction for the two star detectives. You got to be praised once again and that's all that mattered. He was convicted of murder, Robert. He was given the death penalty for something he didn't do. No one gave him the benefit of the doubt, no one including that pathetic excuse for a jury. My brother was classed as a monster. A jealous, murderous monster.' She paused to take a deep breath. 'And I lost my entire family because of you, your partner and that fucking, useless, waste-of-space jury. They couldn't see the truth if it'd danced naked in front of them.' Her eyes burned with rage.

Hunter gave her a puzzled look.

'Twenty days after John committed suicide my mother passed away from heart sorrow. Do you know what that is?'

Hunter didn't answer.

'She didn't eat, didn't speak, didn't move. She simply sat in her room staring out the window with John's picture in her hands. Tears rolling down her face until she had none left to cry. The anguish and pain in her heart eating her away from the inside until she was too weak to fight back.'

Hunter kept silent, his eyes following her as she slowly paced around the room.

'It didn't end there.' Brenda's voice was now dark and somber. 'Thirty-five years, Robert. My parents had been married for thirty-five years. After losing his son and his wife in such a short space of time, my father started to succumb to a never-ending sadness.'

Hunter already guessed the end to this story.

'Twenty-two days after burying my mother. After the real killer was finally caught, his depression got the best of him and my father followed my brother's way out. I was alone . . . again.' The anger in her was almost palpable.

'So you decided to take your revenge on the jury,' Hunter said, his voice still weak.

'You finally figured it out,' she replied calmly. 'It took you long enough. Maybe the great Robert Hunter isn't so great after all.'

'But you didn't go after the jurors themselves. You killed someone close to them. Someone they loved,' Hunter continued.

'Isn't revenge sweet?' she said with a frightening comfortable smile. 'An eye for an eye, Robert. I gave them back what they'd given me. Heartache, loneliness, emptiness, sadness. I wanted them to feel a loss so great that every day would become a struggle.'

Not all the victims had been directly related to one of the jurors from John Spencer's case, but it was easy to figure out why. Some of them were lovers. Forbidden lovers, illicit affairs, even gay lovers. Hidden relationships that were impossible to trace back to any of the jurors. A loved one nevertheless.

'I dedicated my life to finding the right person. The one they loved the most. I took my time following them. I studied their routines. I found out everything there was to know about them. Places they liked to hang out. Secrets about their past. I even went to some filthy sex parties just to get closer to one of them. I must admit though, watching the jurors suffer with every new murder was reinvigorating.'

Hunter threw her a worried look.

'Oh yes, I took the time to observe them after every kill,' she explained. 'I wanted to see them suffer. Their pain gave me strength.' She paused for a moment. 'Three of the jurors committed suicide, did you know that? They couldn't take the loss. They couldn't take the pain, just like my parents couldn't.' She laughed an evil laugh that darkened the room. 'Just to prove how incompetent the police are, I left a clue with every victim, and you still couldn't catch me,' she continued.

'The double-crucifix on the victims' necks,' Hunter confirmed.

She gave him a malicious nod.

'Like the tattoo your brother had on the back of his neck?'

Another surprised look from Brenda.

'I checked your brother's records after I found out about the jurors. I remembered that on the arresting report, under identifying marks, the officer in charge had noted down several tattoos, but he never fully described them. I had to check the autopsy report to find out what they were. A double-arm crucifix to the back of the neck was one of them. You were giving every victim your brother's mark.'

'Aren't you clever? I tattooed the double-crucifix on my brother's neck myself,' she said proudly. 'John loved the pain.'

Hunter felt the air inside his living room go cold. As Brenda recalled putting her own brother through pain, the pleasure in her voice was chilling.

'But why frame Mike Farloe? He had nothing to do with your brother's case,' Hunter asked, trying to fill in one of the gaps he still didn't have an answer to.

'He'd always been part of the plan,' she shot back matter-of-factly. 'Frame someone believable after the last kill and no one would've carried on snooping around. The case gets closed and everybody's happy,' she said grinning. 'But unfortunately I ran into a small problem. The framing had to be put forward.'

'The seventh victim!' Hunter said.

'Wow. You *are* quick.' She put on an impressed face.

Mike Farloe had been arrested just after the seventh victim was found. An aspiring young lawyer, daughter to one of the jurors. The closest relation to a juror out of all the victims. With just a little more time Hunter and Wilson would surely have hit upon it, but why try to establish a link between victims when they already had a self-confessed killer in custody? With Mike's arrest everything about the Crucifix Killer's investigation came to a halt.

'She was supposed to be my last victim,' Brenda snorted. 'But how was I to know she had a photographic memory? She recognized me from the courtroom when I first approached her. She even remembered the clothes I wore. She became an immediate threat, so I had no choice but to move her up on my list. After that I needed time to reorganize my plan. Framing somebody at the end of it all was always my intention. I found Mike Farloe preaching the gospel on the streets just after I killed that piece of shit accountant.'

The fifth victim, Hunter thought.

'Mike was easy. A sick pedophile who idolized the Crucifix

Killer. I prepped Mike for months, feeding him all the necessary information. Just enough for him to sound convincing when caught. I knew he was ready.' She shrugged her shoulders. 'I wasn't counting on him confessing though, that was just a bonus. It completely stopped the investigation dead. Just what I needed,' she said with a chuckle. 'But with his arrest came the opportunity for me to get to someone else on my list. One of the main protagonists of my suffering . . . your stupid fucking partner.'

Hunter's eyes filled with sudden horror.

'Oh, I forgot,' she said with a frozen smile. 'You didn't know that was my doing, did you?'

'What was your doing?' Hunter asked with a trembling voice.

'That little boat explosion.'

Hunter felt his stomach churn.

'With the end of the Crucifix Killer's case I wasn't surprised when you and your partner decided to take a break. It was only fair after such a lengthy investigation. All I had to do was follow him.' She paused and watched as Hunter battled with his own repugnance. 'You know, they invited me up onto their boat. You can always count on a cop to help someone in need, especially a woman. Once on board, the killing was child's play. I had him tied up, just like you are now, and then I made him watch. I made him watch while I made the little bitch suffer. There was so much blood, Robert.' She stared at Hunter for a moment, savoring his pain. 'And yes, I knew she was your only cousin. That gave me even more pleasure.'

Hunter felt nauseous, a sick taste regurgitated into his mouth.

'He begged for her life. He offered me his in exchange for hers. The ultimate love sacrifice, but that was no good to me. I had his life in my hands anyway.' A short silence followed before she continued. 'She died slowly while he cried like a baby. I didn't kill him straight away you know. I left him for a few hours so he could soak in the pain of her death. After that, the only thing left for me to do was bring some fuel barrels from my boat onto his, create a little leak, set some timers and . . . boom. The fire would destroy any evidence I missed.'

The pleasure in her voice was arctic.

'The greatest thing after that was watching you take the ride straight to rock bottom, it was beautiful. After their deaths I thought you would do it. I thought you would give in and blow your brains out. You were close to doing it.'

Hunter could voice no reply.

'But then you were given a new partner and it looked like you were starting to bounce back. I still had two more on my list, not counting you, so I figured it was time for us to start playing our game again.' She ran her hand through her hair in an overly casual way. 'You were a tough one to get to. A real loner. No wife, no girlfriend, no children, no lover and no family. So I created Isabella, the slut. The one who'd pick you up from a sleazy bar. The one who'd make you fall in love with her.' Her arrogance was majestic.

'Do you have any idea what it's like to go to bed with someone you despise? To allow that someone to touch you, to kiss you?' She contorted her face into a disgusted look. 'Every second we were together made my skin crawl. Every time you touched me I felt violated. Every time you left I'd wash myself clean for hours, scrubbing my skin until it was red raw.' She took a deep breath to calm herself. 'You were supposed to fall in love with her. She was the one you were supposed to risk your life for. She was the one who'd rip your heart from you before killing you. Can you see the irony, Robert?'

Hunter didn't shy away from her stare.

'But you ran away from romance like the devil from a cross,' she continued in a calm voice. 'You couldn't see how special she was, could you? Were you too good for her? Is that what you think? The great Robert Hunter was too good for little, fragile Isabella, is that it?' she said, mockingly putting on a sad child's face.

'That was my mistake. I should've spent more time with Isabella.'

Brenda looked deeply into Hunter's eyes and held them for a while. 'I know what you're thinking. You're thinking that if you had spent more time with her you would've figured her out.' She laughed. 'I've got news for you, Robert. You could've spent months with her and you still wouldn't have a clue. Isabella was perfect. I made her perfect. I spent over a year creating her and living her life before finally approaching you. I acquired new mannerisms and habits. I started from scratch. New life, new apartment, new job, new everything. Psychological immersion. You know what that is, don't you, Robert? I actually became two different people. Nothing linked Isabella to me.'

Hunter could see she was right. The way she walked, her gestures, her posture. Everything was different.

'No matter how good you are Robert. You're no clairvoyant. You can't see what's not there. No one can. Isabella gave nothing away. No mistakes, no slip-ups. As I've said, I made her perfect.' She allowed Hunter to dwell on it for a few seconds before continuing. 'Anyway, I was running out of time. I had to adapt my plan. Since you didn't fall for Isabella, I had to find someone to take her place. Someone you'd risk your life for. Someone who you cared about, but there's no one, is there, Robert? The closest person to you was your new partner, so he became the obvious choice. I had to act quickly.'

Hunter thought of Garcia lying in a coma. His only fault had been being assigned Hunter as a partner.

'I have to admit I had my doubts. I didn't think you'd risk your life to save his. I didn't think you were capable of such an act. I thought you'd walk away and leave him to die alone. I was sure you'd protect your own skin and that's all.' She paused and gave Hunter an irreverent shrug. 'Robert the martyr, huh? What a fucking joke.'·

Brenda was so different from Isabella it was frightening. Hunter studied her for a few seconds, analyzing her movements. She was getting agitated.

'But somehow you managed to beat the clock twice and still save your partner. You did well, but did you think you'd beat me?' she asked with a farcical smile as she bent down and stared into Hunter's tired eyes. 'You'll never beat me, Robert. I'm better than you. I'm more intelligent than you. I'm quicker than you and I don't make mistakes. You are no match for me. My plan was perfect. I'm perfect.'

Hunter lost sight of her as she walked around his chair. The unmistakable sound of a blade being sharpened came from behind him and his heartbeat peaked. He knew he'd run out of time. She was getting ready for the last kill.

Sixty-Nine

'And now it's time you finally paid for what you've done. For your incompetence, for all the pain you've given me, Robert. I figure I probably have a couple of days alone with you. After what's happened today, I'm sure your captain told you to take a day or two off. No one's expecting to hear from you so soon. Your partner is out of action. No one will miss you, Robert. By the time they come looking for you . . .' She didn't have to finish her sentence.

'Let me give you an idea of what's gonna happen to you. First, I'll put you to sleep so I can operate on your throat. Nothing fancy. Actually, it will be pretty rough. Just enough for me to sever your vocal cords. I can't have you screaming in here for two days.'

Vroooom. Hunter heard the piercing sound of an electric drill come from behind him. He took a deep breath, but he could feel the fear taking over.

'Then,' she continued. 'When you are awake again, I'm gonna drill holes through your kneecaps, your elbow and your ankle joints. That will shatter the bones into hundreds of little sharp pieces. Any tiny movement, even breathing will cause you incredible pain. I'll savor the moment for a few hours before moving on.'

Hunter closed his eyes and tried to control the shudder spasms that had started running through his body.

'After that, I'll start experimenting with your eyes, your teeth, your genitals and your exposed flesh.' She grinned. 'But don't worry, I'll keep you alive and suffering until the last second.'

Hunter twisted his neck, but he couldn't see her. Doubts were flooding his mind. Fear had settled in and he started to regret his decision. Maybe his plan wouldn't work out.

'But there's something I need to do first,' Brenda whispered.

Unexpectedly he felt his hair being grabbed from behind with tremendous force. His head violently jolted forward. He tried fighting back but he simply didn't have the strength, the energy. The steel blade against the back of his neck first felt cold as ice, then it burned like volcanic fire. Not a deep cut, he sensed. Just enough to scar the flesh.

The double-crucifix, Hunter thought. I'm being marked for death.

'Wait . . .' he called. His voice was still fragile, his throat still too dry, burning with a feverish heat. He had to do something. Buy some time. 'Don't you wanna know where you made your mistake? Don't you wanna know how you're gonna lose?'

He felt the blade moving away from his neck. Her unsettling laughter echoing throughout Hunter's small living room. 'You don't even know how to bluff, Robert. I never made a mistake. I never left anything behind. My plan has always been flawless,' she said with patronizing arrogance. 'And I think you're starting to go delusional. Let me describe the situation for you. I've got you tied up, alone and weak as a wounded animal. I'm the one holding all the knives and you think I'm gonna lose?'

'See, you're almost right,' he said, moving his head back up. He could feel the sting of the flesh wound she'd made on his neck. 'But earlier tonight, when I found out about your revenge, about the jurors, about who you really were, I also found out that today would've been your brother's birthday.'

Brenda had moved from behind his chair and was facing Hunter once again. A glistening blade in her right hand, an intrigued look on her face.

'So I figured out you wanted it that way,' Hunter continued. 'The final revenge on your brother's birthday. The perfect finale.'

'Very good, Robert,' she said, clapping her hands. 'Too bad you decided to start doing all your detective work on the day of your death.'

'So . . .' Hunter quickly carried on, 'before I left the RHD, I placed a call to my captain explaining what I'd found out and he placed a watch on me.'

Brenda frowned. A speck of doubt in her eyes.

'When I got home, I knew something wasn't right, I knew someone had been here. That someone had to be you. You knew I'd have a drink or two tonight, so you drugged every bottle of whisky I have because you didn't know which one I'd go for. But you should've placed them back in the correct order.'

Brenda's eyes moved from Hunter to his small bar and then back to him.

'They've been in the same order for years. I never move them.'

'If you knew the bottles were drugged, why drink it?' she asked insolently.

'Because I knew you wouldn't poison me to death. It's not your style. It wouldn't be revenge if I died without knowing why.'

Hunter could sense Brenda was getting agitated. His heart was in overdrive but he kept his voice calm.

'I knew you were in my apartment, I could feel your presence. I knew you'd be watching me so I pretended to check
my phone by pressing a few keys when in reality I was dialing
my captain. If you look inside my pocket, you'll find that my
cell phone is still on. If you look out the window, you'll find
that the building is surrounded. You can't get out of here. It's
over.'

Her eyes rested on the window behind Hunter. An edgy and
disturbed look on her face. She had underestimated him and
she knew it.

'You're bluffing,' she said in a nervy voice.

'Check the window,' he replied sturdily.

She didn't move. Her hand was shaking from all the adren-
aline. 'Nothing is over,' she finally shouted back in rage,
moving around Hunter's chair.

Unexpectedly and with a loud crash Hunter's living-room
door swung open. Wood splinters flying through the air from
the broken hinges. In a fraction of a second three STU agents
had come through the door. Their laser sights placing three red
dots over Brenda's heart.

'Drop the knife! Drop it now,' the first officer commanded in
an authoritative voice, but Brenda had already positioned herself behind Hunter. She had kneeled down sheltering most of
her body behind his. The knife she had in her right hand was
now being held with both hands, its entire blade pressed hori-
zontally against Hunter's neck, as if she was about to garrote
him with it.

'Drop the knife,' the officer ordered again.

'Wait . . .' Hunter called. He knew what she'd done. She'd
positioned herself in such a way that her entire weight was
pulling her backwards, away from Hunter's chair. With the
blade against his neck in a strangle position, Hunter knew if she

fell back, she'd almost decapitate him. If she died, he'd die. 'Lower your weapons,' Hunter said.

'No can do, sir,' came the immediate reply.

Hunter knew the officers wouldn't back off; they lived for moments like this one.

'Isabella, listen to me . . .' he whispered. He didn't want to call her by her real name. He hoped there was something of Isabella left in her. 'These guys have itchy trigger fingers. They won't hesitate to shoot you. They won't hesitate to shoot me to get to you.' Hunter kept his voice as calm as possible. He understood stressful situations. He knew people had a tendency to match the anxiety of those around them. 'Please don't let it end like this. There are people who can help you, people that wanna help you. I understand the pain you've been through, but the pain doesn't have to go on.'

'You'll never understand the pain,' she whispered back.

'I do understand it. You saw it, you said so yourself. After I lost my partner and my only cousin the pain almost ate me alive. I did hit rock bottom, but I didn't stay there. Give us a chance to help you.'

'You wanna help me?' her voice just a little tender now.

'Yes, let me help you. Please.'

'Like you helped your partner today, Robert?' Her Italian accent was back. Hunter sensed that the woman behind him wasn't Brenda anymore.

'Yes . . . like I helped Carlos.' No hesitation in Hunter's voice.

He felt the blade being pressed just a little harder against his neck and the skin starting to rupture.

'Would you do the same for me, Robert?' she whispered into his right ear. 'Would you risk your life for mine?'

'You have three seconds to drop the knife before we shoot

you where you stand,' the officer instructed again, this time with overwhelming irritation.

Hunter knew he didn't have much time.

'You're not gonna answer me?' she asked again.

A split second of silence followed.

'Yes . . .' he whispered back. 'I'd risk my life for you.'

Hunter sensed a timid smile on her lips before she pulled the blade away from his neck. In a lightning movement she stood up and before the STU team had a chance to discharge their weapons she had plunged the knife deep into her own abdomen. The laser-sharp blade sliced through skin and muscle with incredible ease and surgical precision. Hunter felt a gush of warm liquid strike him in the back of the neck.

'No!' he croaked.

'Jesus Christ!' the STU leader shouted, lowering his weapon. 'Get the paramedics up here . . . now,' he ordered. They all rushed towards Hunter and Brenda who was now on the floor. The pool of blood that surrounded her body was increasing with incredible speed.

As fast as he could, the STU leader used his own knife to cut Hunter free who immediately fell to his knees, his body shivering.

'Are you OK, sir?' the officer asked.

Hunter didn't respond. His eyes were fixed on Brenda's limp body. An STU agent was now holding her head in his hands. Hunter could sense the life draining out of her. The look on the agent's face told him what he already knew.

Seventy

Four days later.

Hunter slowly opened the door to Garcia's room and peeked inside. Anna was standing next to his bed, her hand gently stroking his arm.

'Is he awake?' he whispered.

'Yes, I'm up,' Garcia replied with a frail voice, turning his head to face the door.

Hunter gave him a wide smile and stepped into the room. A box of chocolates under his right arm.

'You're bringing me presents?' Garcia asked with a worried look.

'Hell no . . . this is for Anna,' he replied, handing the chocolates to her.

'Oh! Thank you very much,' she said accepting the gift and giving Hunter a peck on the cheek.

'What's going on here?' Garcia asked. 'Chocolates . . . kisses . . . next thing you know you'll be coming over to my house for dinner.'

'He will be,' Anna confirmed. 'I've already invited him. As soon as you're back home.' She smiled a sweet smile that seemed to light up the room.

'How're you feeling, partner?' Hunter asked.

Garcia lowered his eyes to his bandaged hands. 'Well, apart from the unwanted holes through the palms of my hands, the deep scratches on my head and feeling like I've been dropped from the top of the Golden Gate Bridge I feel peachy, how're you doing?'

'Probably as good as you,' he replied without much conviction.

Garcia shifted his stare towards Anna who understood the signal.

'I'll leave you two alone for a moment. I wanna go down to the cafeteria anyway,' she said, bending down and giving Garcia a soft kiss on the lips. 'I've got some chocolates to attend to,' she teased him.

'Save me some,' Garcia said, giving her a quick wink.

After she left, Garcia was the first to speak.

'I've heard you caught her.'

'I've heard you don't remember much,' Hunter replied.

Garcia slowly shook his head. 'I have no recollection of anything concrete. Little flashes of memory, but I wouldn't be able to identify the killer if it came to that.'

Hunter nodded and Garcia noticed a hint of sadness in his eyes. 'I figured it out, but I didn't catch her,' he said, taking a step closer to the bed.

'How did you do it?'

'Joe Bowman . . .'

Garcia frowned, trying to remember the name. 'The gym manager? Steroid man?'

Hunter nodded. 'I knew I'd seen him before, but he'd convinced me that it'd been in some fitness magazine. It didn't really click until D-King mentioned something about being the jury, the judge and the executioner.'

'D-King?' Garcia said with surprise. 'The drug dealer?'

'Long story, I'll tell you later, but that's what revived my memory about John Spencer's case. Joe was one of the jurors. He looked pretty different then. No steroids, a lot smaller, but I knew it was him.'

Garcia's facial expression urged Hunter to carry on.

'From that, I found out all the victims were linked to the jurors, some of them family, some of them lovers or affairs, just like Victoria Baker was. She was Joe Bowman's lover remember, he's married.'

Garcia agreed in silence. 'And George Slater?'

'He had a gay lover. Rafael, one of the jurors. We talked to him yesterday.'

'Does his wife know?'

'I don't think so. I don't think she needs to know. It would only sadden her further.'

'I agree. And we were right about him having a lover.'

Hunter nodded. 'My problem was figuring out the killer. It was obvious that this had all been about John Spencer's case, about revenge, but who?'

'Family,' Garcia said.

'There's no love stronger than family love,' Hunter agreed. 'But a further check revealed that the only family he had left was his sister . . . his adopted sister.'

'Adopted?'

Another nod. 'Brenda was adopted at the late age of nine. Not because she was an orphan, but because she'd been taken away from her overly abusive biological family by the Department of Health and Human Services. John's family took her in and gave her the love she never had. She felt protected, she felt secure with them. They became the family she'd never really had. Their deaths triggered something in her subconscious memory. Maybe a scared feeling of being without a family again. Maybe the memories of all the abuse she'd received when she was young. Maybe the fear of being taken away and returned to her original family.'

Garcia looked confused.

'In traumatic situations like the one she'd been through,' Hunter explained. 'Losing her entire family in such quick succession, it's not uncommon for the brain to make no distinction of age. It simply retrieves the memories from the subconscious. All the fear and anger she felt as a child would've come back with the same intensity if not stronger, making her feel like a little lonely girl once again. That might've awakened some sort of rage, some sort of hidden evil inside her. She blamed everyone involved in her brother's case for taking her family from her. Especially the jury, Scott and I. She couldn't allow it to go unpunished.'

'When did you know it was Isabella?'

'When I found out about John Spencer. With his sister being the only living relative, all that was left for me to do was to find out who she was. A new search revealed that she'd been committed shortly after her father's death.'

'Committed?'

'In San Francisco, that's where she lived. After her father died, rage took over her and she apparently lost her mind . . . went crazy, destroyed her apartment and almost killed her boyfriend. They lived together at the time.'

'So she was arrested,' Garcia stated more than asked.

'At first, yes, and then taken to the Langley Porter Psychiatric Hospital where she stayed for a couple of years. I called the San Francisco Police Department and they sent me a fax of the arresting report. She looked very different in the picture. Different color and length of hair, in fact she looked older, as though what she'd been through had knocked the life out of her. But there was no doubt. I knew who she was then.'

Hunter walked over to the window and had a look outside. The day looked perfect, not a cloud in the sky. 'And then I remembered her CD collection and whatever doubt I still had just disappeared.'

'CD collection?'

'The first night I had dinner with Isabella at her place, for some reason I checked her CD collection.'

Garcia made a face that silently asked 'How did that help?'

'Her entire collection was comprised of Jazz CDs, with the exception of a handful of rock albums, all of them auto-graphed, not by the band, not by the musicians, but by the producer – John Spencer. What I didn't know at the time was that John never signed his name as John Spencer, that's not how he was known in the music industry. He signed his auto-graphs Specter J. His rock pseudonym or something, I found that out on the internet. That's why when I read the autograph inscriptions that night it never occurred to me. The inscrip-tions said something like, "From Big B with eternal love." I just assumed that was one of these weird names artists give them-selves nowadays, you know like Puffy, or LL Cool J. Specter J and Big B didn't ring any bells then.'

'Big Brother?' Garcia half asked, half concluded.

Hunter nodded. 'John Spencer was a year older than Brenda.'

'So her time in psychiatric care gave her all the time in the world to hatch her plan.'

'A couple of years,' Hunter confirmed.

'And that explains the time difference between John Spencer's case and the first Crucifix killing.'

Another nod from Hunter. 'And yesterday I found out about her military past.'

'Military?'

'Well, sort of. She was a surgeon, a very talented one according to what I found. At the beginning of her career she spent two years in Bosnia and Herzegovina with US forces and the medical team helping landmine victims.'

'You're kidding?' Garcia's eyebrows rose in surprise and then in realization. 'The explosives?'

'That's where she would've gained knowledge of them. It's part of their training, understanding about mines, explosives, detonating mechanisms, velocity and power of explosion . . . things like that. She would've had every manual available to her then.'

'So it would've been just a case of knowing where to look, who to talk to and she would've easily obtained the raw materials she needed.'

'Precisely.'

A short silence followed. 'The sketch she gave us?' Garcia asked, already guessing the answer.

'To throw us off course. That night, without realizing, I'd drawn a doodle of the double-crucifix. An unconscious reflex as my mind had been totally absorbed by the case. Isabe . . .' Hunter paused and thought better of what he was about to say. 'Brenda,' he corrected himself, 'was a very clever woman and with some very quick thinking she saw the perfect opportunity to send us on a wild-goose chase, so she came up with that fictitious story about meeting someone in a bar. Someone with the double-crucifix tattooed on his wrists. She then only needed to give us a bogus description and the investigation would take a wrong turn.'

'We wasted a couple of weeks running after that bogus description.'

'And we would've wasted more,' Hunter agreed. 'We had no reason to doubt her. We assumed we were on to a good thing.'

'And how did you know she would come after you that night?'

'Three things. One, there were no more jurors left to take revenge upon.'

'But she'd only taken nine victims; there are twelve jurors in total.'

'The other three were already dead from natural causes. She couldn't hurt them anymore. Scott, my partner, the other arresting detective, was also dead.' Hunter stopped for a moment remembering what Brenda had told him four days ago. After a deep breath he continued. 'I was the only one left.'

'Not a great position to be in,' Garcia joked.

Hunter agreed. 'Two, it was John's birthday. For her, the ultimate revenge day. The ultimate present to her brother and her family.'

A long pause followed.

'And three? You said there were three things,' Garcia questioned.

'Me carrying your cross.'

'Huh? I don't follow,' Garcia said, shifting himself on the bed, trying to get into a better position.

'The biggest analogy of someone's last day on earth.'

Garcia thought about it for a few seconds. 'To carry a cross on your back. Jesus's last day on earth,' Garcia said, realizing Hunter's point.

Hunter nodded again. 'I knew I only had a few hours to think of something. I knew she'd be coming after me.'

Hunter turned to face the window again and his stare seemed distant and alienated. He gently touched the back of his neck and felt the scar which hadn't fully healed yet.

'If you had a strong suspicion it was Isabella, why did you go through all that? Why did you risk your life allowing her to get to you? Why not just arrest her?' Garcia asked, shifting his body once again.

'I had no proof, only suspicions. Just a crazy theory about revenge. As you know we had nothing on the killer, no DNA or fingerprints, nothing that could link her to any of the victims or crime scenes. If we took her in, she would've walked, and I'm sure we would've lost her forever. My only hope was to allow her to come to me.'

'So you set a trap. A dangerous trap.'

Another nod. 'I could think of nothing else, I was running out of time.'

'How could she be capable of all those killings, all that evil?' Garcia asked.

'We'll never be able to say for sure, but when alone with any of the victims, she became a different person. She burned with rage and evil. She was capable of anything. I know it. I saw it in her eyes. I could literally sense the rage that surrounded her.'

Garcia observed his partner for a few silent seconds. 'Are you OK?' he asked.

'I'm fine,' Hunter replied confidently. 'I'm glad it's over.'

'You can say that again,' Garcia said, lifting both of his bandaged hands.

They both laughed.

'As long as Captain Bolter doesn't assign me a paper-pushing job.'

'Not a chance,' Hunter confirmed. 'You're my partner. If I'm going after the bad guys, you're coming with.'

Garcia smiled. 'Thanks, Robert,' he said in a more serious tone.

'That's OK. I wouldn't let the captain give you a desk job anyway.'

'Not for that . . . for risking your life . . . for saving mine.'

Hunter gently rested his hand on his partner's left shoulder. No words were said. No words needed to be said.

Doctor Winston opened the door to his autopsy room in the basement of the Department of Coroner and ushered Captain Bolter inside.

'So what have we got?' the captain said without wasting any time. Like most people the basement autopsy room gave him the creeps and the quicker he got out of there, the better.

'Cause of death was severe laceration of the stomach, intestines and aortic aneurysm together with massive hemorrhage. As she plunged the knife into herself she managed to drive it across from left to right. A little like the Japanese ritual,' the doctor said directing the captain to the body on the steel table.

'Disembowelment?'

'Not exactly, but achieving the same final effect. She knew she'd be dead within a minute. No chance of survival.'

They both stared at the body in silence for a moment.

'Well,' the captain said. 'I have to admit I'm glad this is all over.'

'Me too,' Doctor Winston replied with a smile. 'How's Carlos doing?' he said changing the subject.

'Getting better. Give him time and he'll be alright.'

'How about Robert?'

'He's still a little shook up. He's blaming himself for not figuring it out earlier.'

'It's understandable. The killer got close to him, too close in fact. Emotionally and physically. But I don't know any other detective that would've come out of it alive.'

'Me neither.' Captain Bolter's eyes moved back to the body. 'Well, she's dead. Robert will be over it and onto the next case by next week.'

'I'm sure he will, but, anyway, that's not why I called you here.'

Captain Bolter frowned with interest, waiting for Doctor Winston to carry on.

'Robert will wanna see the autopsy report.'

'So?'

'I think I should alter it.'

Captain Bolter shot him a worried look. 'Why would you wanna do that?'

Doctor Winston took a piece of paper from his desk and handed it to Captain Bolter who read it attentively. His eyes stopped moving halfway down the page and widened in surprise.

'Are you sure about this, Doctor?'

'As sure as I can be.'

'How old?'

'Judging by the size of the embryo, no more than four or five weeks.'

Captain Bolter ran his hand through his hair before rereading the autopsy report. 'That's about when they met isn't it?'

'That's what I thought,' the doctor replied.

'Do you know for certain it's his?'

'No . . . not without a DNA test, but she had one agenda in mind. She doesn't strike me as the type who'd sleep around, not when all her efforts were on avenging her family's death and getting to Robert.'

Captain Bolter placed the report back on the doctor's desk. A minute of silence went by before he spoke again.

'It would do Robert no good if he found this out.'

'I agree. This is the last thing he needs.'

'Who else knows about this?'

'You and I, that's it.'

'Let's keep it that way then. Alter the report,' the captain said firmly.

'I heard you're getting a commendation from the Chief of Police and the Mayor himself,' Garcia said as Hunter poured himself a glass of water from the glass jug by Garcia's bed.

'So are you.'

Garcia raised both of his eyebrows.

'We're partners remember? We were on the case together.'

Garcia smiled.

'Not bad for your first case as a RHD detective,' Hunter teased.

'Yeah, not bad for someone who can now use his hands as whistles.' Garcia lifted his right hand and moved it back and forth in front of his mouth pretending to blow on it and making a quick whistling sound.

They both broke into laughter.

A gentle knock on the door grabbed their attention. 'I could hear you two laughing halfway down the hall,' Anna said as she entered the room. 'It's great to see both of you laughing.'

'It certainly is,' Hunter said, resting his hand on Garcia's arm. 'It certainly is.' ✆